PRAISE FOR
AMERICA LIBRE

"An engaging, fast-moving story of love, intrigue, and personal and ethnic conflict, wrapped in rich, thought-provoking political and cultural commentary."
   —Richard W. Slatta, PhD, professor of Latin American history, North Carolina State University

"Thematically similar to T. C. Boyle's enormously popular *The Tortilla Curtain*, Ramos's AMERICA LIBRE is a story of what we all struggle with when we decide where we stand on the issue of immigration."
   —Professor Edward J. Mulens, University of Missouri-Columbia

"A window into the despair, brought about by racism, faced by many of our Hispanic neighbors."
   —Miguel De La Torre, PhD, director of the Justice and Peace Institute, Iliff School of Theology

"In such explosive times as ours, it is rare to discover a novel that captures fanaticism in all its extremes and tells a story as thrilling and vibrant as AMERICA LIBRE. Future and history collide in a cautionary tale of a new Civil War on American soil. A must-read for all, no matter where you draw your line in the sand."
   —James Rollins, *New York Times* bestselling author of *The Last Oracle*

AMERICA
LIBRE

Raul Ramos y Sanchez

GRAND CENTRAL
PUBLISHING

NEW YORK   BOSTON

Grand Central Publishing
Hachette Book Group
237 Park Avenue
New York, NY 10017

Visit our Web site at www.HachetteBookGroup.com.

Printed in the United States of America

First Edition: July 2009
10 9 8 7 6 5 4 3 2 1

Grand Central Publishing is a division of Hachette Book Group, Inc. The Grand Central Publishing name and logo is a trademark of Hachette Book Group, Inc.

Library of Congress Cataloging-in-Publication Data

Ramos y Sánchez, Raúl.
    America libre / Raul Ramos y Sanchez.—1st ed.
        p. cm.
    Summary: "How will today's immigration crisis shape our nation? Fast-paced and action-packed, America Libre is a wake-up call to the dangers of extremism—on both sides of this explosive issue."—Provided by the publisher.
    ISBN 978-0-446-50775-2
    1. United States—Emigration and immigration—Fiction.   2. United States—Ethnic relations—Fiction.   3. Illegal aliens—United States—Social conditions—Fiction.   4. Hispanic Americans—Crimes against—Fiction.
5. Insurgency—United States—Fiction.   6. Political violence—United States—Fiction.   7. Social change—Mexican-American Border Region—Fiction.   8. Domestic fiction. gsafd   I. Title.
    PS3618.A4765A44 2009
    813'.6—dc22

2008038746

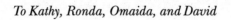

To Kathy, Ronda, Omaida, and David

ACKNOWLEDGMENTS

Every author's work is an unpaid debt. We borrow ideas, time, information, even love, in quantities we can never repay. Let this page serve as an accounting of the debits of appreciation accrued in the making of this book.

I owe my agent, Sally van Haitsma, for her faith, patience, and unflagging determination.

I owe my partners and siblings, Ronda and David, who take care of business at BRC Marketing while I cavort with the muses.

I owe my editor at Grand Central Publishing, Selina McLemore, for the trust she placed in my work and her sage editing of the GCP edition. GCP's Latoya Smith has been a pleasure to work with as well.

I owe Dr. Miguel De La Torre and Dr. Edward Mullen for their time and generosity in reviewing this work.

I owe James Adams, Barbara Estes, and Jason Johnson for their help in research. I also owe the scholastic work and counsel of Dr. Oscar Alvarez Gila, Dr. Miguel De La Torre, Dr. Franklin W. Knight, and Dr. Richard W. Slatta.

I owe Rueben Martinez, founder of Libreria Martinez, for his generous support of a first-time author and for nominating *America Libre* for the 2008 International Latino Book Awards.

I owe my mother, Omaida, for a lifetime of support and an example of courage and will.

Most of all, I owe my wife, Kathleen, who never fails to encourage me while enduring my circadian rhythms, which she's convinced are from a planet with a rather eccentric spin rate.

AMERICA
LIBRE

THE RIO GRANDE INCIDENT

THE RIO GRANDE INCIDENT:
Day 1

The origins of any political revolution parallel the
beginnings of life on our planet. The amino acids and
proteins lie inert in a volatile primordial brew until a
random lightning strike suddenly brings them to life.
                                    —*José Antonio Marcha, 1978*
                                    Translated by J. M. Herrera

The trouble had started two weeks earlier. Enraged at
the fatal police shooting of a young Latina bystander during a
drug bust, a late-night mob descended on a Texas Department
of Public Safety complex and torched the empty buildings. By
morning, a local newscast of the barrio's law-and-order melt-
down mushroomed into a major story, drawing the national
media to San Antonio. Since then, the presence of network
cameras had incited the south side's bored and jobless teenagers into nightly rioting.

Seizing the national spotlight, the governor of Texas
vowed looters would be shot on sight. Octavio Perez, a radical community leader, angrily announced that force would
be met with force. He called on Mexican-Americans to arm
themselves and resist if necessary.

Disdaining Perez's warning, Edward Cole, a twenty-six-year-
old National Guard lieutenant, chose a provocative location
for his downtown command post: the Alamo.

"This won't be the first time this place has been surrounded by a shitload of angry Mexicans," Cole told his platoon of weekend warriors outside the shut-down tourist site. A high school gym teacher for most of the year, Lieutenant Cole had been called up to lead a Texas National Guard detachment. Their orders were to keep San Antonio's south side rioting from spreading downtown.

Now Cole was fielding yet another call over the radio.

"Lieutenant, we got some beaners tearing the hell out of a liquor store two blocks south of my position," the sentry reported.

"How many?"

"I'd say fifty to a hundred."

"Sit tight, Corporal. The cavalry is coming to the rescue," Cole said, trying his best to sound cool and confident. From a two-day training session on crowd control, he'd learned that a rapid show of strength was essential in dispersing a mob. But the colonel who had briefed Cole for the mission had been very clear about the governor's statement.

"It's not open season on rioters, Lieutenant. Your men are authorized to fire their weapons only in self-defense," the colonel had ordered. "And even then, it had damn well better be as a last resort. The governor's statement was meant to deter violence, not provoke it."

Lieutenant Cole had never seen combat. But he was sure he could deal with a small crowd of unruly Mexicans. After all, he had eight men armed with M16A2 semiautomatics under his command. Cole put on his helmet, smoothed out his crisply ironed ascot, and ordered his men into the three reconditioned Humvees at his disposal.

"Let's move out," he said over the lead Humvee's radio. With the convoy under way, Cole turned to his driver. "Step on it, Baker. We don't want to let this thing get out of hand."

As the driver accelerated, the young lieutenant envisioned his dramatic entrance:

Bullhorn in hand, he'd emerge from the vehicle surrounded by a squad of armed troopers, the awed crowd quickly scattering as he ordered them to disperse...

Drifting back from his daydream, Cole noticed they were closing fast on the crowd outside the liquor store. Too fast.

"Stop, Baker! Stop!" Cole yelled.

The startled driver slammed on the brakes, triggering a chain collision with the vehicles trailing close behind. Shaken but unhurt, Cole looked through the window at the laughing faces outside. Instead of arriving like the 7th Cavalry, they'd wound up looking like the Keystone Kops.

Then a liquor bottle struck Cole's Humvee. Like the opening drop of a summer downpour, it was soon followed by the deafening sound of glass bottles shattering against metal.

"Let's open up on these bastards, Lieutenant! They're gonna kill us!" the driver shouted.

Cole shook his head, realizing his plan had been a mistake. "Negative, Baker! We're pulling out."

But before the lieutenant could grab the radio transmitter to relay his order, the driver's window shattered.

"I'm hit! I'm hit! Oh my God. I'm hit!" the driver shrieked, clutching his head. A cascade of blood flowed down Baker's nose and cheeks. He'd suffered only a gash on the forehead from the broken glass, but all the same, it was as shocking as a mortal wound. Never one to stomach the sight of blood, Baker passed out, slumping into his seat.

Cole couldn't allow himself to panic; with no window and no driver he was far too vulnerable. Mind racing, he stared outside and soon noticed a group of shadowy figures crouching along the roof of the liquor store. *Are they carrying weapons?*

"Listen up, people. I think we might have snipers on the roof! I repeat, snipers on the roof!" Cole yelled into the radio. "Let's lock and load! Have your weapons ready to return fire!"

On the verge of panic, the part-time soldiers fumbled nervously with their rifles as the drunken mob closed on the convoy, pounding against the vehicles.

The window on Cole's side caved in with a terrifying crash. The rattled young lieutenant was certain he now faced a life-or-death decision—and he was determined to save his men. With the radio still in hand, Lieutenant Edward Cole gave an order he would forever regret.

"We're under attack. Open fire!"

When it was over, twenty-three people lay dead on the black pavement beneath the neon sign of the Rio Grande Carryout.

***

"The Rio Grande Incident," as it came to be known, led every newscast and spanned every front page from Boston to Beijing. Bloggers went into hyperdrive. Talk radio knew no other subject. Protests erupted in many American cities, usually flash mobs that drew a wide spectrum of extremists.

Outside the U.S. embassy in Mexico City, tens of thousands chanting "Rio Grande" burned American flags alongside an effigy of Texas governor Jeff Bradley. Massive demonstrations multiplied across Latin America, Asia, and Europe in the days that followed. The prime minister of France called the confrontation "an appalling abuse of power." Germany's chancellor labeled it "barbaric." Officials in China declared it "an unfortunate consequence of capitalist excess."

Fed by the media frenzy, the destruction and looting on San Antonio's south side escalated. In less than a week, riots broke out in other Hispanic enclaves across Texas, New Mexico, Arizona, and California.

Many Americans were shocked by the sudden turmoil in the Southwest, yet in hindsight, the origins of the discontent were easy to see.

As the United States entered the second decade of the twenty-first century, a severe recession was under way. With unemployment benefits running out, millions of Americans sought any kind of job, saturating low-rung job markets. From farms to fast-food chains, Hispanics were pitted against mainstream workers in a game of economic musical chairs.

Only a few years earlier, the election of the nation's first African-American president, Adam Elewa, had brought hope to Hispanics and all minorities. But Elewa was voted out after one term following a renewal of terrorist attacks on U.S. soil. Elewa's successor, Carleton Brenner, resumed what many were calling the War on Terror II. With widespread public support, Brenner quickly launched a wave of overseas military deployments and stiffened border security.

The tighter borders stemmed the flow of illegal immigrants. But the presence of millions of undocumented Hispanics already within the country was a political quagmire that remained unresolved. More significant, Latinos born in the U.S. had long overtaken immigration as the prime source of Hispanic growth thanks to birth rates that soared far above the mainstream average. The nation's Hispanic population had exploded—and the lingering economic slump had created a powder keg of idle, restless youth.

Fear of this perplexing ethnic bloc among mainstream

Americans had given rise to an escalating backlash. Armed vigilante groups patrolling the Mexican border had shot and killed border crossers on several occasions. Inside the border, anyone with a swarthy complexion was not much safer. Assaults by Anglo gangs against Hispanics caught in the wrong neighborhood were now commonplace. "Amigo shopping," the epidemic of muggings on illegal immigrants who always carried cash, was rarely investigated by police. Graffiti deriding Hispanics was a staple in schools and workplaces. Another burning cross in the yard of a Latino home was no longer news.

Meanwhile, politicians had discovered a wellspring of nativist passion. In a scramble for votes, a deluge of anti-immigration and "English only" ordinances had been passed over the last decade by state and local governments as Washington's inability to resolve the thorny immigration issue continued. Most of these laws were struck down by federal judges. Yet local politicians persisted in passing new ones. The strident nativist vote was too powerful to resist. This conflicting patchwork of laws created an unforeseen side effect. Fleeing the legislative backlash, most Hispanics—both legal and illegal—were now concentrated in "safe haven" communities, usually in crowded urban areas.

Outraged by the growing attacks against Hispanics and seeing the anti-immigrant laws as thinly veiled bullying, Latino community leaders in the Southwest had grown increasingly militant. Protest marches and rallies were on the rise. Hispanic separatists, once only fringe groups at the marches, were visibly growing in number. A favorite banner at many of these events reflected an attitude gaining in popularity: "We didn't cross the border. The border crossed us."

Now, in a sweltering July, these long-smoldering elements were reaching the flashpoint in the nation's teeming barrios.

THE RIO GRANDE INCIDENT:
Day 12

Manolo Suarez awoke to the crash of breaking glass.

Through the bedroom's lone window, opened to the stifling heat, he heard the shrill wail of a burglar alarm and loud, angry voices. Mano glanced at the glowing clock. It was 12:27 a.m.

Rosa lay naked against his side, using his brawny biceps for a pillow. Mano gently moved his wife aside and stepped out of bed.

"Wake up, querida," he said, pulling a T-shirt over his chiseled torso.

Rosa stirred, still torpid from their lovemaking less than an hour earlier. "Mano? What's going on?"

"There's rioting outside. I'm going to take a look. Move the children into the living room—away from the windows," he said as he finished dressing.

From the courtyard of his apartment building on East Fourth Street in Los Angeles, Mano watched the mob, surprised by its makeup. The main source of violence was a few dozen teens at the edge of the crowd. They were hurling bricks, bottles, and stones at the shops along Fourth Street. Behind the teenagers were small groups of adults shouting encouragement, waiting for a chance to grab anything of value. Most people on the street were simply milling around, watching curiously, drifting with the action.

Near the back of the crowd, Mano spotted a familiar face. Eddie Paz was loitering with two other men, sharing swigs from a bottle of Cutty Sark. Eddie had been a lot boy at the dealership where Mano worked as a mechanic—until the business had gone under five months earlier.

"Suarez!" Eddie slurred. "Come here, man!"

Hoping to learn more about the mob, Mano waded into the mass of bodies. At six foot three and a hard two hundred sixty, he plowed easily through the crowd.

"Take a swig!" Eddie said, holding out the bottle as Mano approached.

"No thanks, Eddie," Mano shouted over the noise. "How long has this been going on?" he asked, gesturing to the chaos around them.

"I dunno, man," Eddie said, staggering closer, booze on his breath. "Me and the guys were tossing down a few back at Paquito's and heard all this racket about an hour ago. Been checking out the scene ever since."

"I'm surprised to see you out here doing this, Eddie. You've got a family to support."

"Hey, man, I think it's a shame these kids are tearing up the barrio," Eddie said indignantly. "A lot of these businesses are owned by Latinos. They don't deserve this shit. But what can I do about it, man?"

"What you can do, Eddie, is go home. Hanging around out here only gives these cholos safety in numbers," Mano said and walked away.

Rosa used her nightgown to wipe a tear from Elena's cheek. The trembling five-year-old clung to her mother on the worn living room couch, terrified by the angry screams and crashes outside.

"Where's Papi?" the half-awake child asked, suddenly noticing her father's absence.

"Papi will be back soon," Rosa cooed soothingly, hoping it was true. She knew Mano could take care of himself on the street. He'd done it all his life. But this rioting was something new, something that made no sense.

Rosa glanced at Pedro and Julio tucked into the pallets she'd laid out on the living room floor. The noise outside had energized her sons, their brown eyes flashing with each new swell in the din.

When Mano entered the front door, Rosa stifled a sigh of relief to avoid alarming the children.

"Make the people stop, Papi," Elena cried, pointing outside.

Mano stroked his daughter's cheek. "It's OK, m'hijita. You're safe in here. No one's going to hurt you."

Ten-year-old Pedro sat up excitedly. "I want to go out and riot with you, Papi."

"Me, too," said Julio, who, at eight, was always eager to follow his big brother.

"I did not go outside to riot, Pedro. I went outside to make sure we weren't in danger."

"But everybody at school says rioting is tight, Papi. You know, so people will listen to us Hispanics. It's on the news and everything."

"What they're doing outside is senseless, Pedro," Mano said calmly. "They're attacking places that provide us jobs.

Rioting isn't going to make people listen to Hispanics, m'hijo. It's going to make things worse."

Rosa stroked her son's forehead. "Pedro, you've seen your father looking for work every day for the last five months. Do you think this rioting is going to help him find a job?"

The boy lowered his eyes. "No, Mami," he said softly, settling back under the covers.

Rosa could sense the tug of excitement the rioting had on her boys, an undertow she would have to guide them to resist. Drugs, crime, the gangs, and now this pointless violence—it was one more danger her kids would face. Asking God for the strength and patience to protect them was always first in the prayers she said daily. "Close your eyes, m'hijo," she said, gently smoothing Pedro's blankets.

The boy blinked drowsily a few times—then his eyes widened suddenly as the shriek of sirens joined the din outside.

"All of you stay here," Mano said, rising to his feet. "I'm going to see what's going on."

Without a view of the street from the living room, Mano went to the kitchen window. The pulsing red lights of emergency vehicles glowed against the wall of the warehouse next door. Moving to the bedroom window at the back of their apartment, Mano was alarmed to see the flickering yellow reflection of flames on the building behind them.

Trying to determine the source of the fire, Mano heard a series of dull thumps coming from the street. He recognized the sound of tear gas canisters and could tell from the sudden drop in voices that the crowd was in retreat. Soon pale smoke was seeping into their apartment.

By the time Mano reached the living room, Rosa and the

children were already coughing. "Get the children into the bathroom," he called out to Rosa. "Seal the door with wet towels, then wet down some washcloths and breathe through them." Mano leaned close to Rosa, speaking softly so the children could not hear. "I saw flames outside. Keep the children ready to move in case the fire spreads."

Rosa's eyes flared with alarm for a moment, then she composed herself and nodded calmly. She led the children into the bathroom and closed the door.

Feeling as if his eyes were being boiled, Mano rushed into their bedroom and ripped the sheet from the bed. After soaking the fabric in the kitchen sink, he jammed the dripping cloth under the front door. From a wet kitchen towel, he fashioned a gas mask for himself and began patrolling the windows.

Inside the cramped bathroom, Rosa coughed violently as she prepared wet-cloth masks for the children before making one of her own. She sealed the bathroom door, then herded the kids into the bathtub, trying to keep them comfortable but alert. Sitting on the edge of the tub, she began a familiar nursery rhyme. "*Palomita blanca, pico de coral,*" she recited, playfully patting each of their heads in time with the verse. "*Pidele al Señor que no llueva más.*" The children giggled and joined in, their squeaky voices muffled by the cloths. For the next hour Rosa led them through the many cancionitas she'd learned from her mother.

Although Rosa spoke little Spanish and barely understood the meaning of these nursery rhymes she'd passed on to her children, their familiar rhythm was always reassuring—especially tonight. After more than an hour, the children were struggling to stay awake, their heads lolling. Rosa was relieved when she heard Mano's voice from the other side of the bathroom door.

"It's OK. You can come out now," he said.

Moving away the wet towels, Rosa cautiously opened the door. The noise outside had ended and the air was clear. With gentle pats and soothing whispers, she led her exhausted children to their bedroom, tucked them in, and returned to the living room.

"Ay, Dios mio, look at this mess," Rosa said, shaking her head. While stanching the gas, Mano had toppled her shrine to Our Lady of Guadalupe. The painted statuette had survived the fall, but the glass-encased votive candle flanking La Virgen Morena had shattered, littering the floor with globs of wax. Stuck to the hardening mess were grains of rice from the small offering of food Rosa kept at the shrine. "Our Lady fell but she didn't break. That's a good sign," Rosa whispered as she began cleaning up.

"Leave that for the morning, querida. It can wait," Mano said and then patted the cushion next to him on the frayed red couch. "Come here, Rosita. Sit with me."

Rosa settled next to her husband, leaning her head on his beefy shoulder as Mano kissed her hair softly. They said nothing, content with the warmth and nearness of each other. During their twelve years of marriage these intimate moments of silence had become a refuge, an escape from stress and worries.

But tonight their closeness did not calm Rosa. This rioting was threatening her family—and she could not understand why the people in their barrio seemed bent on such mindless destruction. *Of course life is hard for Latinos; it always has been. So why start burning and looting now?* she wondered.

Rosa knew she made little effort to keep up with events outside their home. She rarely watched the news or read a paper. Her world was her family. She had three children and a husband to feed and keep healthy. She trusted God to take care of the rest. Her isolation was born out of long habit. The only child of a single parent, Rosa had spent much of her childhood caring for her mother, who'd been paralyzed by MS when Rosa was eight. Only after her mother's death had she consented to Mano's patient courtship, giving her life a new focus.

Even today, her travels in the barrio were along well-worn paths between home, shopping, and church. This rioting, however, was forcing Rosa into a realization she was not eager to accept: there was something going on around her she had not yet grasped.

She raised her eyes to meet her husband's. "All this rioting, Mano…What's made people so angry?"

Mano slowly rubbed his jaw, mulling her question. "I think it's more than one thing, Rosita," he said softly. "To begin with, I'm not the only one who's looking for a job."

"Yes, I know that, mi amor. But the streets have been full of teenagers with nothing to do for the last few years. Why now?"

Mano stared at the ceiling for a moment. "I've heard some people say that shutting down the Metro lines in L.A. was done to spite Hispanics…and to keep our kids out of the malls."

"Do you think that's true?"

Mano shrugged. "I don't know, querida. But I think this trouble has been building up for a while. A lot of hotheads were upset when they cut off Social Security for non-citizens last year. And there are people who think all these 'English only' laws are a slap at Latinos, too."

"Yes, but is that any reason to riot?"

"Life has always been tough for Hispanics, querida. And right now, it's hard to find work. I can understand why a lot of Latinos are angry. But destroying other people's property isn't going to make things easier."

Rosa stared at her hands and sighed. "What are we going to do, Mano?" she asked. "It could be a long time before you find another job."

Mano smiled. "The only way to find work is to look for it."

His confidence lifted her mood. "Well, if you're going to look for work tomorrow, it's way past your bedtime," Rosa said, patting his muscled back. "What time should I wake you up, mi amor?"

"The same time as always."

"Mano, you can't get up at five forty-five after being up half the night."

"My job now is to find a job, remember? That's been our game plan and we should stick to it," Mano said, then effortlessly lifted her from the couch and carried her to their bed. "You lay down, querida. The kids are going to need you tomorrow. I want to stay up for a while."

After Rosa was asleep, Mano returned to his rounds, scanning the darkness for signs of trouble until the glow of dawn emerged above the buildings. Convinced the danger was finally over, he moved to the living room and turned on the television, keeping the volume down.

"...the East Los Angeles area now appears calm after the second night of rioting," the newscaster was saying. The camera panned across Mano's neighborhood from a high point downtown. Several plumes of dark smoke were rising in the hazy dawn. "The LAPD is advising commuters to avoid the area…"

Mano stared absently at the TV. For a long time, he'd dreamt of buying a house, a place with a bedroom for each child and a yard where they could play. This morning, as he sat on the wax-stained couch, the dream seemed blurry and distant. This barrio was already a dangerous place for his family. The rioting would only make it worse.

When the TV station cut to a car commercial, a chilling thought crossed Mano's mind. Had their station wagon survived the riot? His family's only vehicle was parked around the corner of the building, out of sight from their apartment.

Locking the door behind him, Mano made his way through the courtyard of the apartment complex, pausing at the threshold. Fourth Street was deserted, its pavement blanketed with stones, bricks, and bottles. Every street-facing window was broken. Several cars were overturned and torched, black smoke rising from their smoldering tires. Mano broke into a run. Rounding the corner of his building, he was devastated by what he saw.

All four cars in the parking lot had been torched, including the aging Taurus station wagon for which he still owed eleven payments.

Mano was now without wheels and jobless in Los Angeles—a city that had ended all public transportation.

As San Antonio's turmoil spread from Los Angeles across the Southwest, publications of every political stripe offered explanations for the disturbances.

The *Washington Post* claimed the rioting had been triggered by a recent congressional bill making English the nation's official language, in effect eliminating all Spanish-language versions of public documents and ending national support for bilingual education. Coming on the heels of earlier legislation that terminated Social Security benefits for non-citizens, the *Post* said these new laws "exposed the hidden rage lurking in the barrios."

The *Wall Street Journal* suggested that our once-porous borders and unrestricted immigration were responsible for "the crowded, crime-ridden ghettos within our cities, now erupting into violence."

An article in *Time* countered that Hispanics had not yet learned to flex their political muscle. The rioting was "an unfocused attempt to voice the nascent political influence of this emerging power bloc."

Blogs cited a long list of combustible elements for the disturbances, including the high unemployment rate the last six years, an exceptionally hot summer, and even Mayan prophecies about the end of time. Many found parallels to similar movements around the world—the Basques in Spain, Tamil rebels in Sri Lanka, the Quebecois in Canada, the Kurdish rebellion in Turkey, the implosion of the Soviet Union, and the ethnic clashes of the Balkans.

Whatever the causes, two months after the Rio Grande Incident, riots were now nightly events in many barrios of the U.S. Southwest.

THE RIO GRANDE INCIDENT:
Month 2, Day 4

The vu-phone rang, playing the opening of Beethoven's *Für Elise.*

Ernesto Alvarez flicked aside his half-smoked Kool and flipped open the vu-phone's cover. Instead of a live image of the caller, the words "secure mode" flashed on the display. Nesto brought the toy-like instrument to his ear.

"Yeah," he said with studied nonchalance. Under the streetlights, he listened distractedly, admiring the collection of crude tattoos on his hand. "Cool," he said finally and slipped the vu-phone back into his baggy pants.

"It's set," Nesto announced to the three teenagers slouching against the playground fence. A faint orange glow washed over their pubescent faces as they dragged hard on their Kools. None of them were over sixteen.

Tonight would be their salto, an initiation to prove they were daring enough to become vatos in Nesto's gang, El Farol.

El Farol had emerged in East Los Angeles during the early '80s as families fleeing the death squads of El Salvador found another source of intimidation in their new home—Mexican street gangs. The gang's current mero mero, Nesto, had already instructed the boys on their salto—and they were eager to begin.

"De verdad, Nesto? The guns will be ready?" asked Freddie Estevez, oldest of the boys.

Nesto moved within inches of Freddie's face. "I'm only going to tell you this once, Frederico," he whispered. "In El Farol, you never question the word of your mero mero. Entiendes?"

"Sí, Nesto," Freddie said, lowering his eyes.

"OK, now get the fuck outta here. You know what you need to do."

After the boys hurried away, Nesto silently asked himself again if he was making a smart move. This gig could bring some major heat down on El Farol—and on him. But the opportunity was too sweet to turn down. First, there was the money. The twenty thousand he'd been offered to stir up some trouble had been impossible to resist. But the brilliant part was in taking this play far beyond its original intent and turning it into a warning to the other gangs crowding his turf. The sheer cojones of this salto would send a message to his rivals: El Farol is too tough to be messed with.

Sure, it was risky. But Nesto knew the gangs would honor their code of silence. And with all the rioting and looting, there was little chance of being caught.

Ten minutes after leaving Nesto, the boys reached their destination: the roof above the Casa Mia restaurant. As Nesto had promised, the black plastic garbage bag was already there and Freddie opened it eagerly. Inside were three loaded .38s.

After Freddie distributed the revolvers, the boys squatted behind the low wall along the front of the roof, their eyes fixed on the Best Help drugstore across the street, already closed for the night. Before long, a rusting Mercury Cougar pulled into the drugstore's parking lot.

A man emerged from the car and methodically doused the vehicle with a can of gasoline. After throwing the empty can into the backseat, he struck a match, flung it at the car, and casually walked away.

As Nesto had predicted, the burning car quickly drew a crowd. Freddie recognized several members of El Farol shouting angrily among the onlookers, trying to incite them. It wasn't difficult.

Someone smashed a window, triggering the drugstore's burglar alarm. The impotent ringing did little to deter the mob. More windows were broken and several men assaulted the front door.

When the boys heard sirens in the distance, they dropped to their bellies. By the time the fire and police vehicles arrived, the would-be vatos at the edge of the roof were peering through the drainage holes in the wall like troops at the gun slits of a fortress.

Nesto had told them to choose targets without body armor and wait until the police were firing tear gas to mask the sound of their shots. Freddie would give the command to fire.

To Freddie, the policemen visible through the small opening were unreal figures—shooting at them was like playing *Vice City 5*. As he'd done countless times at the arcade, he lined up the target's torso in his gunsight.

"Now!" Freddie shouted and squeezed the trigger.

The man in his sight arched his shoulders and slumped to the ground. "Let's go!" Freddie said after hearing the guns of the boys beside him. Nesto had been clear: take one shot and get out.

The boys crawled away from the wall, dropped into the

alley behind the restaurant, and ran. In a secluded gravel lot two blocks away, Nesto waited for them in his car. Driving away slowly, Nesto said solemnly, "You have brought honor to El Farol. You are now men, and my brothers, carne de mi carne."

THE RIO GRANDE INCIDENT:
Month 2, Day 5

Like the thirteen English colonies huddled along
the coast of North America in 1776, the countries
of Latin America will one day reach an epiphany of
consciousness and unite into a single nation. This is
their inevitable destiny.

> *—José Antonio Marcha, 1982*
> *Translated by J. M. Herrera*

The nation's television networks interrupted their regular programming to report on the shooting of three policemen outside a Best Help drugstore in East Los Angeles. Two officers were pronounced dead at the scene; another was in critical condition. The talking heads somberly said the shootings appeared to be a premeditated attack against law enforcement personnel—a first in the current wave of rioting.

Two days later, a sheriff's deputy was shot during a disturbance in El Paso. Over the next week, police and firefighters were fired on throughout the Southwest.

The new hit-and-run tactics sparked a national debate. Were these the actions of isolated individuals, an organized national resistance, or the work of foreign enemies?

To America's pundits, the tragic events unfolding in the

Southwest demanded a more momentous cause than the lashing out of bored, frustrated, jobless teens with nothing to lose. This search for a grander meaning would elevate an obscure intellectual from Chile into the figurehead of an international movement.

José Antonio Marcha y Huber was a senior aide to Chile's foreign minister in the government of Salvador Allende when a 1973 CIA-sponsored coup overthrew Allende's leftist regime. Accompanied by his wife and children, Marcha sought refuge with a sister in Los Angeles. Inside "the belly of the beast," as he put it, the former government policymaker was forced to support his family with the only work he could find—as a hotel clerk.

Despite his reduced circumstances, Marcha wrote voluminously on a battered Smith Corona, chain-smoking Salems late into the night. Without any prospects of publication, Marcha authored a long series of treatises on the history and politics of the Americas. After his death in 1997, his manuscripts were published on the Internet by his children to honor his memory. In this fashion, his views acquired a modest circulation among a small group of academics and intellectuals.

Central to Marcha's theories was an obscure idea that the media would designate as the cause célèbre for the current civil disturbances: La República Hispana de América—the Hispanic Republic of America.

Marcha's vision for the Hispanic Republic of America was inspired by his love/hate relationship with the United States. Before settling in North America, Marcha thought of himself as a Chilean. But after living in the U.S., Marcha discovered he had another identity. He was also a "Hispanic." It was in the U.S. where Marcha first began to feel solidarity with other Latin Americans. The transformation was not simple.

Marcha was deeply steeped in Chile's rivalry with its neighbors, Bolivia and Peru. The enmity between the nations harkened back to a bitter, five-year border war that began in 1879. Putting aside these regional rivalries was only part of Marcha's conversion.

Like most upper-crust Chileans, José Antonio Marcha was of European ancestry. He held a smug and barely concealed sense of superiority over the indigenous people and mestizos in his country. A blueblood in his own land with a German-born grandfather, Marcha was appalled to learn that as a Hispanic living in the United States, he was lumped into the same racial category as the people he once disdained.

Marcha's eventual sense of kinship with all the races of Latin America was forged by the pressure of American prejudice. He began to see himself the way most Americans saw him—as a member of a downtrodden minority.

At the same time, Marcha also marveled at the diversity and vastness of the United States. In spite of its mélange of people and unwieldy size, the U.S. had managed to create a nation that spanned a continent. This observation sparked a question in Marcha's mind: *Could Latin America ever transform itself from a collection of separate states into a single nation?* In time, he came to believe that the unification of Latin America was not only possible, it was the region's inevitable destiny.

He spent the rest of his life on this quest.

Most of Marcha's writings were impeccably researched, supported by numerous references and sources. But buried within his tedious prose was an idea that threatened to engulf the United States in a bitter civil war.

Marcha asserted that large portions of Texas, California, Florida, New Mexico, and Arizona belonged to the people of the Hispanic Republic of America, and he demanded reclamation of these territories. His work pointed to several historical precedents, among them the creation of the State of Israel based on the Zionist movement's prior claim to Palestine.

There was no denying that all five U.S. states had, at one time, been under Spanish or Mexican control. And, with the exception of Florida, this was precisely where the turmoil was taking place today. The cause for the calm in Florida lay ninety miles south of Key West.

Since the end of the Castro regime, the predominantly Cuban community of South Florida had been embroiled in a thorny tangle of property disputes in Cuba. The returning exiles and their descendants were fighting in the courts—and sometimes in the streets—to reestablish property rights more than sixty years old. It was apparent that Cuban-Americans were one Hispanic group with a separate agenda. However, within most other Hispanic communities in the United States, the words of José Antonio Marcha would soon become a siren song.

THE RIO GRANDE INCIDENT:
Month 2, Day 7

Mano could make out the downtown skyline behind the badly faded sign of the Ultra Care Car Wash. A clear day in August was rare in the valley and Mano tried to convince himself it was a good omen.

He needed a lift. After eleven years as a mechanic, he couldn't imagine being back where he started, looking for work at a car wash.

Inside the door marked "Office," Mano found a cramped foyer dominated by a bulletproof reception window. With no one in sight, he rang the speaker box on the wall, and a metallic voice replied from the unit.

"Yeah?"

"I'm looking for work, sir," Mano said into the microphone.

"Fill out an application. They're on the table," the voice said.

After completing the application, Mano buzzed again. A balding, middle-aged Anglo appeared at the window—and was immediately startled by Mano's intimidating size. "OK, big fella, let's take a look," he said warily.

Mano passed the application through a curved slot below the window. The manager grunted as he skimmed the form. "You got work papers?" he finally said.

Although born in Los Angeles, Mano was used to the question. He had swarthy skin and a Spanish surname. "Yes, sir. Here's a copy of my honorable discharge from the Army," he said, producing the folded document from his pocket.

The manager looked over the photocopy, furrowing his brow suspiciously. He then pointed to Mano's application. "It says here you worked as a mechanic, Suarez. But I don't need a mechanic, see. All we do here is wash cars. Comprende?"

"That's OK. I'll work washing cars, sir," Mano said, trying not to take offense. Like most third-generation Chicanos, Mano spoke English far better than Spanish.

"Well, that's the thing, see. The minute a mechanic job opens up, you're gone."

"With all due respect, sir, would you rather hire some crackhead who's going to quit the next time he makes a big score?"

"All right, all right, big guy, I'll put you on the list. But I gotta tell you. Business ain't so good and I got about fifteen guys ahead of you waiting for the next opening. Comprende?"

"Yes, I understand," Mano said calmly. "Thank you for accepting my application."

"Yeah, sure." The manager sounded relieved.

Mano returned to the pavement outside the car wash. The bright sky was doing little to raise his mood.

When the Ford dealership he worked at for eight years had gone out of business, Mano had stayed hopeful. He combed the want ads each day, looking for other dealership positions. When that failed, he tried garages and gas stations, often appearing in person. When his tools were repossessed, he gave up on work as a mechanic and applied at department stores, restaurants, even fast-food joints. No luck. Absolutely nada. If La Migra hadn't put an end to it years ago, he would have joined the illegals outside a Home Depot and taken day work. Now, after nearly six months of rejection, his confidence was fading.

There's no one else to blame, he told himself. This country gave a man the freedom to shape his own destiny—for better or worse. Still, he could not figure out where he'd gone wrong. For sure, his luck had not been good.

The insurance company had declared his family's station wagon destroyed in "an act of civil unrest" and nullified the claim. Since then, he'd been forced to search for work on foot.

Mano stared at the cracks in the sidewalk. This job opening had been his last hope. Now he'd have to tell Rosa about the grim deadline that loomed next week: the end of his unemployment benefits.

Looking up from the pavement, Mano saw the spires of Holy Trinity Church glinting in the sunshine above the clutter of signs along the street. Without knowing why, he began walking in their direction. A short while later, he stood in front of the church.

Mano had never been devout. He relied on Rosa to tend to the religion for the family. On the day he'd lost his job, Rosa lit a votive candle on the family's small shrine to La Virgen Morena and had prayed over it daily ever since. Maybe it was time he prayed as well. *There's not much left for me to do*, he told himself, entering the carved wood door.

Kneeling in the empty church, Mano heard footsteps behind him. "Good morning," a warm voice said from the aisle.

Mano turned and saw a blond-haired man in his mid-thirties wearing the collar of a priest. "Good morning, Father," Mano said, feeling strange calling a man his own age "Father."

The priest extended his palm. "I'm Father Johnson."

Mano stood and shook his hand. "My name is Manolo Suarez."

"Please, sit down," the priest said, settling into the pew next to Mano. "What brings you to church so early on such a fine day, Manolo?"

Mano did not want to air his problems, but he could not bring himself to lie. "I felt a need to pray," he said finally.

"Most people come to pray during Mass. I've found that those who come in to pray at other times are usually facing something serious," the priest said slowly.

"I'd rather not talk about it, Father. It's nothing."

"Then why not talk about it? Sometimes talking helps."

Father Johnson's calm and open manner put Mano at ease. Speaking quietly, he told the priest about his six-month struggle to find a job, the loss of his car, and the end of his unemployment benefits next week. "I've used up all my ideas, Father. So I figured there was only one thing left that could help my family...and that was to pray. That's why I'm here."

The priest put his hand on Mano's shoulder, showing no fear of his bulk. "May I tell you a story about prayer, Manolo?"

"I think that's your job, isn't it, Padre?" Mano answered with a small smile.

The priest laughed. "You haven't lost your sense of humor, Manolo. I think your family is in good hands."

"I don't know, Father. Lately, I haven't done so well," Mano said, looking down.

"Is that your fault? Did you ask to lose your job? Haven't you looked for work every day? You're doing everything you can, Manolo. It's our society that's letting you down," the priest said with a sudden burst of passion.

"With all due respect, Padre, no one owes me anything. It's *my* responsibility to take care of my family."

"You're right, Manolo. You do have a personal responsibility. But perhaps it's your duty to make the world a better place for everyone, not just for yourself and your family."

"I'm not sure I understand."

"Let me tell you my story about prayer, Manolo. Perhaps that will help. There once was a woman who wanted very badly to win the lottery. Every morning, she would kneel by her bed and pray. 'Lord, please, please, please let me win the lottery so I can buy a home for my poor parents.' Every night, she would pray again. 'Lord, please, please, please let me win the lottery. It's not for me—it's for my poor parents who don't have a home.' This went on for months. Every day without fail, she would pray, morning and night. And then one day, the Lord finally answered her prayers. He said, 'Give me a break, lady. Buy a lottery ticket.'"

Mano laughed harder than he had for quite some time.

And then, without warning, he felt the shame and despair he'd been holding back for months flood over him. He covered his face and wept quietly.

When he finally composed himself, he was surprised to find his confidence returning. "Thanks, Padre," he whispered.

"Don't thank me. You've bought a ticket, Manolo," the priest said gently. "But it might be in the wrong lottery."

"I still don't understand you, Father."

"I'm going to put you in touch with someone who can explain it to you . . . and perhaps give you a job."

Mano strode briskly across the weed-choked turf of Belvedere Park, still wondering why Father Johnson had insisted he memorize his destination rather than write it down. He repeated it to himself once again: *Joe Herrera, Cielo Azul Bookstore, four blocks north of Belvedere Park.*

Crossing Fisher Street, he saw the bookstore. The shop was undamaged by the rioting, its large front window stacked to the ceiling with a haphazard clutter of books that blocked the view inside.

A mild chime rang as Mano opened the door and stepped slowly into the dimly lit shop, the air pungent with the smell of moldy books.

"Buenos días, señor," said a voice from the darkness.

As Mano's eyes adjusted to the gloom, he saw a man behind a counter at the back of the room. The shopkeeper looked well over sixty, his gray hair pulled back into a ponytail. The man's high cheekbones and bronze skin revealed a blend of Spanish and Native American ancestors.

So this is Joe Herrera, Mano thought as he walked forward and extended his hand over the counter. Though his own beefy grip engulfed the smaller man's hand, he found the shopkeeper's handshake surprisingly firm.

"Hello, sir. I'm Manolo Suarez."

"What can I do for you, Mr. Suarez?" the older man said in perfect English.

"Father Johnson sent me. He said you might have a job

available, but he wasn't very clear about what kind of job it might be."

"Father Johnson has sent people to us before. They're usually looking for answers they can't find in a church. Are you one of those people?"

"I'm not looking for answers, sir. I'm looking for a job."

"You're also a man who comes right to the point, I see," he said, breaking into a smile.

"Yes, sir. And right now I'm wondering what kind of job a mechanic would find in a bookstore."

"Well, let's start by finding out more about you. We should have our employment applications around here somewhere," he said, crouching behind the counter. "Ah, here they are."

The application was far simpler than any of the hundreds Mano had seen over the last six months. He stood at the counter and quickly completed the form.

"I'll take your application into the office and have it processed," the older man said, carrying the sheet toward the steel door behind the counter. "Our decision won't take long. If you'd like to wait, you're welcome to sit down," he said, gesturing toward a pair of upholstered chairs in the corner of the shop.

"You mean I'll know today if you're hiring me?"

"Yes, that's very likely."

"Then I'll be glad to wait. Thank you, sir."

Too excited to sit, Mano began wandering around the room. With the exception of those crowding the front window, the books in the room were carefully arranged, their subjects neatly labeled along the edges of the shelves. African-American

Studies. Aromatherapy. Astrology. To Mano, the subjects seemed out of place for a barrio bookstore. Then again, *any* bookstore was rare in East Los Angeles. Except for the large number of titles in Spanish, he would have expected to see a store like this in Venice Beach.

The books in the room did not hold his attention. He'd never had much time for reading, but he did have an eye for detail. It didn't take Mano long to realize that from where he stood, there was an eye-level gap in the clutter of books along the front window. The space provided a view of the eastern approach to the store. *Is this intentional?* he wondered. He ambled along the pile of books and, at about three paces from the front door, he saw another gap with a view toward the west. *Is there a purpose for these peepholes?*

Before he could explore this mystery further, Mano heard the steel door open behind him. Emerging from the office was a tall woman with long honey-blonde hair. Even across the shadowy room, Mano could see her ice-blue eyes. She appeared to be in her early thirties, with a complexion and features he would have expected to see in Beverly Hills instead of East Los Angeles. Despite a drab T-shirt, faded jeans, and spare makeup, her raw beauty would have turned any man's head.

"Buenos días, Señor Suárez. Bienvenido a nuestra tienda," the woman said. Although Mano spoke only a handful of words in Spanish, he'd grown up hearing it and knew immediately Spanish was her native tongue.

"Hello, ma'am," Mano replied. "As I told Mr. Herrera—"

"I'm sorry. There's no Mr. Herrera here," the woman interrupted in flawless English.

"But I'm certain Father Johnson told me to come see Joe Herrera…at the Cielo Azul Bookstore."

"Yes, he did. I'm Jo Herrera…*Josefina*," she said, pronouncing her first name—*Ho-say-FEE-nah*—with its Spanish inflection.

"I'm sorry. I meant no disrespect, ma'am."

"It's OK—you're not the first."

"When Father Johnson said 'Joe Herrera,' I figured—"

"Mark—*Father Johnson*—has a sense of humor. And besides, he may have thought you might be reluctant to apply for work at a business run by a woman."

"No, ma'am. That's no problem. My last CO in the Army was a woman. But I'm a mechanic. I'm not sure what I can do in a bookstore."

"Besides this bookstore, I own a recycling business. We keep our trucks in a garage on the other side of the alley," she said, gesturing toward the back door. "The business is growing and we're going to need another driver soon. We could also use your skills as a mechanic to keep the trucks running."

"I have a California CDL, so I'm licensed to drive up to thirteen tons," Mano said eagerly.

"Yes, I know."

"You didn't ask about my CDL on your application. How did you know?"

Jo tapped her fingertips together. "For now, let's just say we have certain resources."

Although Mano found this answer puzzling, the prospect of finding a job overrode his misgivings. He was elated at the chance to work again. "Is there anything else you need to know?"

A soft smile crossed Jo's face. "Can you start Monday?"

Mano walked home with a jaunt in his stride that had been missing for quite some time. To celebrate their good fortune, he stopped for a modest bouquet of flowers for Rosa and a cake for the children. After six months of scrimping, the time had come to splurge a little.

Since losing his car, Mano had grown closer to the soul of his barrio. The riots had not changed the daily pulse of life amid the bungalows, bars, body shops, apartments, and weedy vacant lots. Dusk was a time when those heading home from work crossed paths with the ever-present teens and people of the night—the gangbangers, drug dealers, pimps, and prostitutes.

Near his apartment, Mano saw the Jimenez twins playing hopscotch on the crowded sidewalk with a crushed Budweiser Tall Boy can.

"Hi, big guy!" one of them called out, giggling.

Mano waved, feeling a pang of pity. Although the girls were only five, they were on the street alone. Both their parents worked, and their nana—as grandmothers were called in Chicano households—often let the twins wander outside while she did her chores.

Mano had no such worries about his own children. Each day at five, Rosa would bring the kids inside, prepare the food, set the table, and wait until Mano was home before serving their evening meal. The family ritual was now unquestioned.

Entering the courtyard to his apartment, Mano recognized the throaty growl of a V-8, accompanied by an odd series of pops. He turned and saw an SUV speeding down the crowded street, bright muzzle flashes coming from its windows. For a heartbeat, he stared in disbelief. *They're shooting at us.*

Acting on instincts honed in combat, Mano dropped his packages and dove into the courtyard. On his belly, he watched in horror as the vehicle raced down the street, firing at anyone in sight. People on the crowded sidewalks tried to run, but few made it to safety. The bullets found their marks in a sickening array. Some victims seemed to be performing a spastic dance, twitching awkwardly before falling. Others simply collapsed like marionettes with severed strings.

Before Mano could make a move to help, it was over.

The roar of the engine faded, replaced by raw cries of pain. Mano looked around, stunned. His neighbor, Lourdes Echeverría, was crawling toward the courtyard, her face drenched in blood. Near her, an elderly man stood motionless, transfixed by the bodies littering the sidewalk.

"Mano!" Rosa called out, emerging from their apartment behind him. "What happened?"

Mano rose to his feet and stopped her in the courtyard before she could reach the street. "Go back inside, querida. People have been shot and there may be more trouble." He led Rosa to the entrance of their apartment and found Pedro, Julio, and Elena gathered at the door, drawn by the commotion.

"There's been an accident," Rosa said to the children. "We need to stay inside and keep out of the way."

When Mano moved back toward the street, Rosa reached for his hand. "Where are you going?"

"The wounded need help."

"Your children need you, too."

"Don't worry, mi amor. I'll be careful," he said before turning away.

Nearing the street, Mano noticed the bouquet he'd been carrying was now strewn along the pavement. The flower petals were blowing toward a sight he'd never forget.

Slumped against a wall were the Jimenez twins, their frail bodies riddled by bullets, blood seeping into the crudely drawn squares of their hopscotch game. They had died embracing each other.

Mano stared, numb with horror, oblivious to the chaos around him until the panicked screaming on the street finally broke his trance. With a shudder, he looked away from the twins and noticed the confusion swirling around him. People trying to help the wounded were rushing frantically among the victims scattered along the street.

Mano grabbed a trash can lid, moved to a stretch of street without any parked cars, and began banging on the metal lid furiously with a stone. The faces in the crowd quickly turned toward the noise. "Listen to me!" he called out. "Move all the injured here so the medics can treat them in one place when they arrive," he yelled, gesturing to the sidewalk in front of him. Minutes later, the wounded that could be moved were placed along the open stretch of street. After what seemed a very long time, the wail of sirens joined their cries.

On the narrow streets approaching the shooting scene, news vans jockeyed for position with emergency medical vehicles rushing to treat the injured. Despite the gallant efforts of Mano and his neighbors, several victims bled to death before the medical crews arrived. An angry mood swirled through the crowd. Before the last of the ambulances pulled away, a vacant building three blocks away was set ablaze. By the time

Mano returned to his family, more fires had been set and several businesses set upon. The arson and looting continued through the night.

The shooting spree on East Fourth Street had left eleven dead and twenty-eight wounded. The following day, another drive-by shooting on Pico Street killed eight more. Television interviews with eyewitnesses at both East Los Angeles locations revealed a common detail: the men in the vehicle appeared to be Anglos. Putting a new twist on a frontier term, the media immediately dubbed the attackers "vigilantes."

THE RIO GRANDE INCIDENT:
Month 2, Day 10

Jo was behind the counter at the bookstore when Mano arrived for work on Monday morning. "The first thing we'll do is introduce you to the other drivers," she said, leading him out the back door. Following his new boss, Mano tried not to stare at the slim and sensuous body under her tight jeans.

Crossing the alley behind the bookstore, they approached a large concrete garage in a compound enclosed by a high chain-link fence. Above the building's main entrance, someone had hand-painted "Green Planet Recycling Company" in olive-colored letters. The rest of the walls were a variety of gaudy shades. "We hire kids from the community to paint the building every few months. I let them pick the colors," Jo explained. "We're due for another coat, but after the shootings this weekend, I'm not sure it's going to be safe for them to work outside." She opened the gate and added bitterly, "These attacks were horrible...but I'm not completely surprised. It was only a matter of time before this kind of vermin crawled out of their holes."

Mano said nothing. He had no desire to relive the attack.

Jo stopped suddenly and turned to face him. "Hey, I just remembered something from your application," she said, her eyes widening. "Wasn't the first attack near your home?"

"Yes," he said after a moment's pause.

"Did you see what happened?"

Mano's face tightened. "I'd rather not talk about it, ma'am."

"Of course, Manolo. I understand," she said, nodding. "Let's go inside."

Mano was grateful to Jo for not prying. When he'd returned from Afghanistan, people had pressed him for details about his combat experiences. Like most soldiers, Mano had learned to put the horrors behind him and move on. It was the only way to survive. The vigilante attack was no different. Surprisingly, Jo seemed to respect that.

Inside the garage, three men sat sipping coffee at a small table near their trucks. Two of the drivers, Pepe and Luis, were Chicanos. The third was a black man wearing a do-rag. When Jo introduced him as Jesús Lopez, Mano tried to hide his surprise. Although he'd soldiered with a black Puerto Rican, Mano had never met an Afro-Latino in East Los Angeles. Until this moment, he'd never questioned why.

Once the introductions were over, Jo seemed eager to leave. "Why don't you start by taking an inventory of our parts and tools, Manolo?" she said, walking toward the door. "I'll be in the office if you need me."

After watching Jo leave, Luis addressed the newcomer. "You know anybody that went down, Manolo? From the vigilantes, I mean. My neighbor lost his brother Saturday night. They shot him in the belly and he bled to death—right on the street, man."

"I'm sorry to hear that," Mano answered.

"That was some wrong shit, man," Luis added. "I brought my piece," he said, patting his pants pocket. "Those fucking vigilantes mess with me, I'm gonna be ready."

Pepe leaned forward, his eyes eager. "Let me see, Luis. Show it to me."

Luis reached into his pocket and produced a cheap .25 caliber pistol. Mano knew this puny Saturday night special would do little to stop the heavily armed vigilantes.

"I'm getting me some hardware, too," Pepe said excitedly. "We can't just take this bullshit."

Although he shared their outrage, this bravado worried Mano. "I want to stop them as much as you do," he said evenly, "but a gunfight in the street might get more innocent people killed. Stray bullets don't know the good guys from the bad guys."

Luis scowled. "What are we supposed to do, man? Lay down like a bunch of jotos?"

Before the confrontation could escalate, Jesús raised his coffee cup toward Mano in a toast. "Estás bienvenido, Manolo. Por seguro necesitamos un mecánico."

"I'm sorry, Jesús. I don't speak much Spanish."

"You welcome here," Jesús said in a thick accent. "We much need a mecánico."

Pepe and Luis grudgingly nodded in agreement.

"Thanks, Jesús. I'm glad to have the job. Have you been working here long?"

Jesús held up a pair of fingers. "Two jeers."

Studying the man's friendly face, Mano wondered how Jesús had dealt with the brewing tensions between Latinos and African-Americans. "I guess you're not from Mexico," he said, offering Jesús an opening.

"No. I from Panama," Jesús answered, his features suddenly tight.

Sensing the driver's uneasiness, Mano changed the subject. "You like working here?"

Jesús's face brightened again. "Josefina is good boss, man," he said, smiling. "She very rich. She no have to come to el barrio. Josefina start business here because she want justicia."

Mano's eyebrows knitted. "What is 'hoos-tee-see-uh'?"

Jesús shrugged. "I don't know how to say in English."

"Justicia means justice," Luis offered.

"You won't work for anybody better, man," Pepe chimed in. "I mean, she a chick and everything. So we gotta do some silly shit sometimes. But Jo looks out for our people."

Mano nodded. "That's good to know."

Their gruff formalities complete, the drivers climbed aboard their trucks and roared out of the garage, leaving Mano to his inventory project. He dove into the task like a man who'd stumbled onto a cool pond after a long stretch in the desert. Shortly after 3 p.m., he knocked on the bookstore's heavy steel door. "Excuse me, ma'am. I'm done with the inventory. Here's the report. Is there something else you need me to do?"

Jo took the paper from his hand. "Not right now, Mano. Why don't you take a seat until something comes up?" she said, pointing toward the chairs in the corner. "You're welcome to borrow any of the reading material."

Alone in the shop, Mano glanced restlessly through the books, too anxious to sit down and read. Having nothing to do was a bad sign. A few minutes later, he returned to the garage, determined to find a productive task. He could not fail his family again.

Rosa Suarez knew her husband's habits. Every Wednesday after the children were asleep, Mano worked out with the barbells stored in their closet. The rhythmic clinking of his free weights was a comforting cadence for Rosa, a familiar ritual that marked the passing of another week. But this Wednesday was different. Mano had come home with a six-pack. After dinner, he'd remained at the table, staring out the kitchen window, drinking methodically.

Once the children were in bed, Rosa approached her husband.

"Que te pasa, Mano? Is something bothering you?" she asked, clearing the empty cans from the table.

Beer sprayed onto the floor as Mano popped the top on the last can. "Everything's fine, querida," he answered, slurring slightly.

"Are you sure, mi amor? You've never brought home liquor before." The only time she'd seen her husband drink alcohol was at parties and weddings.

"This?" he said, holding up the beer can. "It's just my way of celebrating," he said dryly.

"People don't celebrate by drinking alone, Mano. What about this new boss of yours—what do you call her? Jo? Is she being difficult?" Rosa didn't know what to make of this odd woman. To Rosa, Jo had intruded in the world of men—something bound to cause trouble.

Mano shook his head. "No. Jo seems OK. She's started a business in East L.A. that's created jobs. Not a lot of rich Hispanics doing that."

"What is it, then? You finally found work, mi amor. I thought you'd be happy."

"It's hard to be happy when our neighbors are buying coffins," he answered before taking another long swallow.

Rosa made the sign of the cross. "We can't change what's happened, Mano. It was God's will. I've been praying every day for—" Before she could finish, there was a knock on the door. "I'll get that," she said, moving quickly toward the entrance. She did not want anyone to see her husband like this.

Ignoring the murmurs from the doorway, Mano brought the can to his lips again, a distant focus in his eyes. *How long will this job last?* He'd asked himself that question countless times over the last three days. Jo seemed a good person, but she was not running a charity. Without more to do, he might be back on the street again any day. And the streets were getting deadly.

Mano was no stranger to death. He'd seen men die shrieking in pain in Afghanistan. But the memory of the Jimenez twins huddled on the sidewalk plagued him in a way the sight of soldiers killed in combat never had. Since the shootings, his dreams had been haunted by the twins—a nightmare that always ended with the bodies of his own children on the bloody sidewalk.

The vigilantes had already struck twice; he was sure they would again. His wife and children were in danger anytime they stepped outside—and not just from the vigilantes. Luis and Pepe were not alone. Working people in the barrios were arming themselves, escalating the risk. The only way to protect his family was to move them out of this place. That would take money, though, which meant his job was their only ticket out of harm's way—if it lasted.

When Rosa returned, she held a small bundle of clothes, her eyes welling with tears. "It was Nana Jimenez," she whispered. "She gave me these clothes for Elena. They belonged to the twins." Tears began a slow path down her cheeks as she looked at the garments. A small yellow Mickey Mouse shirt was folded neatly on top. "What kind of men would do such a thing, Mano?"

Mano drained the rest of the beer as he pondered her question.

The men who'd done the shooting did not care who they killed. To them, one Hispanic was the same as any other—young, old, woman, man, it didn't matter. Mano knew only one thing could create such senseless cruelty. "Men who are afraid," he said at last.

"Afraid of what?"

"Us," he said, crushing the empty beer can.

⸻

During his first four days on the job, Mano tuned up the trucks, reorganized the tool drawers, drew up a vehicle maintenance schedule, and cleaned out the cluttered garage—all on his own initiative. The drivers had seemed glad to have a mechanic. But where was the work they needed? He did not want to ask them the question, fearing the answer.

Until now, he'd clung to the hope that Jo had yet to figure out the best way to use him. But by Friday afternoon, he could no longer deny the obvious: there wasn't enough work for him. Jo had suggested he wait in the bookstore on Monday. Maybe if she saw him sitting idly, she'd find a task for him.

He crossed the alley and entered the bookstore through the back door. Ramon Garcia, the man he'd mistaken for "Joe Herrera" that first day, was behind the counter, reading a book. As soon as Mano sat down, Ramon retreated into the office, leaving him alone.

A week ago, Mano thought finding a job would solve all his problems. How quickly that had changed. Now, the safety of his family depended on keeping this job—a job that looked shakier each day. The uncertainty was a torment more intense than being out of work. Something had to change. The shame in Rosa's eyes when he drank was unbearable. Yet it took a belly full of beer each night to numb his mind enough to sleep. Even then, the nightmares of the twins usually returned.

As the silent minutes passed, Mano imagined Jo's words of dismissal: *I'm sorry, Manolo. This isn't working out. You've seen for yourself why we have to let you go.* He could even picture the pity in her eyes. That was the most painful image of all.

Looking for a distraction, he noticed a stack of pamphlets on the small table next to him. He opened one of the brochures and began reading.

JUSTICIA, by José Antonio Marcha. Edited by J. M. Herrera.

If you are a Latino living in the United States, you are a foreigner in your own country. That's right. You may not realize it, but you are the rightful heir to significant parts of the territory now called the United States.

Look around you. Spanish place names prevail throughout most of Texas, California, New Mexico, Arizona, and Florida. The cities of Los Angeles, San Francisco, San Antonio, El Paso, and Albuquerque are just a few of the many places founded by your ancestors. They came from Spain, merged with the indigenous people of the Americas and the slaves brought over from Africa, and created the Hispanic culture. This was a unique and profound fusion of people and traditions. Nothing like it has ever taken place in the United States.

This new Hispanic culture existed throughout much of North and South America for over four centuries. However, the Hispanic settlements in North America were overrun by the territorial expansion of the United States during the 1800s. These illegal immigrants often squatted on Hispanic lands, then wrested them away by force. The so-called "Battle of the Alamo" is probably the best-known example. The Anglo aggressors crushed the Hispanic societies they conquered, driving away your ancestors or reducing them to positions of servitude.

Over the last few decades, Hispanics have been returning in large numbers to their former homelands through "immigration." Yet Hispanics in these U.S.-occupied territories are relegated to the lowest rungs of the social ladder. They are denied the opportunity to work and live where they choose. Most Hispanics are only hired for menial jobs and then frequently paid unfair wages. Through discriminatory housing practices, they are reduced to living in crowded, filthy, crime-infested barrios. Sometimes the prejudice is overt; at other times, the discrimination is indirect. And most galling of all, this injustice is perpetrated on soil that was once their own.

This must stop. The time has come for you to reclaim the lands that are rightfully yours.

This is treason, Mano thought as he stopped reading. He was a native-born American who'd fought for his country. This pamphlet was an attack on everything he believed. And yet...

The words also captured the frustration he fought every day to ignore.

Despite his rock-hard loyalty to his country, Mano was astonished to find he could not completely reject the ideas in the pamphlet. He was left with a nagging doubt, a feeling gnawing in his belly that something in the words was right. He looked back down at the booklet in his hands and finished reading *Justicia.*

Those eight pages would open the first crack in the foundations of his world.

Ramon was connecting to the Internet when the familiar creak of the steel door announced Jo's arrival. She entered hurriedly, a laptop case slung over her shoulder. As usual on even-numbered days, she carried two Starbucks lattes. She and Ramon shared an addiction to lattes—Jo from her days at Stanford and Ramon from his movie-producer wife. Now that all the coffee joints in East Los Angeles were closed, the two took turns stopping in Santa Monica to satisfy their morning habit.

"Buenos días," Ramon said without looking up from his computer.

"Good morning, Ramon. You and Maggie have a good weekend?" Jo asked, placing the latte on his desk.

"We went to see *Il Trovatore* Saturday night. The singing

was tolerable. But the direction hasn't been very inspired this season. How about you?"

"It was OK," Jo said, meticulously tidying the neat stacks of folders on her desk while the laptop powered up.

"I wouldn't be surprised if you worked all weekend again."

Jo sighed. "Please don't tell me again I work too much, Ray."

"All right, Josefina. We'll skip my weekly sermon on overwork."

"Muchas gracias. So what's on our agenda for today?"

"I think our first order of business is the status of Manolo."

Lattes in hand, the two walked to a corner of the office shielded from the door by a partition. The back side of the partition contained six surveillance monitors. In the upper-right screen, Mano was visible inspecting the trucks in the garage. Ramon twisted a switch and the image of Mano moved rapidly in reverse, the time code in the corner of the screen counting backward.

"He's been arriving every morning before seven-thirty," Ramon said. "So far, his behavior has matched up with our research. He's got all the qualities we're looking for in a bodyguard—intelligence, a clean criminal record, and military experience. I think he's the most promising recruit Mark has ever sent us, Jo."

"What's your take on his politics?"

"Getting him on our side of the fence won't be easy. He served two hitches with the Rangers and saw combat in Afghanistan. That's not exactly the résumé of a radical."

"No, but there's something else, Ray. He saw the first vigilante shooting. He didn't want to talk about it, which tells me it was pretty bad."

"I see what you mean. That'll certainly help us win him over," Ramon said, rubbing his chin. "But I wouldn't bring it up with him, Jo. This could backfire on us if it's not handled delicately."

"Yeah, I feel terrible poaching on a tragedy," she said, suddenly dispirited.

Ramon smiled wryly. "Listen, with all due respect to the feminist deities, I think a woman who looks like a movie star and is smarter than Henry Kissinger is going to be a damn good recruiter, no matter what."

Jo shook her head in mock disgust. "You're a closet sexist, Ramon," she said, smiling.

"Maybe. But I doubt you'll spare the charm to bring an asset like Manolo into our camp. A man like that could help us."

"I wish he spoke better Spanish. Apparently, he only speaks a few words, though I'm sure he understands a lot more than that."

"That's not unusual for a third-generation Chicano. The genealogy databases show his grandfather came to the U.S. as a field laborer under the Bracero program during World War II. He must have been one of the few who didn't get sent back to Mexico after the GIs returned. That man must have been one hard worker."

"The work ethic must run in the family. It took a full week without specific assignments to get him into the bookstore to read the material."

"He's had the weekend to mull it over. I expect we'll get his reaction this morning."

"You're usually right about these things, Ramon. It will be interesting to see how Señor Suarez feels about Señor Marcha," Jo said, taking the first sip of her latte.

For the third time that morning, Mano scanned the parking lot behind the bookstore. This time, Jo's Volvo sedan was there. The time had come to confront his boss.

Even as he walked across the alley, Mano wasn't sure what he would say. One thing was certain: he needed this job. But he felt himself drawn to this encounter by his sense of duty, a need to defend the principles of his country. He entered the bookstore and saw Jo behind the counter.

"Buenos días, Manolo," she said with a smile.

Without preface, Mano pulled the *Justicia* pamphlet from his pocket and thrust it toward her. "Ma'am, do you support what's written here?"

"Yes, Manolo," she answered calmly. "In fact, I translated and edited *Justicia*."

Mano looked at the cover of the pamphlet. *Edited by J. M. Herrera*, it read. He had not noticed the editor's name. "No disrespect, ma'am, but I've been trying to figure out whether this is treason or just plain crazy."

"There isn't a third alternative?"

"What would that be?"

"That it's the truth."

Mano shook his head, struggling to find the right words. "No, ma'am, it can't be true. I don't know how to explain it. But, it's...it's just not the way things are."

"Manolo, long ago, a wise person said, 'Time makes more converts than reason.' Hispanics in America have come to accept the way things are, not because they're fair or just, but because it's the way things have been for a very long time."

"That sounds anti-American."

"The man who said this was Thomas Paine, one of the patriots of the American Revolution...although the Tories considered him a traitorous rabble-rouser."

Stymied by her answer, Mano tried another argument. "What you're proposing isn't legal, ma'am. You can't just barge in and take away people's property."

"Do you think the Anglos did anything different? The ground you're standing on belonged to Hispanic settlers when your great-grandfather was alive. The gabachos didn't ask permission to come here. They swarmed over the land and overran the locals by sheer numbers. And the Anglo takeover didn't just happen in California. The first illegal immigrants in Texas came from Tennessee."

"Why haven't I heard this before?"

"The history they teach in American schools glosses over the fact that most Anglo families in Texas were uninvited squatters. The Anglos not only grabbed up Mexican land, they refused to pay taxes on it. That's why General Santa Anna marched his army to a place called the Alamo—to evict the illegal immigrants."

"No matter how we got the land, there's no other country on earth where people are as free as the United States."

"That's true, Manolo," Jo agreed. "But did you know that England was the most progressive nation in Europe at the time of the American Revolution? No other monarchy had an active parliament and a Magna Carta protecting the rights of its citizens. Yet all those privileges didn't stop the American colonists from asserting their independence." Jo paused, letting her words sink in. "Do you think our cause seems any less justified than that of the American colonists?"

Mano knew he was outmatched in a debate with Jo. His

strongest argument came from the gut, and it told him her ideas were dangerous. "I don't have your education, ma'am. But I still believe you're wrong," he said tersely.

"I realize I'm not going to change your views, Manolo," she said gently. "I can see you find Marcha's ideas difficult to accept."

"I think they border on treason."

"Surely you agree that people have the right of free speech in this country."

"Treason is not protected by any rights, ma'am."

Jo reached for the *Justicia* pamphlet he was holding, gently cradling his hand in her own. "Look at this, Manolo," she said, pointing to the back cover. "The works of José Antonio Marcha are registered with the Library of Congress. If there was anything illegal in his writings, I wouldn't be allowed to publish them."

The warm softness of her hand left him speechless for a moment. "I . . . see your point," he finally managed to say.

"So you agree this document does not break any laws?"

"Apparently not."

"That's good to hear. From what I know about you, I can't imagine you'd work for an organization that did something illegal," she said with a soft smile.

Mano's throat tightened. Talk of ending his job was territory he did not want to cross.

Without waiting for an answer, Jo continued. "Manolo, I realize Marcha's ideas seem strange to you. But you should know there are a lot of others who share them—and I have a suggestion that may help. There's a community rally ncxt Saturday at Salazar Park. Why don't you come and listen to the speakers? After that, if you feel that working here compromises your principles, you can quit. What do you say?"

"Look, ma'am, I'm starting to think there won't be a job for me here much longer anyway."

"Why?"

"How long can you carry a salary for someone who isn't doing very much?"

"You let me worry about that, Manolo. I know we haven't had much for you to do yet. But that's temporary. We're planning to expand our routes. Your job is safe."

Mano rubbed his face, trying to mask his relief. He'd listen to these crazy ideas if it meant a chance to protect his family. After all, Jo seemed to mean well—the drivers certainly believed that. Besides, attending a rally didn't mean you supported the cause. "I suppose it wouldn't hurt to go," he said finally.

"I'm very glad to hear that," Jo said, leaning closer. "I'll be driving with Ramon to save parking space. Do you want a ride?"

"Thanks, but I think it'd be best...for family reasons, if I walked, ma'am." The thought of Rosa seeing him get into Jo's car made him uneasy.

"I understand," she said, nodding. "There's something else, though. This 'ma'am' thing is starting to get very old. Would you mind calling me Jo?"

"Sure...Jo," he said, almost whispering her name. "Most people call me Mano."

She reached out and shook his hand firmly. "It's a deal, Mano," she said, meeting his gaze. "I think you may be surprised by what you hear at the rally."

THE RIO GRANDE INCIDENT:
Month 2, Day 22

Intellectuals are the prime ingredient of social ferment.
Their ideas are the yeast that raises the masses into
rebellion.

—*José Antonio Marcha, 1979*
Translated by J. M. Herrera

I don't understand why you have to go to this rally," Rosa
said, bringing her husband an espresso. She'd risen at 6 a.m.
to prepare Mano's breakfast, making this Saturday morning
feel like a workday.

Mano reached distractedly for the small cup. "I gave Jo my
word."

"It doesn't seem right, Mano. A boss shouldn't force her
politics on you."

"That's not what Jo is doing."

"No? Then what do you call it?" she asked, buttering slices
of toast.

"She wants to make sure I'm OK with the things she
believes."

Rosa looked up suspiciously. "Why is it so important to her
what you think?"

"Because she doesn't want me to quit my job," he said, staring straight ahead. "Do you?"

Without answering, Rosa placed the toast in front of him and retreated to their bedroom. Mano finished his breakfast alone and quietly left the apartment. The walk to Salazar Park would take a good part of the morning.

Turning west on Whittier, Mano saw fresh evidence of rioting. The blackened husk of a warehouse was surrounded by piles of ashes still soggy from the fire department's hoses. *Such a waste*, he thought, walking past the burned-out building. Destroying businesses was no way to bring jobs to the barrios. Yet he had to admit his own feelings were no less confused. He was troubled by Jo's ideas but wanted desperately to keep his job. These conflicting thoughts swirled in his head as he paced steadily toward the rally.

It was almost noon when he reached Salazar Park. Although a gray sky threatened rain, the crowd was nearly shoulder to shoulder. Above the sea of bodies on the scruffy grass, he saw a large banner behind the makeshift grandstand.

RALLY FOR JUSTICIA
Unity. Community. Strength.

A couple dozen Anglos with professionally lettered signs supporting the rally stood near the large media contingent ringing the platform. The rest of the crowd appeared to be Eslos—Chicanos from the barrios of East Los Angeles.

As he walked toward the grandstand, Mano spotted several bands of young men in sports jerseys, many in the 49er uniforms of the 19th Street Gang, as well as the UNLV gear worn by their bitter rivals, the Pachucos. Ordinarily, this would have meant heavy trouble, but for some reason, the vatos seemed content to coexist today.

Deployed in a ragged line along the west edge of the park were over a hundred LAPD officers in riot gear. Their slumping postures worried Mano. He knew exhausted men had short fuses.

Near the east stairway to the podium, where Jo had arranged to meet him, Mano saw a posh group of people who looked like dignitaries. Suddenly, a woman among them waved to him.

"Mano...over here," she said. It was Jo.

She wore an elegant blue dress, her golden hair styled in an upward sweep that showcased a gleaming pearl necklace and matching earrings. Ramon, standing beside her, was also transformed, his denim and fatigues replaced by a tweed sports coat and maroon tie, which gave his graying ponytail a look of scholarly sophistication.

Mano was suddenly embarrassed. He'd worn a freshly pressed dress shirt and slacks, the outfit he'd used for his many job interviews. But compared to those in this crowd of dignitaries, he felt coarse and out of place.

As if reading Mano's mind, Ramon produced a handful of silk neckties from his briefcase. "I haven't got a coat that would even come close to fitting you, Mano, but I did bring along a few ties. Maybe you'll find one you like."

Mano ran his calloused fingers hesitantly over the sleek fabric, not sure if he remembered how to tie a knot. The last time he'd worn a tie was for his Army portrait.

"Here...this gray one goes well with your blue shirt," Jo said, looping the tie around his neck. Mano stood frozen as she wove the tie into a knot. "I always loved doing this for my father," she said, smoothing the tie down after she'd finished, lightly caressing Mano's muscular chest. The trail of her fingers left an electric tingle on Mano's skin. Against his will, he looked into Jo's eyes. She met his gaze steadily. "How does that feel?"

Mano cleared his throat. "Fine. Thank you."

"Good. Let's meet the other speakers."

"Other speakers? Are you speaking today, Jo?"

"No, Mano," Ramon answered. "I am."

Mano's eyes widened. Clearly, Ramon Garcia was more than a clerk in a bookstore. He should have noticed that before.

"I see you're surprised," Ramon said, smiling.

"Yes," Mano admitted as an angry chant erupted from the crowd. He nodded toward the Anglo contingent making most of the noise. "What wouldn't surprise me is if there's trouble here today. Do you have a plan in case things get out of hand?"

Jo gave Ramon a knowing look before answering. "Do you have any ideas, Mano?" she asked.

"If trouble breaks out, it's likely to start around the people with the signs over there," he said, pointing toward the Anglos. "The police will probably chase them along the front of the grandstand. Our best bet would be to leave toward the north, behind the stage. That way, we'll avoid the police—they look tired, and tired cops are likely to start beating anyone who isn't wearing a badge."

"That sounds like a good escape plan," Ramon replied. "But we need to find a way to avoid any violence today. Politically, it would be best if this rally remains peaceful."

"In other words," Jo added, "we need to demonstrate that we can control our people when we want to."

"*When you want to?*" Mano repeated. "Are you saying there are times when you *want* people to riot?"

"Mano, do you think all these people and the media would be here today if there hadn't been violence in the past?" Jo asked.

"No," Mano admitted. "But that still doesn't make it right."

"You're a rare person, Mano," Jo said, smiling. "That's why I think you can help our people. Your ethics and discipline can help create justicia," she said. "Maybe you'll find the answers to some of your concerns after you've heard the speakers today. Right now, though, we need to sit down." She took Mano's beefy hand and led him up the grandstand steps.

Appeased, Mano followed quietly as Jo guided him to a row of folding chairs beside the podium. Looking down at the crowd, he suppressed a surge of pride. In the last two weeks, he'd gone from desperate unemployment to a place among the dignitaries at a community rally.

A deejay from the local Radio Única affiliate introduced the rally's first speaker, Octavio Perez, a community leader from San Antonio whose name drew a loud, sustained cheer. Mano had never heard of Perez, but he was unmistakably popular with many Eslos.

Perez began by accusing the Texas National Guard of murdering twenty-three people at the Rio Grande Incident. He then linked those deaths to the vigilante shootings in Los Angeles.

"Where is justice? Where is the protection of the law? Who is responsible for the slaying of these innocents? I lay the blame squarely on the heads of the agents of repression, the thugs with badges who call themselves 'policemen.' Their hands are drenched in blood," Perez shouted into the microphones.

The crowd cheered, many shaking their fists toward the police lines. The officers bristled in response.

Mano leaned toward Jo and whispered, "If you want to avoid trouble, you need to shut this guy up, Jo. He's getting people pretty worked up."

"We can't control what the speakers say. Perez was scheduled to appear before the vigilante shootings started."

Drawing his speech to a close, Perez worked the crowd with the rising cadence of an expert orator. "We are a people joined by heritage, by language, and most of all, by the bonds of oppression. Across this land, let us raise our voices together and speak out against injustice. Let them hear us say: No más!"

The crowd exploded into applause.

Mano was relieved when Perez's tirade against the police ended without incident. But drenched in the ovation directed toward the grandstand, Mano could not help feeling stirrings of sympathy for Perez's message, especially when he recalled the horrific deaths in his own neighborhood.

After the speech, an aging ranchera band took the stage. In the middle of the group's second song, the emcee broke in to announce the arrival of the next speaker—United States congressman Phillip Benitez.

"I didn't know Congressman Benitez would be here," Mano whispered to Jo.

"Didn't you read the flyers and posters we printed?"

"I don't pay much attention to political stuff," Mano said. "How did you manage to get him here?"

"He needs us right now as much as we need him."

Although Mano made little effort to keep up with politics, he knew Benitez was a controversial figure. The congressman had been accused of receiving unreported campaign contributions from a farm workers' union, but was cleared after a lengthy investigation. More recently, he'd seized the national spotlight with his heated opposition to legislation that had made English the nation's official language.

Even to those familiar with politics, Benitez's appearance at the rally was something of a surprise. When the rioting had erupted in San Antonio, Benitez had publicly condemned it as "the work of idle fools." Now, with anger growing among his constituents, Benitez was apparently embracing the cause of justicia, though many in the crowd clearly doubted his sincerity on any issue.

A canned patriotic jingle preceded the congressman's arrival, masking the lukewarm reception he received from the crowd. Mano watched as the short man, dressed impeccably in a blue suit, jauntily climbed the steps to the grandstand. He waved energetically, a smile frozen on his makeup-coated face.

Benitez's arrival at the podium triggered four sets of thousand-watt floodlights and a barrage of shutter clicks from the media contingent. After a half minute of smiling and waving to a crowd that had long since stopped applauding, the music was turned off and Benitez began his speech.

At first, Mano was more absorbed by what Benitez was doing than what he was saying. In an impressive display of media savvy, Benitez was striking a series of photogenic poses, holding each one a few seconds, then quickly switching to another, never missing a beat as he spoke. Mano realized his technique was guaranteed to produce a flattering photo.

While Benitez was delivering a sensational performance for the media, his connection with the crowd was another matter. Even through the glare of the lights, Mano could tell the audience was becoming restless.

"I'm here today to let you know that your voices will be heard in Washington. And come November, we must harness this community support into votes. Viva justicia! Viva the United States!" Benitez said as he struck his final pose.

The canned music began again, and Benitez went into another round of vigorous waving to the tepidly applauding crowd. With a final wave, he disappeared down the grandstand steps and dashed into a waiting limousine.

With many of the media crews packing their equipment, the radio deejay rushed back onstage. "Our final speaker is a man who has worked tirelessly for justicia in Los Angeles and across the nation. I'm proud to introduce Ramon Garcia."

Ramon walked confidently to the podium and, after a few preliminary phrases, launched into the heart of his talk.

"We've heard the word 'justicia' a lot today. What is justicia?" Ramon asked and then paused. "Many of our people work long hours to provide decent homes for their families. Yet we are not welcome to live in other parts of this city. Is this justicia?"

"No!" a few in the crowd shouted in response.

"Our children are forced to attend schools that are underfunded. Yet the affirmative action laws that can help them get an equal education are repealed. Is this justicia?"

"No!" cried more voices.

"Our hermanos and hermanas who struggle to find work

with only a bare knowledge of English are told that federal job applications may no longer be printed in Spanish. Is this justicia?"

"No!" they screamed back, louder still.

"Legal residents working in this country are forced to pay Social Security taxes—without being able to draw a penny of it in retirement benefits. Is this justicia?"

"NO!"

"Latinos walking to work are beaten to death because they dared to walk in the wrong neighborhood. Is this justicia?"

"NO!"

"We've seen armed vigilantes drive through our barrios, gunning down innocent men, women, and children. But the police have yet to catch any of these cowards. Is this justicia?"

"NO!"

The passion in Ramon's voice rose. "The soil on which we're now standing was once the home of the Californios— Hispanics who settled this land more than three hundred years ago. This land was wrested away from them and annexed into the United States of America. Today, on this very soil, the descendants of the Californios are denied equal rights and privileges. Is this justicia?"

"NO!"

"In the words of José Antonio Marcha"—Ramon paused as many in the crowd cheered lustily at the mention of Marcha's name—"in the words of José Antonio Marcha, the day will come when Hispanics unite and reclaim the territory that is rightfully ours. Is this justicia?"

"YES!" roared the crowd.

In a spontaneous outburst, they began to chant, "*JUS-TI-*

CIA! JUS-TI-CIA! JUS-TI-CIA!" Their voices echoed throughout the park and the adjoining streets, growing louder with each repetition. Mano felt the hair on his neck rise.

"*JUS-TI-CIA! JUS-TI-CIA! JUS-TI-CIA!*"

The chant washed over Mano with an energy so great he gripped the edges of his chair, bracing himself against its power.

Ramon held up his hands, quelling the chant, bringing the crowd back under his spell. "We can no longer rely on the current power structure to protect us. Therefore, we're launching La Defensa del Pueblo, a community organization to patrol our barrios. Will you support it?"

"YES!"

"If we are united, the power of justicia will be invincible. But in the struggle ahead, how we use our power will be continually tested. Today's test is our ability to lift our voices together—without violence. We need to show our opponents that if they respond to us with reason and peace, we can do the same." Ramon paused. "Will we show the world we can do this today?"

"YES!"

"Some will tell you that your votes will help us in this struggle. And I say to you, yes, that's true. But remember this: In the end, our struggle will only be won with sangre, sudor, y dolor." Mano recognized the words of Winston Churchill being spoken in Spanish—blood, sweat, and tears.

Ramon defiantly thrust his fist in the air. "Viva justicia! Viva La República Hispana de América!"

The applause was thunderous.

Mano sat in awe, overwhelmed by the ovation. As the wild cheering continued, he felt something extraordinary. For a moment it seemed he and the crowd were somehow a single entity, their voices a presence he could feel in his chest. This strange oneness faded with the cheers, leaving him with a warm glow he could only compare to the bliss after sex.

Mano glanced at Jo. Her lips were parted slightly; her eyes glazed in a half-closed stare. She turned toward him and their eyes met. In that instant, he knew she'd felt the same climax of energy. Embarrassed, he looked away.

As the crowd slowly quieted, Ramon returned from the podium, shaking hands with the others on the stage. Most of the people began leaving the park peacefully, but Mano saw trouble brewing.

Surrounded by TV news crews, the Anglos he'd spotted earlier were taunting the police along the west edge of the park. Mano left the stage and moved toward them swiftly, assessing the situation.

A young man with blond braids, about ten paces from the police line, appeared to be leading the demonstrators. "Hey, pig! Were you one of the vigilantes?" he shouted at the police. "You like to go around shooting women and children? Maybe it's because your dick is so small and you can't satisfy your wife. You bring her to me, man. I'll show her a good time!"

Mano grabbed the young man's arm below the armpit and lifted him like a naughty schoolboy, his toes barely touching the ground. "We've had enough trouble around here. Please don't start any more," he said calmly.

"Easy, bro, easy," the young man said, suddenly deflated. "I haven't got a beef with you, man. We're out here for *your* people, you know."

"If you'd really like to help, the best thing you can do is tell your friends to go home quietly like everyone else."

"OK, dude. All right. It's cool, man."

Mano released his grip and the young man immediately called out to his cohorts, "All right, people. It's over. We're cutting out."

As the protesters retreated from the police lines, the TV crews turned off their cameras and called it a day. Hanging around until the end had not paid off as they'd hoped. The rally had ended peacefully.

———

Even the rain couldn't dampen Jo's mood.

As she powered the Volvo into the fast lane toward Bel Air, the clunk of the wipers seemed to be playing a conga rhythm with the clicking of her turn signal. *Thump. Tock. Tock. Tock. Thump. Tock. Tock. Tock.*

While Jo cheerfully tapped out a counterbeat on the steering wheel, Ramon's vu-phone rang. He flipped open the silver clamshell and saw his wife's face in the display panel.

"Hi, Maggie," he said into the unit.

Ramon's wife, Margaret Zane, was on a location shoot in New Zealand. Now nearing fifty, Maggie had risen from publicist to senior producer at Lion Pictures thanks to her uncanny ability to twist arms without making enemies. *Not bad for a working-class kid from Pittsburgh born Margaret Zembrowski,* Jo thought.

"Hello, sweetheart," Maggie said. "We're on a break between shots. How did it go?"

"I'd say it went well," Ramon replied, the corners of his mouth arching slightly.

"He's being modest, Maggie. Your husband was magnificent!" Jo called out. When Jo had moved to Los Angeles three years earlier, she'd sought out Ramon Garcia for his connections within the Eslo community. His power as an orator had been a pleasant surprise.

Ramon angled the vu-phone toward Jo.

"That's wonderful, Jo," Margaret said from the small screen. "I wish I could have been there."

Jo flashed a smile into the display. "Somebody's got to keep those flamboyant directors in line," she said.

"This one likes to spend money like he's van Gogh heaping paint on a canvas...except he doesn't have near the talent. If he keeps it up, *I'm* the one who's going to cut off his ear. In fact, I might even start lower on his anatomy," Maggie said.

"Hang on, I'm going to switch over to secure mode, Maggie," Ramon said, pressing the button that encrypted their connection and blacked out their visual contact. "Everything went according to plan," he said into the vu-phone's mike. "The gangs kept their truce."

"That's good," Maggie said with relief in her voice. "Frankly, I was worried—especially when you told me there would be families at the rally. God knows enough people have been killed in East Los Angeles lately."

"The last thing we wanted to do was to jeopardize innocent lives," Jo said hurriedly. "If we'd had trouble break out in front of the media, it would have looked like we were inciting violence. That's not the public image La Defensa del Pueblo needs to cultivate right now."

"You have a gift for politics, Jo," Margaret said. "I'm just glad no one was hurt."

"I wasn't surprised the gangs honored the truce," Ramon said. "They can be vicious, but they also value honor. Each mero gave me his word there wouldn't be trouble, and they all kept it. Of course, spreading a little cash among them always helps."

Jo's expression turned grim. Ramon's words reminded her of the business with Nesto and the cops. The mero had taken things too far; she'd never intended for him to kill the cops. Still, the results had been good for their cause—today's turnout was proof of that. *The momentum for justicia is growing—but does that justify murder?* Jo buried her remorse once again and turned her attention back to Ramon and Margaret.

"Did it help to have Benitez there?" Margaret asked.

"You were right about inviting him, Maggie," Ramon replied. "He really brought out the cameras."

"Every share point in ratings is worth a thousand bullets," Jo added.

Margaret laughed softly. "You certainly have a colorful way of putting it, dear."

Jo smiled. Maggie's celebrity connections had once again helped their cause. "I wish you could have seen your husband on the podium, Maggie. He was in total control today."

"Thanks, Jo," Ramon cut in. "But let's give credit where it's due. I don't think the responses from the audience would have happened on cue if you hadn't arranged for a few of our friends in the crowd to get them started. It was a brilliant idea."

"Well, congratulations to you both," Margaret said. "It sounds like you pulled off a minor miracle today. Look, I hate to run, but I've got to lean on my little prima donna. If he doesn't get this crew back to work soon, we're going to lose the light and fall another day behind schedule. I'll call you again tomorrow, Ramon."

"Bye, love," Ramon said and disconnected. After returning the phone to his pocket, he looked out the window. "You know, Jo, our cause hasn't had an opportunity like this since the sixties. I feel like a young radical again."

"That's a good thing, viejo. We've got a lot of work ahead of us. Getting La Defensa del Pueblo in place is going to be a grind over the next few months. But today, I think we seized the day."

"Yeah, we even caught a break on the rain. I doubt if anyone in the crowd got wet...except maybe Mano. He's got a long walk home."

"Coño!" Jo cursed, pounding the steering wheel with her fist. "I've been so giddy over the rally, I forgot about Mano. I offered him a ride, but I think he's worried his wife will get jealous."

"Wasn't Mano great at the rally, though? Dios mio, he's got the instincts of a sheepdog. It's like he's hardwired to protect his flock. I know you noticed it, too. He immediately worked out an escape plan for us, without being asked."

Jo nodded. "I was amazed at how quickly he calmed down the group from UCLA."

"Yeah, I saw that. He spotted the leader, confronted him, and hasta la vista, the trouble was over."

"I'd love to know what he said."

"I don't think it really mattered much. A man who can lift you off the ground with one hand can be pretty damned persuasive."

Jo laughed, then suddenly got serious. "We seem to be getting through to him, Ray. I watched him during the speeches. He was moved by what he heard today."

"I hope you're right. We're going to need more people like

Mano—and soon. As Marcha said, 'Wars are won by moral men who can kill in cold blood.' "

⸻

Mano walked upright in the downpour, untroubled by the wet clothes clinging to his skin. The rain had chased the evening crowds indoors, transforming the barrio's familiar streets into a strange and silent place. Although he was getting closer to home, everything seemed changed in a way he could not describe—including his outlook. The uncertainty that had plagued him for the last few days was nearly gone. In its place was...well, if not clarity, at least calm. He knew the rally had something to do with it, but as yet had not figured out why.

Striding along the empty street, Mano remembered the early years of the new century when East Los Angeles, like many Hispanic communities across the country, had been the target of a massive ad blitz. Sparked by the 2000 U.S. Census that showed the soaring growth of the Latino population, the advertising was usually stupid and insulting, often awkwardly translated versions of English-language campaigns. Before long, the advertisers discovered that the "bonanza" of the Hispanic market was empty hype touted by ad agencies desperate for new revenues.

The only corporate presence in his neighborhood these days was the perennial liquor, beer, and cigarette videoboards. The commercial giants whose brands dominated the urban landscape of the American mainstream had once again shunned the barrios of Los Angeles. Outside the barrios, national franchises were ever-present on most main thoroughfares. The streets were lined with a jangling array of electronic signs that continually flashed, blinked, and pulsed, beckoning consumers with jingles and video-animated messages. In the barrios, these slick displays were rare.

Then Mano noticed something he never had before: almost every building was covered with images made by a human hand—the crude signs of mami-and-papi businesses, the murals of aspiring artists, the placas of the gangs. He'd known these streets all his life. But tonight, for the first time, Mano saw more than the surface of the motley walls. He could sense the people who created them.

The people of his barrio lived in a world of stark contradictions. Dreams flourished alongside despair. Honor was twisted into the self-destructive violence of the gangs. The fast lane for great ambitions was often the sale of drugs. The family was revered, but many women raised their children alone.

Mano had always believed most Hispanics worked harder than Anglos. Yet in pay, in education, even in dignity, they seemed continually mired in second-class status. They were not welcome to live outside the crowded barrios. Only last week, Mano had seen innocent people gunned down in the street. Their only crime had been their heritage—*his* heritage.

That thought brought Mano to a disturbing realization. Although he'd never been ashamed of his ancestry, Mano could not truly say it had ever been a source of pride. Being Latino was something he'd simply learned to endure with dignity, like a handicap. The revelation shamed him. The people at the rally were his own. He could not escape who he was.

Almost home, Mano stopped where the Jimenez twins had

been killed and stared at the pavement. The neighbors had tried to scrub away the stains, but the concrete was still tinted brown with their blood.

Moving away won't save my children, he realized suddenly.

The vigilantes had only one goal: to attack Hispanics. Today it was in the barrios. Tomorrow it could be anywhere. Moving away from here would not change who they were. As long as these killers were loose, his wife and children were targets.

Until now, Mano had disdained Hispanics like Jo and Ramon who shouted about prejudice and injustice. He'd considered them whiners, too weak to overcome the adversities fate had dealt them. He still felt Jo and Ramon were wrong about a lot of things, but they were right about one: those in danger had to defend themselves from the vigilantes. That was something in their cause he could support.

THE RIO GRANDE INCIDENT:
Month 2, Day 25

In every revolution, patriots rise from the least likely
of places. Men and women who have never taken an
interest in political processes become infused with
passion. They find a wellspring of duty and devotion
they never knew existed within them.

—*José Antonio Marcha, 1986*
Translated by J. M. Herrera

Henry Evans II stared at the glut of unopened e-mails
and sighed. Although it was not yet nine on Monday, he was
already exhausted. Over the last year, Evans had grown pale,
overweight, and nearly bald—hardly the look that would help
the regional director of the CIA move up the government
services ziggurat. But then again, the last eleven months had
been unlike any other in Evans's twenty-six-year CIA career.

According to many outsiders, the previous year's merger
of all federal security organizations into the Central Intelligence Agency was a shrewd power move by President Carleton Brenner—a former CIA director. Promising a leaner,
meaner federal security effort, the president had ordered
the FBI, NSA, ATF, and Department of Homeland Security
to cease operations as independent entities.

In reality, the consolidation was a bureaucratic nightmare.

The CIA had been forced to keep each organization's leadership, setting off endless turf battles. And with the restrictions on domestic surveillance Congress had imposed after the early excesses of the war on terror, even routine investigations became mired in legal bottlenecks. As a result, Evans had seen his workload explode and his budget slashed.

The Agency faced another loathsome burden: it had been enlisted to conceal the extent of U.S. military involvement overseas. The memos circulated by Brenner appointees emphasized this was to keep our enemies in the dark, but Evans knew better. The American public was the real target of the misinformation campaign. *They aren't even called wars anymore*, Evans thought, *just another "military intervention."*

When his desk phone rang, Evans glared at the archaic device, galled that the CIA was still saddled with voice-only telephones. Congress had cut the upgrade to vu-phones from the consolidation budget. After several rings, Evans listlessly reached for the phone. "Evans," he answered mechanically.

"G'morning, Hank. It's Maria Prado. I've got a report for you on a rally in East L.A. Saturday. There are some new bogeys on our radar screen you should know about. I e-mailed you a photo of them just a few minutes ago."

A veteran field agent, Prado had been hounding Evans for weeks with reports on the disturbances in East Los Angeles. After decades as a CIA officer dealing exclusively in foreign intelligence, Evans looked dubiously at domestic surveillance. To him, this urban violence was the work of hooligans and petty criminals—a matter for the police, not the CIA.

"Hang on a minute," Evans replied, scrolling through hundreds of new messages. "Here it is," he said, double-clicking on the attachment.

The image showed a group seated at a grandstand with three heads circled in red. Marked in the front row was a slender man, probably in his late sixties, dressed in a tweed jacket and sporting a gray ponytail. Circled in the row behind was a burly man in his mid-thirties, along with a striking blonde about the same age.

"What's the scoop?" Evans asked after glancing at the photo.

"The guy in the front row was one of the speakers, a real rabble-rouser, too. His name's Ramon Garcia. No priors, but he's a sixties radical who's resurfaced. The FBI started a file on him in '71, when he worked as an aide to Cesar Chavez. Turns out he's now setting up a group called La Defensa del Pueblo in response to the vigilante shootings."

"Can this guy cause any trouble?"

"Well, he's connected to some serious cash. His wife is Margaret Zane, a producer for Lion Pictures. They live in a Bel Air mansion big enough to house a regiment. I checked this guy out, Hank. He's got connections within the Eslo community—and around the country, too. If you ask me, he's worth watching."

"Is the blonde in the back row his wife?"

"No, that's Josefina Herrera. She's a dual citizen of the U.S. and Uruguay. Made a pile of money with a med-tech start-up while she was pre-med at Stanford, then sold her shares just before the biotech bust. She's either very smart or very lucky. Anyway, she moved to the L.A. area three years ago and runs a bookstore and a recycling business. They seem to be mostly hobbies for her. My guess is she's a rich liberal who's fond of bankrolling do-gooder causes. You know the type: likes to slum with the masses during the week so she feels better about the Brie and Chablis aboard her yacht on Sunday."

"Who's the muscle?"

"We don't have much on him. The Face ID unit says he's Manolo Suarez. Worked as a mechanic until six months ago—been unemployed since. He was a sergeant in a Ranger support unit. Got the Bronze Star in Afghanistan for carrying a guy more than a mile to an aid station after their Humvee was hit."

"You know we've got a lot on our plate right now, Maria. Do you think this organization poses a serious threat?"

"Well, their rally could have turned ugly, Hank. But they went out of their way to keep it peaceful. They don't seem to be an overt threat. Still, I think we need to keep an eye on La Defensa del Pueblo."

"What's your recommendation?"

"I can sniff around. Maybe we can get a mole inside this group."

"Let's just keep an eye on them for now, Maria. Quite frankly, I haven't got time to read another field report on a bunch of small-time barrio radicals," Evans said wearily before hanging up.

THE RIO GRANDE INCIDENT:
Month 2, Day 29

It was after seven when Mano pulled the Mack into the garage, tired but content. He'd gotten lost twice in the northern suburbs, setting him back a couple of hours, but on the whole, his first day as a driver had gone well. He looked forward to two weeks of real work while Jesús Lopez was on vacation.

While locking the compound gate, he noticed Jo beside her Volvo.

"Mano, do you have a minute?" she called out across the alley.

"Sure," he answered, walking toward his boss.

"Did you have any trouble with the special addresses?"

"No. Your directions were very clear, Jo. I tagged the bags from those houses and locked them in the storeroom."

"Good, I'll take care of them from here."

"It may be none of my business, but why don't we recycle the material from those homes like the others?"

Jo hesitated. "It's for security reasons," she said guardedly.

"For whose security?"

"Mano, the very nature of security involves discretion. That's all I can tell you. Look," she said, placing her hand lightly on his arm, "I'm sure it's been a long day for you. Would you like a ride home?"

"No...no, thanks. I'd rather walk," he said, unnerved by her touch.

"Mano, I feel badly about last Saturday. I invited you to the rally and you wound up walking home in the rain. I'd like to make it up to you."

"That's not necessary."

"OK, I'll be blunt, Mano. I know you're worried about what your wife might think. So let me drop you off a few blocks from your apartment. If you walk home now, you'll hardly get to see your kids before bedtime. What do you say?"

Mano had little doubt Rosa would be jealous if she saw Jo drive him home. On the other hand, accepting Jo's ride would avoid a very late supper for his family. Rosa always made the kids wait until he was home before they ate—even when he called to say he'd be late. In any case, there was little chance his wife would see Jo if he walked the last few blocks. "It *is* getting late," Mano agreed reluctantly.

"Then hop in," Jo said, unlocking the sedan.

Once inside the Volvo, Mano was surprised to see his address already entered into the driving directions on the top-of-the-line GPS array. "I see you were pretty sure I'd accept your invitation," he said, gesturing toward the display.

Jo smiled sheepishly, starting the engine. "It always helps to plan ahead. I hope you don't see anything sinister in it."

"No, but I *am* surprised someone who seems like a tree hugger would drive a car with 326 horses."

"There are times when the extra power can...well...get you out of trouble," Jo said, choosing her words carefully.

While weighing Jo's cautious reply, Mano was struck by an intense sensation. The Volvo's crisp, new-car smell had been replaced by a sweet, musky scent, thrilling him in a way that was almost primal. It was coming from Jo.

From the corner of his eye, he saw Jo casually move her smooth, slim arm onto the center console, only inches away. Against his will, he was aroused by her nearness. He squirmed his large torso against the door frame, trying to increase the space between them.

"Have you thought any more about Marcha's ideas since the rally, Mano?" Jo asked, merging into the traffic on Fisher Street.

Mano looked through the Volvo's tinted window. Outside were the hand-painted signs and graffiti he'd walked past in the rain two days before. "Well, I still don't think this country belongs to Hispanics, but I believe we need to protect our people from the vigilantes. We can agree on that much."

"If you're interested in protecting our people, Mano, there's work you can do that's more important than recycling trash or fixing trucks."

"What kind of work?"

"I can't tell you everything. For now, the important thing is to know you're committed to our cause."

"I want to help our people, Jo, but you have to tell me what you intend to do."

"We need to unite our people, Mano. When we finally join together, we'll earn the dignity that's rightfully ours—and protection from attackers like the vigilantes," she added quickly. "But first we need to build a coalition with true political power. Intellectuals, community organizations, labor unions, the church—even the gangs. We all need to join forces. That's what the movement for justicia is all about—justice."

"And exactly how do you see me fitting into those plans?"

"When the time comes, you'll see just how important your contribution can be. But for now, knowing you're committed will be enough." She turned and met his eyes. "Can Ramon and I count on you?"

Mano didn't have an answer. Two weeks earlier, he would have immediately rejected Jo's request. Since then, though, the world no longer seemed so simple. "I want to help our people, but I can't promise I'll go along with everything you ask."

A smile spread across Jo's face as she returned her eyes to the road. "That'll work for now," she said. "The GPS says we're getting close to your apartment. We can talk more about this later."

At an intersection two blocks from Mano's apartment, Jo pulled the sedan smoothly to the curb.

"Thanks for the ride, Jo. I'll see you tomorrow."

"Buenas noches, Mano."

As Mano emerged from the car, a small figure watched him through the window of the Laundromat across the street. It was Nana Jimenez, the grandmother of the slain twins.

THE RIO GRANDE INCIDENT:
Month 4, Day 3

The call came on a Saturday afternoon. Rosa answered their ancient voice phone, then handed it to Mano after only a few words. "It's Felipe," she said, covering the mouthpiece. "He sounds upset."

"Lucia…was…shot, Mano," Felipe said, fighting back sobs. "The vigilantes killed her." In a voice choking with grief, Mano's brother-in-law gave him the details. Mano's sixteen-year-old niece had been killed near a Wal-Mart on Washington Boulevard. Lucia had died trying to shield her younger siblings from the gunfire. "I'll let you know when we'll have the funeral Mass," Felipe said before hanging up.

Mano sank back in his chair, eyes hollow with shock. It was clear the police could not stop these shootings—or maybe they didn't want to, as many in the barrios believed.

In the three months since the first drive-by raids, the vigilantes had launched five more attacks in East Los Angeles. The LAPD had formed a special task force to find the perpetrators. But the only lead so far was a dead end: an SUV and a sedan fitting the descriptions of those used in the latest raid were found torched in the San Gabriel Mountains. Both had been stolen shortly before the attack. Now the vigilantes had killed again—this time someone of his own blood.

Mano heard the voices of his children playing outside in the courtyard. A cold knot formed in his belly as he realized only luck had kept them safe so far.

Three days later at Holy Trinity Church, Mano sat in the pew behind his sister, gently stroking her trembling shoulder. Teresa's veiled head was bowed, a handkerchief pressed against her face. She'd struggled to keep her composure during the opening of the Mass, but as Father Johnson started her daughter's eulogy, Teresa began to weep.

"Lucia was a gentle girl. She was quiet and never asked much for herself," the young priest said from the pulpit. "Her joy came from the happiness of others. As the oldest of Teresa and Felipe's six children, she was like a second mother in the family, mature beyond her years. In her last act on earth, she gave her life to protect her brothers and sisters. Her loss will be felt deeply by so many.

"We are told that God has plans for all of us. What was God's plan for Lucia? Perhaps it is not for us to know yet. Her young life was ended by men filled with hatred, men who killed without question, men who knew nothing about Lucia except one thing: she was not like them. And that was enough to condemn her in their eyes."

Mano felt a hot swell of anger fill his chest. He pictured these men who fancied themselves heroes, laughing and swilling beer, bragging with one another about their deeds. They would strike again—he was sure of that.

Father Johnson's voice became hoarse with emotion, drawing Mano's attention back to the pulpit. "Like our heavenly

Father, Lucia was an innocent who gave her life to save others." The priest paused, raising his gaze to meet the eyes of those gathered in the near-empty church. "Let us pray that her death was not in vain."

As Mano bowed his head, an audacious plan began to form in his mind.

————

On the following morning, Jo steered the Volvo into the parking lot behind the bookstore and saw Mano standing near the back door.

"Buenos días, Mano," she called out, waving through the window.

Mano stood erect like a soldier coming to attention when she stepped out of the car. "Good morning," he answered dryly, eyes focused in the distance.

"Well, as usual, I can see you haven't come to chitchat," she said, trying to soften his serious mood. "I'm sure you have something important to discuss."

"That's right."

"Would you like to come in and sit down?" she asked, nodding toward the door.

"No, this shouldn't take long."

Jo lowered her sunglasses, exposing her bright blue eyes. "All right. I'm listening."

"Last week you said there was other work I could do to help protect our people."

Jo waited for him to say more, to ask what she had meant, but Mano only stood there, silently staring at her. She answered the question he wouldn't ask. "Yes, there is. In fact, Ramon and I have been discussing it. We're looking for a security director for La Defensa del Pueblo and thought you might be a good candidate."

Mano's eyes narrowed with interest. "What kind of work would that be?"

"The primary duty of the security director would be to keep the leaders of the DDP safe from any kind of threat. There are a lot of other functions, but that's the most important one."

"You mean like a bodyguard?"

"That's an oversimplified description, but yes, like a bodyguard."

"How does that help our people, Jo?"

Jo smiled, disarmed by Mano's directness. "The mission of La Defensa del Pueblo is to protect our people. We plan to organize the barrios so the vigilantes won't catch us off guard again. By keeping the leaders of the DDP out of danger, you're helping that mission."

"How much authority will the security director have?"

"This is a very important position with a great deal of autonomy. After all, our lives could depend on the person who holds this job." Jo paused. "It also pays a lot more than you're making now," she added.

"Can the security director also look for ways to protect our people from the vigilantes?"

"Yes. Establishing community security would be one of the other functions."

"In that case, I'd like to apply for the job."

"I'm very pleased to hear that. Mind telling me what's sparked your interest?"

Mano lowered his gaze. He did not want Jo to know about the death of his niece. Jo might turn him down if she felt this was something personal. "Is that important?" he said at last.

"No, I suppose not," she answered. "Let me discuss this with Ramon. We'll give you a final answer tomorrow."

Mano nodded in thanks and left for the garage.

When Jo entered the bookstore, she found Ramon already behind the counter.

"He's with us," she called out, smiling.

THE RIO GRANDE INCIDENT:
Month 4, Day 11

It's mine?" Mano asked, staring at the gleaming black Audi hybrid parked beside Jo's Volvo.

"Absolutely," Jo said, opening the driver's door. "The new director of security for La Defensa del Pueblo is going to need reliable transportation."

Mano shook his head. "I appreciate your gesture, Jo, but I can't accept this car. It's too much."

"This isn't charity, Mano. Ramon and I made it part of the position. Anyone we hired as security director gets the car, fully insured." Jo paused, running her fingers slowly along the sleek lines of the fender. "It has a state-of-the-art security and communications system and comes with a Priority One gas ration card," she said, handing him the keys. "Get in and see how it feels."

Mano took the driver's seat, fondling the leather-wrapped steering wheel. "I never expected anything like this, Jo."

"Trust me, amigo. You're going to earn it," she said before entering the passenger's side. She activated the GPS array and brought up a preset location. "Let's head here," she said, tapping a map point on the LCD screen.

"Where are we going?" Mano asked, pulling out of the parking lot.

"This is your first assignment as security director—helping us choose a new location for the headquarters of La Defensa del Pueblo."

"Why not keep the office here at the bookstore?"

"We need room to grow...and a place the vigilantes can't shoot up too easily. We're going to become a prime target soon," Jo explained. "I found several locations online that might work. Let's go take a look at the bricks and mortar."

After visiting all the sites Jo had researched, they settled on a vacant three-story office building on East Olympic Boulevard that had been spared from the rioting. Like the Cielo Azul Bookstore, it was centrally located within the Eslo community, something high on Jo's list of priorities. More important to Mano, the site was defensible, nestled in the center of five connected buildings, providing ample protection from the flanks. In his eyes, the location had just one flaw.

He led Jo back to the building's ground-floor entrance. "All this glass worries me," he said, nodding toward the two plate-glass doors flanked by window panels. "People working near this entrance would be easy targets. We'll need to replace this glass with something solid—although we should leave some view ports to watch anyone approaching."

"That's not a problem. We'll get some steel doors and put in remote cameras, too. The whole interior will need to be gutted and rebuilt anyway."

Mano's brow creased. "Can you afford all this and still keep the businesses running?"

"It's time you knew some things about the bookstore and my recycling business, Mano. They were never meant to be moneymaking ventures."

"What do you mean?"

"I opened the bookstore to raise community awareness for justicia and to establish contacts in the Eslo community. I started the recycling business because I want to help the environment—it also turned out to be an effective way to gather information."

Mano's face tightened as he recalled the "special addresses" on his recycling route. "So you've been spying on American citizens."

"Mano, your moral sense is even stronger than your body," she said, smiling. "I admire that very much."

"I'm serious about this, Jo."

"All right," she said, suddenly terse. "It's quite simple, Mano. We need to gather intelligence to protect our people—even if it means doing something distasteful. Didn't your unit in Afghanistan rely on spying to survive?"

"Enemies in a war have no rights. American citizens do."

"You think we're not at war? The vigilantes are not common criminals, Mano. Their killings are indiscriminate. And they're motivated by ideology. I call that war—or genocide. Take your pick."

"I agree the vigilantes are our enemies. That doesn't justify spying on anyone you suspect might be against you."

Jo's face softened again. "Innocent people are dying," she said, placing her hand on his shoulder. "We're beyond justifications, Mano. Our enemies are using every means possible to get information about us. Do you expect us to do anything less?"

Mano pondered her question. He'd joined the DDP to stop the vigilantes. Was he willing to walk away from Jo and Ramon's considerable resources over this?

"Spying on American citizens is wrong, Jo," Mano said

firmly. "But if it helps stop the attacks, I can live with it—for now."

Jo smiled. "I'm glad to hear that," she said, then tapped on one of the glass doors. "You want to replace this door with steel but still leave us a way to see what's going on outside. What we're doing at Green Planet isn't really any different. We need to keep an eye on our enemies to protect ourselves. This conflict is going to get a lot worse, Mano—and very soon."

Four months after the first drive-by raid, the death toll from the vigilante attacks stood at forty-one. Copycat shooting sprees by vigilante convoys had struck El Paso, Houston, Brownsville, and San Antonio. The civil disturbances in those Texas cities escalated following the attacks. Looting no longer seemed the prime motive for the turmoil. The violence now appeared to be directed against visible symbols of government power.

The wave of vigilante attacks swelled the ranks of La Defensa del Pueblo in Los Angeles. Soon, similar organizations were sprouting in Hispanic communities throughout the Southwest.

During a heavily attended press conference, the chief of the LAPD declared that La Defensa del Pueblo was a "hotbed for terrorism" and ordered its leaders to disband or face arrest. The ACLU quickly filed a federal injunction, preventing the chief from carrying out his threat. Chastened but not deterred, the chief vowed that if any DDP members were caught carrying weapons, their entire leadership would be jailed. La Defensa del Pueblo responded by posting road-blocks at key intersections on routes into East Los Angeles.

Wearing sky blue armbands, unarmed DDP volunteers challenged suspicious vehicles entering the barrios. Three days later, a convoy of vigilantes attacked one of the road-blocks, killing four DDP sentries and two bystanders. The slayings made martyrs of the DDP volunteers, raising the organization's stock within the Eslo community.

Outside the nation's troubled areas, people watched warily, hoping the violence would not spread to their back-yards. The media did little to dispel their fears.

ABC launched a daily thirty-minute news special titled *Rampage in the Barrios* after its regular evening newscast. Featuring an animated logo with a grave musical theme, the show was packed with lurid footage of the recurring violence. Ratings were meteoric and the other networks quickly followed suit. NBC named their daily show *Streets of Turmoil.* CBS called theirs *Crisis in Our Cities.*

For the first time in nearly a decade, viewership of the broadcast networks rose.

THE RIO GRANDE INCIDENT:
Month 5, Day 12

Our tactics have to change!" Ramon yelled over the burst of a jackhammer. "We need to give our people weapons, or pretty soon wearing a DDP armband will be like having a target on your back!"

In spite of the jackhammer, Jo and Mano listened intently. It was their first meeting in the new headquarters of La Defensa del Pueblo. The air in the small second-floor conference room was thick with the acrid smell of fresh paint and the sweet tang of newly cut two-by-fours.

"We can't do that yet, Ramon! If we arm"—suddenly the jackhammer stopped and Jo lowered her voice—"if we arm our people, we're going to be fighting a battle on two fronts at once: one with the vigilantes and the other with the LAPD."

The jackhammer started up again. The renovations on their new headquarters were running behind schedule.

"I'm aware that the top cop of our fair city vowed he would never allow the DDP to carry weapons!" Ramon yelled in response. "But what's to stop us from keeping our weapons concealed?"

The jackhammer stopped.

"If the vigilantes think we're unarmed, they'll continue to

attack our roadblocks," Mano said softly. Until that moment, he had been listening wordlessly. Hearing him speak startled the others more than the sound of the jackhammer.

Jo nodded. "Mano's right. We may surprise the vigilantes the first time we fight back. But once we use our weapons, the game's over. We'll all be arrested."

"And there will be no one left to protect our people," Mano added.

"What else can we do?" Ramon said with a sour look. "We can't sit back and do nothing while our people are gunned down in the streets."

"We can go after the source. Take out the vigilantes," Mano said calmly.

Jo and Ramon looked at each other in astonishment.

"Estás loco, hombre?" Ramon finally said. "That's impossible, Mano. To begin with, how do we find them?"

"We set a trap, take some prisoners, and find out who their leaders are."

"Could it work?" Jo asked, her eyes brightening.

Ramon crossed his arms and frowned. "Of course not. It's ridiculous."

The jackhammer rattled to life again. Mano sat silently, waiting for it to stop. "Yes, I think it could work," he said after the noise ceased. "The most difficult part will be setting the bait—to lure them into attacking someplace where we're ready for them."

"It can't be any kind of event that draws the cops," Jo said, quickly grasping Mano's plan. "The vigilantes won't risk getting busted."

"OK, suppose you can draw the vigilantes into a trap. Then what?" Ramon asked.

"Once we take some prisoners and find out who their leaders are, we launch a counterstrike."

Ramon threw his hands up. "A trap…taking prisoners…a counterstrike…Dios mio, Mano, it's too much. The logistical preparations are enormous. Most of our people don't have your military training. We can't pull this off."

"I know this operation will take a lot of work," Mano said. "I'm willing to do this on my own time. It won't interfere with my main duties, Ramon."

"Taking time away from your work isn't what worries me, Mano."

Jo rose to her feet. "Right now, we don't have any better options, Ramon. I know it's a long shot, but I say we go for it."

Mano sensed Ramon was losing face—and his resolve. "Ramon, you and Jo have done a lot of good things over the last few months, things that have helped our people. They haven't been easy, but you got them done. This won't be easy either, but it's something we have to do." It was the longest speech Jo or Ramon had ever heard Mano make.

As if on cue, the jackhammer started up again. Jo waited for it to stop before she spoke. "It seems like you've been thinking about this plan for a while, Mano."

"I'm the director of security for the DDP. I've got to earn my keep."

"I get the feeling there's something more than professional pride behind this, Mano," Ramon observed. "Is this something personal?"

Mano's eyes narrowed. "I'd like to meet the men who did these things—face to face," he said, his voice nearly a growl. It was the closest thing to anger Jo and Ramon had ever seen from him.

Ramon whistled softly. "If your plan works, I almost pity them."

———

Lying awake in the darkness, Rosa heard the faint click of the deadbolt on the front door. She looked at the glowing dial of the clock by the bed. It was 2:11 a.m. She followed the sounds of her husband's movements through their apartment. When Mano entered their bedroom, she turned on the lamp.

"You're awake," Mano whispered in surprise.

"How long is this going to last, Mano?" Rosa asked without rancor. "This is the third time this week you've missed dinner. Each time, I made the children wait until nine to eat a cold meal. And now Pedro is following his father's example—he's started hanging out on the street. It's a constant battle to get him inside before dark."

"I'll talk to him."

"You really think that's going to help? You always said children need examples, not lectures."

"Don't do this, Rosa. You know I've got a lot of work to do right now."

"I still don't understand what kind of work needs to be done at a recycling company at two in the morning."

Mano exhaled slowly, trying to stay calm. Preparing his trap for the vigilantes was taking longer than expected. Still, he could not risk telling Rosa about the plan. The less she and the children knew, the less danger they were in. "Rosa, we've been over this before," he said evenly. "It's not something I can talk about. You have to trust me."

"I want to trust you, mi amor, but it's a struggle. I try not to listen to the gossip. But when you bring home a fancy car and then stay out late, night after night—"

"What do you mean, Rosa?" Mano interrupted. "What kind of gossip?"

"It's foolishness. It's nothing."

Mano stroked his wife's cheek tenderly. "Please, tell me what people are saying that's bothering you, Rosita."

"Well, Jorge Pujols, the cashier at the grocery store, told me Nana Jimenez is spreading gossip. She's telling people she saw you getting out of a classy new car driven by a beautiful blonde."

Mano had not expected this. His attempt to prevent a misunderstanding now looked like something furtive. At the same time, he could not deny the growing attraction he felt for Jo.

"Rosa, I want you to listen carefully. What Nana Jimenez said is true."

"Que dices?"

"The woman she saw was Jo. She gave me a ride home from work a while back."

Rosa was stunned. "You never told me that Jo was a beautiful blonde," she said, wrapping the covers around her torso. Rosa had always pictured Jo as one of those mannish women with close-cropped hair she'd seen once on a trip to Venice Beach.

"It never seemed important," Mano said, knowing that was not completely true.

"What else have you been keeping from me, Mano?"

"I've told you everything that's important."

"Then tell me why you have to hide what you're doing late at night."

"I'm trying to protect you and the children."

"How?"

"That's all I can tell you."

"But Mano..."

"Please, Rosa. Don't ask me any more about this," he said sternly and began to undress.

Rosa watched him silently from under the covers until he turned out the light and crawled into bed.

"Good night, querida," Mano said, then kissed her passionlessly and turned away.

Rosa stared into the darkness. For weeks, she had been trying to suppress the notion that Mano might be seeing another woman. Now, it seemed, her worst fears might be true. Mano had never lied to her, but it was impossible not to doubt him. Why else would he need to keep secrets from her?

She probed her memory in desperation, trying to understand what had driven them apart. None of it made sense. Mano finally had a job; they had a little money. Things should be better, not worse. Yet when Mano had been out of work, they'd pulled together, giving each other hope and strength.

Looking back, it seemed the troubles in her family had started with the turmoil in the barrios. She'd tried to ignore the world outside, to keep her home normal and safe. It was useless. Pedro was on his way to becoming another cholo hanging out in the streets—and Julio would follow him before long. Worst of all, the rioting had brought *that woman* into their lives. Josefina had money, an education, and now it seemed she was beautiful as well. But that wasn't enough. It seemed she wanted Mano, too.

Rosa wasn't sure how, but she had to find a way to protect her family from this woman. Tomorrow she would place fresh offerings on her shrine to Our Lady and pray for guidance. She would not give up her husband without a fight.

—————

Keith Sawyer was wringing out a fetid mop when the bright yellow poster on the bulletin board caught his eye. After a second look, the school janitor recognized the familiar face on the placard and pushed his wheeled bucket closer toward the wall. The brightly printed poster read:

Benefit Performance for La Defensa
del Pueblo of Los Angeles
featuring
TOMAS CRUZ!
Time: 8:30–10:00 p.m. Saturday, January 12
Place: El Lobo Club—112 Agnes Street

"Stupid, flashy-assed greaser. What's he up to anyway?" Sawyer muttered to himself—a habit he had acquired after sixteen years as a night janitor at Cesar Chavez High School. Like almost everyone on the planet, Sawyer knew that Cruz was a Latino pop singer who had made it big in Hollywood, but he was surprised that a big star like Cruz would appear at a small local club in East Los Angeles. Most of all, it infuriated him that Cruz was doing it to help La Defensa del Pueblo—a group Sawyer considered the lowest kind of traitors.

The paunchy janitor fumed as he imagined the crowds of drooling chicas Cruz would attract. Then an idea surfaced in Sawyer's mind. Maybe there was a way to fix the smart-ass beaner—and his good-for-nothing fans, too. Walking briskly down the empty halls, Sawyer entered the janitor's room, fished a number from his wallet, and dialed his ancient cell phone, grinning in satisfaction as the line rang.

"Hello?" answered a man's voice.

"I've got news on a little shindig coming up here in greaser land that you might want to know about."

———

"There they are," Ramon said, tilting his head toward a group of vatos nearly a hundred meters away. "Nesto is the shortest one."

Across the litter-strewn length of Belvedere Park, Mano saw the outlines of six young men slouching on a row of benches under the glare of the streetlights.

Walking toward the group, Mano was again pleased by Ramon's change of heart. After initially opposing the proposed move against the vigilantes, Ramon had arranged tonight's meeting to prepare for the ambush.

"Y que, Nesto?" Ramon said to the mero as he and Mano approached the group, their sullen postures matched by menacing stares.

"Y que?" the slender gang leader answered, staring past Ramon with a look of indifference. The greeting was the latest insider's idiom in the ever-changing slang of L.A.'s gangbangers.

Ramon nodded in respect. "As I told your runner, we have some business to discuss. Podemos charlar un poco?"

Nesto pointed with his chin toward the center of the park and sauntered in that direction, Mano and Ramon in tow. After a dozen paces, Nesto stopped, just far enough to be out of earshot from his vatos, but near enough to remain within their protection.

"So what's up, ese?" the mero asked Ramon.

"Well, my young friend, we need weapons and some men for a job next week."

Nesto stared at Ramon, his head cocked insolently. "Keep talking."

"We want six men—four with AKs, two with RPGs."

Nesto scratched his chin. "Fifty Gs," he said after a moment. "Twenty-five up front."

"That's agreeable," Ramon answered quickly. "Send a runner over tomorrow for the money."

"Small bills this time, ese—small bills. You got it?"

"I understand, Nesto. Now let's discuss the details. This is Manolo Suarez," Ramon said, gesturing toward Mano. "He's the mastermind behind our plan."

For the next hour, Mano outlined his plan to the gang leader. In spite of the mero's impudent façade, he caught on quickly.

"Then we're set for next Saturday," Ramon concluded. "Send a runner if you have any questions, Nesto."

"Hey, it's cool, man. Just be sure you bring the rest of the money," Nesto called over his shoulder, swaggering away.

Once outside the park, Mano could no longer contain his curiosity. "AK-47s...rocket-propelled grenades...where does an L.A. street gang get that kind of firepower, Ramon?"

"The members of El Farol are sons of refugees from El Salvador. Many of their parents were leftist sympathizers who came here fleeing the death squads. The insurgents in El Salvador were supplied with Russian weapons by Cuba and Nicaragua—when they were still socialists. Many of those weapons are still floating around in El Salvador. That's Nesto's weapons pipeline."

THE RIO GRANDE INCIDENT:
Month 6, Day 3

A revolution is like a hand grenade. Once the pin is pulled, it must be thrown. There is no turning back.
— *José Antonio Marcha, 1982*
Translated by J. M. Herrera

Mano walked across the rooftop, the stiff fabric of his new black fatigues hissing rhythmically with each step. Near the center of the building, he met Nesto. "Are we ready?" he asked.

"Everything is set, man," the mero said, nonchalantly flicking the remnants of a cigarette into the darkness.

"Let's take a look," Mano said, walking toward the orange glow of the streetlights at the edge of the roof. Shrugging in disgust, Nesto followed.

The building below them had once been occupied by a collection of retail shops and offices that lined the south side of Agnes Street. The block-long structure was now empty and gutted, its tenants driven away by the rioting.

Mano scanned the two-lane street below: an urban canyon formed by an unbroken row of two-story buildings hugging both sides of the sidewalk. He was glad to see the street deserted.

One block west was the blinking neon sign of El Lobo Club.

Although Tomas Cruz's show would not start for nearly an hour, a queue had already formed in front of the nightclub.

"Let's go over the deployment of your people, Nesto."

"Look, ese, I told you and Ramon where my vatos would be when we made the deal. This is bullshit, man."

"There's something you have to understand," Mano began, stepping next to Nesto and slowly putting his arm around the mero's shoulders. "If you screw this up, innocent people could get hurt." He squeezed Nesto against his side in a one-armed hug. "Do you want to see that happen?"

Nesto struggled for breath against the pressure, pinned helplessly against Mano's rock-hard torso. He didn't want to find out if Mano could squeeze hard enough to break his ribs. "No, man...That...wouldn't be cool," he grunted.

"All right, then," Mano said, releasing his hold. "Let's review the positions of your people."

"OK, man," Nesto said, trying to regain his composure. "Like I told you, my vatos are set up in four positions." He pointed right. "I've got two guys near the east corner of this building ready to go with AK-47s. Across the street on the east corner, I've got two more dudes with AKs." He pointed left. "On the west end of this building—and across the street—I've got our lights-out punch, baby. Two teams of vatos with RPGs."

Mano followed Nesto's gestures, making out the shadowy figures at each position. As he watched the men huddled in the darkness, he was again amazed at the firepower in the hands of these ordinary street thugs. He was glad to have the men and their weapons tonight, but they had to be kept under tight control and discipline; his plan left little room for error.

Mano heard the soft crunch of footsteps on the gravel behind him. A slim figure walked briskly toward them through the darkness. It was Jo, dressed in black fatigues, her golden hair braided and pinned close to her head.

Nesto looked surprised, then his expression changed to anger. "What's she doing here?"

"I keep asking her the same question," Mano said.

"Look, Mano, I know it's your job to protect me," she said. "But this action overrides that directive. So what's the situation?"

Nesto sighed loudly.

"I've checked our communications links twice," Mano reported. "We're ready."

Jo nodded. "Where are the lookouts?"

"Our main lookout is two blocks east. That's him in that pickup truck parked near the corner. We've got two other lookouts north and south of that position."

Mano and Jo were betting the house the vigilantes would approach from the east. Their research into previous vigilante raids had shown the attacks had always taken place in the direction of a freeway entrance to ensure a quick getaway. An entrance to I-710 lay two blocks west.

"The trucks?" Jo asked.

"They're parked along the cross street to the west."

"Crowd control?"

"DDP members are stationed along each corner with orders to keep people away from this street."

"It sounds like everything's in place," Jo said with a tight smile.

"The only question left is *when*," Mano said. "My guess is they'll hit us when the show is over."

"That makes sense. Traffic will be lighter on the freeway—people will be caught off guard."

Mano looked at his watch. It was 8:16. "The show starts in less than fifteen minutes. We better get ready," he said, nodding to Nesto.

Nesto understood Mano's gesture and walked behind a cooling unit nearby, returning with a gray duffel bag that he unzipped before them. In the glow of the streetlights, Mano could make out the dull sheen on the black barrels of three AK-47s. Slinging one assault rifle over his shoulder, Nesto handed Mano another, along with a belt of six curved ammo clips.

Nesto pointed down at the remaining assault rifle. "Ramon said you wanted two extra AKs. Who's this one for?"

Jo reached for the weapon. "It's for me."

Nesto jumped to his feet. "Que dices? Are you shitting me, man? Forget it. I'm not going to turn over one of our weapons to a woman."

Jo stepped close to the mero. "What's the problem, Nesto? Que te pasa?" she asked, coolly staring into his eyes, which were several inches below her own.

Nesto began to wilt. "You're the problem. You don't know what you're doing," he said, his voice losing its edge.

With her eyes still locked on Nesto's, Jo reached down, picking up the AK-47 and the ammo belt near her feet. With confident precision, she withdrew a clip from the belt, angled the rifle a quarter turn, slapped the clip home, and pulled back the action to place the first bullet in the chamber.

"The Kalashnikov AK-47 fires a 7.62-millimeter round at a rate of six hundred rounds per minute and has an effective killing range of three hundred meters," Jo said steadily. Then she raised the weapon skyward, released the safety, and took two steps backward, giving her room to level it. "Would you care for a personal demonstration of my marksmanship?"

Nesto had not become the leader of a violent gang through bravado alone. He knew when to make a strategic retreat. "Oooh, so this chica knows something about guns," Nesto said with a smirk. "OK, niña, you want to play with the boys, be my guest, but be careful you don't get hurt." He walked away, leaving Jo and Mano alone.

Mano opened his backpack and began methodically arranging its contents. On the right, he placed his walkie-talkie, a pair of binoculars, and a battery-powered spotlight. He then loaded the AK-47 and laid the rifle to his left.

"Now we wait," he said.

Mano crawled to the edge of the roof and looked west. Most of the people who had lined the sidewalk outside El Lobo an hour earlier were now inside, but a sizable overflow remained around the front door, reveling in the music drifting outside.

"Paloma, this is Oso. Anything?" Mano said into his walkie-talkie.

"Nada," the voice of his lookout squawked back.

Mano retreated from the edge and joined Jo, who was sitting with her back against a ventilation unit, the AK-47 positioned casually across her lap. Mano seldom made small talk. But tonight, like his days under fire in Afghanistan, he felt a need to.

"It seems like you've done this kind of thing before, Jo."

"I was born in Uruguay, Mano. My father was a Tupamaro."

Mano shrugged. "I don't know what that means."

"The Tupamaro party has a long history of resisting the government in Uruguay—and it hasn't always been peaceful," Jo said, absently rubbing the barrel of the rifle. "Although my father is a doctor, he made sure his children learned how to defend themselves."

"How did you wind up in a Los Angeles barrio?"

Jo hesitated, clearly uncertain how much she could trust him. "My mother wanted to be an actress. Then she met my father. They were married while he was still in medical school, and I was born two years later. Around that time, my father became active with the Tupamaros and started taking on clandestine missions. My mother got scared and divorced him. She came to Los Angeles, hoping to make it in the movies. I used to spend the summers here with her... until she died of a drug overdose. I was seventeen."

Sensing her lingering grief, Mano changed the subject. "So that's how you learned to speak English so well."

"Yes, that's right."

"What brought you back to Los Angeles?"

Jo leaned back, staring into the sky. "My father sent me to pre-med at Stanford. While I was in Palo Alto, I met Mark Johnson. He was a seminary student back then. Mark introduced me to the work of José Antonio Marcha and it changed my life. I realized who I really am—and the destiny of our people. Before I read Marcha, my world revolved around the Tupamaro struggle in Uruguay. But Marcha showed me that I'm a Hispanic and I share a legacy much bigger than Uruguayan politics. After Mark was ordained and started his mission in Los Angeles, I decided this was a good place to join the struggle of all Latinos—for justicia."

"Sometimes it's hard for me to understand why you're doing this, Jo. You don't even look like a Latina."

Jo shook her head, suddenly animated. "That's where you're wrong, Mano. There are plenty of people who look like me all over Latin America."

"I've never seen them."

"Like most people in the States, your image of Hispanics comes from television and movies, and they invariably typecast us as bronze, swarthy types. What's ironic is white Hispanic actors are often given Anglo roles because most producers just don't think a U.S. audience will recognize characters as Latinos unless they fit the brown-skinned stereotype. The same holds true for black Hispanics."

"I see what you mean. When I first met Jesús, I had no idea he was Latino."

"Few Norteamericanos understand the racial diversity of Latin America. For example, there are more blacks living in Latin America today than in the United States. Most people in this country believe the U.S. was responsible for importing the vast majority of African slaves in the Americas. The truth is that only five percent of the slaves brought to the New World came to the United States. The rest went to the Caribbean and South America. But when was the last time you saw a black Latino in a movie or a TV show?"

Mano stared back in surprise. "Why don't more people know about this?"

Before she could answer, the walkie-talkie crackled to life.

"Oso, this is Paloma. I think we've got something. Three vehicles coming down Agnes, a Suburban in the lead."

From the front passenger's seat of the Chevy Suburban, Gary Putnam selected the "voice only" mode on his vu-phone and dialed. "C'mon, goddammit. Pick up," he muttered as the line rang. He tapped impatiently on the barrel of the M16 nestled between his knees.

After the fourth ring, Putnam heard a voice on the line.

"This is Wally."

"Wally, this is Gary. I think we got us a problem over here."

"What? You're calling me on an unsecured line, you idiot!"

"I know—I know. But this is important. Darren said he thought he saw somebody leaning over a roof as he was casing the street. What if they're ready for us?"

"You're worse than an old woman, Gary. You know that? Now stop and think about it. How in the hell would a bunch of dumb-ass taco benders be smart enough to figure out when and where we're coming from?"

"I don't know. But isn't it Darren's job to drive ahead of us and let us know if there's gonna be any trouble?"

"Darren's job is to look for cops and let us know if any goddamn media types are crawling around. As much as I'd like to see their worthless guts smeared on the sidewalk, killing reporters would be bad for our side," Wally said. "Buck up, Gary. Most real Americans would give us medals for what we're doing."

"But just suppose they're ready for us. What do we do then, Wally?"

"If they've got the balls to mix it up with us, then I say, bring it on. But believe me, Gary, the greasers will never know what hit 'em."

As Wally disconnected, Gary Putnam adjusted his thick horn-rimmed glasses and turned to the driver of the SUV. "Wally says we go," he said, his mouth suddenly dry.

Mano's pulse was racing. Lying near the edge of the roof, he focused his binoculars on the three approaching vehicles. Nesto and his men had already been alerted and were poised to strike on his signal. Mano would have to decide in the next few seconds.

"Do you think it's them?" Jo asked, lying next to him.

"We have to be sure," he said softly.

The vehicles were two blocks away, traveling at a normal speed, but staying suspiciously close together. A Chevy Suburban led the pack, followed by a Camry sedan and a ragged Chrysler minivan.

"We're running out of time," Jo said through gritted teeth.

Mano's heartbeat was now thundering in his ears. If he made the wrong choice, innocent people would die. Then he saw the proof he'd been waiting for. As the convoy gained speed, gun barrels emerged from the windows of the vehicles.

"Signal the trucks," Mano said with a calm that belied his pounding heart.

"Go, Go, GO! HURRY!" Jo yelled into her vu-phone.

The vigilante vehicles were now racing past Mano's position near the middle of the block, bearing down on the crowd outside El Lobo. On the cross street just ahead of the convoy, two Mack trucks trundled into the intersection from opposite directions and stopped, forming a roadblock. The neat line of the convoy became a swirl of vehicles fishtailing wildly as they slammed on their brakes.

"Open fire," Mano said into his walkie-talkie.

The syncopated barking of assault rifles erupted in the concrete gorge. Mano heard Jo's AK-47 firing beside him in short, controlled bursts as the pockmarks of bullets began to cover the vehicles.

The driver of the Suburban floored the SUV in reverse and succeeded in ramming a utility pole. The Camry, its windshield shattered, rolled to a stop. The minivan managed a U-turn and began retreating from the ambush, a panicked shooter firing wildly into the night from its rear window.

Mano's fire plan for the RPGs was devastatingly simple. Holding the battery-powered spotlight by its pistol grip, Mano directed a thirteen-million-candlepower beacon onto the roof of the minivan. Two seconds later, a rocket-propelled grenade struck the front of the minivan on the passenger's side. A second shot missed, striking the pavement behind the vehicle, but it didn't matter; the minivan, still rolling, burst into flames.

Mano then turned his spotlight on the Suburban, which was pulling forward for another try at an escape. The first grenade struck near the rear wheel of the vehicle, destroying its axle and leaving the SUV foundering. The second hit the vehicle dead center on the driver's side, sending a shower of flying metal whirling over Mano's head. All three vehicles had been neutralized.

"Keep them pinned down," Mano said into his walkie-talkie. "We're headed for the ground."

With the chatter of AK-47s echoing below, Mano and Jo donned black masks and scrambled down the fire escape at the building's west end. After reaching Agnes Street, Mano peered carefully around the corner of the building. The minivan was engulfed in flames—no chance of survivors there. But there was still movement inside the sedan and the SUV.

"Cease fire," Mano said into the walkie-talkie.

The shooting died away, leaving a stillness broken only by the crackle of flames from the minivan. "Come out with your hands up," Mano yelled.

A man wearing thick glasses emerged from the Suburban, stumbling on a wounded leg, frantically waving his hands in the air. "Don't shoot! Don't shoot! I'm not armed, see?"

Then the door of the Camry opened slowly and a tall, rangy man stepped silently into the street, his hands above his head.

Less than six minutes after the first shots were fired, La Defensa del Pueblo had taken its first prisoners.

———

The slam of the massive door echoed throughout the vacant building.

"They're on ice," Nesto announced after locking up the prisoners. "I say we start with the big one. He's gonna be a lot more fun to mess up."

Nesto, Jo, Ramon, and Mano were gathered outside their makeshift jail—the steel-lined impeller test chamber at an abandoned jet engine plant. This was the moment Mano had been waiting for. He was face to face with the men who had slaughtered so many innocent people—the Jimenez twins, his neighbors, his niece—people he'd known and loved. Still, there were some things Mano could not bring himself to do.

"We're not going to torture the prisoners," Mano said.

Nesto laughed in derision. "Are you shittin' me, man? You're not gonna get anything out of these guys without some major pain."

"Mano, this has been your operation from the start," Ramon said. "In my opinion, you should decide how to interrogate these men."

"I agree," Jo added.

Mano stared at the floor. The time to help his people was here. Just as in Afghanistan, the speeches and patriotic words were gone. All that remained was the raw truth of life and death. He was beyond hatred and vengeance now. These men were a cancer, a sick cluster of cells that had to be removed. Turn them over to the police and they would alert the others, the ones who really pulled the strings. It was up to him to put an end to this. As he'd been trained in the Rangers, he had to put aside his feelings and act with the cold swiftness of a surgeon. "I think we can make the one with the glasses talk," he said finally.

―――

The vigilantes were seated on the floor in opposite corners of the test chamber when Mano and Nesto entered the steel-lined room.

Mano approached the tall vigilante holding his Glock-32. "I want to know who organized these raids."

The vigilante spit at Mano's feet. "Go to hell, greaser. If I'd known it was you that attacked us instead of the cops, you'd never have taken me alive."

Mano pulled the man to his feet and pressed the gun under the man's chin. "I'm going to count to three," he said with ice in his voice. "If you don't tell me who organized these raids, you're dead."

The tall man quivered but maintained a defiant look. In a soft voice, Mano began a slow count. "One...two...three—"

He squeezed the trigger.

Blood and tissue from the man's head splattered the steel wall and sprayed the others in the room.

Mano turned to the other vigilante, his thick glasses now spotted with blood.

"Oh my God, please don't shoot!" the man shrieked, holding his hands up and turning his face away.

Mano pulled the vigilante to his feet and gently held him against the wall, keeping the gun pointed toward the ground.

"Who is responsible for organizing these raids?" Mano asked him softly.

"O'Connor...Wally O'Connor," the vigilante replied in a hoarse whisper, tears streaming from his eyes. Mano released him, and the man slid slowly down the wall until he lay, sobbing, on the floor.

Mano crouched beside him. "Are you telling me the truth?"

"I swear it. I swear it," he whimpered. "Wally's a real estate agent—got an office in El Segundo. He brought us all together and bankrolled the whole deal."

Mano, Nesto, and Ramon huddled around the Volvo while Jo sat inside navigating through the touch-screen Internet feed on the dashboard.

"It checks out," Jo said. "Walter O'Connor is a Realtor,

affiliated with Hopewell. Rather successful, too. He grossed over sixty million in sales last year. Not bad for an ex-con. He spent three years in San Quentin for armed robbery and was paroled in '98."

"I did some time in San Quentin," Nesto said. "The place is lousy with guys from the Aryan Fatherland. Sounds like we know where this dude went to school."

"It all fits," Ramon agreed. "A group like the Aryan Fatherland would do anything to incite a race war."

"Are we sure this is our man?" Mano asked.

"That dude with the glasses looked too terrified to lie, ese," Nesto said. Then he turned to Mano. "You're one bad motherfucker, man."

Mano's face was expressionless. "The tall one was never going to talk. Executing him in front of the other one served its purpose. That's all."

Ramon pointed to O'Connor's address on the display. "It's too bad this guy's house isn't on a Green Planet pickup route. We could learn a lot from his garbage."

"He don't seem like the type that recycles his Kentucky Fried Chicken buckets, you know what I mean?" Nesto said with a sneer.

"Even if O'Connor isn't their top leader, he could lead us to the others," Mano said.

Jo nodded in agreement. "I say we move on O'Connor."

"In that case, there's one more thing I need to do," Mano said, walking back toward the test chamber. A few moments later, the trio outside heard the muffled pop of a gunshot. Then Mano emerged from the building.

Jo and Ramon exchanged glances. In that moment, they both knew Mano had become more than a hired bodyguard.

This deed had committed him to their cause in a way no oath of loyalty could have.

"He would have alerted O'Connor if we'd turned him over to the police," Mano said, his voice chillingly sober. "The man was a criminal. We have no courts to try him. For now, this is our only choice for justicia."

As the others stared at him in stunned silence, Mano realized he'd crossed a threshold from which he could never return.

———

Arriving on the scene shortly after the skirmish on Agnes Street, the LAPD found eight bodies amid the charred wreckage of three vehicles. The names of those killed were withheld pending notification of next of kin. No weapons were found, but the police conjectured they'd been carried off by the winning faction.

The only public record of the event came from an E! Network camera crew shooting a puff piece on Tomas Cruz's appearance at El Lobo. After hearing gunfire and explosions outside, the E! crew emerged from the club in time to film two masked figures, both in black fatigues and armed with AK-47s, sprinting past the corner of a building. The exclusive footage would be showcased with stunning impact.

Twenty-four hours after the clash, NBC aired a special report titled *Attack on Agnes Street.* Using the E! crew's footage and archival images of urban guerrillas from Belfast to Beirut, the NBC program sensationally documented the new phase in the unrest: a coordinated paramilitary attack by the insurgents.

THE RIO GRANDE INCIDENT:
Month 6, Day 5

Mano's mind was churning as he entered the DDP conference room. His plan to locate the leader of the vigilantes had gone well enough, but a major hurdle still remained. How would they get to Walter O'Connor? He hoped this meeting would sort that out.

Ramon, already seated at the oval table, held up a copy of the *Los Angeles Times* as Mano sat down. "Your attack on the vigilantes has really helped our cause, amigo. This publicity is a godsend."

Dominating the paper's front page was a grainy still-frame image from the E! footage. It showed Mano and Jo in black fatigues peering around the corner of a building, weapons at the ready, faces hidden behind black masks.

"I'm more concerned with catching O'Connor."

"Jo says she's got a plan in mind. She'll be here soon."

Despite his focus on O'Connor, Mano's thoughts wandered to Jo. She was unlike any other woman he'd known. Yes, she was achingly beautiful, but it was more than that. Jo's rare mix of courage and class made her seem raw and silky all at once. He found the contradiction strangely seductive.

Mano pointed to the newspaper. "I asked Jo why someone

with her kind of money would get involved in this stuff, but I didn't really understand her answer."

"This isn't the first time Jo's picture has made the front page."

"What do you mean?"

"I met Jo's father in Uruguay a few years back and he told me an interesting story. When Jo was nine, she talked a group of children in her neighborhood into attending a Tupamaro demonstration against the government in Montevideo. It turns out over four hundred thousand people showed up. The next day, a picture of Jo and her friends holding their hand-lettered signs was on the front page of the paper in Montevideo. The photo eventually appeared on TV shows, magazines, and posters. It became a symbol of government resistance. It's hard to forget that kind of excitement. Jo's father was a rebel, too. She grew up with revolution in her baby formula. Jo tries hard to look like a rich liberal. But believe me, Mano, that's a pose. Jo's got a fire in her belly."

"She's no stranger to guns."

The sound of footsteps in the hallway announced Jo's approach. "Ah, I see the fair damsel from Montevideo has arrived," Ramon said with a mock bow as she entered the room.

Jo smiled. "Cut the bullshit, Ray. I've got a plan to nab O'Connor that I want to discuss—and we don't have much time."

At the CIA, Hank Evans tossed a copy of the *Los Angeles Times* toward Maria Prado, a blurry picture of two black-masked guerrillas on the front page. "It looks like we've got some commando wannabes in East L.A., Maria. Any idea who they might be?"

Prado leaned back, thrusting her chin in the air. "If I recall," she said, "you felt my investigation of the Eslos wasn't a high priority."

"OK, Maria, maybe I was wrong."

"Maybe?"

"All right. I admit it. You warned me and I blew it off. Now, help me out here. This is starting to look serious."

Satisfied by his admission, Prado began briefing her boss. "Well, as always, I think it comes down to means and motive. The gangs certainly have the means—but I can't see their motive here. A number of the gangs are extremely well-armed, but this operation seems out of character," Prado said, tapping the newspaper photo. "The gangs are driven mostly by profit. Some call them the barrios' best entrepreneurs. And everybody knows the gangs fight each other for turf. But what most people overlook is that the turf they fight over is an exclusive franchise to traffic in drugs, prostitution, gambling, and extortion. That produces some serious cash. But there's no money in taking out a bunch of rednecks," Prado said, her enthusiasm growing.

"Then there are the radical groups—and there's a lot of them, too. Student groups, union groups, community groups—they're coming out of the woodwork in East L.A. They've got the motive but not the means—most of them are just hot air. They prefer to fight in the courts and in the media. La Defensa del Pueblo is probably the most visible of these radical groups right now."

Hank nodded. "Yes, I remember your report on them."

"If a group like the DDP could somehow enlist the help

of the gangs, that could be real trouble. You'd have a hybrid group with both means and motive. I think that's what we're seeing here, Hank."

"You still want to get a mole into La Defensa del Pueblo?"

"I do," she replied quickly. "The DDP seems the logical place to start. But I'm not certain they're the ones behind this violence. The leaders of the DDP appear way too effete for wet work. At the very least, a mole at La Defensa del Pueblo will help us rule them out, and maybe lead us to the real troublemakers."

"You have my authorization. Get on it, Maria, and keep me posted."

Pedro made sure his mother was busy in the kitchen, then carefully unfolded the cover page from the *Los Angeles Times* stashed in his math book. "Here, Julio. Lamp this," he said, passing the torn-off page to his brother.

"Tight!" Julio replied excitedly, staring at the photograph of the guerrillas.

Pedro pointed to the weapons held by the pair in the photo. "Those are AK-47s," he said, trying to impress his sibling.

"I know that," Julio said indignantly. "Everybody in school was talking about Agnes Street."

"Yeah, that was way tight."

"The big guy in the picture sorta looks like Papi."

Pedro sneered. "Papi? He was probably with his guerra again."

"Where did you hear—" Julio stopped in midsentence as Rosa entered the living room.

Pedro hurriedly folded the newspaper page and tucked it back in his book. The furtive gesture caught Rosa's attention.

"What have you got there, Pedro?" she said, drawing closer.

"Just something from school."

"What is it?"

"Nothing, Mami."

Rosa held out her hand. "Let me see."

His head bowed, the boy gave her the newspaper page.

Rosa unfolded the sheet and scanned the front-page article. At the bodega, she'd overheard people talking about the gunfight on Agnes Street, but this was the first time she had seen any news coverage on the event. She crumpled the paper and held it away from her like something rotten.

"These men are not heroes, do you understand?" Rosa said sternly. "They're fools—and they're going to get more people killed in the barrios. This is why I won't let you bring any newspapers into this house. The people who write this don't care how it affects kids like you."

"But, Mami, the gabachos had it coming," Pedro protested.

Rosa's face hardened. "Pedro! You will never use that word again, do you hear me? You're insulting yourself when you use words like that. How can you expect to be treated with dignity if you don't do the same?"

Pedro stood silently for a moment, then sulked into the bedroom. Julio quickly followed him.

Rosa sighed heavily. Mano's example was hurting their sons. Staying out late at night was not how a decent man behaved. Even if Mano was doing nothing wrong, everyone gossiped and assumed the worst. She could see Pedro's respect for his father fade more each day—and the influence of the streets grow in its place.

She walked to her shrine, knelt before the figurine of La Virgen, and made the sign of the cross. *Thank you, Señora, for your blessings*, she prayed. *You brought us Mano's job and the new car. But I would give it all back if you'd let my husband be a good father to his children again.*

THE RIO GRANDE INCIDENT:
Month 6, Day 9

Jo parked the rented Chrysler Sebring facing away from the Hopewell Realtors storefront and fussily adjusted her pinned-up hair in the rearview mirror, giving her a chance to survey the strip mall. There were no uniforms or plainclothes security lurking outside Walter O'Connor's realty office.

As she approached the storefront, Jo saw two conservatively dressed young men with shaved heads sprawled indolently across couches in the lobby. One was flipping through a magazine while stroking his goatee. The other was immersed in a game on his vu-phone. O'Connor was apparently taking the precaution of a personal security detail, but judging from the caliber of his bodyguards, he was not taking the threat too seriously.

As Jo opened the door, the young men glanced up, then ignored her. Crossing the lobby, she heard a voice from somewhere deep in the office. "Is she here yet?"

"Yeah," the young man nearest her shouted back without looking up from his magazine.

"Why the hell didn't you tell me?" the voice said, louder now.

"I'm not your receptionist, OK?"

Walter O'Connor burst into the room and glared at the two young men. He was a man who would have blended into the landscape anywhere in the United States. Around forty, average in height and build, O'Connor was wearing a tan sports coat over a buttoned-up white polo shirt and black pleated trousers. His brown hair was streaked with gray and parted neatly on the side.

"I'll deal with you later," O'Connor said to the young security guard, then turned toward Jo with a smarmy smile. "Mrs. Steele"—he extended his hand—"I'm Wally O'Connor. Please let me apologize for our trainees; they're just getting started in the business and they ain't learnt their manners yet. Won't you please come on in?"

Jo returned the smile. "Please, Wally, my mother-in-law is Mrs. Steele. Call me Bonnie," she said, entering his private office.

O'Connor gestured to one of the chairs in front of his desk. "You mentioned on the phone that Colonel Steele's just been transferred to the base out here, right?" he said, dropping into a high-backed swivel chair.

Jo folded her hands on her lap. "Yes. Frank wanted me to get started on our house hunt right away. He's still back in Dayton finishing things up at Wright-Patt."

Jo had selected her clothes for this role carefully. Her silk blouse, calf-length skirt, modest gold necklace, and black leather purse projected the conservative style O'Connor would expect from the wife of an Air Force colonel. From her research on O'Connor, Jo knew he'd see a colonel's wife as a plum client—he normally worked with blue-collar customers.

"Do you know this area at all, Bonnie?"

"Not really. Frank has a friend who was transferred out here a few years back. In fact, his friend recommended the house I mentioned when I called."

"Well, that's why I asked you if you knew the area. You see...well...your husband's friend, is he a...a...person of color, by any chance?"

Jo had not expected O'Connor's question. "I'm not sure—I've never met him myself. Frank just said his friend assured him this property was a good deal."

"OK, Bonnie, now, I'm gonna tell you something I'm not supposed to." O'Connor paused, lowering his voice. "There's a bunch of people in Washington that believes Realtors shouldn't be allowed to tell the truth about certain neighborhoods. You understand what I'm saying?"

Jo knew exactly what he was saying. O'Connor was redlining—steering Jo away from a neighborhood with a large population of Hispanics. His bigotry had not hurt his realty business, Jo supposed.

"No, Wally, I'm not sure I do."

"I've made a good living by treating people fairly, even if that means breakin' the rules. So I'm gonna tell you straight out. That neighborhood's not fit for decent white people like you and your husband."

Just to see the look on O'Connor's face, Jo was tempted to say her husband was black, but instead she continued her charade, producing a slip of paper from her purse. "What's wrong with the neighborhood at this address?"

"It's north of Long Beach, see, and most people who live there these days ain't white—they're Hispanics. Now there's some folks, mostly liberals, who like to look down on me for telling you this. But I've noticed one thing, Bonnie: even the liberals won't buy in a neighborhood where they know the property values are gonna go down. They don't want to send their kids to schools with a bunch of greasers who're gonna cut up their sons and molest their daughters."

She masked it well, but Jo was stung by O'Connor's comment. Her own home was in Beverly Crest—an area with very few Hispanics. Still, she was risking her life and spending her fortune for the cause of *justicia*. *That's what truly counts*, she told herself.

"I appreciate what you're trying to do for us, Wally. But I have to honor my husband's request to look at this property. It's a Christian wife's duty."

O'Connor nodded solemnly. "I understand, Bonnie. It's God's will that a wife obey her husband. I'll show you that property, but then we'll look at some other homes in a more fittin' neighborhood."

O'Connor opened the door to the lobby and, with an exaggerated sweep of his hand, gestured for Jo to pass. Following her, he glanced at the guards and jerked his head toward the front door. The two rose to their feet.

"You don't mind if we take along my trainees, do you?" O'Connor asked. "The boys are following me around to learn the business."

"No, of course not," Jo replied. She'd debated with Ramon and Mano as to whether O'Connor would bring his guards with him. It turned out that Mano was right. She would need to alert him.

"This here's Darren," Wally said, pointing to the young man with the goatee, "and this one's Michael."

Jo smiled at the young men, both of whom nodded indifferently, seemingly more interested in the carpet pattern than in making her acquaintance.

Now, walking ahead of Jo, O'Connor led her to the front passenger's seat of his Ford Expedition. The two guards took seats in the row behind her. A few minutes later, they were cruising north on I-405.

O'Connor glanced toward Jo. "That's an unusual ornament on your necklace, Bonnie. I've never seen anything like it before."

"Oh, it's something I picked up at a little shop in Dayton," Jo said, improvising.

"Did I mention I'm from Ohio, too? Portsmouth. Did you ever get down to Portsmouth?"

Jo knew she was on thin ice. There hadn't been much time to prepare for this role. "Frank was only stationed at Wright-Patterson a couple of years. With two kids at home and Frank away a lot, I didn't get out much."

"Well, you ought to see Portsmouth, Bonnie. It's God's country down there. The river and the cliffs—"

"Excuse me, Wally," Jo interrupted. "Could we make a stop somewhere? I need a chance to...freshen up."

After they pulled into a gas station at the next exit, Jo entered the restroom and called Mano. "I hate to admit it, but you were right. He's got two goons with him."

"We'll be ready. Thanks for the call."

Mano's calm tone filled Jo with confidence. Her attraction to him was growing steadily, she admitted to herself. He'd become a pillar in her life she'd not even known was missing.

As Jo opened the restroom door, she was startled to see

Darren standing outside. Had he been listening? For the first time on the mission, Jo felt the cold chill of fear.

Seeing her shocked expression, Darren offered an explanation. "Wally asked me to escort you back here. He says this is a rough area."

Jo was still suspicious. If Darren was on to her, he would have to report it to Wally. She would need to keep an eye on him.

When she returned to the SUV, O'Connor again acted like a royal footman, opening the door with a great deal of pomp. Jo watched Darren walk around the rear of the vehicle and exchange a few words with Wally before they both got inside.

Dammit, Jo thought. *This doesn't look good.*

She lowered the sun visor, pretending to inspect her makeup in the mirror while keeping an eye on Darren. After touching up her lipstick, she left the handbag open on her lap. She didn't want to use the six-shot Beretta inside, but she might have no choice.

O'Connor eased the SUV in front of a modest ranch home on a wooded cul-de-sac. "Well, this here's the place, Bonnie," he said. "It's vacant and been on the market for quite a while. Notice how most of these houses around here are vacant? Like I told you, with all the beaners moving in, this neighborhood is just about ready to go to hell in a handbasket. You think we need to go inside?"

Jo was relieved they'd made it this far. Maybe Darren hadn't overheard her call after all. "I promised Frank I'd look at this house, Wally, and I intend to keep my word."

"I can't tell you how much I admire a Christian woman who's obedient to her husband—even if it *is* a waste of valuable time. It's the way all wives should be. I'd be honored to show you the inside, Bonnie."

O'Connor unlocked the front door with a key from a combination box hanging on the doorknob and gestured for Jo to enter. *With all three of them here, this is going to be tricky,* Jo thought. *The timing will have to be perfect.*

She walked casually through the living room and made her way down the hall, O'Connor in tow. She was relieved when the two guards remained behind.

O'Connor made another wide sweep with his arm. "See how shabby the place is? The family of a United States Air Force colonel deserves better than this."

"I don't know, Wally. I think some fresh paint and wallpaper could really cheer the place up. Let's see what the other rooms are like." Jo walked into the first bedroom with O'Connor close behind her.

He went to the far corner of the bedroom and opened the closet. "I wouldn't be surprised if this place is crawlin' with roaches. You know how these people live," he said, peering inside.

Jo moved quickly toward the doorway, cutting off O'Connor's path to the exit. The Realtor gasped in shock as Jo produced the Beretta from her purse and leveled it at his chest.

"Not a peep, Wally, or you're dead," she said very softly.

Reaching down, she brought the pendant to her lips. The shrill sound that followed made O'Connor cover his ears.

When he heard Jo's whistle, Mano was in position outside the front door. Entering the house with his Glock drawn, he saw the two guards in the living room staring wide-eyed in confusion.

"Hands up!" Mano shouted, training the pistol on them.

Hearing footsteps from the hallway, Mano turned and saw Nesto run into the living room, his pistol drawn. Distracted, Mano felt a hard slap on his gun hand as the man closest to him bolted for the door. Glancing left, he saw that Nesto had already secured the other guard. It was up to him to catch the fugitive.

Dashing outside, Mano aimed his Glock at the man's back…and broke into a run, unable to pull the trigger. After a burst of speed, he was nearly on the thug as he reached the street. The young man dropped to the ground in a catlike reflex, sending Mano hurtling through the air over his body. The guard sprang to his feet, trying to run again, while Mano—still rolling—leg-whipped him, fracturing the goon's tibia. The young man went down screaming in pain.

On the ground, the guard drew a pistol from his sports coat, but before he could aim, Mano pounced, landing heavily on his chest. With his left hand, he grabbed the guard's gun hand and pinned it to the ground. He then brought his bulky right forearm crashing down on the man's throat, violently compressing it against the pavement. The guard's head twitched spastically, his pupils rolled out of sight, and bloody foam oozed from his mouth. The blow had crushed his larynx and severed his spinal cord.

Breathing heavily, Mano rose to his knees and stared down at the lifeless body, feeling numb.

Jo's voice broke his trance. "Get up, Mano. We've got to get out of here—now."

Guided by the moonlight, Jo reached the edge of the sea-side cliff. "This is far enough," she said, the crash of waves a distant murmur far below. Behind her, Mano led two bound and gagged captives at gunpoint—O'Connor and his guard. Jo nodded to Mano and he removed the duct tape from O'Connor's mouth.

"What's a white woman doing with scum like this?" spat the president of the Aryan Fatherland. "Don't you have any pride in your race?"

Jo laughed. "I was born in Uruguay. My name is Herrera," she said, pronouncing her name with the distinctive trill of a native Spanish speaker. "But you and your kind are too igno-rant to realize Latin Americans are no different than North Americans. We're not a race, we're a people."

O'Connor's eyes widened in astonishment, but his hatred seemed to trump all reason. "Call yourself what you like, bitch."

Jo stared at him calmly. "O'Connor... that's an Irish name, right?"

O'Connor jutted out his chin. "My father was Irish and my mother was German. I come from pure Aryan bloodlines."

"Did you know that the Irish were considered a separate and inferior race by many people in this country until the late nineteenth century?"

"That's a lie."

"Is it? Then you probably won't believe me when I tell you that Ben Franklin once complained about a horde of non-whites breeding so fast they were overrunning the British colonies—tawny-skinned people who wouldn't bother to learn English." Jo paused, waiting for her next words to sink in: "the German immigrants of Pennsylvania."

"You're right about *one* thing, cunt: I *don't* believe you," O'Connor said, the tendons of his neck bulging. "You're nothing but a bunch of worthless, third-world terrorists trying to destroy a nation built by the superior intelligence and Christian values of the white race."

"And you believe it's your duty to preserve these values, right, Wally?"

"You're damned right."

"It doesn't seem like you've done a very good job so far."

"We've killed over forty of your useless fucking mud people."

"Yeah, but don't try to take credit for something you didn't do, Wally. Somebody a whole lot smarter than you set it all up."

"No, sister. I'm the—" O'Connor stopped, suddenly realizing Jo had baited him into a confession.

"You're what, Wally?" Jo asked, finally venting her fury. "You're the man who arranged for his lackeys to gun down more than forty unarmed men, women, and children? Is that what you were about to say?"

O'Connor didn't reply, but simply stared at Jo, hatred burning in his eyes.

Jo turned slowly toward the sea. "He's the one," she said to Mano, her voice emotionless.

On a foggy spring morning, an Orange County deputy, responding to a call from an Iowa tourist, found the bodies of three men at the foot of a cliff along a deserted stretch of shoreline. Two of the men had been shot in the head in what appeared to be execution-style slayings. One was identified as Walter O'Connor, age forty-three, a Realtor from El Segundo. The other was Darren Strachan, a twenty-three-year-old convicted felon paroled from San Quentin five months before. The third body was that of Michael Walker, twenty-five—another felon recently released from San Quentin. The cause of Walker's death was listed as "blunt force trauma." Although authorities later found O'Connor's realty office ransacked, the motive for the killings remained unclear.

Over the next two weeks, the greater Los Angeles area was hit by a wave of similar killings. All eleven of the men slain were former San Quentin inmates.

Shortly thereafter, the vigilante raids into East Los Angeles ceased.

Across the rest of the Southwest, however, the drive-by shootings by Anglos continued, spawning a vengeful spiral of violence. Each vigilante attack triggered more protests and rioting; each disturbance in the barrios provoked more attacks by the vigilantes.

Even in Los Angeles, where the vigilante attacks had stopped, rioting still broke out in response to Anglo raids in other cities.

Three months after the notorious ambush on L.A.'s Agnes Street, local authorities throughout the Southwest were confronting a surging tide of anarchy. Government buildings, utility companies, malls, corporate offices, colleges, and sports stadiums all became the scenes of demonstrations that often turned violent.

THE RIO GRANDE INCIDENT:
Month 9

Repression is a revolutionary's best recruiter. It
will create more converts than a thousand rousing
speeches.

—José Antonio Marcha, 1978
Translated by J. M. Herrera

Rosa emerged from the bodega keeping Elena close
by her side. The chance of trouble was growing worse each
day, but bringing her five-year-old shopping seemed less
risky than leaving her home alone. She scanned the street
and noticed a patrol of six National Guardsmen moving in
her direction. Fearing the soldiers might attract trouble, she
went back inside the store.

Through the front window, she watched the heavily armed
men draw closer until they were just outside the store. One of
the Guardsmen drifted away from the others and approached
Sofia and Julie Cardona as the teenagers walked by.

The soldier tilted back his helmet and leered. "Hello,
pretty señoritas," he said, revealing a row of crooked teeth.

The young girls giggled, whispered something to each
other, and kept walking.

"Hey, I'm talking to you," he said, his tone suddenly harsh.
"Halt!"

The girls froze, suddenly uncertain.

"Don't you bitches play hard to get with me," he sneered. "How much? I'm ready to do both of you if the price is right."

Sofia and Julie stared back in shock.

"Come off it," the soldier said. "I know this innocent bit is a trick to jack up the price. What's it gonna cost me?"

The girls looked at the ground, too embarrassed to speak.

"What's the matter, don't you know English? You understand this, don't you?" he yelled, grabbing his crotch.

Sofia covered her face, suddenly in tears.

Another soldier approached them. "C'mon, Davis," he said, pulling his comrade toward the rest of the patrol. "Leave these skanks alone. We'll find us some good whores back at the base."

Davis turned to the girls again. "What? You beaners think you're too good to fuck a white man?" he yelled before returning to the other soldiers.

Rosa found herself trembling with rage. She knew Sofia and Julie Cardona well. They were decent girls from a good family. She did not want to hate the soldiers, but it was impossible to forgive their abuse. These men had terrified the girls—and insulted their parents who were working hard to raise them right.

Elena tugged on her hand. "What were they doing, Mami?"

Rosa's heart sank. She'd been too stunned by the encounter to realize her five-year-old was witnessing the ugly scene. "It was nothing, m'hijita. Just a silly game," she answered quickly, guiding her away from the window.

Looking at her wide-eyed daughter, Rosa wondered if

Elena would someday be accosted by ignorant men like these.
The likelihood seemed very real. War often turned men into
animals. And war was the only way to describe the conditions
around much of the country.

For the first time in her life Rosa was paying attention to
events outside her home. She had tried to resist. But the brutal deaths around her had revealed a painful truth: ignoring the outside world would not spare her family from its
dangers. She now watched the television news while the boys
were in school and Elena was napping. The entire country
had changed for the worse—and very quickly.

———

Nine months after the Rio Grande Incident, the barrios of
the Southwest were becoming battle zones where insurgents,
vigilantes, police, and National Guard troops waged a bitter
conflict. Hate crimes against Hispanics by the KKK and other
white supremacist groups multiplied outside the Southwest,
stirring more friction.

Damage to public structures was now so common that a
new style of architecture was evolving in urban areas throughout the Southwest. Glass was disappearing from public buildings, replaced by hasty patches of concrete, stone, or brick.
In the interim, sandbags were being piled inside windows.
National Guard troops in combat gear were now permanent
fixtures of the urban landscape. "Homeland Security" was
taking on an alarming new meaning in the national lexicon.

The apparent inability of the government to maintain
order—or capture the vigilantes—was widely publicized by
the media. The bloggers were particularly vitriolic. Local,
state, and federal law enforcement agencies were routinely

roasted for incompetence and accused of collusion with the vigilantes. Some radical-left publications called them government death squads despite their obviously random attacks.

Many Americans were too afraid to leave their homes, let alone shop. Each passing week saw more retail stores shuttered. Local economies that were already weak went on life support. With gasoline already rationed as a "strategic resource" in the war on terror, workers moved closer to their jobs, sending once-prosperous suburbs into decline.

As the months passed, the scope of the violence mounted. Attacks by small armed cadres erupted, the insurgents often wearing black, emulating their brethren who had ambushed the vigilantes in Los Angeles.

In El Paso, four armed men stormed a local television station and fought a SWAT team to their deaths while the station's cameras rolled.

The residents of Corpus Christi awoke to the sound of automatic rifle fire when insurgents staged an early morning assault on a National Guard detachment camped on the outskirts of the city.

Explosions rocked the morning calm of Santa Fe as three homemade bombs were detonated in the portals of New Mexico's iconic Capitol Building. A group calling itself the "Latino Liberation Front" claimed responsibility.

Eager to cash in on the ratings windfall, the broadcast networks hired extra camera crews to keep up with the escalating violence, vying with one another to air the most sensational footage. Their constant reports of turmoil inflamed opinions on both sides of the widening divide between Hispanics and the rest of the nation.

Seeking the limelight, a number of pundits and politicians

began parroting an alarming prediction: A full-scale Hispanic rebellion was imminent. A growing segment of mainstream America quietly feared the prophecies were true. Nine months after the Rio Grande Incident, their fears would find a voice in an obscure congressman from Louisiana.

———

A cascade of camera flashes greeted the Nationalist congressman from Louisiana as he stepped behind the podium on the steps of the Capitol. Melvin Bates looked out across the expanse of the Mall, savoring the moment. He'd waited years for an opportunity like this.

The Nationalists had gained eight seats in the last election, and today's announcement could vault the fledgling party into national prominence. Although Bates knew the resolution he was about to propose had little chance of being ratified, he was convinced it would create an immense number of new supporters for the Nationalists...and help fill the coffers of his party's reelection war chest. Played right, the Nationalists could become power brokers, able to tip the scales between the two major parties.

Looking down, Bates saw the elite of the Washington press corps arrayed before him in a rectangle of folding chairs. Flanking them were the TV crews, their cameras and microphones facing him like nestlings with begging maws. Through his aides, Bates had leaked the volatile subject of this press conference to a number of reporters. Judging by the media turnout, the tactic had been effective.

Bates cleared his throat and began his opening statement.

"My fellow patriots, our nation faces a challenge unlike any other in our proud history. We are besieged by an enemy within our borders who is brazenly moving among us in military formations with the avowed objective of sedition and conquest. These unprecedented and heinous deeds are tearing at the very fabric of our society.

"To protect our homeland, some misguided Americans have taken the law into their own hands. They have struck back blindly against these terrorists. However well-intended, the righteous fury of these misguided patriots is bringing us to the brink of anarchy. We cannot allow our nation to continue suffering under these conditions.

"The insurgency we face today has a decidedly foreign presence. Those who are perpetrating these acts of terror speak another language. Many were not born within our borders. What we face today is nothing less than a conflict with foreigners on our own soil.

"I fully understand that those committing these deeds of aggression represent only a small minority of the Hispanics in our land, and let me make this perfectly clear: the majority of the legal citizens of the Hispanic race are loyal, law-abiding Americans.

"Therefore, for the protection of our faithful Hispanic citizens and to help root out the terrorists within our borders, I will be proposing to the members of Congress a resolution of Quarantine and Relocation."

Bates paused and looked beyond the teleprompter. He felt a rush of delight at the astonished expressions among the press corps.

"First, this bill will mandate the immediate deportation of all Hispanics who are not naturalized American citizens. Next, the bill calls for the creation of Relocation Communities where loyal Hispanic-Americans can be protected from the wrath of misguided citizens. These Relocation Communities will not only protect innocent Hispanics, but they will also help us isolate the terrorist minority within Hispanic areas and choke off their lifelines of support. In addition, the relocation will aid authorities in locating and deporting the vast number of illegal aliens still within our borders.

"Until the Relocation Communities are ready for occupancy, the bill calls for the creation of Quarantine Zones around Hispanic areas within our cities. This will help quell the domestic violence running rampant in many urban zones in our nation.

"These are dire times; they call for dire measures. I urge all patriotic Americans to join me in support of this resolution to restore the peace and tranquility of our nation.

"Thank you and God bless America. I'll take your questions now."

On the day following Congressman Bates's press conference, the headline of the *Washington Post* read, "Ethnic Cleansing in the U.S.?" It was the first salvo in a massive barrage of media coverage. By week's end, Bates's proposed "Quarantine and Relocation Act" had sparked a heated national debate.

Opponents saw the relocation as a clear violation of Hispanics' First Amendment rights. Supporters countered that Hispanics had become enemy aliens, no longer entitled to constitutional protections.

The proposed resolution was hardening positions on both sides of the Hispanic issue. Any middle ground was rapidly disappearing.

Two months after Melvin Bates's public proposal, opponents of the resolution readied a massive protest in the nation's capital. Orchestrated by a broad coalition of Latino groups, the event would be labeled the "Forum for Justice."

Mano reached high above his head, groping blindly through the clothes and blankets stacked on the top shelf of the closet until his fingers recognized the familiar stiff canvas of his Army duffel bag.

Retrieving the carryall, he noticed the dank smell of mold. *Dammit*. He'd have to buy a new travel bag now. He dreaded spending the money, but was certain Jo and Ramon would find it embarrassing to fly with a security chief carrying worn, smelly luggage.

He stared at the khaki duffel bag wistfully. The last time he'd flown was on the way home following his discharge. He'd worn his fatigues on the plane, although Army regs said he could go civvie. The airlines offered discounts to soldiers flying in uniform and he wanted to save the money. This flight would be quite different. Jo and Ramon had chartered a private jet for their trip to Washington, and all his expenses would be paid.

Mano was refolding the duffel bag when Rosa entered the room.

"What are you doing with that?" she asked. Mano's presence in their bedroom in the middle of the day had piqued her curiosity.

"We need to throw it away. It's moldy."

"All right. But why did you get it out?"

"I've got a business trip next week."

"Business trip?" she said warily. "Where are you going?"

Mano knew he could not hide his involvement with the DDP any longer. Rosa would find out soon enough anyway. News of Jo's high-profile role in the Forum for Justice would spread quickly in the media. Thankfully, the threat of vengeance from the local vigilantes was no longer a factor.

"Rosa, it's time I told you what I've been doing," he said, sitting down on the bed. "Come here. Sit with me," he said, patting the mattress beside him.

Rosa remained standing, frozen with apprehension. "It's that woman. I know it," she said, her voice breaking with emotion.

"Yes, Jo is involved." Mano nodded calmly. "But it's not what you think."

"What is it, then?"

"I'm the security director for an organization Jo founded with Ramon Garcia—La Defensa del Pueblo."

"Dios mio, Mano! That's one of the crazy groups making all the trouble," she said. "Why didn't you tell me?"

"Because I thought anything you knew might put you and the children in danger."

"I don't understand you, Mano," she said, wringing her hands. "If you thought it would put us in danger, why did you join up with these people?"

"To protect you."

Rosa's eyes began welling with tears. "That doesn't make any sense, Mano. You're lying to me. What are you really doing with that woman?"

"Stop it, Rosa! Stop inventing things and calm down," he said, rising to his feet. "What I'm doing is helping the DDP protect our community. I can't say anything more without endangering other people. Can't you understand that?"

Rosa stiffened, drawing her arms against her chest. "I see," she said, sounding unconvinced. "That's very convenient."

"You don't believe me?"

"What you've told me is not very easy to believe. You're not political, Mano. You've always said people like Josefina are troublemakers with nothing better to do. Now you tell me you work for her as a...what is it?"

"Security director."

Rosa laughed bitterly. "I don't even know what that means."

"It means that I'm using my military training to help people here at home."

"How? By stirring up more trouble?"

Mano clenched his fists, frustrated by their impasse. "I've told you all I can, Rosa. But what I've told you is the truth."

"Even if it is the truth, what you're doing is wrong, Mano. You said it was foolish to riot. But this DDP of yours is constantly stirring people up."

"No, Rosa. You don't understand," he said, shaking his head. "Besides, this job is giving our family a chance to get ahead. Do you want me to quit?"

Rosa moved closer. "I know Josefina pays you well, Mano. But look what it's doing to our family. You can find another job, mi amor," she said, her voice pleading. "You always have before."

Mano rubbed his temples, considering her words. He knew the chance for a job with the pay Jo provided would probably never come again. All the same, what Rosa said was true. Their family was falling apart. "I've promised Jo I'd go on this trip," he said. "When I get back, we'll talk about this again."

"Is the destination of this trip a secret, too?"

"I'm going with Jo and Ramon to a rally in Washington, D.C. We leave next Thursday."

Rosa stared at her hands for moment. "I'll pray for your safe return," she said coldly and then left the room.

THE RIO GRANDE INCIDENT:
Month 11, Day 4

Looking out from the grandstand, Mano was edgy and tense.

Although the first speech of the Forum for Justice was still two hours away, the area in front of the brightly painted podium at the foot of the Lincoln Memorial was already packed as early arrivals pressed impatiently for choice vantage points. Behind them, around the six-hundred-meter-long Reflecting Pool, surged more people.

The bodies in the restless mass roiled like a turbulent sea, banners and placards snapping in the brisk May breeze. Responding to the call for Relocation Communities, an angry chant rang spontaneously through the crowd: "Hell no! We won't go! Hell no! We won't go!"

Mano knew the buildings lining both sides of the Mall held law enforcement officers monitoring the agitated crowd. However, in the great open space at the Mall's center, the police were noticeably absent—and Mano understood why. If trouble broke out, any officers in the middle of the crowd would be cut off and surrounded.

Mano turned to look for Jo and spotted her at the rear of the grandstand, preparing for the ceremonies. She was engrossed in a flurry of logistical details and ego tussles with the staffs of the celebrities and politicos who would occupy the podium. As they traveled together, his attraction to Jo had reached the point of delicious discomfort. He relished following her with his eyes, yet was stung by guilt when his gaze lingered. Despite himself, there were times when he imagined—

"Mano!" Margaret Zane called out, drawing closer. "Have you got a minute?" Ramon's wife asked.

Margaret was a striking presence, striding confidently in a sheer peach gown that streamed in her wake, her bright orange hair piled precariously in the "Tower of Pisa" look that was the rage on Rodeo Drive. Mano knew Margaret was largely responsible for the demonstration's immense turn-out. She'd sweet-talked or strong-armed most of the celebrities into attending the demonstration, then cajoled her studio's top publicist into sending out a blitz of press releases on the event.

Walking alongside Margaret was a tall brunette in a tight metallic-gold jumpsuit.

"Hello, Ms. Zane," Mano said.

"Oh, Mano, you are so gallant. I just love it! But please, call me Maggie," she said with a gleaming smile.

"OK, Maggie. What can I do for you?"

"Manolo Suarez, this is Estelle Clark," Maggie said, gesturing toward her companion. "Estelle is an executive assistant for Ben Torres, and she has some concerns about security. So I thought we should talk to you."

Mano didn't watch much television, but even he knew Ben Torres was the star of *Salsa on the Side*, a hit sitcom about a Latino detective in New York's posh East Side. Mano also understood why Torres might be worried about security—he was the event's opening speaker.

Estelle stepped forward, flashed a perfunctory smile, then got down to business. "Ben is going to be escorted by his two security regulars, but he's never done an event like this before and he has some concerns. To begin with, what precautions have you taken to protect the speakers?"

Mano waved his arm toward the buildings lining the Mall. "There are federal officers in every structure you can see from here, Ms. Clark. The chances of a sniper using any of them are very small. And the podium is bulletproof. The level of security for the speakers here today matches the president's."

Estelle's face warmed slightly. "Ben also wants to know what's being done about crowd control."

"There are probably more than two hundred thousand people out there already, ma'am," Mano said, turning toward the crowd. "There's going to be a lot more by the time Mr. Torres starts to speak. Nobody can control a crowd that size. But you can assure Mr. Torres that we have an evacuation plan in place. If there's any trouble, our contract guards will form a corridor behind the grandstand and escort the dignitaries toward the river. We have a number of boats waiting there to get everyone away safely."

"Isn't Mano wonderful, Estelle?" Maggie said. "I told you we're in good hands. Ramon goes on and on about how carefully Mano plans these kinds of things."

"Thanks, Mr. Suarez," Estelle said, this time with a genuine smile. "I'll let Ben know about your arrangements. It sounds like things are under control here." Her business concluded, Estelle turned and began a sensuous walk back across the grandstand.

Maggie sighed after Estelle was out of sight. "That's a

relief. I'm glad we didn't run into Ramon. He thinks Ben's show is trash and exploits Latino stereotypes—I'm sure he would have let Estelle know it, too. By the way, you handled her quite well, Mano."

"Thank you, Maggie. All I did was tell the truth."

Maggie seemed suddenly nervous. "Your plan is just a precaution, right, Mano? You don't really think there's going to be trouble?"

Mano glanced at the mass of humanity on the Mall, their number swelling by the minute. He couldn't put his feelings into words, but Mano's defensive instincts were aroused. "We all need to stay alert today, Maggie. With this many people in one place, I don't know what to expect."

Even on an overcast afternoon in May, the Forum for Justice event drew more than one million people to Washington, D.C.

Thanks to a podium studded with celebrities, the demonstration was broadcast live by every major network. An array of camera towers normally used to cover golf tournaments loomed over the crowd at key locations on the Mall while a specially approved blimp provided aerial views in the normally restricted airspace of the capital. As the broadcast began, the network anchors were calling it the largest public gathering in the history of the nation's capital.

Minutes after television star Ben Torres began his speech, shots rang out. On a side street near the Vietnam War Memorial, a counterdemonstration by members of the Ku Klux Klan and the American Nazi Party clashed with the outer edge of demonstrators on the Mall. Many in both camps were armed. Both factions would later claim the other side fired first.

The shooting sent a chain reaction of panic and anger through the massive crowd. Many bolted away from the gunfire. Others charged into the fray. Even as Torres called desperately for calm from the podium, the confrontation exploded into a chaotic street battle captured by the cameras of the national media.

An aerial view showed the two opposing groups clashing, the border between the angry masses marked by a jagged line of flailing limbs. In another view, taken from a tower, two men were seen in a gun duel, puffs of smoke bursting from their weapons with each shot. A telephoto lens captured a close-up of a woman kneeling beside a bleeding man, begging for help from passersby. Another camera recorded a circle of men mercilessly kicking a prone victim. A pan of the Mall showed it littered with unmoving bodies.

One network anchor was left speechless by the violence. Another tried to keep up a commentary, adding a surreal, blow-by-blow description of the frenzy. Millions at home watched in shock and horror.

When the violence was quelled forty minutes later, more than six hundred people lay dead. More than two thousand were wounded. Most of the victims were unarmed demonstrators caught in the crossfire.

The rest of the ceremonies were cancelled. The Forum for Justice was over before the first speech could end.

The mood of the crowd ranged from anger to dismay as the demonstrators cleared the Mall. Many felt cheated of their chance to protest an unjust resolution. Many more felt deep despair at the senseless carnage. Most Latinos watching at home shared their outrage and grief.

The mainstream public saw the incident differently. The demonstrators, they believed, had provoked the attacks. If the Hispanics and their supporters had stayed home, they reasoned, the violence could have been avoided.

As the sun began to set on that cloudy Saturday, there seemed to be only one point of consensus about the tragic event: the Forum for Justice had been a bloody public spectacle that had driven a wedge between the nation's rapidly cleaving factions.

As the first anniversary of the Rio Grande Incident approached, the U.S. was dividing into two hostile camps.

Before entering the Beech 400A, Ramon turned for a last look at the Washington Monument. In the horizon beyond Dulles Airport, the floodlit obelisk with its distinctive red lights pierced the dusk.

His footsteps silenced by the shrill whine of the engines, Ramon slouched dejectedly into the chartered plane and found his wife already inside. "What a disaster, Maggie," he said, making his way aft. "I'll be glad to get out of this town."

Margaret, wearing a T-shirt and cut-off jeans, was cradling a tumbler of scotch, her gown and hairpiece safely packed away. "I've never seen anything so horrible," she said, filling her glass with another shot of Chivas. "The violence was bad enough, but a lot of people on that podium had important things to say."

Ramon dropped heavily into the seat next to her. "This is going to set back our cause."

"Thank God Mano got the dignitaries out safely. Think about the bad press that could have—" But before Maggie could finish, Jo entered the plane.

"Sorry I'm late," Jo said, slinging herself into one of the seats. Unlike her companions, she seemed energized and excited. Without pausing, she picked up the phone to the cockpit. "We're all on board now, Captain. I'm sorry for the delay," she said into the receiver. A few seconds later, the co-captain emerged from the cockpit and closed the plane's door.

"Where's Mano?" Ramon asked.

Jo's face hardened. "I couldn't get him to leave," she said, trying to mask her irritation as she fastened her safety belt. "He's staying behind to help the medical teams carry away the wounded. He'll catch a commercial flight back later."

"You made a wise choice in hiring Mano, Jo. That kind of man is very rare."

A slight smile warmed Jo's face. "You're right, Maggie. I should know by now that Mano is going to be Mano. I'm just disappointed because we've got so much to plan, and not a lot of time."

Ramon looked puzzled. "I don't understand, Jo. What's so critical right now?"

Jo swiveled in the leather seat to face him. "When the shooting started today, I saw all our work to derail the Bates resolution go up in smoke, Ray. I was sure it was a catastrophe for our cause. But then something happened that changed my mind." The roar of the engines grew louder and Jo's voice rose in response. "I saw a group of elderly women on the Mall charge into the skinhead line, swinging their sign poles like Vikings. They were angry, Ray, and they were fighting back. That's when I remembered something Marcha wrote: 'Repression is a revolutionary's best recruiter.' Don't you see, Ramon? If the Bates resolution is inevitable, we need to make the most of it. The deportations, the quarantines, the relocations—these things are going to make our people angry. It could turn out to be a golden opportunity—if we're ready to seize it," Jo said, almost shouting. "What happened today might turn out to be a godsend."

As the small jet began climbing into the air, Ramon noticed the glimmer of a smile on Jo's face.

THE RIO GRANDE INCIDENT:
Month 11, Day 8

Nearing the door to his apartment, Mano stopped to compose himself. He did not want to bring his problems home to Rosa and the children.

Since returning from Washington two days ago he'd made an effort to get home on time, but it was stressful leaving work with so much undone. Tensions were escalating daily, and there never seemed to be enough time to oversee security at the five DDP locations spread across the city. Making matters worse, the trip east had put him further behind. By force of will, he relaxed and cleared his mind before unlocking the door.

The children were sprawled on the couch, watching television, when he entered the living room. Mano knelt on the floor near them and spread his arms. "Who's going to challenge the linebacker?" he asked with a mock growl.

"I will! I will!" Elena and Julio shouted in unison. Pedro ignored his father, his eyes locked on the television.

"All right, Elena—on three. Hut…Hut…Hut…"

Elena cradled an imaginary football, lowered her head, and charged into her father's chest.

Mano made a big show of being bowled over by the five-year-old. After squirming past him, Elena pretended to spike the ball and raised her hands in triumph, grinning widely.

Mano let his shoulders sag theatrically. "All right, show-boat," he said to her. "Act like you've been in the end zone before."

Rosa, in the kitchen preparing supper, peeked out and smiled. It had been months since Mano had played the Line-backer with the kids.

Julio looked at his father, his face serious. "Play for real. OK, Papi?"

"Bring it on, big guy," Mano answered, thumping his chest. "On two."

Grim-faced, the boy took a three-point stance as Mano began the cadence.

"Ready…Set…Hut…Hut…"

Julio charged but feinted left then veered right, forcing Mano to reach for him. The boy ducked under Mano's arm and spun past him.

"What a move, ladies and gentlemen!" Mano said, now an announcer. "Suarez has scored to give USC the lead!"

Julio and Elena exchanged high-fives as the eight-year-old strutted victoriously, nodding his acknowledgment to the imaginary crowd.

"C'mon, Pedro," Mano said to his oldest son. "The line-backer's ready for you."

"I don't want to play," Pedro answered without looking away from the screen.

Mano tugged playfully on Pedro's leg. "What's the matter? Don't think you can get past the linebacker?"

"This is stupid. You're just pretending that we win."

Mano sighed, his energy suddenly drained.

Julio put his arm around Mano's bulky neck. "It's OK, Papi," he whispered. "Pedro's mad because he misses you."

Mano felt his throat tighten and his eyes grow moist. "You're a good son, Julio," he said softly.

Julio took his hand. "C'mon, Papi. Watch the show with us," he said, leading his father toward the couch.

Once Mano sat down, Elena and Julio huddled against him on the sofa. After a while, Pedro moved to the floor and nestled between his father's legs. At six on the dot, Rosa called them to the table for dinner. After the meal, they cleaned up the kitchen together. Later, Rosa and Mano helped the boys with their homework, and by nine-thirty all three kids were in bed.

After her usual evening shower, Rosa found Mano in the living room tinkering with the window air conditioner they'd purchased recently—another by-product of Mano's increased pay.

"We need to talk, Mano," she said, fastening a towel around her hair.

"I'm trying to fix this condenser. It leaks when the humidity gets too high."

"Mano, you promised we'd discuss your job when you got back from Washington. You've been home four days now."

Mano put down his wrench and exhaled slowly. "What do you want me to say, Rosa? I've been trying to get home earlier and spend more time with the kids."

"I want you to say you're going to look for another job."

"You've got to stop being jealous, querida. There's nothing between Jo and me." Even as he said it, Mano knew he could not deny a mounting attraction to his boss. All the same, he was certain he'd never allow himself to act on it.

Rosa took Mano's hands in hers. "Look, even if there's been something between you and Josefina...well, if you end it, we'll get through that," she said almost in a whisper. "But you've got to get away from her, Mano. She and her kind are trouble. They're the reason we have all this fighting in the barrios—and the soldiers," she added, recalling the crude Guardsmen who'd harassed the Cardona girls. "This DDP business is dangerous, mi amor."

"Rosa, La Defensa del Pueblo has saved lives. I know it."

"Saved lives? Look at all the people who were killed at your rally in Washington."

"What happened in Washington was a tragedy, Rosa. But it wasn't wrong. Our people stood up for their rights—and they did it under the law."

"All it's done is stir up more trouble."

"We have to raise support against the Bates resolution, querida. I won't deny it's dangerous. But a man has a duty to do what's right for his people."

Rosa pulled her hands away. "Can't you see what she's doing, Mano? She's got you wrapped up in this whole Hispanic business. Why should you risk your life for a bunch of strangers just because your parents spoke Spanish? Your family comes first."

"That's true, mi amor. But there's something you need to understand," he said, taking her hands again. "It doesn't matter how you and I feel about other Latinos. People like Bates will hate us anyway. Don't you see? You, me, the children, and every other Hispanic are all the same to them. They want to lock all of us up inside these Quarantine Zones—and they're not going to stop and ask if you supported the Latino cause."

Rosa turned away, closing the collar of her robe. "You don't sound like the man I married anymore."

"This country's changed, mi amor. I don't like it—but helping the DDP is what's best for our family. We don't have any other choice."

"Where does it stop, Mano? They're radicals. I've heard people talk about this Marcha and his ideas for a revolution. Just because you won't tell me everything doesn't mean I don't know. How far will you go with these people?"

"Trust me. I would never do anything to betray our country."

Rosa turned and looked into his eyes. "They'll lead you to treason, Mano," she said softly. "I just hope you can still recognize that when it happens."

In the week following the aborted Forum for Justice, rioting flared in the barrios of Atlanta, Charlotte, Chicago, Cleveland, Des Moines, Miami, Minneapolis, New York, and Tampa—the first Hispanic disturbances outside the Southwest. Attacks by vigilantes also spread, repeating a destructive pattern.

Hastening the cultural fracture, the major Spanish-language television networks began broadcasting editorials for the first time. These highly rated programs presented a decidedly pro-Hispanic view of events.

Street interviews on the major broadcast networks seemed to suggest most mainstream Americans were fed up with the Hispanic issue. They simply wanted an end to a thorny and intractable problem. Among large numbers of scared and frustrated citizens, the simplicity of the Bates resolution was growing in appeal.

A Gallup poll taken before the Forum for Justice showed thirty-seven percent of Americans favored the Quarantine and Relocation Act. One week after the bloody spectacle on the Mall, the number rose to sixty-four percent. Ironically, support for the bill was strongest in areas unaffected by the turmoil.

Sensing the changing mood of the American public, the Brenner administration announced its support for the Quarantine and Relocation Act. Twelve days after the bloody demonstrations in Washington, the bill was ratified by the House of Representatives. Still, many doubted it would make it through the Senate.

Then the fate of a suburban family from Indiana sealed the bill's fate.

"Ron, I don't see any gas stations around here," Cristy Davis said nervously, toggling through the GPS display on the dash of their Envoy.

"Will you relax?" her husband answered testily from behind the wheel. "You know how those damned things work. If you don't pay to advertise, they won't list you. There's gotta be a filling station somewhere around here."

Cristy glanced again at the gas gauge. "We're getting really low, Ron. If we'd stopped at that exit outside of Gary like I asked you to, we wouldn't be doing this."

"Dammit, Cristy! Proving you were right isn't going to help right now. Why don't you do something useful? Try to figure out what our next exit is because I'm gonna take it. I don't care what the GPS says."

In the rear seat of the SUV, eleven-year-old Kasey Davis pulled off her headphones. Although she'd not heard her parents' conversation, the tension on their faces alarmed her. "What's the matter, Mommy?"

"It's nothing, Kasey. Everything's fine, honey. Why don't you take some more movies of our vacation to show Grandma?" Cristy said, hoping to distract her daughter.

Since they'd left their home in Connersville that morning, Kasey had spent a good part of the drive capturing the rural countryside on her new digital camcorder. As they neared downtown Chicago, the view outside had changed drastically. There were closely packed buildings of every shape and size as far as she could see.

Kasey raised the camcorder and began to record.

After exiting I-55 in search of a gas station, the Davis family found themselves in the middle of a confrontation between Hispanic rioters and police on Chicago's southwest side. Some eyewitnesses claimed the driver of the SUV panicked after seeing the crowd and swerved into an alley, running down a child and prompting the angry mob to turn on the cornered vehicle. That story was contradicted by other witnesses, who said the mob fell upon the vehicle without any provocation. When the police finally forced the crowd back and reached the SUV, all three members of the Davis family were dead. The camcorder disc shot by Kasey Davis was recovered by an opportunistic Chicago resident who immediately posted it online.

Over the next two days, the horrifying footage was viewed by millions on the Internet and broadcast repeatedly by the networks. The blurred and jerky recording showed an angry horde swarming the SUV, pounding on the vehicle and screaming at its occupants. At that point, Kasey dropped the camera on the floor, but it continued to record. What happened next was not totally clear.

The sound track was what made the recording so haunting. The angry shouts of the mob, the panicked voices of the family, and their final, desperate screams left an indelible mark on every person who heard it.

The fate of the Davis family was the nightmare of most mainstream Americans. They feared the growing bloodshed would soon reach them. The reaction among non-Hispanics was now almost unanimous: the violence in the barrios must stop. A *USA Today* poll taken two days after the Davis tragedy showed ninety-one percent of non-Hispanics now favored the Bates resolution.

In the days that followed, all congressional resistance to the Quarantine and Relocation Act evaporated. The uncanny progress of the controversial bill left Washington insiders stunned. Among those most surprised was its original sponsor, Nationalist congressman Melvin Bates.

Jo walked purposefully into the conference room and sat down at the oval table.

"Sorry to keep you waiting, hermanos," she said to Mano and Ramon. "I've been tied up with our friends in Palo Alto. I swear, sometimes I think computer geeks live on a circadian cycle from Mars. Anyway, I'm happy to report our stealth pipeline to the Web is under way. How are we coming with the dummy businesses, Ramon?"

"Excellent," Ramon said. "I've got three different lawyers setting up a string of LLCs. By the end of the week, we'll be ready to start buying the materials on our list—very discreetly, of course."

"I don't understand all this, Jo. What's going on?" Mano asked.

"I'm sorry, Mano. Ramon and I had to keep this from you. It's sensitive information and you had no need to know until now," Jo explained. "As I'm sure you've heard, the Quarantine and Relocation Act looks certain to pass in the Senate. Once the quarantine is in place, the government is going to surround the barrios with troops. We need to start our preparations to resist the quarantine right away."

"Resist?" Mano asked.

Jo's eyebrows arched in surprise. "Are you opposed to resisting the quarantine?"

"Rallying votes to stop the Bates resolution is one thing. But this is a nation of laws, Jo. Once the majority votes for something, the rest of us have to go along—whether we like it or not. I won't resist the Bates resolution if it's passed by Congress."

Ramon swiveled his chair toward Mano. "You didn't have any qualms about 'resisting' the Aryan Fatherland, amigo."

"That was different. We stopped the murder of innocent people. The Bates resolution isn't putting anyone in danger, *and* it's the will of the people."

"You forget about the Bill of Rights, Mano," Jo said. "You see, the Founding Fathers were a pretty cautious bunch of radicals. They were just as worried about a dictatorship by the majority as they were about the dictatorship of a monarch. That's why they made sure the rights of individuals were guaranteed by the Constitution—regardless of the whims of the public. The Quarantine and Relocation Act clearly violates several amendments in the Bill of Rights."

Ramon leaned forward, eager to weigh in. "If the Supreme Court wasn't stacked with hard-line conservatives right now, this resolution would be ruled unconstitutional overnight. But the Supremes serve for life. So it may be decades before enough of the current court members die and moderates can reverse the decision, Mano."

"Until that happens," Mano said, "you're breaking the law."

"If you took a vote on the Bates resolution here in East Los Angeles, do you think it would pass?" Jo asked.

"No," Mano admitted.

"Now suppose the people of East Los Angeles were a separate nation. Wouldn't their votes count?"

Mano raised his palm in protest. "But this is not a separate nation, Jo. It's part of the United States."

"Weren't the thirteen American colonies part of England until they asserted their independence?"

Mano sighed. "Look, Jo. Even if it was right to resist the Bates resolution, we'd be opposing U.S. troops," he said. "I served in that uniform. I could never fight against the people who wear it."

"Mano, you remind me of a great military leader who once faced a similar decision," Ramon said.

"Who was that?" Mano asked, trying to stifle a surge of pride.

"Robert E. Lee—the finest military mind of his time," Ramon said, sipping his latte. "Lee graduated from West Point and served in the U.S. Army for over twenty years. In 1860, Lee was forced to make a big decision. Did he owe his allegiance to the U.S. government or to his native Virginia? It was a difficult choice. Lee knew that, either way, he'd be fighting against comrades he'd served with for decades. His decision to fight for the South eventually came down to a single reason: he felt his native state needed him more."

Jo leaned close to Mano, locking him in her gaze. "Who needs *you* more, Mano?"

Mano looked back into Jo's intense blue eyes, a tingle in his chest. *Is there another meaning to the question?* Jo excited him, and this growing passion was complicating his decision, leaving him baffled and uneasy.

"I'm going to have to think about it," he said.

"Mano, we don't have the luxury of time," Jo said, leaning forward in her chair. "We have to make plans and make them fast. I wish we could give you more time to decide, but we can't afford to wait any longer."

Mano stared at the tabletop as Rosa's words echoed in his head: *They'll lead you to treason. I just hope you can still recognize that when it happens.* Was resisting this unjust law treason? Maybe not—but his loyalty to the troops who wore the uniform was too strong. "I can't do this," he said at last.

"Mano, I'm going to be closing down the recycling business," Jo said. "You'll be out of work. Think of the consequences for your family."

"We'll manage."

"You'll manage?" Ramon said skeptically. "Where are you going to find another job—especially after they wall us in? How are you going to—"

Jo interrupted him with a soft touch on the shoulder. "Save your breath, Ray," she said. "You and I both know Mano.

Arguing is not going to change his mind. Look, Mano, if you feel differently about this later, come and see me. The door will always be open."

She and Ramon then rose wordlessly and walked out of the conference room.

THE RIO GRANDE INCIDENT:
Month 12, Day 17

The tragedies of struggle forge heroes from common men.

—*José Antonio Marcha, 1987*
Translated by J. M. Herrera

Thanks, Vargas," Mano said to the driver of the aging Chevy before the sedan pulled away, leaving him on the crowded sidewalk.

Entering his apartment's courtyard, he found his elderly neighbor Guillermo Ortega on a folding chair facing the street.

"You're back early. Doesn't look like you had much luck," Guillermo said.

Mano shook his head glumly. "No, the docks didn't have any temp work today."

"Didn't I tell you not to listen to Mario Crespo? That pinche cabrón likes to sound important, telling people he knows where they can find work."

"Crespo was only trying to help, viejito," Mano said, patting the old man's stooped shoulder.

"Only trying to help, eh? Did Vargas ask you for gas money?" Guillermo said, referring to the driver of the car that had taken Mano and four other men to San Pedro Bay in search of work.

"Vargas didn't have to ask. I gave him twenty dollars for gas."

The old man sneered. "That Vargas is a sly one. I think he's got something going with Crespo. One makes up stories about finding work, and the other one charges people money to drive them there. Did Vargas collect gas money from everybody else?"

"Yes," Mano said, realizing the old man might be right. He and the four other men desperately looking for work had probably been suckered. Mano's shoulders slumped. The prospects of finding a job seemed hopeless.

It had been three weeks since he'd quit La Defensa del Pueblo, and the consequences of his decision were beginning to sink in. Although they'd managed to put away some of his pay, it was only a matter of time before their savings would run out. Then he and his family would be reduced to the fate of so many others in the barrios—standing in line at the food pantries, dejectedly waiting to take home a cardboard box of withered vegetables, dented cans, and second-hand clothes.

Mano looked at his apartment door. He could not bear facing Rosa with another excuse, another failure. "I'm going for a walk, Guillermo."

"Keep your eyes open, muchacho. I've heard talk that tanks have been running through the barrio. There must be big trouble somewhere."

"We're falling behind!" said the voice in Sergeant Brewer's earphones. "Close it up, Brewer!" his vehicle's commander ordered.

Wesley Brewer accelerated the M113, struggling to control the armored personnel carrier in the tight confines of South Mott Street. His brief experience driving the tanklike M113 had been in the high desert around Fort Irwin, where his National Guard unit trained. In fact, counting the last twelve minutes, the young sergeant had logged less than two hours behind the steering yoke of an M113. Now Brewer was driving second in a convoy of four, rushing to a disturbance at East Los Angeles College, where automatic weapon fire had been reported.

Brewer cringed as he peered through his periscope. Ahead of him, the lead vehicle turned right and disappeared behind a building. Brewer had come to dread the nearly blind right turns of the M113.

Racing around the corner behind the lead unit, Brewer felt the rear end of his vehicle begin to slide. *Shit. I'm going too fast,* he realized as the thirty-three-ton vehicle careened across the narrow street, slamming into the front of a burned-out bakery.

"Goddammit, Brewer. You're making us look like idiots!" the vehicle's commander barked into Brewer's earphones, his own periscope fixed on the lead M113 rapidly pulling away. "Get us back in convoy formation, NOW!"

The damage to the vehicle was minor, but restricted by their scopes, the crew members never saw the small red-jacketed figure standing in front of the store. The M113 hurriedly backed away from the rubble and continued down East Second Street, trying desperately to keep up with the lead unit.

The sight of the armored vehicles had mesmerized the eight-year-old boy standing in front of the store. They were the last thing Julio Suarez would ever see.

Mano drifted along the teeming street, plagued by the questions he'd been asking himself for days. *Does my loyalty have a price tag? Who do I owe my loyalty to? Could Marcha be right?*

In a search for answers, he began sorting through his life, recalling his days in high school. Although he'd done well in his classes, he'd been steered toward vocational training. *Would I have gone to college if I'd attended high school in an Anglo neighborhood?* His time in the Army raised similar questions. He'd served two hitches and made master sergeant. *Why didn't I consider applying for Officer Candidate School?* Weighed against his own life, Marcha's ideas had an element of truth. The question was, how much?

As Mano turned north on Ford Boulevard, his vu-phone rang—an extravagance he'd maintained to help him find work. When he saw "home" on the phone's exterior display, he knew the call was important. Rosa hated to use the phone—they were being charged by the minute. Perhaps she had a lead on some work. Mano tried to quell his excitement as he connected the call.

Rosa's face was a mask of anguish in the display.

"Rosita, what's the matter?"

"Mano," Rosa wailed. "Dios mio, Mano—"

"Calm yourself, mi amor. Tell me what's happened."

"It's Julio . . . Julio was killed by the soldiers."

Rosa sat on the edge of the couch, her arms folded tightly, red-rimmed eyes staring at the floor.

Standing before her, his head bowed with respect, Jorge

Pujols said, "I'll stay until your husband arrives, Señora." While walking home from work, Jorge had witnessed the armored vehicle crash into the burned-out bakery. Recognizing Julio, the grocery clerk had rushed to their apartment.

When Mano entered the apartment a short while later, Jorge intercepted him at the door. Speaking in whispers to spare Rosa the pain of reliving the tragedy, he told Mano what he'd seen.

In the small apartment, it was impossible for Rosa not to overhear Jorge. The account he gave her husband had many more grisly details. "They never stopped, Mano," Jorge concluded. "The soldiers ran over the boy and never even stopped." The words pierced Rosa's heart once more.

Mano shook the grocery clerk's hand. "Thank you, Jorge, for coming to us. I know it wasn't easy."

"You're quite a man, Mano. You just lost your son and you're thanking me for bringing you the news," Pujols said, looking up in awe. "May God keep you, Señora," he called out to Rosa before leaving the apartment.

Mano crossed the living room, hugged Rosa tightly, then gently raised her face. "Querida, I'm going to have to leave you for a while. Do you understand?"

They both knew why Mano had to go: he had to recover Julio's body. But neither of them could say it aloud without breaking down.

"Go. I'll be all right," she answered finally. "I left Elena and Pedro next door with Guillermo and Juana," she said, rising from the couch. "I'll bring them back. It's time to eat and I know they don't have anything to feed the children."

Mano drew her tightly against him. "I'll be back as soon as I can," he said before stepping away.

She watched Mano close the door. Alone for the first time since receiving the news of Julio's death, Rosa felt her legs quiver and fell to her knees, anguish and pain eclipsing all else. She covered her face and wept. *Julio, my son. You hurt no one. There are so many things you'll never know, so many things you should have done. You'll never...* She suddenly shook her head. *No, you cannot do this.*

Rosa stood, wiped away her tears, and walked toward the door.

She had no time for grief. She needed to feed her children and put them to bed—then prepare her son's body for burial.

———

The barrio's familiar streets no longer seemed real as Mano walked in the gathering dusk. *Could it really happen? Could an American military unit run over a child and not stop or call for help? Have U.S. troops become so blinded by hate that innocent lives no longer matter?* Part of him refused to believe it. Men who could do such a thing, even if they wore the U.S. uniform, were without honor.

Rounding the corner on Dougal Street, Mano saw the vacant bakery, its caved-in façade gaping like the maw of a bent-toothed monster.

"That's the father," whispered one of the neighbors gathered around the building. The words stung Mano. Although he knew it wasn't rational, he still wanted to believe this was all a mistake.

A hush fell over the onlookers as Mano stopped in front of the bakery. After hesitating, he forced himself to look inside. Beneath a tangle of masonry and splintered lumber was a small, broken body. Mano recognized Julio's red jacket.

A surge of pain began in Mano's throat and continued downward through his chest. He braced himself against the wall, hot tears clouding his sight. Closing his eyes, a question rang through the darkness: *Why my son? Why my son?* Slowly, the words changed to a vision. He was back on Fourth Street, helplessly watching the vigilantes gun down his neighbors. He had risked everything to protect his family—and it had been useless. In the end, his former comrades had taken his son's life.

Lost in shock, Mano knelt near the pile of rubble as his neighbors watched in silence. Then a distant roar broke the stillness—the unmistakable rumble of a tank.

The vehicle was out of sight but getting closer, its clatter assaulting Mano like an angry fist pounding inside his head. The sound became a taunt, mocking his futile efforts to protect his family, fueling his growing sense of betrayal.

Mano rose and pushed his way through the crowd, charging toward the sound. He wanted to drag the men out of the tank and kill them with his bare hands, or be killed—it didn't matter which. These men were no longer his comrades; they were his enemies. Exhaling white-hot anger with each breath, he ran toward the roar. For a block he raced ahead, each footfall stoking his anger. Then the faces of Rosa, Pedro, and Elena flashed through his mind.

The images tempered his fury, bringing him to his senses. Gasping for breath, he stopped. He had a wife and two other children who still depended on him. Throwing away his life would not bring his son back. He had no weapons and no plan.

Mano walked back slowly to the bakery and began clearing away the debris that covered Julio's body. Several of his neighbors joined him in the grim task, some offering condolences, others cursing the heartless men who could kill a child and flee. Mano could not bring himself to reply.

As he tore through the rubble, Mano found his way blocked by the remains of an interior wall. Grabbing a severed section of pipe, he swung it viciously, pulverizing a large section of sheetrock. In an eruption of rage, he struck the wall again and again, his frenzy growing with each blow until the wall finally collapsed.

Breathless, his fury spent, Mano stared at the pipe in his hand. *I do have a weapon to avenge my son*, he realized suddenly. *La Defensa del Pueblo.*

"Jo!" Ramon called out as she hurried past his office at DDP headquarters. "Sonia says there's someone to see you in the conference room."

"I'm really swamped right now," Jo said, pausing at the doorway. "Can Sonia reschedule whoever it is?"

Ramon grinned slyly. "Oh, I think you'll want to take this meeting."

"Who is it?"

"Mano."

"I knew he'd come back," she said before dashing toward the conference room on the floor below.

Jo's jubilant mood ended when she entered the conference room and saw Mano seated stiffly at the oval table. He seemed a different man, his eyes sunken, his face harder.

"You don't look well, Mano," she said gently. "Is everything OK?"

Mano stared at the tabletop. *She doesn't know about Julio.* That was not surprising. Another child's death in the barrios wasn't news these days. The few people outside his family who'd shown up for Julio's funeral were proof of that. One thing was certain. Julio's death was a family matter—and that's how it would remain.

"You said the door would still be open," he said at last.

"Of course, Mano," Jo said, sitting down. "I think you made a wise decision coming back."

"Have you hired a new security director?"

"We've looked. I'm doing the job for the moment—although not very well." She smiled and added, "I suppose I shouldn't say that. Now you'll want more money."

"You paid me well, Jo. I don't want more money."

"That's a relief. The government's trying hard to choke off our funds."

"Whatever you can pay me is fine."

"We can talk about that later. What I want to know now is the reason you came back."

Mano studied the table again. "I changed my mind."

"I see," Jo said, leaning closer. "Can you tell me why?"

"I'd rather not."

"Mano, a man like you doesn't wake up one morning and suddenly change his mind. You had some very serious qualms about resisting the Bates resolution."

"I don't anymore. Isn't that enough?"

"Look, I don't want to pry, but I need to know why you're doing this. Frankly, bringing you back could put our security at risk. How do we know you haven't gone over to the other side?"

Mano managed a weak smile. "If I'd turned against you,

you'd be under arrest by now, Jo. I already know enough to get *all* of us locked away."

"That convinces my mind," Jo said, looking deep into his eyes. "But it doesn't convince my heart."

Mano lowered his gaze, trying to hide a sudden rush of excitement. His grief and anger had dulled his infatuation with Jo. In one look, his passion for her was back. Along with it came a wave of guilt. "This is wrong," he said, rising from the table. "I should go."

"No, wait," she said, reaching for his hand.

Mano stopped, held by her feather-light touch.

"I shouldn't have doubted you," she said. "I'm sorry."

"That's not why I should go."

"What is it, then?"

"I don't know how to say this, Jo . . . I love my wife, but—"

"Mano!" Ramon called out, entering the conference room. "It's good to see you, hombre!" he said, then looked him over and added, "Although you look like hell."

Mano was startled by the interruption, then relieved. "You don't look so great yourself," he replied, his face warming into a small smile.

"I'm glad you're back," Ramon said, clapping his shoulder. "We could sure use your help again."

"Mano's not sure he wants to come back, Ray."

"What?" Ramon said, frowning. "Mano, you're not one to make social calls. Why else would you come?"

Jo answered for him again. "It's my fault," she said. "Mano agreed to join us. But I pressed him for his reasons and now he's balked about coming back."

Ramon turned to Mano. "Whatever reasons you have for joining us again are good enough for me, amigo."

"That goes for me as well," Jo added. "I was wrong to question your motives."

"Well?" Ramon asked, spreading his palms. "Are you with us?"

Mano glanced at Jo. Her eyes were on the floor. He could do this; he *had* to control his impulses. There was no other way to avenge his son's death. "I can start whenever you need me."

Ramon beamed. "Good. Because we've planned some very special surprises for Mr. Bates and his friends once the Quarantine Zones are in place."

THE RIO GRANDE INCIDENT:
Month 12, Day 29

Walking across the defunct railway bridge, Mano gazed at the Los Angeles River below, wondering why Jo had asked to meet here. He wasn't familiar with this area of the river, which abutted the rail yards of the Southern Pacific.

For most of the year, the Los Angeles River was an oversized, graffiti-covered culvert with a meandering trickle. As a kid, Mano had often played on the river's paved channel—it was one of the best places around to skate and play stickball.

Mano's memories of childhood reawakened the pain of losing Julio. The twelve days since his son's death had been the most agonizing of his life. As he'd done in the past, Mano dulled the pain by burying himself in work. Rosa, consumed by her own grief, didn't question his actions.

In anticipation of the quarantine, Jo had launched a flurry of preparations for self-sufficiency. Throughout the barrios, they were already stockpiling caches of food, water, medical supplies, and gasoline, purchased through the dummy businesses set up by Ramon to avoid suspicion.

Halfway across the bridge, Mano saw Jo and a stranger waiting on the other side. Walking closer, he recognized Ramon—without his ponytail.

"I imagine you're wondering why I asked you to meet us

here—and maybe why Ramon cut his hair," Jo said after Mano reached them.

"Both those questions crossed my mind."

"Well, to begin with, Ramon has gotten way too easy to spot with that infamous ponytail of his," Jo explained, smiling.

Ramon also grinned. "We kept the hair, though. I'll keep wearing my fake ponytail in public and take it off when I need to go undercover."

"As for you," Jo said to Mano, "you're going to need a new identity to travel outside the Quarantine Zone." She reached into her backpack and handed Mano a rolled-up piece of khaki fabric, about six inches in width.

"What's this?"

"It's your turban. Once you grow a beard, you'll be ready to pass for Mr. Ajitkumar Singh," Jo explained. "I think you'll look pretty dashing as a Sikh."

"Sikhs are tall and warriorlike," Ramon added. "You should fit the part well."

"We didn't have to meet here for you to tell me this."

"That's true," Jo agreed. "Look around, Mano. What do you see?"

"The L.A. River. Is there something else?"

Jo nodded. "I see a lifeline for our barrios once the quarantine begins."

Mano gazed up and down the river. "Yes, I see what you mean. The river and these railroad tracks cut right through the middle of Los Angeles. The government will have to keep this area open after the quarantine."

Jo smiled, impressed by Mano's strategic grasp. "That's right. This corridor can be our pipeline to get people out and supplies in."

Sensing the possibilities, Mano pointed toward the succession of mammoth drainage pipes lining the concrete riverbank. "Those storm sewers feed into the river from every part of the city. If we connect some new tunnels to them, we'll have an invisible supply network."

Ramon grinned wryly. "It sounds like you've just outlined the plans for the East L.A. version of the Ho Chi Minh Trail."

THE QUARANTINE AND RELOCATION ACT

THE QUARANTINE AND RELOCATION ACT:
Day 1

Leon Trotsky said war is the mother of revolution. He might have added that government repression is usually the midwife.

—*José Antonio Marcha, 1989*
Translated by J. M. Herrera

On a rainy Tuesday in July, the U.S. Senate convened a special session. Four months after the Quarantine and Relocation Act was first proposed by Melvin Bates, eighty-two of the nation's senators voted in favor of the bill. With unprecedented swiftness, President Brenner signed the act into law the same day. On Wednesday, the ninety-point headline on the front page of the *New York Post* read:

THEY MUST GO

Overnight, one of every six people on U.S. soil was designated Class H—"H" as in "Hispanic." This classification was given to anyone with a Spanish surname or at least one parent of Hispanic origin. Anyone with a Hispanic spouse was also included.

The ACLU and the National Council of Churches contested the classification in a case taken by the Supreme Court. As expected, it was to no avail. Meantime, lower federal courts were swamped with thousands of cases in which families with culturally ambiguous names like Estes, Marin, and Martin requested an exemption from Class H designation.

Class H status included two categories: citizens and noncitizens. Immediate deportation awaited anyone designated Class H who was not an American citizen.

To expedite their relocation, Class H citizens were required to register their home addresses within thirty days with the CIA. Failure to comply would bring a ten-thousand-dollar fine and three years' imprisonment.

With the enactment of the law, teams of government bureaucrats began the arduous task of determining the boundaries of the temporary Quarantine Zones around Hispanic urban enclaves. The construction of the first Relocation Communities also became a priority. With these plans under way, a purge began of the Class H population from government positions of power and influence.

Class H government employees were required to reapply for security clearances. None received a "secret" clearance after reapplying. Class H bureaucrats at every level were assigned to nonessential projects. The secretary of housing and urban development, Judith Ramirez, was no exception. She was no longer allowed to attend cabinet meetings in which matters of national security might be discussed, in effect making her a figurehead with no real authority. Class H judges at the federal, state, and local levels were banned from adjudicating criminal cases. From privates to generals, military personnel with a Class H status were reassigned to maintenance units with no access to weapons or military intelligence.

Class H citizens were allowed to vote, but only for congressional representatives within the Quarantine Zones and Relocation Communities. Congressional representatives from these areas would hold non-voting seats in the House of Representatives.

Within two months of the Quarantine and Relocation Act's adoption, the first walls began to rise around the nation's forty-six Quarantine Zones—and the neutralization of Hispanic political influence in the United States was well under way.

THE QUARANTINE AND RELOCATION ACT:
Month 2, Day 2

Your purpose for entering the Quarantine Zone, ma'am?" asked Private First Class Paul Little as he examined the three-day pass issued to Emily Barnett.

"I'm a deaconess of the First Apostolic Church," answered the primly dressed blonde. "We have a congregation in the zone."

Private Little jerked his thumb toward the steel gate behind him. "There's not much hope of saving any souls in there, ma'am. They're all scum. A white woman alone around these people had best be careful."

"Cool it, Little," said the other guard at the fortified checkpoint.

"Nah, man. The lady oughta know what she's getting herself into."

"Ma'am," the other guard said to Emily. "My squadmate's just an ignorant redneck. There's good folks in there that need all the help they can get."

"Yeah, and she's going to find out how good when some Pancho pulls a knife and rapes her."

Emily retrieved her pass from the soldier. "Thank you for your sensitively expressed concern, Private," she said, and entered the North Gate into Quarantine Zone B.

The government bureaucrats had split Los Angeles into two Quarantine Zones divided along the L.A. River—Zone A in the west and Zone B in the east. Wedged precariously between the zones was downtown Los Angeles.

Walking into Zone B, Emily glanced at the graffiti-covered wall behind her. Erected only two months earlier, the wall facing the central business district had been the first section completed—a ten-foot barrier of stacked concrete slabs topped with concertina wire. Work on the wall along the eastern and southern boundaries of Zone B was still under way. In those areas, dense coils of concertina wire served as an interim barrier.

After walking two blocks, Emily turned east, out of sight of the checkpoint guards, and entered a black Audi sedan parked along the street.

"The pass worked perfectly, Mano!" Jo said, climbing into the Audi's passenger seat. "The guards never raised an eyebrow. Ramon's document team did an exceptional job."

Mano started the Audi and pulled away from the curb. "Ramon's people are already working day and night. How much longer do we wait?" he asked, rubbing the new growth of beard on his chin.

"I'm glad you're eager to start our operations, Mano. But we shouldn't make any moves until we're ready. Once the government opens the Relocation Communities, all Hispanics will be moved into quarantine. That means Ramon and I are going to lose our homes outside the zone—and that's going to make it much harder for us to travel. We all need identities that will hold up. Otherwise our plans will be worthless."

"Maybe we should take on one of these guard posts along

the wall while we're waiting. We'll need to test their defenses eventually."

"No. An attack might draw a military crackdown in the zones before we're ready. We need to be patient."

I've been patient. Very patient, Mano said to himself. But as the launch of their operations grew closer, he ached for the chance to lash back at the soldiers. Still, he knew Jo was right about striking too early. "I see your point," he said aloud.

They traveled several blocks in silence before Jo spoke again, almost in a whisper this time. "Mano, there's something else...something personal," she said, nervously stroking her hair.

Her intimate tone made Mano's pulse quicken. His love for Rosa was unshaken, but his infatuation with Jo was becoming a live wire, something sparking wildly inside him. The idea Jo might share his attraction filled him with delight—and dread.

"I think your wife and children will be safer in one of the Relocation Communities the government's building in the Dakotas. Once we start our operations, it's going to get pretty dangerous for us here."

Mano was thunderstruck. The thought of separating from his family had never crossed his mind. "What makes you think Rosa and the children will be safer in a camp?" he said, bringing the Audi to a stop along the curb.

"The U.S. government can be repressive, Mano, but it's rarely cruel. As Marcha pointed out, most Americans are decent people. Living in a camp won't be pleasant, but your family won't be mistreated. On the other hand, the leadership of the DDP will need to go underground once the relocations begin. We're going to be in extreme danger...at all times."

"How long will we be apart? How do I know I'll ever see them again?"

"I can't answer that, Mano. If we win—*when* we win—there will be negotiations to return those who were relocated. But that could take years. It's your decision, of course. But I think your wife and children run a greater risk staying here."

Jo's words rekindled a hurt never far from Mano's heart. Julio's death had been like the loss of a limb. Although the most intense pain had faded, Mano knew the feeling of being incomplete would stay with him forever. Looking back, he now realized his wounded pride had driven him to keep the news from Jo.

"You may be right, Jo," he said softly. "My youngest son was killed by the soldiers."

Jo gasped, startled by the news. "Dios mio, Mano!" she said. "When?"

"Just before we were quarantined."

"That was two months ago."

"I know. I should have told you," he said, lowering his eyes.

She touched his shoulder tenderly, her eyes welling with tears. "I understand, Mano. People think it helps to talk about a tragedy. Sometimes, though, it only makes the pain worse. I found that out when I lost my mother."

The warmth of Jo's hand melted his last resolve of silence. In a voice hoarse with emotion, he told her about Julio's death at the hands of the convoy. "They left my son to die," he said, almost whispering. "I didn't want to believe it. American troops weren't like that in my day."

Jo withdrew her hand to wipe away her tears. "That's the reason you came back, isn't it?"

"Yes," Mano said without looking up.

"Now I understand why you didn't want to tell me. I'm sorry. I had no idea."

"Not many people knew. The funeral was very small."

Jo stared at the floor for a moment. "Look, Mano," she said uneasily. "You've become more than an employee to me. What we're doing together . . . well, it's not just a business relationship anymore."

"What are you trying to say?"

"God, this is getting complicated," Jo said, chewing her lip. "What I'm trying to say is that I care for you—and your family. You've already lost a child, Mano. I couldn't live with myself if anyone else in your family was hurt by our work with La Defensa. That's why I think you should move your wife and children away once the quarantines begin."

Mano looked into her eyes. "Are there any other reasons you want me to do this?"

Jo turned away, tugging at a strand of hair. "Even if there are, those reasons shouldn't matter," she answered softly. "Any feelings we may have are not important, Mano. We have a duty to our people. But if your family stays here after the quarantine, they'll be in more danger than ever," she said, facing him again. "Please promise me you'll think about sending them away."

Mano started the engine and pulled away from the curb. "When the time comes, I'll consider it," he said, staring straight ahead.

The CIA's regional secretary had just bitten into his third donut of the morning when the phone rang.

"Humph Evunhs," he said into the phone, chewing furiously.

"Hello?" said the voice in his earpiece.

"Hank Evans," he said after swallowing.

"Good morning, Hank. Bill Perkins," Evans's deputy said hurriedly. "Have you gone through your e-mail yet?"

"No. What's up?"

"Washington issued a new directive this morning. All Hispanics in the intelligence community are being reassigned to non-critical areas. They're no longer cleared for any information rated 'secret' or higher. They're saying it's—you know—security issues."

Evans's face reddened. "That's absurd. Everything we touch is rated 'secret.' A Hispanic won't be able to walk into any of our offices—or even file a field report."

"I know, Hank."

"Well, the politicians who hatched up this half-baked scheme are in for a rude surprise," Evans said, the rolls of flesh under his chin quivering. "We're going to have some very serious 'security issues' if we turn every Hispanic in the intelligence community into a cook or a janitor."

Since the passing of the Quarantine and Relocation Act, Evans had done an about-face on the threat from radical Hispanics. Thanks to the chaos caused by the Bates resolution, he had come to believe the Hispanic issue was now the most serious security challenge the nation faced.

"What do you want us to do, Hank?"

Evans's mind began to work again after venting his wrath. "Maria Prado has been working on getting a mole into La Defensa del Pueblo. You need to pick up the ball on that."

"Right, Hank. I'll get started on it as soon as I can," Perkins replied and hung up quickly.

Evans picked up the rest of his donut and started to hurl it into the trash can, then changed his mind. He may have lost his temper, but he hadn't lost his appetite.

As Phil Saunders eased his rig into the parking lot of the SmartStop near Culver City, California, the sun was setting into the smog-banked horizon. He'd made over five hundred miles today and was going to reward himself with a good dinner and a solid night's sleep.

After killing the diesel, Phil climbed down from the cab and made a quick scan of his rig. The bags of fertilizer on his stake bed were still tightly stacked. Satisfied with the condition of his load, he headed for the restaurant.

As he walked past the long line of rigs, a svelte redhead leaning seductively against a GMC pickup flashed a big smile and crooked her finger enticingly. *Well, now. Maybe there's an extra treat in store for ol' Phil tonight,* he thought, turning toward her.

Finding a hooker at a truck stop was not unusual. But this one stood out from the mostly overweight and cheerless women who worked the eighteen-wheel circuit. Not much older than thirty, she wore a tight halter top and cut-off shorts, her crimson hair a curly mass towering above large hoop earrings. She was every trucker's dream.

"Hello, darlin'. My name's Phil," he said in his best Burt Reynolds voice.

"Hi, there," she said with a sultry smile. "You look like a fella who could use some company."

"I guess that depends on how much it costs, honey."

"It'll cost you a hundred," she said sweetly, then looked at her watch. "But I haven't got much time."

Phil winked, a gleam in his eye. "Why don't we go back to my rig? Ol' Phil's got him a sleeper."

"Why, that sounds real cozy," the redhead said, slinging her small purse over her shoulder and taking Phil's arm.

After reaching the truck, Phil unlocked the cab. "Here we are, darlin'," he said, gesturing toward the open door, admiring the redhead's slim figure as she climbed into the cab. *This is one lively little hottie.*

Following her inside, Phil was stunned to find the redhead pointing a silver revolver at his face. The steadiness of her hand left little doubt she knew how to use it. "There's been a little change in plans, darlin'," the woman said calmly. "Put your keys on the console—nice and slow—and step back into the sleeper."

Seconds later, Phil saw a man's face appear at the window of his cab. Keeping her gun trained on Phil, the redhead let the man in. Phil tried to memorize the man's appearance, hoping he'd survive the ordeal. The man was black, below average in height, with a slight build, his hair done up in a once again fashionable Afro. A brightly patterned shirt open at the collar revealed a heavy gold necklace that glistened against his dark skin.

Without a word, the man took the keys from the console and deftly guided the eighteen-wheeler out of the truck stop and onto I-405 South. *This pimp must have made an honest living at one time*, Phil noted silently.

An hour later, Phil found himself bound to a chair in an abandoned gas station outside Compton, a swath of duct tape covering his mouth. In the dim streetlight entering through the windows, he spotted a broken pneumatic pipe fixture protruding from the wall. After hearing his rig pull away, he began rocking the chair toward the wall. If he could get the tape binding his hands against the sharp edge of the plug, he might be able to free himself.

Inside Phil's semi, Jo removed the red wig and said, "That should hold ol' Phil for a while," as Jesús Lopez pulled the truck away from the gas station. After a ten-minute drive, Jesús stopped the rig in an alley along the L.A. River and killed the lights. Moments later, a group of men emerged from a storm sewer along the riverbank and began unloading the truck, feverishly passing the bags of fertilizer hand-to-hand in a line leading into the drain. In less than two hours, the ammonium nitrate was stockpiled in a vacant textile warehouse inside Quarantine Zone B.

Drenched in sweat, Mano approached Jo and Ramon. "We're done," he said, breathing heavily.

"It's a good thing that stuff only explodes when you mix it with oil," Ramon said, smirking. "With the heat your team worked up, we could have all gone up in a bang."

Mano rolled his eyes. "That might possibly be funny if you'd actually done any work, old man."

"Any idea how much am-nite we have?" Jo asked.

"Not as much as we'd like," Mano answered. "I'd guess around ten tons."

Jo nodded. "That's cutting it close, but it should do."

"You see," Ramon said defensively, "I still think it would have been better to buy this stuff through one of our dummy companies."

"Let it go, Ray. You were outvoted," Jo shot back. "You

agreed any big purchase of ammonium nitrate would have sent up a red flag with the government. Mano and I felt this way was less risky. Besides, Mano came up with a great plan to ditch the truck."

"Oh? What brilliant idea did our resident tactical genius concoct?"

Jo nudged Mano with her elbow. "Tell him."

"Jesús is going to drive the empty truck to Compton and torch it."

"Well, well... I must admit, that's not a bad red herring, amigo."

Ramon knew the truck driver would identify Jesús as an African-American to the authorities. Ditching the stolen truck in predominantly black Compton would deflect the investigation away from them.

"OK, let's face it," Jo said soberly. "We didn't get as much am-nite as we wanted. So we damn well better make what we have count."

After returning from lunch, Hank Evans double-clicked on Bill Perkins's e-mail with the subject line "DDP." An e-mail message was a red flag—Evans knew his deputy would have delivered any good news on the investigation in person.

> Hank,
> Wanted to bring you up to speed on the DDP surveillance. They seem to be keeping their noses clean. Their main activity still appears to be community service, i.e., ferrying food and medicine delivered by the Army for distribution within the Quarantine Zones. Their organization is tight and has been difficult to penetrate. We

are continuing with our efforts at securing a mole. Our progress in
the zones is slow as it is hard for any of our people to blend in.

—Bill

Evans noted that the worst news was buried in the middle
of the poorly constructed paragraph. They had not yet found
a mole.

THE QUARANTINE AND RELOCATION ACT:
Month 4, Day 11

Chuckie Buster was seething. Straddling his Dyna Glide, idling at the curb on Temple Street, he revved the throttle again and looked over his leather-clad shoulder. Arrayed in a neat line behind him, eleven other riders waited impatiently to roll, the roar of their Harleys echoing in the nearly empty streets of downtown Los Angeles. *Where in the hell is Stratton this time?* Buster fumed as a lone Neon crawled by.

Buster was the leader of the Wanderers in the Desert, a Christian motorcycle club from the First Church of Christ. The Wanderers had been waiting more than half an hour to start an after-service ride to Lake Elsinore, but they couldn't leave without Stratton. After mechanical breakdowns had ruined rides in the past, the members had agreed never to ride again without someone driving a chase van, and Stratton was the only one in the club willing to endure that humdrum task.

Buster turned off his bike, dropped the kickstand, and gave a throat-slash sign to the members behind him. The rumble of the Harleys died away and the usual Sunday morning stillness returned to downtown Los Angeles.

Mano's turban rubbed annoyingly against the roof of the rented Neon as he cruised along Temple, making a last check of the blast zone. Ahead of him, he spotted a line of motorcyclists parked along the street and pulled to the curb a block ahead of them. With only seconds left to act, he scanned the laptop beside him and disabled the charges set for that section of street. Muttering a prayer for the bikers, he pulled the Neon back onto the road and drove away.

Walking toward the bike behind him, Chuckie Buster was stunned by a blinding flash, followed by a blast of heat that singed his beard. Instinctively, Buster dropped to the pavement. The thunder of multiple explosions shook the ground, seeming to come from everywhere at once as Buster huddled against the curb and prayed.

When the blasts finally ended, Buster raised his head warily. Black smoke billowed skyward, gradually revealing the devastation. For blocks in every direction, traffic lights lay scattered like cordwood along the streets, a blackened crater marking the base of each pole. Dotting each intersection was the mangled yellow carcass of a fallen traffic signal. Miraculously, the poles where the Wanderers were parked were the only ones intact. They had somehow been spared.

Chuckie Buster saw it as a sign from God.

THE QUARANTINE AND RELOCATION ACT:
Month 4, Day 12

On the last weekend in September, the Sunday morning calm of downtown Los Angeles had been shattered by a wave of explosions.

Beginning precisely at 9 a.m., a series of blasts destroyed an electrical relay station, four power-line towers, and nineteen traffic signals in the downtown area. From unexploded charges at the base of two utility poles, the LAPD determined the explosives were made with ammonium nitrate, a commonly used fertilizer. There were no casualties as a result of the attacks, but much of downtown Los Angeles was left without power. A special evening edition of the *Los Angeles Times* called the bombings "Blackout Sunday."

During Monday morning rush hour, traffic in the central business district went into gridlock, snarled by the absence of signals and a redeployment of traffic police to security duty. The situation worsened when car bombs exploded in three downtown parking garages exactly at noon. Although the blasts caused no injuries, news of the bombings sent panicked office workers scrambling out of the city. In the exodus, many commuters, trapped in the traffic, abandoned their cars and fled on foot.

They were the first to leave downtown Los Angeles in panic. They would not be the last.

―――――

Hank Evans sat at his desk, fighting a severe case of drowsiness. He'd overdone the spiked Christmas eggnog in the officers' mess during lunch, and now he was paying the price.

This depressing place could drive anyone to drink, Evans thought, looking around at his new office. It was barren, harshly lit, and smelled of crayons and mold.

After the attacks on downtown Los Angeles, the CIA had evacuated its regional headquarters. Much to Evans's dismay, his office was moved from a stately federal high-rise overlooking the National Cemetery to an abandoned elementary school at the center of Army Outpost Bravo, just outside the northern border of Quarantine Zone B.

Evans leaned over the desk, hands propping up his chin, staring dully at the pile of reports from his field agents in the zones. Reading them would be a long and useless task—he knew their efforts had been futile.

The loss of all Hispanic operatives had crippled the CIA. Few Anglos possessed the language skills and cultural subtleties to penetrate the growing number of rebel groups surfacing within the zones. In Evans's opinion, the CIA had better information on the numerous foreign enemies the nation faced than the Hispanic insurgency at home.

As the domestic situation had worsened, the bloated CIA bureaucracy finally began to shift its attention away from its foreign operations to the escalating crisis. Evans felt it had taken too long. As it was, the CIA was barely keeping up with the overseas conflicts. This growing challenge on the home front was stretching the Agency's resources to the breaking point. Some hard decisions would need to be made in Washington. Given its present resources, Evans knew the Agency could not sustain intelligence networks on this many fronts at once. It was impossible—and demoralizing.

He needed more coffee. As Evans rose to get another cup, Bill Perkins popped his head into the doorway. "Hank, I've got some good news," he said, smiling. "We might just have ourselves a mole at La Defensa del Pueblo."

"Come in. Sit down," Evans said, retreating to his chair, grateful for the distraction. "What's the scoop?"

"I told the Army intel guys to keep their eyes open for me and they came up with someone who looks promising. His name's Ernesto Alvarez. He's a gangbanger they busted for trying to bribe a trooper on guard duty. He wanted the soldier to make himself scarce for a while. My guess is he had a shipment of drugs coming in. Anyway, after they nabbed him, Alvarez told the intel guys he'd give them information on the leaders of La Defensa del Pueblo if they'd release him. The names he provided check out—Ramon Garcia and Josefina Herrera."

"That's no big secret, Bill," Evans said, recalling Maria Prado's report on the rally in Salazar Park. "Garcia and Herrera have both appeared publicly at DDP functions in the past. Anyone could have that information."

Perkins looked crestfallen. "Well, it's the only break we've had so far, Hank."

Evans didn't want to disappoint his subordinate. He knew Perkins, juggling overseas assignments, had scrambled to come up with something. "Well, there's a chance this gangbanger might be able to help us. Like you said, we haven't got any other leads or inside sources right now."

Perkins seemed relieved. "I'd like to put him on a retainer, Hank. I'm worried that if I turn this guy loose, he'll bolt and we'll never see him again."

"How much?"

"Well, if he's a dope dealer, it'll take some serious coin to keep him coming back. I'd say ten thousand a month."

Evans considered the request. Their funding was being cut again. But with so little being produced by their fieldwork, their budget allocation for this type of intelligence gathering was still pretty much intact. *Better to use it than to lose it*, Hank told himself.

"OK, Bill. I'm going to go with you on this one."

"I'll get on it. My gut tells me this guy's the real deal," Perkins said as he rose from his chair.

"Let's find out. And soon."

THE QUARANTINE AND RELOCATION ACT: *Month 8, Day 6*

Mano stared at the tops of the skyscrapers visible over the west wall. Without their once-familiar lights, the buildings were hazy silhouettes against the night sky. Had it been worth it? They'd succeeded in depopulating downtown Los Angeles; there was little doubt of that.

In the weeks following Blackout Sunday, they'd detonated a succession of bloodless explosions in downtown parking lots. Wells Fargo had been the first company to announce they were relocating their corporate headquarters to a more secure location. Other downtown companies soon followed.

As Jo had predicted, the flight of the corporations was the start of a stampede. Worried parents insisted USC close its downtown campus. The Los Angeles Library moved its collection to regional branches, shuttering its landmark highrise. The Opera and the Philharmonic discontinued their seasons. Without clientele from downtown workers and arts patrons, most restaurants and bars closed their doors.

Now, less than four months after Blackout Sunday, the central business district of Los Angeles had become a ghost town—every day of the week.

But their strategic victory came with a price. An Army

patrol had stumbled onto one of their explosive-making centers near Montebello last week. The young vatos at the site tried to put up a fight, using handguns against automatic rifles. All four were killed.

They'd paid with their lives for plans that they'd had no part in shaping. Although the four young men had not worn uniforms, Mano knew they'd been soldiers all the same.

From his backpack, Mano produced four small wreaths and placed them solemnly against the wall. After saying a prayer, he began walking toward his apartment feeling both proud and ashamed.

Back home, as he crawled silently into bed beside Rosa, he once again recalled Jo's advice about sending his family away. After almost six months, he was still no closer to a decision. With the first Relocation Communities now complete, waiting any longer made no sense.

Six sleepless hours later, as the first glimmer of daylight crept into the room, Mano had made up his mind. Now would come the hardest part yet: breaking the news to his wife.

Rosa stirred slightly and Mano let his hand wander along her undulating body. She still had curves in all the right places—even after three children. He felt the warmth and smoothness of her skin and sighed. His decision involved many sacrifices. A very long time might pass before he and Rosa would share a bed again. He embraced his wife gently, savoring her nearness.

Although not fully awake, Rosa turned toward Mano and began caressing him. It was not unusual for them to make love at dawn, before the children awoke. Mano was becoming aroused, his breath beginning to quicken, when a thought crossed his mind that instantly diminished his fervor.

Lovemaking would not be a good preface to the news he was about to give Rosa.

He took her hand, brought it to his lips, and kissed it gently. "Rosita, we need to talk," he whispered.

"What is it, mi amor?" Rosa said, stretching languidly.

"They're saying the first Relocation Community in North Dakota will be ready next month."

"Uh-huh," she replied without opening her eyes.

"When the camp is ready, you and the children will have to go."

"Dios mio, Mano, what are you saying?" Rosa asked, suddenly wide awake.

"You and the children will be safer in a Relocation Community."

"What about you?"

"I can be more useful staying here."

"What are you saying, Mano? What kind of man would abandon his wife and children at a time like this?"

"Los Angeles is already a dangerous place, Rosa. It's going to get worse."

"But why can't you go with us? What good can it do for you to stay here?"

"I can fight," Mano said simply.

"Fight for what, Mano? What reason is there for you to risk your life?"

"Look around you, Rosa. What's the name of this city? What's the name of this state? Our people named these places. This was *our* country once. And now we're being penned up and carted away like criminals." Even as he spoke, Mano was surprised at his own words. He had never said these things out loud before. It was like listening to someone else. "Marcha was right, Rosa. It's time for us to take our country back."

"What's gotten your head full of these ideas, Mano?" Rosa asked angrily. "It's that woman, isn't it? She's the one who's got you believing this nonsense."

"At first, I thought it was nonsense, too. And then I realized we have a duty to our people, Rosa. I wish I had the words…"

"Mano, you've always looked out for this family. What about your children? Don't you care what happens to them?"

"It's for our children that I'm doing this," Mano said with an air of finality.

Rosa stared at her husband, knowing more words were useless. From twelve years of marriage, she had come to know Mano as a man who made few demands, but once his mind was made up, no amount of arguing would change it.

At that moment, Rosa realized she had lost Mano. Josefina was breaking up her family. She was rich and beautiful. But that was not enough. She wanted her husband, too. Now Josefina would have Mano to herself while she and the children rotted away in a camp. Without another word, Rosa put on her nightgown, walked quietly into the bathroom, and turned on the faucet to mask the sound of her weeping.

Maria Prado read the letter again. There had to be some mistake.

During a fourteen-year CIA career, she'd learned it was easy to misinterpret the tortured, arcane prose of government documents.

After the second reading, the message of the certified

letter from the Department of Homeland Security was still the same: her family had fourteen days to move out of their home in La Mirada and report to temporary quarters in Los Angeles Quarantine Zone B until assignment to a Relocation Community.

Maria reached for the vu-phone.

Professor Francisco Prado saw his wife's face appear in the vu-phone on his desk. "Hello, dear," he said.

"Frank, we're being relocated."

"What? How can they do that?" Francisco shouted, losing his typically calm demeanor. He switched off the vu-phone's speaker and picked up the receiver. "You work for the CIA, for Chrissake," he said, lowering his voice.

"I don't think that matters anymore, Frank. First they stripped away my security clearance, and now this."

"They can't just take away our house and kick us out like that."

"We're Class H, Frank. Our constitutional protections have been revoked. And they're technically not taking away our house. The letter says we'll be compensated under eminent domain laws. It's hogwash, of course, but it's all legal."

"We can fight this, Maria," Francisco said with a sudden burst of conviction. "We've got powerful friends. They can't do this to us."

Sixteen days later, three new names were added to the roll call of Temporary Housing Unit 11 in Quarantine Zone B, a crowded tent city erected on the grounds of Evergreen Cemetery—Francisco Prado, Maria Prado, and their daughter, Andrea.

THE QUARANTINE AND RELOCATION ACT:
Month 9, Day 2

Mano entered his apartment and saw a row of mismatched suitcases lined up neatly near the door. Rosa and the children were ready to leave.

Looking around the empty living room, he realized it was probably the last time he'd ever see the place—not that he would miss it much once he went into hiding. But this dark and cramped apartment was the only home his children had ever known. Leaving it would not be easy for them. God only knew what kind of place Rosa and the kids would find at the Relocation Community. Mano's sole hope was that it would be safer than staying here.

"Papi, you're home!" Elena yelled as she and Pedro ran out of the bedroom, dressed in their church clothes. Mano knelt and embraced the children, feeling their fragile arms around his neck. It was a moment he wished would last forever.

He had never imagined it would come to this; he was about to part with the core of his life. Holding Elena and Pedro, he wanted to tell them how much they meant to him, how their absence would leave him hollow, but he held back—it would only make parting more difficult for the children.

He gently stroked Elena's hair. "All ready for your trip?"

"Yes, Papi," she said eagerly. "Mami bought me a new doll. Her name is Sonya."

Mano was grateful that Rosa was doing all she could to make this easier for the children. They would need her strength more than ever.

He turned to his son. "What about you, m'hijo?"

An older Pedro was not so easily distracted. "Why aren't you coming with us, Papi?"

"There are important things I have to do here, Pedro. I can't explain them right now. We'll be together again when I'm done. You have to trust me."

The boy lowered his eyes. "I wish Julio could have come with us. I won't have anyone to play with on the trip...I miss him, Papi."

Mano lifted the boy's chin. "Be strong, m'hijo."

The boy looked silently at his father, fighting back tears. Mano knew there was nothing more he could say; Julio's loss was a pain they would have to endure.

"Your mother and I have some things to talk about," Mano said after a moment. "Why don't you two go out in the court-yard and play?"

Once the children were outside, Mano pulled an envelope from his pocket and handed it to Rosa. As she looked, her eyes widened in astonishment. The envelope was stuffed with hundred-dollar bills—more money than she had ever seen. "It's twenty thousand dollars," he said.

Rosa's face hardened. "I don't want this money," she said coldly.

"Why not, querida? What's the matter?"

"It came from *her*. She thinks she can buy you with it."

"You're wrong, Rosa. This money is an advance on my pay."

"I don't want it. I don't want it," she said, throwing the envelope to the ground and bursting into tears.

Mano retrieved the envelope and held it out to her again. "Rosa, please take the money. The children are going to need it."

Rosa stared at the envelope for a long time before finally stuffing it into her purse.

Mano encircled her in his arms. "I don't know how long it will be before I see you again, querida. But once this is over, nothing will keep me away."

Rosa said nothing, weeping softly, head bowed against his broad chest. After a time, she broke their embrace and started for the door. "I shouldn't leave the children outside alone too long," she said, drying her eyes.

Thirty-five minutes later, Rosa and the children were on a bus headed for North Dakota.

A hard rain drummed on the roof of the former Greyhound coach, pelting the windows and blurring the view outside. With the air brakes hissing in protest, the driver brought the aging bus to a stop and turned off the engine. In a protective cage at the front of the bus, an armed guard beside the driver stared warily toward the locked passenger compartment holding forty-six detainees—including Rosa Suarez and her children.

"Mami, I think we're stopping for gas again," Pedro said, his forehead pressed against the window. Rosa leaned forward, looking for her daughter and found her playing dolls with another girl two rows ahead. "Elena, come back to your seat, m'hijita. We'll be getting off the bus in a while." After seven days on the road, the routine at fuel stops was a familiar ritual for everyone aboard the bus.

Rosa's bus was part of a motley convoy of six civilian buses led by an Army truck carrying a squad of soldiers and a Humvee bringing up the rear. Each time the column stopped for gas, the Army truck would discharge its soldiers to form a containment perimeter around the detainees getting off the bus for rest breaks. Fearing the nearly three hundred detainees being transported by the six buses might overwhelm the eighteen soldiers escorting them, each bus was unloaded separately as it took on fuel.

Assigned to bus number five, Rosa knew their chance to use a real restroom and wash up was still nearly an hour away. Nonetheless, she rose and dug through the suitcases on the rack above their seats for the children's rain gear. She wanted to have the kids ready. Once the gas tank was full, everyone would be ordered back on the bus, whether they'd used the facilities or not.

After a week in the squalid interior, Rosa no longer noticed the foul smell of the broken restroom at the rear of the bus. But each time they stepped outside and the soldiers turned away from them in disgust, she was reminded that the stench had permeated everyone aboard. Adding to the humiliation, some of the soldiers wore surgical masks; whether to shield them from the smell or to protect them from disease, Rosa wasn't sure.

As bad as it was, Rosa was grateful she'd been assigned to one of the many Greyhound buses commandeered by the government for the relocations. The unfortunate detainees assigned to former school buses were forced to use a chemical toilet at the rear of the bus without any privacy at all. Rosa had heard the government's huge new fleet of buses was at work constantly, transporting Class H citizens to the camps or heading south with the millions being deported.

The sound of the rain let up slightly and Rosa glanced outside. From what she could see through the downpour, the landscape had not changed. For the last day, the countryside had been the same: a flat, featureless grassland stretching to the horizon. Except for a lonely cluster of trees every few miles, nothing broke the monotony. "It's a green desert," Rosa had overheard someone say. "Nobody can survive out there alone." The only human signs they'd passed were the gray, splintered remains of two abandoned farms.

Pedro pointed to a series of dark shapes on the other side of the bus. "What's that, Mami?"

Rosa squinted, trying to make out the semicircular objects in the heavy rain. "I think they're some kind of buildings, m'hijo."

"Listen up, people," said the guard over the bus's scratchy speakers. "Collect all your belongings. This is Relocation Community Number Eight."

Emerging from the bus in the downpour, Rosa was surprised to find the camp had no fences. Carrying her suitcases with the children in tow, she followed the other detainees as they were herded into a line before a pair of military clerks seated under a tent. For two hours, they waited in the rain to be processed. Rosa was grateful the children had ponchos, but they were still shivering in the cold April air. Unable to hold their suitcases aloft any longer, they were forced to place them on the ground, which the crowd had churned into mud.

While they waited, Rosa got a better look at the odd-shaped buildings they'd seen from the bus. They looked like giant half-buried soup cans lying on their sides. A man near her said they were called Quonset huts.

"I'm hungry," Elena said, tugging on Rosa's skirt.

Glancing at her watch, Rosa saw it was after five. There was not much chance they'd get fed anytime soon. "Here," she said, handing Elena and Pedro the packages of peanut butter crackers she'd been saving in her travel bag. "This is an emergency. Don't expect food like this every day."

The rain was down to a drizzle when Rosa and the children finally reached one of the clerks. After wordlessly shuffling through her documents, the soldier pecked at his laptop and said, "You're assigned to Dormitory 171."

"Can you tell me where that is, please?"

"Just follow the line and ask somebody," he answered without looking up, then called out, "Next!"

The sky was dark when Rosa finally found Dormitory 171, a newly built Quonset hut at the far edge of the mile-wide camp. Opening the door, she saw scores of women and children milling lifelessly amid two rows of bunk beds in a long, dimly lit room. Apparently she had been assigned to the single mothers' quarters.

She found three empty beds near the fire exit. Not surprisingly, they were quite far from the bathrooms. While she unpacked her mud-caked suitcases, a woman approached her.

"You better get your kids ready for bed, chica," she said. "The lights go out at eight on the dot."

Rosa looked at her watch, suddenly alarmed. She had ten minutes. "Would you watch my suitcases while I take my children to the bathroom?"

"Sure. You go right ahead."

When Rosa returned, she hurriedly got out pajamas for the children and dressed them for bed. She put Pedro in the bunk above her and Elena on the bed beside her. As she was tucking in her daughter, an alarm bell sounded. Seconds later, the lights went out.

"I don't like this place, Mami," Elena whimpered in the darkness. "When are we going home?"

Rosa stroked her daughter's hair, trying to hide her own despair. They no longer had a home—but there was no reason to burden her child with the truth. "We'll be home soon, m'hijita," she whispered soothingly. "We'll be home soon."

THE QUARANTINE AND RELOCATION ACT:
Month 13

A government is an illusion, a collective idea that resides primarily in the public imagination. Few realize how quickly this fragile fantasy can evaporate.

—José Antonio Marcha, 1981
Translated by J. M. Herrera

Crouching low to avoid being seen, Nesto led Mano to the crest of the hill. "There it is, ese," the mero said, pointing toward the military facility on the other side of the slope.

The garrison in the scrubby valley below looked like a miniature diorama. Except for an irregular cluster of buildings at its center, the facility was laid out with the military's fondness for symmetry—rectangular wire fencing, tidy rows of Quonset huts, and neatly parked military vehicles, all laid out in textbook precision.

"So this is Outpost Bravo," Mano said, studying the camp. "What are the buildings in the middle? They don't look military."

"I think it used to be some kind of school. That's what Tony said, anyway."

Mano's eyebrow rose in suspicion. Nesto's story of how he'd learned about the location of the garrison had sounded doubtful from the beginning. "This is pretty far outside Zone B for your boys to wander."

"Hey, ese. I was just doing like you said. Sending out my vatos to scout the area."

"All right," Mano said, unconvinced. "I'm grateful you brought me here."

"So what are you gonna do?"

"I don't know yet," Mano said, rubbing his chin. *Even if I did, I wouldn't tell you.* "We should head back. I'm sure they patrol this area."

As they retreated through the deserted neighborhoods, Mano weighed what he had seen. The site for the garrison was a smart choice, he had to admit. It stood between Zone B and the mountains to the north, an ideal place to wage a guerrilla war. Just the same, Outpost Bravo was a sign of the precarious situation the government now faced in Southern California—a change that had come faster than anyone could have imagined.

———

Just over two years after the Rio Grande Incident, a transformation of unprecedented proportions was under way in Southern California. Triggered by the Blackout Sunday bombings that had rocked downtown Los Angeles four months earlier, a massive exodus was vacating what had once been the sixth most populous area on the planet.

It began in the beach communities west of the L.A. Quarantine Zones.

Fearful of the insurgents' continuing forays outside the walls, homeowners began a wave of panic selling. Property values plummeted, but sellers found few takers. The desperation spiraled.

Neighborhoods dwindled daily, creating a shortage of moving vans and rental trucks. Those left behind became frantic. Eventually they simply abandoned their homes, hauling away all the belongings their vehicles could hold and joining thousands of others jamming the freeways heading north. Left without customers, area merchants and businesses pulled up stakes.

The pattern of flight in the beach communities quickly spread to other affluent areas. The mass departures in suburbia also uprooted working-class enclaves around the Quarantine Zones.

The working poor were forced to head north in search of jobs. Households dependent on government aid saw their subsidies disappear as government workers fled the region and postal service became unreliable. Like predators following the migration of their prey, criminals followed their victims north. Before long, only a few isolated individuals remained, scavenging the desolate urban landscape to survive. Most were indigents who soon acquired the name "dregs."

The events in Los Angeles were not unique. Similar diasporas were taking place around the Quarantine Zones in Albuquerque, Brownsville, Dallas, El Paso, Houston, Phoenix, San Antonio, San Diego, Santa Fe, and Tucson.

In Atlanta, Chicago, Charlotte, Miami, New York, and Tampa, the areas adjacent to the Quarantine Zones remained relatively stable, but with preparations for additional Relocation Communities lagging far behind schedule, government control within the Quarantine Zones was rapidly deteriorating.

Most Washington insiders knew the Hispanic issue had always been a sideshow for the Brenner White House.

President Brenner felt his success in the global arena would be his true legacy. In spite of the extensive media coverage given to the turmoil, the administration's sights had remained on the loftier stage of international affairs. Now the Hispanic issue was escalating into the central crisis of the Brenner administration. The Hispanic unrest was changing from a thorn in their side to a dagger at their throat.

THE QUARANTINE AND RELOCATION ACT:
Month 13, Day 3

Walking along the narrow dirt path, Rosa tried to brush the dust off the sleeve of Elena's white dress, but her efforts were useless. Each step she and the children took stirred up more of the powdery soil that seemed to cling to everything.

When Rosa and the children had arrived last April, the problem at Community Number Eight had been mud. Back then, the rain-soaked clay had clung to their shoes in heavy clumps. Now, in late July, the obstinate soil had transformed itself into a gray powder sent airborne by the slightest provocation and transported into every crack by the perpetual wind.

"Tuck your shirttail in, Pedro," Rosa said to her son, who complied without protest. They were nearing the Prados' trailer, and Rosa was eager to make a good impression.

Unlike the rest of the camp's detainees, who were packed into communal Quonset huts, the Prados had somehow managed to obtain their own dwelling. By outside standards, it was a pitiful place. The trailer's faded sides were rusted and dented, the glass of its small windows replaced by yellow plastic sheeting. But in Community Number Eight, the trailer was a choice residence.

Rosa looked west, beyond the trailer. In the distance, she

could see a large fenced-in compound. Patrolled by guards, it was where more Quonset huts were under construction. The authorities wanted to keep construction tools out of the hands of the Community members, afraid the implements might be used as weapons. Outside the construction areas, the Community was still without walls or fences. The nearest town was a trek of nearly sixty miles over a waterless prairie. Even if someone trying to escape had reached a settlement, the clannish locals would have immediately spotted an outsider.

Rosa's visit to the Prados had been prompted by Elena. Maria Prado had approached Rosa as she was picking up Elena at the camp's preschool the week before.

"Hola!" Maria had said cheerfully. "I'm Maria Prado. You must be Mrs. Suarez. My daughter Andrea has really taken to your Elena. She's insisting that Elena come to her birthday party. It's this coming Saturday at two. Do you think you can make it? You can bring your son as well if you like," Maria said, gesturing to Pedro.

Rosa was flattered. The Prados appeared to be among the elite of the Community.

"Thank you very much, Mrs. Prado. I'd be happy to bring Elena."

"Please, call me Maria."

"Thanks, Maria. My name is Rosa."

"Wonderful, Rosa. We'll see you Saturday."

Shortly after agreeing to the visit, Rosa began having second thoughts. What could she possibly give the Prado child as a birthday present?

Rosa had left Los Angeles with twenty thousand in cash. Three days after arriving at the camp, she awoke to a demoralizing blow: the suitcases under her bunk had been stolen during the night, including the scuffed brown Tourister in which she had placed the money. The only possessions she and the children had left were her gold wedding band, the clothes on their backs, and her statuette of Our Lady of Guadalupe. Not wanting to frighten the children, she endured the setback without complaint.

By this time, Rosa had become accustomed to being penniless. Thankfully, hunger was not a problem—the Community's kitchen served adequate portions of tasteless but nutritious food. But the absence of the minor luxuries of life Rosa had always taken for granted—like gentle soaps, deodorant, makeup, and skin cream—made for a grim existence.

Elena finally solved the problem of a gift for her friend with the uncanny insight of a young girl. Two days before the party, she brought a drawing to Rosa.

"It's a Priscilla Percival doll," Elena announced, thrusting her artwork toward Rosa. "Andrea said it's what she wants for her birthday. I know we can't get Andrea a real one, so I made her this one instead."

"I think Andrea will love your present, Elena."

Approaching the door to the Prados' trailer, Elena carried the Priscilla Percival drawing wrapped in an ancient Sunday comics page adorned with a bow made from a discarded dressing gown hem.

With her two children flanking her, Rosa knocked on the trailer's door.

"Buenos días," Maria said, smiling as she opened the door. "Come in. Come in. It's hot in here, but it sure beats standing outside in the dust."

On the kitchen counter was a small cake with six candles. Rosa had no idea how Maria had managed this extravagance, but she was grateful Maria was willing to share it with her children.

"Francisco, this is Rosa Suarez, Elena's mother," Maria said to her husband.

"Welcome to our home, Señora," Francisco said politely, then retreated to the small bedroom at the back of the trailer, leaving the main room to the women and children.

After occupying the youngsters with a game, Maria took a seat next to Rosa. Following a few pleasantries, Maria startled Rosa with the direction of her conversation.

"I think I'm familiar with your husband, Rosa," Maria said, lowering her voice. "He's Manolo Suarez, right? He worked for the Green Planet Recycling Company?"

"Oh…yes," Rosa said, the questions about Mano making her uneasy.

Maria leaned closer. "Well, I just want you to know that if you want to get in touch with him, I have a way of getting messages out of this place without the censors getting their hands on it."

"I don't know where he is or how to reach him, Maria," Rosa said truthfully. She knew her husband was involved in the resistance, but she wasn't sure in what capacity.

"OK, OK, I understand you might be reluctant to tell me where he's hiding. But if you change your mind about contacting him, just let me know."

The way Maria had steered their conversation made Rosa wary. Something about this situation did not add up. The separate quarters, the extra food, the perks—all clearly suggested the Prados were in the good graces of the authorities. Yet Maria seemed to imply she was somehow part of the resistance.

Then the answer struck Rosa. *Maria is a snitch.* This had to be the source of these petty privileges. Rosa's invitation to this party was probably a scheme to uncover Mano's whereabouts.

Rosa suddenly rose from the bench and called out to her children. "Elena...Pedro...it's time for us to go."

Maria begged her to stay, but Rosa politely insisted.

Walking back toward her dormitory, Rosa wondered once again about Mano.

Was he alive? Clearly, the Prado woman believed that. Even so, he was probably with *her.* Would she ever see her husband again? Her life seemed on hold, suspended by events beyond her knowledge and control. The sense of unreality had not ended there.

Since arriving at the camp, Rosa had found something inside her missing, a thing she'd taken for granted like the air or the sun: the feeling of having a country. Being treated like an enemy who could not be trusted was a constant reminder that she was an outsider. Rosa knew most of the soldiers were not really cruel. They were simply doing a job and had little time to be personal. All the same, their mistrust had taken its toll.

The soldiers no longer considered her an American—and now she felt the same.

THE QUARANTINE AND RELOCATION ACT:
Month 13, Day 5

Guillermo walked into the room, proudly carrying a tray with three brimming cups. Delicate wafts of steam rose from the fawn-colored drinks.

"Viejo loco! You forgot the sugar!" Juana yelled, following her husband out of the kitchen with a plastic sugar bowl.

"Go back, old woman. Atras! It's my turn to serve Mano's guests," Guillermo said to his wife, placing the tray on the table before Ramon, Jo, and Mano.

"Buenos días, amigos," Guillermo said brightly to the group, handing each of them a cup. The old man moved nimbly despite his stooped posture, the cups steady in his gnarled hands.

"Ah, café con leche. Guillermo, you spoil us," Ramon said graciously, accepting the drink.

The old man beamed. "You three fight for our people every day. The least Juana and I can do is serve you a little coffee." Guillermo wagged his finger at Mano. "I would be fighting for our people too, if only this one would let me," he said with a smile.

Mano laughed softly. "You've done your share of fighting, viejito. Raising seven children is enough of a battle for anybody," he said, bringing the cup to his lips, warmed by the fresh coffee and Guillermo's rough affection.

Guillermo and Juana Ortega, Mano's former neighbors, had moved into his new house and become Mano's self-appointed housekeepers shortly after Rosa and the children had left for the camp. Without asking for payment, the aging couple had adopted the lone man, taking on many domestic tasks in his house and showering him with affection that fell like fresh rain on parched soil. In return, Mano shared his food with Guillermo and Juana, and that was payment enough for them.

Guillermo and Juana typified the changes the quarantine had brought to Mano's barrio. After nearly a year inside the quarantine walls, a new spirit of harmony was flourishing in a community where people had once been isolated by despair. They now had a reason to pull together. In a society with few role models, the insurgents had become the heroes of the barrios, their exploits talked about and celebrated. Those who fell were mourned as martyrs; those who triumphed were embraced with the fervor of a small town cheering on its football team. The passion was infectious.

Children acted as lookouts. Mothers reported information on government troop movements. Old people ferried messages. Families sheltered insurgents on the run. From active resistance to simply keeping silent, almost everyone was united against government control, which was growing weaker every day.

Peacekeeping in the zones was now the duty of heavily armed troops; ordinary law enforcement was nonexistent. Yet Mano had noticed that crime was diminishing. As supplies dried up, drug abuse had plummeted. Even the gang wars had declined.

Still, life was hard. Most city services had been shut down. Water and electricity were sporadically available, maintained for humanitarian reasons—and to support the troop garrisons surrounding the zones.

Most hospital employees within the zones had stopped reporting for work. A few intrepid nurses and physicians now made up the skeleton crews that offered rudimentary medical treatment. No major outbreaks of disease had been reported, but experts thought an epidemic inevitable.

Food and medicine had become the government's only leverage within the zones. Even here, the government's role was tenuous. Cornmeal, grain, and rice, along with antibiotics and medical supplies, were periodically trucked to delivery points at the periphery of the zones. From there, La Defensa del Pueblo supervised their distribution. This quasi-official role for the DDP was an arrangement the government accepted uneasily. As Jo and Ramon had envisioned, the DDP was filling the power vacuum left by the collapse of city government.

The headquarters of La Defensa del Pueblo was now a well-known site where residents of the barrios sought help and support. The DDP's public facilities, however, were managed by minor functionaries. The real leadership of La Defensa del Pueblo remained behind the scenes.

Today, the leaders of this shadow regime were gathered in Mano's quarters to discuss their agenda. After Guillermo retreated to the kitchen, Jo got down to business.

"When is the next issue of *La Voz del Pueblo* due?" Jo asked Ramon.

"You must not have heard yet. A baldie patrol knocked out our printing facility on Second Street yesterday," Ramon reported glumly.

Mano looked puzzled. "What's a 'baldie'?"

"That's what Spanish-only Eslos have started calling the soldiers," Jo explained with a smile. "It's because of their helmets. A 'balde' is a bucket in Spanish."

"In any case," Ramon continued, "the good news is that with all the abandoned print shops, presses we got aplenty. We're refurbishing another one, and *La Voz* should be out again next week."

"Good," Jo said, handing Ramon a DVD. "When you're ready to publish again, here's an article on vegetable gardening in vacant lots. We've got good soil under all this pavement and a long growing season. We need to find ways to start feeding ourselves."

"That's excellent, Jo," Ramon replied. "It's only a matter of time before the government cuts off the food."

"I've got a long list of items to cover," Jo announced. "Before I get to them, is there anything either of you want to bring up?"

"Yes, I've got something," Ramon said, stirring a spoonful of sugar into his cup. "As you know, we're going to need the manpower of the gangs to continue our resistance. However, several of the meros I recruited earlier have started getting cold feet since the Army began their tank patrols. They won't admit it, but I think they're afraid. Any thoughts on how much more cash we should pony up to persuade them?"

"None," Mano replied.

"What?" Ramon said, almost spilling his coffee. "How can we get the meros to join us if we don't pay them?"

"Take out one of the tanks."

"Que dices, hombre? Are you joking?"

"Once we show the meros we can take out a tank," Mano said steadily, "they'll lose their fear of them, Ramon."

"Did Guillermo put something in your café con leche, Mano? How in the hell are we supposed to destroy a tank?"

"Deploying tanks in a city without infantry support is very risky," Mano explained. "Armored vehicles are built to fight in the open. They can be taken out in a close fight." It had been a lesson drilled into him during his military training.

"And you think we can do this?" Jo asked.

"Yes." Mano nodded. "It won't be easy. But if we can get the RPGs from Nesto again, we have a chance. Four RPGs would work. More would be better."

"That's going to cost us—a lot," Ramon said.

"You're right, Ray," Jo agreed. "But remember, you were ready to pay the meros more money on a regular basis. Paying Nesto once will cost us less in the long run. What do you say, Ramon? Do we have the cojones to do this?"

Ramon scratched his chin. "It's risky, Jo. If we fail, we'll look weak."

"We look weak already," Mano said.

"Mano's right," Jo agreed. "I think it's a risk we have to take."

"There's still a flaw in this plan. Even if we manage to destroy one of the tanks, how will anybody know about it?" Ramon asked. "If the attack takes place inside the zone, the military will do everything they can to cover it up."

All three fell silent, pondering the problem. Then Jo snapped her fingers. "Simon Potts!"

Ramon nodded slowly. "Yes, Simon would be perfect."

"Who's Simon Potts?" Mano asked.

"Potts is a freelance cinematographer Maggie and I know,"

Ramon explained. "He's a real maverick...filmed wars and revolutions all over the world. He'd jump at the chance to shoot an exclusive documentary about us. It'd probably get him an Oscar."

"How soon can we get him?" Jo asked.

"I can have Maggie get in touch with him."

Jo pounded her fist on the table like a gavel. "Then let's do it!"

"All right," Ramon agreed. "I'll talk to Nesto about the weapons, too."

Mano put his hand gently on the older man's shoulder. "There's something else, Ramon. Don't accept Nesto's first price this time; he'll lower it if you bargain with him."

At first, Ramon glared at Mano, but his expression softened when he realized Mano was right—he hadn't haggled with Nesto the last time. This was a luxury they could no longer afford. Anticipating the quarantine, Ramon and Margaret had arranged for a divorce that had awarded her sole legal authority over the bulk of their wealth. No longer married to a Hispanic, Margaret was exempt from the quarantine. This "divorce of convenience," as Maggie called it, allowed her to remain outside the Quarantine Zone—and in control of their money. Maggie's money, however, was available sporadically and only in small amounts. The government kept tabs on the bank accounts of people like her.

Jo had converted most of her wealth into gold bullion and cash. But the government had confiscated a sizable portion of her estate. The compensation process would likely drag on for years. With Jo now underground and unable to recover the money, her wealth had been nearly halved.

"Not haggling with Nesto was a mistake," Ramon said,

managing a tight smile. "Our pockets aren't as deep as they used to be. I'll be more of a cranky old miser in the future."

"One more thing," Mano began. "As long as possible, we need to keep Nesto in the dark about the time and place of the attack. I don't trust him."

Ramon looked at Mano in amazement. "Your instincts are uncanny, Mano. There's something about Nesto we haven't shared with you yet: he was approached by the CIA. He told us about it two days ago."

Mano laughed grimly. "I'm not surprised he told you about it. This way, he gets paid by two sources at once."

"Frankly, that hadn't occurred to me," Ramon admitted.

Jo leaned forward eagerly. "But think of the tactical opportunities, Mano. We can misdirect the CIA through Nesto. It gives us an incredible advantage."

"That advantage won't last long, Jo," Mano said. "After they come up empty, the CIA will figure out Nesto has been lying to them."

"Yes, that's true," Jo agreed. "We'll have to throw them some crumbs from time to time, let the government find some obsolete weapons or equipment...anything that will give them the idea Nesto's tips are leading somewhere."

"Nevertheless, Mano's right, Jo," Ramon said. "Dealing with Nesto will be like surfing on a shark's back. We can't afford to slip. He'll turn on us when things get difficult."

"Or we run out of money," Mano added.

"But the risk is worth it," Jo said, her voice rising. "Nesto can provide us with weapons *and* keep the government looking the wrong way. It's just too good to pass up. Look, when the time comes, we'll deal with Nesto. In the meantime, let's get this operation against the tanks going. I think it's time we gave the baldies a bloody nose."

———

Five days later, with the low rumble of tanks rising in the distance, Mano recalled Jo's words. To give the U.S. Army a bloody nose, they would have to be very good—and very lucky.

Mano peered cautiously through the second-floor window of the vacant building. He saw the squat hull of an M1 Abrams tank appear around the corner, about three blocks away. In less than a minute, four M1s were trundling in a straight line down the two-lane street toward Mano. It was 11:43 a.m. The armored patrol was right on schedule.

"Go, Tony," Mano said to the slender teenager beside him. Antonio Mendez rose and sprinted eagerly to the next room, carrying a HEAT-loaded RPG.

Mano made eye contact with the two RPG teams in the burned-out apartments across the street and pumped his fist. Because the tanks' crews might pick up their transmissions at this range, their attack would begin in radio silence. Crouching in the second-floor windows, Nesto's vatos signaled back, confirming they had detected the tanks. Mano then repeated the procedure with the third RPG team hiding in the sewer drain at the corner. They were ready.

In a conventional battle, as Mano knew, four M1s would be a single platoon for a heavy battalion. On the streets of Los Angeles, however, the four tanks were a major force. Mano imagined the Army's battalion commander felt the mere presence of the tanks would cause the insurgents to flee in fear.

The commander's disdain for the insurgents was also evident in the scheduling of the patrols. It had not taken Mano long to recognize these armored columns, sent to show the flag in the zones, used only three different routes that were repeated in the same sequence. The Army's contempt for the insurgents, and its CO's overconfidence, had made it simple to set up an ambush.

Executing the attack was another matter.

From his Army days, Mano knew the killing power of the M1. The tank's 120mm main gun would be useless in close quarters, but each M1 was still armed with two 7.62mm machine guns and a 25mm chain gun. That firepower alone was enough to outgun the six fighters under Mano's command. The trick would be to hit hard and run fast.

As he waited warily for the tanks to approach his trap, Mano recalled his days in Afghanistan and recognized the irony of the situation. Now he was the insurgent waiting to ambush a U.S. column.

When the first tank reached the fire hydrant that marked the beginning of the kill zone, Mano released the safety on his AK-47 and pulled back the bolt. The tank passed through the kill zone and, as he expected, turned right at the corner and disappeared from sight.

Mano's plan was to wait for the fourth tank to enter the kill zone before they fired. At that point, the other vehicles would be around the corner and his teams could attack the last tank without covering fire from the first three. The kill zone Mano had devised gave his RPG teams overhead a clear line of fire into the vulnerable rear panel of the tank that housed the vehicle's engine.

Mano's breath quickened as the second and third tanks

lumbered through the kill zone and around the corner. Things were going according to plan so far. He was counting on the nerve of men—and boys—he barely knew. The target tank approached the kill zone.

*Wait…Wait…*Mano mentally pleaded with his men. Above the roar of engines, he heard a short hiss followed by a booming crash. His heart sank. *Dammit! Too early.*

Looking down, he saw that a rocket from the vatos in the storm sewer had struck the front drive sprocket of the M1, blowing the treads away and bringing the vehicle to a halt. But the shot had been fired too soon. The tank had ground to a stop about fifteen meters from the corner. From this position, the RPG gunners overhead couldn't get a clean angle on the more lightly armored engine compartment at the rear of the tank.

Mano jumped to his feet and raced into the hall.

Entering the next room, he saw Tony Mendez fire his RPG through the window, filling the space with exhaust from the rocket. Mano stumbled through the smoke, his hand outstretched, and grabbed the teenager by the shoulder. "Your angle is too steep," he said, pulling Tony away from the window. "Move back one more room and fire again."

Mano looked outside. The tank was struggling to move on its one good tread, spinning in a slow circle but getting nowhere. The movement was turning the vulnerable rear compartment away from Mano's side of the street; unless the tank turned back toward him, it would be up to the RPG teams on the other side of the street to take it out. He bolted for the next room to check on Tony.

The burping chatter of machine-gun fire grew louder when Mano entered the room. Tony stood near the window, about to bring the RPG to his shoulder, when he noticed Mano. "Pretty cool, huh?" he yelled with a grin.

Suddenly, the window frame beside Tony splintered as a trail of bullets moved laterally, striking him on the cheek. A small pink cloud of blood formed near the boy's head an instant before he fell.

Mano dove for the floor as bullets buzzed over his head like angry bees, shattering the plaster walls above him. The room had been targeted; staying there would be suicide. He crawled to Tony, gently pried the RPG from his grasp, and slung the weapon over his shoulder.

Moving on his belly into the hallway, he heard the whoosh and boom of two more rockets firing outside. He was heartened that the RPG teams across the street were still fighting. Mano's orders had been to fire two shots and then get out. That meant each of the two RPG teams across the street would fire once more, *if* they could manage to get a shot off under the rapidly increasing machine-gun fire.

In the relative safety of the hallway, Mano realized there was now only one way left to get a kill shot on the tank: he would have to go down to the street.

Arriving at the first-floor doorway, he produced a small mirror from the thigh pocket of his fatigues and peeked outside. The crippled tank was still foundering, struck by several rockets and unable to move. But its turret was still rotating, looking for targets. On the cross street behind the damaged vehicle, the other tanks were laying down protective fire on the apartments. The RPG teams in the windows were either gone or dead. He would have to finish off the tank alone.

Mano knew if he emerged from the doorway to aim his RPG toward the crippled tank, the machine guns would cut him down. The only cover was directly behind the stricken tank itself. From there, he could get a point-blank shot into the tank's rear, but to get there, he'd have to cross ten meters of open ground. His only hope was to reach the safe zone before the tank gunners spotted him.

He took three steps backward to get a running start, then bolted.

Time seemed to slow as he crossed the deadly field of fire, the thudding of his heart drowning out the clatter of the machine guns. With each stride, he wondered if it would be his last. *Keep moving...Keep moving...Dive.*

Mano landed heavily on the pavement, emitting a loud grunt as the breath he'd been holding escaped from his lungs. Time returned to normal as the barrel of the RPG slung across his back slammed painfully against the back of his head.

The bullets pulverized the blacktop around him as the gunners zeroed in. In a matter of seconds, one of the tanks would move and gain a field of fire into his position.

Mano rolled onto his side, cradled the RPG, and crab-crawled left for a better angle. Chips of pavement churned up by the bullets stung his cheek as he brought the rear of the tank into his sights and squeezed the trigger.

For an instant, he thought his shot had failed. Then he was consumed in a bright orange flash. He covered his head as a succession of explosions hurled debris skyward.

When Mano opened his eyes, a dense black cloud filled the air. Under cover of the smoke, he crawled toward the curb, lifted the storm sewer's heavy grate, and lowered himself into the sanctuary below.

Fired at close range, the High Explosive Anti-Tank projectile had ignited the vehicle's ammo supply, popping its massive turret.

The destruction of the M1 would have a profound effect on U.S. military tactics against the insurgents. It marked the last time armored vehicles patrolled inside the Quarantine Zones without infantry support. The rebels had embarrassed the U.S. military—and the nation's defense establishment was determined not to let it happen again.

THE QUARANTINE AND RELOCATION ACT:
Month 15

The appetite for independence will grow quickly after
the people get their first taste of the fruits of victory.
> —*José Antonio Marcha, 1982*
> *Translated by J. M. Herrera*

The rebel assault against the tanks in Los Angeles was part
of an ominous trend. Fifteen months after the Bates amendment had become law, the insurgents were stepping up their
forays outside the Quarantine Zones across the United States.

Chasing the instant fame of Simon Potts, teams of freelance video reporters now continually combed the areas
around the zones, looking for footage that would lead the
evening news. This cash-and-carry journalism was producing a constant stream of shocking images that magnified the
scope of the violence in the national consciousness.

Emboldened by the media coverage given to the raids of
their comrades, rebel bands across the nation now continually probed for weak spots, attacking any military target that
appeared vulnerable. The U.S. military, facing shortages of
manpower, sophisticated equipment, and adequate intelligence, always seemed one step behind the insurgents, now
being called Panchos by the troops.

The pattern of aggression by the rebels varied within each region of the nation. The vast abandoned areas along the southern third of California were a haven for small, mobile cadres of insurgents who struck military targets at random while gleaning food and supplies from the vacated suburban landscape. The only civilians still left in the region were a bastion of hardy souls clustered around San Diego's naval base.

Most non-Hispanics in New Mexico had retreated northward to Colorado, leaving the Rio Grande Valley in the hands of the rebels as far north as Santa Fe. The area's narrow canyons were ideal sites for ambushes on government patrols. To avoid heavy casualties, troops moved sparingly through the highlands, leaving the insurgents free to roam.

From El Paso to Houston, the major cities in Texas became a bloody battleground. Using the Quarantine Zones as unassailable bases, the insurgents launched a string of fierce sorties against the government garrisons surrounding them. Despite being outgunned, the rebels' knowledge of the urban terrain gave them a considerable advantage.

In Arizona, the government was losing control south of the Gila River as rebel bands from the QZs of Yuma, Tucson, and Phoenix took to the hills.

Along the Eastern Seaboard and the Midwest, where the Quarantine Zones were smaller and more isolated, the situation was less dire. In these areas, government authorities were able to maintain control, but at a great cost in lives to both sides.

The United States faced a major dilemma. The bulk of America's combat troops were spread across the globe, leaving the military strapped for qualified personnel to squelch the insurgency now raging at home. In a desperate measure, the Brenner administration extended the active duty of reservists by two more years. The families of those affected began a national campaign to reverse the decision. Administration trial balloons on the reinstatement of the military draft met with fierce opposition. The draft became another controversial issue heightening dissension within the United States.

As the turbulent summer gave way to fall, the U.S. found itself more isolated in the world and more divided at home.

———

Hank Evans double-clicked the video conference icon and the image of the assistant director of the CIA materialized on his computer monitor.

Carol Phelps looked haggard, her heavy makeup unable to mask dark folds below her bloodshot eyes. "There's something I want you to watch, Hank," she said without prelude.

After a moment of static, a news clip appeared on Evans's computer. Shot from a distance, a prone insurgent in black fatigues fired a rocket-propelled grenade into the rear hull of an M1 tank, filling the screen with a blazing flash. Three other widely broadcast TV reports of insurgent attacks in the Los Angeles Quarantine Zones followed.

After the last clip faded, the face of Carol Phelps again appeared. "I know you've probably seen these clips in the media over the last few months, Hank," she said sternly. "I'm showing them to you again because they underscore two unacceptable failures on the part of your office." She paused, waiting for her words to sink in.

"First, you have yet to locate the man who shot this footage. This is particularly galling since virtually every person in the country now knows his name. The circumstances of these 'Potts Shots,' as the media is calling them, make it obvious that Simon Potts has access to the highest echelons of the terrorist leadership in Southern California. It is imperative that you apprehend this man for questioning.

"Second, and even more important, it is evident that the terrorists have compromised your security sphere. They have repeatedly anticipated the movement of our forces in your area and have not only attacked us but have shown the audacity to videotape their attacks and distribute the footage."

After a pause, Phelps took a more conciliatory tone. "I know that terrorist attacks like these have been taking place in all the Quarantine Zones, Hank. The big difference is that in your area, they're being documented and released to the public." Phelps massaged her temples. "Look, in the big scheme of things, this is really penny-ante stuff. We both know we've got truly serious military challenges overseas right now. But the administration's ass is being roasted royally by Congress and the media on this domestic bullshit. I have no choice but to pass on the heat to you."

Evans gripped the edge of his desk, trying to contain his anger. Phelps was a Brenner appointee with no real intel experience. "These are the kind of repercussions we have to expect when we squander intelligence assets for political purposes, ma'am," he said.

"You've made no secret of your opposition to the relocation of Hispanics in the intelligence community, Hank. We can't turn back the clock. We have to move on. I understand you have a mole within one suspicious local group...they're called La Defensa del Pueblo, I believe."

Evans was startled. The assistant director was renowned for her network of informers. He was learning firsthand that her reputation was well deserved.

"Yes...but, frankly, Carol, our mole has been no help so far."

"Have you considered that perhaps your mole has been helping the terrorists?"

"We're not sure the DDP is behind any type of violent activity," Evans said, nervously rubbing his jowls. "In fact, they're helping the Army distribute food and medical supplies inside the zones. Their leaders are a couple of dilettantes. Neither one is really the violent type."

"Well, somebody there is sure knocking the hell out of our people...and it's up to you to find out who it is," Phelps said with a cold glare. "I'm giving you fair warning, Hank. If you don't come up with the ringleaders of these terrorists—and I mean soon—you can start considering what you'd like your next career to be."

The assistant director of the CIA then abruptly logged off, leaving Hank Evans staring in frustration at the CIA logo on his computer screen.

"'All warfare is based on deception,'" Mano read aloud from the worn clothbound book. "'When we are near, we must make the enemy believe we are far away. When far away, we must make him believe we are near.'" Mano's eyes rose from the book. "Ramon, this man really understood our kind of fight."

"What's remarkable about Sun Tzu is that he wrote those words more than two thousand years ago, Mano. *The Art of War* has inspired leaders all over the world ever since."

The two men were seated in Ramon's library, a small climate-controlled haven for two thousand or so of Ramon's favorite books hidden away in the meat locker of an abandoned restaurant. This indulgence to Ramon's passion for literature had been a birthday gift from Jo, who'd appointed the room with two cozy leather chairs, a mahogany side table, and a brass reading lamp.

Mano gently stroked the yellowed pages. "I never knew books like this existed."

"That's not too surprising." Ramon laughed. "This is probably the first time in your life you've had time to read."

It was true. Without the company of his family, Mano found himself with time to kill during the lulls between their forays—and reading was a way to dull the loneliness.

Mano's newfound interest in reading also had another motive: he needed to deepen his knowledge of military strategy. He was now routinely matching wits with professional officers. Although he'd succeeded far beyond his expectations, he knew the challenges ahead would be more difficult. Since Ramon had introduced him to *The Art of War* two weeks earlier, he'd already committed large sections to memory.

" 'The supreme art of war is to subdue the enemy without fighting,' " Mano read aloud again.

Ramon was gratified that Mano had taken to Sun Tzu. He'd figured that the profound yet simple words of the Chinese sage would be a good launching point to advance Mano's military intellect. Ramon himself was essentially self-taught. There was no reason why Mano could not do the same.

"Well, after you've cut your teeth on Sun Tzu, I'll introduce you to a couple of gentlemen named Thucydides and

Clausewitz. They'll give you a Western perspective on military theory."

Mano marked his place in the book and put it down reverently. "Will any of those guys teach us how to fight without weapons?"

"Why do you ask?"

"I think we're better off without Nesto. It's only a matter of time before he turns on us."

"I know that, Mano. But we can't replace Nesto's manpower yet. The meeting we've set up tonight will go a long way toward that. But I don't know where else to get access to his weapons." Ramon glanced at his watch. It was nearly midnight. "Right now, though, it's time we left on our recruiting tour."

Forty minutes later, Mano and Ramon were outside Tavo's, a grimy bar in the heart of Quarantine Zone A. The bar was ground zero in the turf of Los Verdugos, a gang with a lethal reputation.

Ramon had already briefed Mano on Los Verdugos. The gang's members were all recent Mexican arrivals in el norte. Most spoke little English and many were undocumented. At the bottom of the economic food chain and with little to lose, these young men were known to be fearless and volatile. Unlike their more savvy rivals, who usually battled for a piece of the action, Los Verdugos fought for honor and pride. Though few in number, they were given a wide berth by the other gangs.

Ramon hoped these recent arrivals retained some of the traditional respect accorded elders in Mexico. It was their best hope of surviving the encounter.

As the two entered the cantina, several forlorn drinkers slouched against the bar while a paunchy bartender leafed lethargically through an ancient issue of *Vogue*. They all stared in awe at Mano's size as he and Ramon strode through the tavern toward the open doorway at the back of the room.

Finding their meeting site in the bar's back room empty, Mano positioned himself behind a faded pool table with a view of the front door.

After several minutes, the front door of the bar opened and a procession of young men with closely cropped hair slowly entered. Most were bare-chested and powerfully built, though none appeared to be very tall. Mano could see numerous tattoos adorning the bronze skin of their torsos and arms. He counted eight vatos in all.

The young men glared wordlessly as they filed into the back room and surrounded the pool table, cutting off Mano and Ramon from the door. The last vato to enter the room had a large tattoo of an angel on his chest. He glanced at Mano with the cold gaze of a predator, then nodded to Ramon.

"Y que, ese," the young man said.

"Y que, Angel," Ramon replied.

"Bueno, viejo, que quieres?" Angel Sanchez asked, thrusting his chin upward.

"He wants to know what we want," Ramon translated for Mano. *Angel and Mano seem a lot alike*, Ramon observed. *Both of them get right to the point.*

"Tell him we want him and his vatos to join us in fighting for justicia," Mano replied.

"I know English...some," Angel said in a thick accent. He then shrugged derisively toward Mano. "Why we help you?"

Ramon launched into a passionate lecture in Spanish. "Porque tu pueblo te necesita. Esto es una oportunidad para ayudar a otros…" As he spoke, Mano could see the eyes of the young men glazing over. Ramon was not reaching them. When Ramon stopped for a breath, Mano addressed Angel.

"Do you hate the other gangs in this barrio?"

Angel nodded his head.

"Do you hate baldies?"

Angel nodded again.

"Which one is it better to fight?"

Angel measured Mano's words. The big man's logic cut to the heart of the matter.

Angel was a realist. He understood that Los Verdugos battled the rival gangs of his barrio for the meager measure of pride that came with defending their turf. Why should he spill the blood of his people over turf when a bigger enemy threatened them both? Perhaps fighting the baldies could be a greater source of honor.

"I talk with Los Verdugos," Angel said, gesturing toward his cohorts. "Tomorrow we talk again…here." He then looked at his vatos and flicked his head toward the door. The young men filed slowly out of the room with slightly less malice than when they entered it.

After Los Verdugos were gone, Ramon playfully slapped Mano's massive shoulder. "That was remarkable, my friend. I think we made some real progress here tonight."

Mano allowed himself a small smile. "As Sun Tzu wrote, 'He will win whose army is animated by the same spirit throughout all its ranks.'"

THE QUARANTINE AND RELOCATION ACT:
Month 16, Day 7

Another drop of sweat trailed down Jo's forehead, making its way into her eye. Jo ignored the sting, keeping the binoculars trained on Lakeview Avenue. The convoy was overdue.

Perched in the steeple of an abandoned church, Jo could see for nearly a kilometer along the road. But in the unseasonable November heatwave, the vantage point was exacting a stiff penalty. The four-by-four-foot attic was broiling—a condition magnified by the presence of Mano's large bulk.

The Army convoy they were waiting to intercept was ferrying building supplies from the recently reactivated Long Beach Naval Base to a new Army garrison under construction near Yorba Linda. One of Angel's vatos had spotted the route two weeks ago while scouting this vacated area southeast of Zone B. Now the rebels were ready to strike.

"Maybe you should take a break," Mano suggested. Jo had been on her feet for the last forty-five minutes in the oppressive heat, peering between the steeple's ventilation slats, her braided hair a sopping mess and her T-shirt soaked with sweat.

"I can last a little longer," she said.

"You might miss it if you're drowsy, Jo."

"All right. Take over," she said, keeping her eyes on the road while Mano rose to his feet.

As Jo turned to hand Mano the binoculars, her breasts brushed against his torso. Against her will, the sensuous contact sparked a rush of passion that made Jo quiver. Her breath suddenly heavy, she looked into Mano's eyes and saw that he, too, was aroused.

Jo could no longer deny it—she loved Mano and ached for his touch. But she also recognized the cruel irony of her love. To give in to her desires would be to destroy what she loved about him most.

She could not allow Mano to betray his wife.

Jo handed Mano the Bushnells and sat down, carefully avoiding any further contact.

Trying to defuse the tension, Mano changed the subject. "Why do you suppose these people left their homes?" he asked, scanning the abandoned landscape.

Jo collected her thoughts before answering. "It seems to me that, above all else, Norteamericanos are individualistic. Their first instinct is to look out for themselves. When the crisis came, they reacted as individuals. Instead of worrying about the consequences, they sold out as quickly as they could and got their families out of danger."

"You'd think some of these people would have had the courage to stay and fight for their homes," Mano said, keeping his eyes glued to the road.

"I don't think it's a matter of courage, Mano. Norteamericanos are brave—and quite tough in many ways. They may be the most competitive people on earth. But they're accustomed to an easy life, and they have few qualms about moving. Most families in the U.S. move every five years. Very few are tied to an ancestral home—especially Californians. Pulling up stakes and moving on is part of the culture. I believe most of them thought they were simply moving out of a rapidly deteriorating neighborhood, not giving up their native soil." Jo paused. "I think a lot of them are having second thoughts about their actions now."

"You don't think Americans are willing to make sacrifices?"

"Any U.S. politician who advocated sacrifice would never get elected. Their political opponent would simply promise a painless solution, and most people would choose to believe it. You have to go back to World War II—more than four generations ago—to find a time when Norteamericanos had to make any real sacrifices. The U.S. Civil War was the last armed conflict on American soil. Compare that to Europe or Asia—"

"I see them coming," said Mano, calmly interrupting her.

Jo jumped to her feet. "Can you tell how many?" she asked, straining to make out the vehicles without the binoculars.

Mano studied the neat line of vehicles. "There are two Humvees in the lead. It looks like...let's see...eight trucks following and one Humvee as the trail escort vehicle."

"Let's hope the last of our am-nite doesn't go to waste."

––––––

From the passenger's seat of the lead Humvee, Lieutenant Jason Kroy stared blankly at the vacant stores and factories along Lakeview Avenue, his mind far away. A third-generation soldier, Kroy envied his younger brother, assigned to a Ranger unit in Iran. *That's where the real soldiers are,* he said to himself dejectedly.

While pondering the bleak prospects of his own career, Kroy heard a thundering boom from the road behind him.

"What the hell was that?" he yelled to his driver.

"I dunno," the driver said nervously. "It sounded like a bomb or something."

Kroy grabbed the radio's handset. "Convoy leader to all units...Pull over! Pull over!" he yelled into the mike.

Emerging from his Humvee, Kroy saw a large cloud of smoke and dust billowing from the causeway across the lake nearly half a kilometer back. His stomach churning, the lieutenant counted his convoy. There were only seven trucks along the road behind him. The last truck and the T.E.V. were missing.

Kroy ran to the second vehicle. "Contact HQ, Sergeant! Tell them we've been ambushed and the convoy is going to need protection! Have them send air cover if possible. Then escort the rest of the convoy to the garrison. I'm going back to check this out. Have them send me any reinforcements they can!"

While the remainder of the convoy got under way, the lieutenant jumped back into his own vehicle. "Get us turned around, Willard!" he said to his driver. "We're going back to the causeway."

The driver's eyes widened with alarm. "You sure you wanna do that, LT?"

"Willard, shut up and drive," Kroy said and then turned to the soldier in the backseat. "Meyers, man the 50!"

The young soldier climbed onto the Humvee's center platform, peeking cautiously from the machine-gun turret as they sped down the road.

———

"We've got a Humvee coming back," Mano said, looking through the binoculars.

Jo picked up the vu-phone she'd rigged to emit a detonating signal. "I'm ready with charge number two," she said, her finger poised over the final digit that would ignite the explosives.

Anticipating the return of a security detachment from the convoy, Mano had placed a second set of charges in an abandoned car near the causeway to give them another chance at a precisely timed blow. Angel and two vatos were hiding near the kill zone. Their task would be to recover any weapons following the attack.

"They're getting closer," Mano said calmly as the Humvee closed on the abandoned car. "Get ready."

Then, in the corner of his binoculars, Mano detected movement—three ragged figures walking nearby. The Humvee slowed as it approached the men.

Jo could sense the time for detonating the charges was lapsing. "What's the matter, Mano?"

"I think we've got some onlookers. Disable the charges, Jo."

"Onlookers?"

"Yeah, they're dregs," Mano said as he studied the three scruffy men through the binoculars. "The explosion at the causeway must have drawn them."

"Mierda!" Jo cursed, tapping in the abort code.

As Mano watched, the soldiers began frisking the men against the abandoned car. "It looks like the soldiers think the dregs may have been involved."

"Is there anything we can do?"

"Call Angel and tell him and his vatos they need to withdraw. This looks like one fish that's going to get away."

Hours later, as Jo and Mano sat at the DDP conference table planning their next operation, Angel entered the room, followed by three Verdugos.

Walking with ominous slowness, the mero moved very close to Mano and stood before him, chest extended, a cold glare in his eyes. "You...are woman...today," he said bitterly.

Mano rose to his feet and smiled. "If you're trying to insult me, Angel, you'll have to do better than that. There are many women as brave as any man. This is one of them," he said, gesturing toward Jo.

Angel looked at Jo for a moment, then softened his tone. "Why you no attack?"

"Because those three men in the street were innocent. They were not our enemies. We are warriors, Angel. The death of those three men would have made us murderers. Asesinos. Their blood would never wash from our hands. Me entiendes?"

"I join you to fight baldies," Angel said, his anger dissipating. "Not to run."

"You have the heart of a lion, Angel. This war is far from over. You'll get a lot more chances to fight," Mano assured him. "Get some sleep. We've got more to do tomorrow."

Appeased, Angel nodded to his vatos and they exited the room.

"That was scary," Jo said softly. "Can we trust him, Mano?"

"You always know where you stand with Angel."

"That's not a very persuasive argument."

"Some people don't fight for ideas, Jo. They fight because they hate. As long as we have an enemy, Angel won't betray us."

As Mano spoke, he realized how much the words applied to himself as well.

THE QUARANTINE AND RELOCATION ACT:
Month 16, Day 28

Mami, wake up. Come see!" Pedro said, gently shaking his mother's arm.

Struggling to stay warm under a scratchy wool blanket, Rosa rolled toward her son on the hard bunk bed and opened one eye. Across the crowded Quonset hut, she saw the weak light of dawn through a small window.

"Keep your voice down, m'hijo. You'll wake someone," she whispered to her son.

"OK, Mami," the boy whispered back. "But you've got to come see this...Elena, too."

Hearing her brother's voice, Elena stirred in the bed next to Rosa's.

"Just a minute, m'hijo. I need to dress your sister," Rosa said as she rose from the bed. After slipping into a robe, she bundled Elena into several layers of mismatched clothing recently donated to the Community. The early November weather was colder than anything Rosa had ever known. A lifelong resident of Los Angeles, she shuddered at the thought that the year's coldest weather was still ahead.

Once they were dressed, Pedro eagerly took Rosa and Elena by the hand and dragged the sleepy pair toward the doorway.

Rosa gasped as they stepped outside. The camp had been transformed.

Rosa had seen pictures of snow. But firsthand, she found it breathtaking. There was a purity and stillness to the stark landscape that cameras failed to capture. As Rosa turned her head, the glow of the pale morning sun followed her gaze across the white contours of the land, igniting a moving wave of glittering reflections. For a moment, she and the children stood in silent awe.

Then Pedro broke the spell. "Come on, Elena!" the boy yelled, dashing into the knee-deep snow. Elena ran stiffly behind her brother, waddling in her bulky clothes. The children romped in the snow, giddy with joy, their laughter warming Rosa. It was a sound she'd heard rarely since their arrival in the Community.

Rosa's thoughts turned to Mano. She knew her husband would relish this moment of joy with the children. Then the questions that tormented her every day returned. *Is he still alive? Is he with that woman? Will I ever see him again?*

Part of her wanted to put Mano behind her and move on, but she could not. She clung desperately to the belief that their family would be reunited. It was the focus of the prayers she recited daily before her small statue of the Blessed Virgin.

The small offerings of food Rosa laid before her shrine had become true sacrifices. The meals at the Community's mess hall had been adequate at first. But lately, the portions had shrunk severely. Unknown to Rosa, politics and bureaucracy were behind the reduction in their rations.

To mollify the financial obligations of the Bates resolution, the Relocation Communities had been presented to

Congress as self-sustaining entities. The architects of the Quarantine and Relocation Act had assumed most Hispanics were farm laborers who would quickly become adept at subsistence farming. Adequate food supplies, along with seeds and fertilizer, had been allocated to the Communities during the planting seasons of spring and early summer. By fall, government officials expected the Relocation Communities to begin their harvests and become essentially self-sufficient. As a result, food rations were radically curtailed.

In reality, over ninety percent of the Hispanics in the U.S. were urban dwellers with little farming experience of any kind. Nevertheless, many industrious souls within the Relocation Communities had attempted gardens, but their efforts were hampered by a lack of implements. Fearing hoes and rakes would be turned into weapons, the local security forces had withheld the garden tools provided by the planners.

In addition, the Relocation Communities were composed primarily of Hispanics from the suburbs. This had happened because Hispanics like the Prados, who lived outside the Quarantine Zones, were given priority for relocation. As a former inner-city dweller, Rosa was frequently reminded that her background was much less affluent than that of most of the roughly twenty thousand residents of Community Number Eight. She also realized that the Hispanics in the Community were a softer, more docile bunch than the people still in the Quarantine Zones.

Rosa turned her attention back to the children. They had been playing in the snow for over twenty minutes and their excitement had waned.

"I'm cold, Mami," Elena said, walking toward her mother.

Rosa picked up her shivering daughter and noticed her

clothes were wet. Elena's exertions had melted the snow that clung to her, and the damp clothes were cooling rapidly.

"Pedro, it's time to go back inside," Rosa called out to her son.

"Just a little while longer, Mami...please!"

"I need help with your sister, Pedro. She's cold and needs to go inside."

The boy responded immediately, running to Rosa's side and helping her carry Elena inside. *He's like his father*, Rosa thought proudly.

By evening, Elena was beginning to show signs of fever. Rosa gave up her blanket to cover her daughter and sat shivering beside Elena throughout the night, readjusting the covers each time the feverish child tossed in bed.

She took Elena to the Community infirmary the following morning. After three hours in the unheated waiting room, the doctor informed her that her daughter had contracted a virus. "There's no medication that will help," the Army physician said dryly. "It's something going around the camp."

The fever continued for the next three days. Rosa watched her child grow weaker, powerless to ease her suffering. On the fourth night, as Rosa hovered once again by her bed, Elena's labored breathing gradually slowed and finally stopped. Drained and numb after four days without sleep, Rosa watched her daughter's life ebb away, too exhausted to mourn. She lay down wearily next to Elena and held her until morning.

The day that followed was a blur. Accompanied by guards, a doctor came to take Elena's body away. Delirious with grief, Rosa fought to stop them and was held down and sedated.

When she awoke later in the day, she was alone in the dormitory.

Still groggy, Rosa's bleary eyes drifted to the statuette of Our Lady on the cardboard box Rosa used as her shrine. "I've prayed to you every day," she said bitterly. "How could you let this happen?" In a flash of anger, she swatted the statue, sending the ceramic figure to the floor.

The statuette shattered but Mary's face remained turned toward Rosa, her serene smile intact. Looking at the statue's downturned eyes, Rosa's anger vanished.

"You gave up your own child to save the world," she whispered. "Forgive me for doubting you."

As she solemnly retrieved the pieces, Rosa became certain her daughter's death had a purpose. She was not sure of it yet, but that would be revealed to her in time. God watched over his servants on this earth.

Elena was buried the following day.

The crude wooden cross marking her grave was among the first in a small plot designated as the Community cemetery.

It would not be the last.

THE QUARANTINE AND RELOCATION ACT:
Month 17, Day 4

The voice of independence always begins as the whisper of a few. It eventually becomes the shout of many.

—*José Antonio Marcha, 1982*
Translated by J. M. Herrera

Jo leaned against the rail of the *Sea Jay*, the spray of the waves caressing her face. Along the horizon, fleecy clouds shimmered like jewels in anticipation of the sun. Despite the splendor surrounding her, Jo felt empty and alone.

Her melancholy had started the night before.

Shortly after the yacht had set sail at dusk, Ramon and Maggie retired to their cabin. They'd been apart for months, and judging by the sounds from their quarters over the next several hours, they were making up for lost time. Their lovemaking had aroused Jo—and depressed her. Unable to sleep, she'd gone on deck around three and had been topside ever since.

You have no reason to be miserable, she told herself. Much of what she'd struggled for was coming to pass. The conflict had hardened their people, creating a stiff-necked confidence in the Quarantine Zones. Mainstream Americans, on the other hand, were growing weary and distracted.

She'd followed the news reports eagerly. The massive migrations away from the Quarantine Zones had flooded job markets in the other cities with displaced workers, stressing a U.S. economy that was already faltering. Housing shortages were driving the cost of a home beyond the means of many young families. The influx of newcomers had turned many sedate suburban areas into hard, teeming neighborhoods where drug use and crime ran rampant. Outside its borders, the U.S. faced a growing list of challenges.

As American military interventions overseas had grown, so had the anger of U.S. allies. Many saw the U.S. as a faltering superpower, arrogant in its supremacy and drunk on its own might. Tariffs and trade barriers had escalated. Years of rising oil prices were also taking an economic toll.

Meanwhile, the thirst for independence was growing in the zones. Many now believed the time had arrived to fulfill José Antonio Marcha's dream—a Hispanic state in North America.

So why was she depressed?

The sound of footsteps on the deck drew her gaze. Mano was staggering awkwardly along the swaying deck, clinging to the rail. He looked more than a little queasy. She smiled, her gloom lifting. "Something tells me this might be your first time at sea."

"In the Army, we always flew."

"Don't worry. You'll get used to it."

"I'll be fine. But there's something more important, Jo. I still don't know where we're going . . . or why."

"You run the risk of capture almost every day, Mano. That's why Ramon and I have kept you in the dark."

"I understand, Jo. But we're all in the same boat right now."

Jo laughed. "That's pretty good, Mano. I've never heard you joke before."

"Sorry. I wasn't trying to be funny," he said sheepishly. "I just think it's time I knew where we're headed."

"We'll be putting in at Mazatlán tomorrow tonight. From there, we have a full day's drive to Santiago."

"What's in Santiago?"

Jo looked out toward the horizon. "That's where we're going to change the map of the world."

Mano looked around the ancient cathedral in awe.

Clustered in small groups around the pews, over one hundred men and women were arguing loudly, the stone-walled room pulsating with the drone of their voices. Representing Quarantine Zones across the United States, these mostly self-appointed delegates had secretly converged on Santiago, Mexico—a dusty backwater 160 kilometers south of the border. Eager to even the score for past U.S. affronts, the local authorities had agreed to turn a blind eye on this clandestine convention in the colonial-era settlement.

Everywhere in the church, Mano saw energetic gestures—fingers thrusting, hands slashing, exaggerated shrugs, and back-slapping hugs. *There's no doubt these are Latinos*, Mano said to himself.

Yet as he studied the delegates, Mano was amazed at their racial diversity. Jo had told him to expect this, but the reality was still a shock. While the majority of the delegates were bronze-skinned and dark-haired people Mano would have identified as "Hispanic," there were many others he would have labeled as black or white on sight alone.

A screech of feedback pierced the air. "Su atención, por favor. Your attention, please," a voice said over the feeble public address system. The room quieted and all eyes turned toward the carved wooden lectern where Ramon Garcia stood.

"Hermanas y hermanos," Ramon said, smiling. "Call it a wild guess, but I suspect a few of you may have some comments on this document." He paused, waiting for the crowd's laughter to fade. "Now that you've had twenty-four hours to review the first draft, I'm certain all of you have comments about the opening section. I'd like to propose we break up into regional groups and put our comments down in writing."

Over the next eight hours, Mano watched in admiration as Ramon guided the boisterous assembly with an amazing display of wit and diplomacy.

The eloquence of the delegates also impressed Mano. He'd only recently come to appreciate the power of the intellect, and this assembly was like a trip to a NASCAR race for someone who'd just learned how to drive.

At sunset, Ramon adjourned the deliberations and the delegates retired to the unfinished condos they were using as quarters. Abandoned by a bankrupt U.S. company, the condos were rudimentary shelter—cinderblock shells without plumbing or electricity.

Inside their own condo, Mano, Jo, and Ramon unwrapped their spartan dinner—U.S. Army MREs—and ate in silence, glad for a break from the incessant talking. After their meal, Jo started a fire in the stone fireplace to ward off the biting chill of night in the high desert.

Ramon moved closer to the smoky hearth, a sleeping bag

draped over his shoulders like a robe. "I doubt the corporate architect who designed these ornamental fireplaces ever dreamed one day they'd keep a bunch of Latino rebels from freezing their asses off."

"I still wish we could've provided better quarters for the delegates," Jo said, stoking the fire. "I hope no one is offended."

Ramon grinned. "Don't worry. Most of these folks have seen some hard times lately. Three meals a day and free firewood at night is going to seem like a Club Med vacation to them."

"What's next?" Mano asked Ramon.

"Well, by tomorrow we should have the first part of the document wrapped up—an outline of our grievances against the United States. That's the easy part—mostly a matter of making a list and making sure everyone gets a chance to add their beefs."

"Then we get to the big show," Jo said.

Ramon nodded in agreement. "That's when we have to decide what the hell we want to do about these grievances. That's going to be the hard part. We're going to propose independence, but it won't be easy to pass."

"Have you been able to tell who's going to lead the opposition?" Jo asked Ramon.

Ramon rubbed his chin. "Right now, I'd say it'll be the Cubans."

"Why the Cubans?" Mano asked, intrigued by the dynamics of the assembly.

Ramon shed the sleeping bag and began pacing. "If you look at the Cubans in South Florida—along with most of the Hispanic communities along the Eastern Seaboard and the Midwest—you'll notice they all face a similar situation:

they're isolated and surrounded. The Hispanic communities of the Southwest share a border with Mexico. And our communities are denser and closer together, too."

"I understand," Mano said. "The Hispanics in the Quarantine Zones outside the Southwest are in a more precarious position."

Jo smiled. "That's right. While all our communities are in jeopardy, the Latinos outside the Southwest don't feel independence is a realistic option. They want to remain U.S. citizens. They're looking for our document to be a demand for government reforms."

"And you can't blame them," said Ramon. "With the exception of Florida, they're in territories that have never been under Hispanic control. Our historic claim to their areas is not really valid."

"But most of the delegates are from the Southwest. Couldn't you raise enough votes to override them?"

"Yes, we could, Mano. But it's not that simple," Ramon explained. "To succeed, we need the support of *all* the Hispanic leaders of North America. Our ultimate goal is to be recognized as a provisional government by the United Nations. There's little chance of that if the Hispanics of North America don't present a unified front."

Mano recalled the passion of the delegates. "It doesn't look like that's going to be easy."

"Welcome to the goat rodeo of Latino politics, amigo," Ramon said with an impish grin.

On the second day of the assembly, Mano sat through another endless series of speeches and debates in Santiago's ancient church. As Ramon had predicted, at the end of the day there was consensus on only one issue: they all wanted the document to list their grievances against the U.S. government. Beyond that, there was little agreement on what course of action to take. Even the name of the document was a subject of considerable debate.

For the next two days, Jo and Ramon worked the delegates tirelessly for the cause of independence, he from the dais, she behind the scenes. The pair hardly slept as they kept a grueling schedule of private conferences and meetings after the long days in the full assembly. Mano was astonished at their stamina.

By the fourth day, the assembly had coalesced into two factions.

Led by the Cubans, a group calling themselves the Reformers wanted to draft a document that would pressure the U.S. government to repeal the Quarantine and Relocation Act.

The Marchistas, as the other faction was being called, argued for a far more radical agenda—a declaration of independence. Led by Jo and Ramon, it represented the bulk of the Hispanic communities of the Southwest.

The factions had sparred on a number of peripheral issues. But as yet, they'd avoided a direct confrontation.

Jo, Ramon, and Mano emerged from their condo and started the short walk toward the church, the glare of the low morning sun reaching toward them from the mountain-lined horizon.

"Today we end the impasse," Ramon announced, striding briskly.

"I understand," Jo said, nodding. "I'll take care of my part."

"What's going to happen today?" Mano asked.

"You'll see very soon, amigo," Ramon replied.

When the trio entered the church, the delegates were already assembled. The buzz of casual conversations that marked the start of previous days was gone, replaced by a tense silence. Mano sat down in the first pew and was surprised to see Jo continue toward the back of the church rather than take her usual seat next to him.

Ramon rose to the dais. "Hermanas y hermanos," he began grandly, "for the last four days, we've aired the long list of grievances we have suffered at the hands of the United States government. Is there a person in this room who does not agree that our people have been the victims of a monumental injustice?" Ramon paused, sure no one would challenge him. "Then I think it's time we addressed the most critical decision this assembly will have to make. It's simply this: will this document be only a list of grievances by disgruntled citizens of the United States...or the first step in a proclamation of our independence?"

A loud chorus of cheers—along with several shouts of protest—filled the air. Ramon raised his hands to quiet the group.

"All other concerns are immaterial until we resolve this issue. Therefore, I'd like to propose we take a vote on the following question. Independence: yes or no?"

After a chorus of voices shouted their assent, Ramon nodded. "All those opposed to a declaration of independence, please stand and raise your hands."

Roughly two dozen delegates in several pockets rose and

thrust their arms into the air, their pained expressions indicating their realization of being greatly outnumbered.

Ramon waited calmly, saying nothing as the standing delegates noticed the looks of disdain around them. As the silence ground on, the posture of those on their feet began to wither. Several lowered their hands but remained standing. Then the scornful stares began taking their toll. Two of the delegates meekly sat down. Those who remained standing glanced around for support, their expressions almost pleading. They were met with hard looks of contempt.

Three more sat down.

The silence continued.

Four more sat down.

The seconds crawled by in a tense, almost unbearable quiet. Then, with the swift, synchronized motion of a school of fish, the remaining delegates sat down.

"It appears our desire for independence is unanimous," Ramon said with a gracious smile.

His words were like the breaking of a dam.

A cheer burst from the assembly as the delegates rose to their feet in a sea of hugs and handshakes. The celebrations rose to a frenzy as a succession of gongs echoed throughout the church. Someone was ringing the church bell. The archaic gesture was like a stamp of legitimacy, etching their decision into history.

It was a moment no one in the church would ever forget.

After finishing his evening meal, Mano crumpled the MRE package and placed it in one of the two bulging plastic bags in what would have been the kitchen of the condo. One bag was for recyclables, the other for regular trash. *No matter where she goes, Jo is still a tree hugger,* Mano mused.

Returning to the condo's hearth, he stretched out on his sleeping bag, enjoying the solitude after a long and momentous day. He was drifting into sleep when Ramon entered the room.

"What's this? Asleep already? Don't my speeches provide you with ample opportunities for a siesta?"

Mano sat up and grinned. "No, Ramon. It's hard work trying to stay awake during your speeches."

Ramon laughed. "Listen, amigo," he said, his voice turning serious. "There are some people Jo and I would like you to meet. Are you up for a little trip?"

"Sure," Mano said, following Ramon outside.

A waning moon above the eastern horizon covered the desert with a ghostly light that gleamed like silver plating off the agaves and acacias. Ramon led Mano through the dim landscape toward two battered buses Jo had rented to ferry many of the delegates to Santiago. Nearing the weathered vehicles, Mano noticed one of the buses had a number of people inside.

The front door of the bus opened. "All aboard," Jo said, grinning from behind the wheel. "The Santiago Express is about to leave the terminal."

The atmosphere aboard the bus was jovial, almost partylike, as they traveled south on the town's only road. Mano was certain most of those on the bus had not endured the grind of negotiating with the Reformers and were still giddy with the excitement of the morning's proceedings. In the dim light, Mano could make out a number of familiar faces. All of them were Marchistas.

After several miles, Jo pulled the bus onto the shoulder,

lit a gas lantern, and rose to face those aboard. "Hermanos, what we did today will go down in history. You have helped conceive a new nation." Jo's words were delivered slowly, with power and dignity. "I guess that makes you a great bunch of fuckers, eh?" she added sweetly.

The men in the bus went wild at her raunchy joke, laughing so hard Mano found it impossible not to join in.

Jo waved her arms to calm the group down. "I want to salute you for the effort you gave today. Ramon told me the stares you and your people gave the Reformers would have melted ice. This day would not have been possible without you."

"Let's hear it for the lady in the bell tower!" a voice called out, sparking a round of energetic cheers.

So that's where Jo went, Mano realized.

"Thank you," Jo said, acknowledging the applause. "But we still have some unfinished business," she said in a more somber tone. "Creating a declaration of independence is only the first part of the challenge we face. We've asserted our moral right to reclaim our land. In fact, we'll petition the United Nations for recognition as a sovereign state. But we have to back up our declaration with action. If we don't, what we've done today will be just words on a piece of paper."

Jo began pacing the aisle. "Now, let's be realistic. The U.S. government has the resources to outlast us and the power to outgun us. It's not a case of a lightweight in the ring with a heavyweight. This is a fight between a lightweight and Godzilla."

She paused as a number of the men laughed. "But if we don't take action, we'll be ignored by the media. And media attention is how we'll get the U.S. public to say, 'These Hispanics are just too damned crazy. They're too fanatical. Let them have their territory. It's the only way we'll have peace.' And that, hermanos, is how we'll win.

"The U.S. government is overcommitted militarily right now," Jo continued. "Their best-trained and best-equipped troops are overseas. We'll never have a better time.

"That's why we need to plan a national offensive *now*. A day when we strike *together* across the entire United States. It will send a clear and unmistakable message: We are *united*. We are a *nation*," she said, pounding her fist into her palm.

A wave of applause punctuated her statement.

Jo sat down, relinquishing the floor to Ramon.

"This blow we strike together must be seared into the memory of our enemies," Ramon began. "We must choose a day that will be remembered, a day that will define our cause, a day on whose anniversary future generations will speak of our struggle with pride." He paused. "And so I propose that we strike on the twentieth of May—the birthday of José Antonio Marcha."

Ramon's inspiration brought another vigorous round of cheers.

A large, swarthy man rose to speak. It was Octavio Perez, the activist who had spoken at the rally in Salazar Park. "Hermanos, just as we have all gotten behind this declaration of independence, we all must get behind this action now. I can tell you that we, the leaders of the resistance in San Antonio, will lay down our lives if necessary to advance the Marcha Offensive. Is there anyone else with the cojones to join us?"

The swell of assenting voices filled the bus.

"My heart is warmed by your courage," Ramon said humbly. "Now that you've decided to come to the party, amigos, it's time to dance with the devil and work out the details," he said with a grin. "To do that, I'd like to turn these proceedings over to a man whose wits and courage have shown he is eminently qualified to advise us in military matters. For those of you who don't already know him, I'd like to introduce our director of security in Los Angeles, Manolo Suarez—El Grande."

Judging by the loud applause, the people aboard the bus knew something of Mano's reputation. Mano rose and awkwardly acknowledged their tribute.

Ramon then unfolded a large map of North America and addressed the delegates. "We need to coordinate the timing, location, and type of attacks each of our organizations will undertake. I propose that Mano serve as an advisor and have the final decision on any disputes. Do you agree?"

The group shouted their affirmation.

Ramon smiled at them serenely. "Good. Then let's get to work."

At dawn, the ramshackle bus lumbered slowly into Santiago, the passengers weary but satisfied. The tactical plans for the Marcha Offensive were complete.

After nine days of intense deliberations, the assembly in Santiago reached a final agreement. Signed by all the delegates, it was called La Declaración de Santiago—the Santiago Declaration. Authored by Josefina Maria Herrera, the document was divided into four sections.

The first section listed the grievances of North America's Hispanics against the U.S. government. Primary among these injustices was the creation of the Relocation Communities and the Quarantine Zones.

The second section detailed the legitimacy of the Latino

territorial claims to the former Hispanic regions currently under United States control. Large portions of Arizona, California, Florida, New Mexico, and Texas were designated in the claim. Following the stratagem drawn up by José Antonio Marcha, the document used the State of Israel as precedent for a displaced people's historical claim to their former territory. A special note was made that the United States was the first country to recognize the sovereign status of Israel.

The third section outlined the structure of a provisional government, called La Republica Hispána de Norteamérica—the Hispanic Republic of North America. This provisional government would petition for a seat in the United Nations. The delegates elected a rotating set of U.N. representatives, and plans were drawn up for a constitutional convention, followed by popular elections within one year after U.N. recognition.

The final section, as a concession to the Reformers, had two clauses. Clause one stated that if the United Nations did not recognize the Hispanic Republic of North America, it would still grant the signers of the document diplomatic immunity under international law. Clause two explained that in the event the Hispanic Republic of North America received U.N. recognition, any Hispanics who chose to remain in the United States would retain all personal property and avoid criminal prosecution.

A copy of the Santiago Declaration was leaked to a local CBS affiliate in San Francisco two weeks after the document was signed. Its release was delayed to give the delegates time to slip back across the border.

Less than two hours after the document arrived at the Bay Area station, the story was picked up by CBS for its national feed. Before the day was over, the report would snowball into an avalanche of media coverage.

THE QUARANTINE AND RELOCATION ACT:
Month 17, Day 14

Hank Evans's phone had been ringing since he'd arrived at his office twenty minutes earlier. He'd been tempted to unplug the desk unit or disconnect the ringer, but tampering with a CIA phone was a federal crime.

The insistent warbling was irritating, but he knew better than to answer the phone this morning. Following yesterday's release of the Santiago Declaration, a blame storm of epic proportions was brewing at the White House and its fury would be directed squarely at the CIA. With the Brenner team in the middle of a reelection campaign, the media bombshell had been devastating.

Editorials across the nation were accusing the president of being caught flat-footed at home by a preoccupation with his international agenda. One widely distributed political cartoon depicted President Brenner blithely juggling a series of flaming torches labeled Afghanistan, Iran, Iraq, Korea, Pakistan, and Venezuela while a mouse wearing a Mexican sombrero gleefully gave him a hot foot. The media circus also had a serious side.

The *Wall Street Journal* declared the Santiago Declaration the most significant challenge to U.S. sovereignty since the Civil War. Some blamed the administration for responding too timidly to the insurgents. Others claimed repressive government policies had been the cause of the insurgency. Not surprisingly, an overnight *USA Today* poll showed President Brenner's approval ratings plummeting.

Evans had been through this kind of PR nightmare before. You kept low until tempers cooled and then went to work to fix the problem. So he ignored the phone and continued his review of field agent budget reports.

While he was finishing his second cherry danish, his administrative assistant entered the office trembling and near tears. "I'm sorry, Hank," she said, handing him a vuphone set on hold. "It's Mrs. Phelps from Washington. She said if I don't find you right away and put this phone in your hand, I'm gonna be fired."

Evans put down the pastry and reached for the phone in disgust. *It's just like Carol Phelps to bully a GS5*, he thought as his assistant retreated from the office.

"Hello, Carol," Evans said cautiously after reconnecting the line.

"This is the last straw, Evans," said the assistant director of the CIA tersely.

"Now look, Carol," Evans said quickly. "I've thought about it, and there's an upside to this. Now we have the names of all the ringleaders."

"You've had the names of many of these people for nearly a year. How many of them are in custody?"

"We're trying to keep tails on them."

"Keep tails on them? Judging by the smarts you've shown so far, Evans, I wouldn't be surprised if there's a tail on your copious ass right now."

"All right, goddammit! I'm going to give it to you straight,

Carol," Evans shouted angrily. "My people are working as hard as they can under the severe handicap your administration has placed on us. First, you cut our budgets. And then you played politics with our national security by locking up our Hispanic agents—"

Phelps cut him off. "I'm not buying your excuses, Hank. If you need to get tough with your mole, do it. Tell him it's your hide or his."

"What are you saying, Carol? That we should threaten the life of an American citizen if he doesn't cooperate with us? Why not, huh? I mean, we've taken away their political rights. Why not just chuck the whole Bill of Rights?"

"Save your little civics lecture, Hank. We're sending a bill to the Hill tomorrow that's going to make it a capital crime to take part in any kind of terrorist activity. We've had it on the shelf for a while, and after this Santiago business, it's going to pass through Congress faster than crap through a goose. So I'm warning you now, Hank. You won't be able to hide behind the Constitution to cover your incompetence anymore."

"Carol, I—"

"I'm not finished," she snapped. "These embarrassments have got to stop. Do you hear me? We're not going to let a bunch of pissant Pancho Villas make us look like fools in front of the world. This will not be the first administration in American history to cede U.S. territory. You do whatever is necessary to take these people out. I want these terrorists, Hank—and I don't care if it's in a body bag. Do I make myself clear? Or do I need to appoint another director in your region?"

Evans stared back at Phelps, saying nothing. He had known it would come to this. His integrity was at stake.

He would have to resign.

Then a wave of fear flooded his mind, dissolving his will like an acid. *Am I ready to throw away my career? How long will it take me to find another job in this economy? Besides, if I resign, who'll maintain the Agency's integrity?*

"I understand, Carol," Evans finally said, lowering his eyes. "I'll get it done."

"The next time I see any of the names from this god-damned Santiago Declaration, I expect it to be on an indict-ment... or in the obituaries," Phelps said and hung up.

Staring at the vu-phone in his plump hand, Evans felt incredibly heavy, like his bones were filled with lead. He reached for his desk phone and slowly pressed the keys.

"Bill Perkins," said the voice on the line.

"Bill, you need to reach our mole at the DDP right away. We've got to put the squeeze on him—hard."

Nine days later, his computer linked to C-SPAN, Hank Evans watched the Senate vote the Terrorist Arraignment Act into law—exactly as Carol Phelps had predicted. The core of the new legislation called for charges of high trea-son against anyone convicted of fomenting sedition, making their actions punishable by death.

The threat of execution now loomed over every rebel—and anyone who aided them.

———

"What is it, Mami?" Pedro asked his mother. "What's the mat-ter?" The boy had never seen Rosa cry before—not even after his sister's death.

Seated on the edge of her bunk, Rosa was staring at a much-handled newspaper, her eyes red-rimmed and distant. Only last week, she'd heard a frightening rumor spread through the camp: anyone caught aiding the rebellion—in any way—would be charged with treason and condemned to death. The newspaper had confirmed the rumor. They were calling the new law the Terrorist Arraignment Act. But there was something more shocking in the worn copy of the *Bismarck Tribune* being furtively circulated around the camp.

In an adjacent story, the paper had printed the complete text of the Santiago Declaration, including the names of all those who had signed the document. Among the signers was Manolo Suarez.

Thank you, Blessed Virgin, Rosa said silently to the statue's mended remnants. *At least I know he's alive.* But the authorities now had Mano's name. How much longer could he evade them? Although teetering between relief and fear, Rosa found something unexpected welling inside her: pride in her husband.

Pedro touched Rosa's shoulder, drawing her back from her trance. "Why are you crying, Mami?"

Rosa wiped her cheeks and slid the newspaper under the covers. "I'm happy. That's all. Women sometimes cry when they're happy," she said, surprised to find her words were actually true. The bleak news had somehow raised her spirits.

Pedro pulled back the blanket and pointed to the newspaper. "Something you read in there made you happy?"

A sliver of a smile formed on Rosa's face; her son was no longer so easy to fool. "Yes, m'hijo."

"What does it say?"

It was useless to hide the news, Rosa realized. The boy

would find out anyway. "You can read it if you want," she said, handing him the newspaper.

Watching her son scan the page, Rosa felt a sense of revelation. No matter how Mano felt about Josefina, she had no doubts he loved his children. If her husband had willingly parted with Elena and Pedro, it was for something he believed deeply. Mano had never started a fight in his life, but he would never back down from one to protect his loved ones. Now, with her husband's life at stake, she finally understood why he had joined the rebels.

The country had divided and they no longer had a choice.

Like it or not, all Hispanics were her people now. Their fate was her fate. There was no room left in the middle. *It's for our children that I'm doing this*, Mano had told her. She now grasped why. Their future would depend on how all Hispanics were treated. In many ways, she'd sensed it all along. Little by little, since the day she'd boarded the bus for this camp, Rosa had felt herself grow more distant from the country she once called home. She could see now that Elena's death had marked her final break with the Anglo world.

"There's Papi's name!" Pedro said proudly, holding out the paper.

Rosa's face warmed. She could not remember the last time Pedro had shown pride in his father. "Yes, m'hijo."

"I don't get a lot of this stuff written here, Mami. Why is Papi in the newspaper?"

Rosa gently cradled Pedro's face in her hands. "Your father's name is there because he's done something very brave."

THE QUARANTINE AND RELOCATION ACT:
Month 18, Day 5

Mano knocked on the meat locker door and entered Ramon's library after hearing his friend's voice invite him inside.

"I'm guessing you've come to spar about some topic again," Ramon said, seated in one of the room's two plush leather chairs.

Carrying a cardboard portfolio, Mano dropped into the chair opposite Ramon. "Yes, but I think my chances would be better if we arm-wrestled."

Ramon laughed. "So what's the subject this time?"

"I've been reading Marcha," Mano said, pulling out a stack of loose sheets from the folder. "The guy was a loser, Ramon. He was a hotel clerk."

Since parting from his family, reading had become Mano's refuge from the stress of battle and the emptiness of his solitary life. He'd embraced the endeavor with the same methodical discipline he still devoted to his physical training. His frequent debates with Ramon on what he'd read were a natural extension of his competitive nature.

Ramon tapped his chin, gathering his thoughts, and then said, "Mano, are you familiar with Thomas Paine?"

"I remember his name from school. Something to do with the American Revolution, right?"

"That's right. Paine wrote *Common Sense*, one of the most compelling arguments for American independence. He persuaded a lot of colonists to oppose British rule. But what they probably didn't tell you in school was that Paine was penniless most of his life. He died a drunken pauper. But that doesn't mean what he wrote was worthless. Sometimes a man's ideas are far greater than the man himself." Ramon paused. "Jo understood this when she began translating Marcha's writings into English. You should ask her opinion sometime."

"OK, I see your point. But there's a lot more that bothers me about Marcha. For example, he wrote, 'Words that inspire us to valiant deeds can be hindered by petty details.' Wasn't he justifying the use of lies?"

"Bending the truth is a staple of politics, Mano. Do you think any government could operate without lying? Let's take the most honest nation on earth today—the United States. The U.S. went to war in Vietnam over a fabricated incident in the Gulf of Tonkin. And what about Iraq? Has anyone yet found the weapons of mass destruction used to justify that invasion? History is full of half-truths governments have used to rouse their people into fighting."

"You're saying it's necessary for a government to lie?"

"Plato said lying is a privilege that should be reserved only for those who govern—and that was over two thousand years ago," Ramon said, grinning. "Look at it this way. It's impossible to maintain security without withholding the truth. If we revealed our location to the baldies, we'd be in jail before dark, or dead by morning. Every government faces the same challenge. They must keep secrets. Once you're maintain-

ing secrets, the next logical step is to misdirect the enemy
with false information. We've done that, too, through Nesto.
Once you've accepted that kind of truth-bending, it becomes
easier to justify feeding your people half-truths."

"It still seems wrong."

"That's why it's important for citizens to question their
governments. Each person has to think critically about the
real motives behind the patriotic rhetoric of any government. Flag-waving is usually used to distract you from the
real motives of the people in power. It's also a highly effective
motivator."

"Are you saying it's wrong to be patriotic?"

"People are driven to act by emotions, Mano. A well-
reasoned argument may get a person to nod her head in
agreement, but very little else. To get a person to act, you
need to create strong emotions—fear, anger, hate, even love.
Every smart leader knows you can't motivate a person into
action through intellectual arguments alone. That's why they
often resort to emotional patriotic appeals, which by their
very nature are overly simplistic and usually shortsighted."

"So you agree with Marcha? You think that lying is not
only acceptable, it's actually necessary?"

"Yes, put very simply, that's correct, Mano."

"That's dishonest, Ramon."

"Perhaps. But Marcha was expressing an idealized version
of reality. Don't you think Thomas Jefferson idealized reality
when he was drafting the Declaration of Independence? Jefferson wrote, 'We hold these truths to be self-evident. That
all men are created equal.' Yet Jefferson was not only a slave-
holder, he kept in bondage the very children he fathered
with his slave Sally Hemings. That, however, did not stop him

from creating the most beautiful and important words ever written on human freedom. Does the fact that Jefferson was a hypocrite make his ideals any less worthy?"

"Are you a hypocrite, Ramon?"

"There are worse things I could be called."

"What could be worse than being a hypocrite?"

Ramon paused before answering. "Being apathetic. Not fighting for those less fortunate. Ignoring the struggle of our people."

Mano considered Ramon's words. His motives were worthy. But there was a part of Mano that felt the right motives were not enough to justify doing something he knew was wrong.

"There has to be a better way, Ramon."

Ramon yawned. "That's not a problem we'll solve tonight, amigo," he said, rising from the chair. "These old bones need some rest."

"Mind if I stay? I've been wanting to check out the Tolstoy books you suggested."

"You're always welcome, Mano. Stay as long as you like," Ramon said before leaving.

Mano was into the second chapter of *War and Peace* when the room's heavy door opened and Jo stepped inside.

"I thought you might be here," she said, her face pale and strained. "Have you been listening to the news?"

"No," Mano said, raising Tolstoy's novel as an explanation.

"Some BBC reports have been coming out of North Dakota that have me worried."

"What kind of reports?"

"Apparently the government has been covering it up for months, but the story broke today," she said anxiously. "There were over seven thousand deaths in the Relocation Communities last winter."

Mano rose to his feet. "Rosa and the children?"

"I don't know. The BBC reported the number of dead by Community, but they don't have individual names. One of the hardest hit was Community Number Eight. They had more than two thousand deaths."

"That's where..." Mano's voice trailed off, unable to say the words aloud.

"We don't know anything for certain, Mano. Your family may be fine."

Mano stood motionless, his eyes vacant. When he finally spoke, his voice was flat and dull. "You don't understand, Jo—I thought I'd finally found it. Since the day all this killing started, all I wanted was to find a place where my family would finally be out of danger. That was the only thing that kept me going sometimes. But it's gone, Jo. That place is gone now."

A wave of remorse engulfed Jo. "This is my fault," she said as a line of tears began a slow descent down her cheeks.

Her tears tore into Mano's heart as deeply as the news of his family. He met her gaze, eyes alive once again. "You only did what you thought was right," he said gently. "I don't blame you."

"You're a good man, Mano—and I took advantage of that," she said, her lips trembling. "I talked you into sending your family away without really questioning why I did it—or what might happen to them. That was a horrible thing to do."

"Don't do this to yourself, Jo. You couldn't have known this would happen."

Jo shook her head. "No. You trusted me and I deceived

you. I even tried to hide it from myself. But the truth is that I asked you to send them away because I—"

Before she could finish, Mano embraced her.

For a long time, they clung to each other tightly. Holding Jo, Mano found a solace missing since the parting from his family. He let himself bask in the warmth of her touch. Jo's body was supple and yielding; her hands caressed his back. Close against him, the pressure of her firm breasts on his chest, Mano felt the passion rising in his loins. He'd fought back fantasies of making love to Jo. Now the moment that had tortured and tantalized him for so long was finally here.

He wanted Jo. But he wanted to rejoin his family even more.

Rosa might still be alive and he could not betray her.

Mano tenderly lifted Jo's face toward his own. "It's time to go," he said softly. "People are depending on us."

As news of the deaths at the Relocation Communities spread, the consequences of the Brenner team's attempts to cover up the tragedy would reverberate around the world.

Following the BBC reports of massive fatalities at the camps in North Dakota, the United Nations passed an unprecedented resolution. It called for an investigation into charges of genocide by the United States. France and Germany, long estranged from the U.S., led a Security Council coalition leveling the accusations. Within days, teams of investigators from the U.N. and the International Red Cross descended on North Dakota, demanding to inspect the camps.

The response of many Americans was outrage. The U.S. had been charged with committing one of history's most heinous crimes—by an organization on its own soil. Political momentum gathered behind a movement once supported only by the far right: withdrawal from the United Nations.

Congressman Melvin Bates once again stepped into the political maelstrom, proposing a House resolution that would end U.S. participation in the United Nations. Some pundits said Bates, a man addicted to media attention, was grandstanding. Others claimed he was desperately attempting to retain the eroding support of followers disillusioned by the mounting failures of the Quarantine and Relocation Act. The U.N. issue became another hotly debated topic in a nation already racked with discord.

Tensions outside U.S. borders were escalating as well. The often stormy relations between the United States and Latin America were at an all-time low. Under the Quarantine and Relocation Act, not just illegal immigrants were being deported. Green-card-carrying legal residents from Latin America were also banished. The millions of deportees were creating economic havoc in their countries of origin, swamping job markets and depriving these nations of the hard currency their U.S. workers often sent home to their families. A resolution of protest was filed against this new U.S. policy at the Organization of American States.

The widening rift between the U.S. and the European Union was now nearing the breaking point. America's succession of military incursions into Islamic nations was the cause of constant turmoil among the fast-growing Muslim populations of Western Europe. Many pundits claimed the E.U.'s leaders secretly hoped America's domestic problems would slow its military adventures overseas.

Meanwhile, the American government had ceased all

attempts at maintaining control within the Quarantine Zones. Once used as holding areas for Hispanics awaiting relocation, the zones had become insurgent bastions. "The Strategy Backfires," read a *Newsweek* cover featuring a photo of armed insurgents guarding the wall inside San Antonio's Quarantine Zone. The magazine reported that internees in South Texas were defiantly calling the QZ El Nuevo Alamo—the New Alamo.

U.S. military efforts were now focused on stemming the tide of insurgent raids into vacated areas adjacent to the QZs across the Southwest.

THE QUARANTINE AND RELOCATION ACT:
Month 19, Day 5

Community Number Eight's fluorescent mess hall lights flickered back to life, flooding the crowded room with a cold, harsh light. Rising to her feet near a primordial 16mm projector, the female missionary addressed the audience. "On behalf of the First Apostolic Church, I want to thank you for attending tonight's film. We certainly hope you enjoyed it," she said, primly smoothing out her dress.

After a smattering of polite applause, the crowd began clearing the room.

Rosa looked around warily as she shepherded Pedro out of the mess hall. Although the film was a welcome break in their bleak existence, Rosa had been hesitant to attend the missionary's showing of *The Ten Commandments*. Trouble seemed to be looming, despite the easing of the camp's severe food rationing.

Last week, foreigners had visited the camp. Through an interpreter, one of them had asked her questions about living conditions. Rosa had answered cautiously, suspicious of a ploy by the authorities to uncover troublemakers. Perhaps this missionary was part of a similar scheme.

Rosa watched anxiously as the missionary addressed each

family on their way out of the mess hall. There was something contradictory about the tall blonde. Her drab outfit and out-moded glasses seemed almost deliberately unattractive.

As Rosa got nearer the exit, her heart fluttered. The missionary was casting sidelong glances in her direction. *Is she another spy like Maria Prado, trying to find Mano?* One thing was certain. There would be no way to avoid her. The woman had planted herself near the doorway and was speaking to everyone as they exited.

"How do you do? I'm Emily Barnett," the missionary said, extending her hand to Rosa.

"I'm Rosa Suarez," she said coolly. "This is my son, Pedro." As she took the woman's hand, Rosa was startled by a sensation in her palm. The missionary had covertly handed her a folded piece of paper.

"I'll be visiting with families individually, Mrs. Suarez. Perhaps we can spend some time together."

"I'm...I'm not sure that would be a good idea," Rosa replied, keeping the note out of sight.

"Please think it over. I'm staying in the guest cabin at the south end of the camp."

After donning the Army surplus coats Rosa and Pedro had been issued the previous week, the two returned to their dormitory. Once she'd put her son to bed, Rosa slipped into the communal restroom and examined the note in one of the stalls.

Querida,
Josefina Herrera is delivering this note.
Talk to her. She is there to help you.
I am well. My love to you and the children.
—Mano

Rosa's hands trembled as she read the small note. It was Mano's handwriting. A warm flush of joy rose in her chest. He was still alive.

It was the first good news Rosa had received since arriving at the Relocation Community nearly a year ago. She felt light and giddy. She wanted to yell in triumph. Then the doubts crept in.

Was this woman really Josefina Herrera? Having never met Jo, Rosa could not be certain. She would need to meet with the woman again. There had to be some way to confirm her identity.

———

Maria Prado was unable to sleep once again, tossing beside her husband as she relived moments from her CIA career.

It was a melancholy reverie.

She'd had a promising future. Then it had all ended, her career severed with the swiftness of a guillotine—all because a few Hispanic extremists had terrified the nation with their mindless rebellion.

The mugshots of the many Hispanic radicals she'd investigated passed fleetingly through her half-awake mind—a gallery of rogues that tormented her frequently. Then a face drifted into Maria's hazy consciousness that brought her suddenly upright—Josefina Herrera's.

Herrera bore an uncanny resemblance to the missionary who'd hosted the film earlier that evening. If you stripped away the glasses and the dowdy clothes, the woman looked very much like the striking blonde on the podium at the rally in East Los Angeles. Was it really her?

The outline of a plan began forming in Maria's mind. If

it really was Josefina Herrera, and Maria could unmask her, it would prove, beyond any doubt, Maria's loyalty to the U.S. And if she could turn in one of the insurgents' top leaders, she and her family might be released from this wretched place.

Tomorrow morning, she'd find out more about this "missionary."

―――――

Arriving in the early morning frost, Rosa knocked hesitantly on the guest cabin's wind-worn door. She'd slept little, weighing the risks of visiting this woman whose cabin was next to the guard station. In the end, the chance for news of Mano had swept aside her qualms.

"Good morning, Mrs. Suarez. How good to see you," the blonde said warmly after opening the door. "Won't you please come in?"

"Good morning—"

Before Rosa could say more, the woman raised her index finger to her lips, pointed to her ear, and waved her hand around the room. Rosa immediately understood her message. The room was bugged.

"I walk every morning. Good for the figure, you know. Would you care to join me?" the blonde asked, reaching for her coat.

"Yes...all right."

The two women left the cabin, wordlessly following the frosty trail along the edge of the camp. Patches of morning fog hung over the flat plain that receded into the distant horizon.

"Who are you?" Rosa asked once she was sure they were out of earshot.

"I'm Josefina Herrera. I'm here because Mano is worried

about you and the children. We got the news last week about all the deaths in the camps."

Rosa was still uncertain. This woman certainly fit the description of Jo reported by Nana Jimenez. But Rosa's experience with Maria Prado had made her leery.

"Why should I believe you?"

"Mano warned me that you'd be cautious," Jo said, smiling. "He told me your younger sister named her first kitten Felix. Then it turned out Felix was a girl."

Rosa looked into the woman's ice-blue eyes, still not certain she could believe her.

"Mano said you two met at his cousin's wedding," Jo continued.

Rosa gazed back, saying nothing.

"You were your cousin's bridesmaid," Jo added. "Mano asked you to dance and you said no. It wasn't until you were properly introduced by his aunt that you agreed to dance with him."

Rosa remained impassive.

"OK, here's my last card, Rosa: your first dance with Mano was to 'Loving Feeling' by the Righteous Brothers. That's it," Jo said with a grin. "If you don't believe me, I'm going back to Los Angeles."

Rosa's expression at last softened, then hardened again. "You have a lot of nerve showing your face here," she said coldly.

"Yes, I do, Rosa. If I'm caught, I'll probably be executed."

Rosa lowered her eyes in shame. "I'm sorry. I should have realized you're here trying to help."

"There's no need to apologize, Rosa. I can't begin to imagine how much you've suffered."

"How is Mano?"

"He misses you and the children very much, Rosa. When he heard how many in this camp had died, he was ready to come here himself. It took a lot of arguing, but I finally convinced him there was much less of a chance that I'd get caught."

"Thank God you did. Once his mind is made up, it's hard to change."

"He's as strong as two mules...and just as stubborn."

The women shared a soft, knowing laugh.

"You've brought me good news, Josefina. I'm happy to know Mano is still alive. It's been so long since I heard from him, I was starting to lose hope."

"I want to take back good news to Mano. But yesterday I only saw Pedro," Jo said, unable to put the dreadful thought into words.

"Elena died last November," Rosa said, her voice quaking. "It was a virus. She didn't suffer, thank God."

The words staggered Jo. "I'm sorry, Rosa. I'm so sorry," she said, tears welling in her eyes. "I would give anything...anything...to bring your child back. It's my fault, Rosa. I told Mano you and the children would be safer here...and I was wrong."

Jo covered her face with her hands and wept. News of Elena's death laid bare her ruthless zeal. Worse still, she knew the news would devastate Mano. The thought of hurting him deepened her pain.

Rosa clasped Jo's shoulders tenderly. "I've known for a long time that you wanted us sent here, Josefina," Rosa said, then gently turned the blonde toward her until their eyes met. "What I've realized today is that you truly believed it was for our own good."

"There's more, Rosa," Jo said, still weeping softly. "When the riots were just starting in the barrios, I paid a gang leader to provoke more trouble. I thought more rioting would help our cause. Later I found out the mero I paid killed two policemen in cold blood. God help me, Rosa. I never intended for those men to die."

Rosa said nothing. Like most women, she understood Jo did not need someone who would judge her—just someone who would listen.

"Don't you see, Rosa? Those deaths were more than cold-blooded murder. They provoked the vigilante attacks, and that's led to so much killing...even the deaths of your children."

Rosa slipped her arm under Jo's and began pulling the blonde on the trail alongside her. "Josefina, the deaths of my children were God's will. We're all his instruments. You don't need to torture yourself about it...or flatter yourself, chica. You're not as powerful as you think," she added with a small smile.

For several minutes, the two women walked quietly, their arms interlocked. After the trail dipped into a low spot, Jo reached under her coat and produced a money belt. "There's thirty thousand dollars in here, Rosa," she said, opening one of the bulging pouches.

This time, Rosa did not spurn Jo's generosity. "Thank you, Josefina. Things have been hard here—this will help," She said, slipping the belt under her coat.

"I have to leave tomorrow, Rosa. The longer I stay, the more dangerous it gets."

"Keep your eyes open for a woman named Maria Prado. I think she may be a snitch," Rosa said as they walked back toward the compound.

"Gracias, mi hermana," Jo replied, squeezing Rosa's arm affectionately.

"Tell Mano I miss him and I pray every day we can be together again soon. But tell him I know that won't happen until the struggle for justicia is over."

"Rosa, there's something I want you to know," Jo said and then paused, searching for the right words. "Mano is still your husband. And he always will be."

Spying on the guest cabin from a crowded place near the mess hall, Maria spotted the "missionary" returning to the shabby hut alongside another woman. As the pair drew closer, Maria recognized the blonde woman's companion. It was Rosa Suarez.

That proves it. This has to be Josefina Herrera, thought Maria, recalling the photo of Herrera and Manolo Suarez on the podium at the East L.A. rally. Now she needed to trick the blonde into revealing her identity.

Maria watched as Rosa and Herrera parted. The blonde then returned to her cabin. A few moments later, Maria knocked on the door.

"Good morning. I'm Maria Prado. We met last night," Maria said politely as Jo answered the door.

"Good morning, Mrs. Prado. What can I do for you?" Jo said, standing in the doorway.

"There's something urgent I need to discuss. May I come in?"

"Yes, of course," Jo said, stepping back from the door.

Maria closed the door behind her and looked out the window before addressing the blonde. "Look, I can't tell you how I found out, but I know you're Josefina Herrera."

"I'm sorry," Jo said slowly. "I don't know what you're talking about."

"It's OK. You can cut the act with me. I'm here because I want to help our cause."

"I'm sorry, Mrs. Prado. Apparently you have me confused with someone else."

"You don't trust me. I understand. Listen, I was with the CIA for fourteen years. But I don't support the government anymore. I'm on your side now."

"I don't know what you're talking about, ma'am. But I'm afraid I'm going to have to ask you to leave."

"Don't be a fool, Herrera. I'm ready to give your side secrets about the government's intelligence community."

Jo picked up the phone on the small table by the bed. "If you don't leave this minute, Mrs. Prado, I'm going to call security."

"Go ahead, Herrera. Call security. You're the one they're going to take away. I know all about you and—"

Before Maria could finish, the front door flew open and two burly guards burst into the room. In a blur of motion, one of the men wrestled Prado to the floor and handcuffed her.

"Let me go, you idiot! I'm with the CIA!" Maria screamed as the men dragged her outside.

"Sorry about this, ma'am," the other guard said to Jo. "These people have some nerve, don't they? Imagine her thinking you was a beaner like her. It's no wonder we had to lock them all up. You can't trust any of 'em."

THE QUARANTINE AND RELOCATION ACT: *Month 19, Day 11*

Refried beans are just not the same without manteca," Juana muttered to herself while blending a brown paste of cooked pintos in a bowl. A staple of most Mexican dishes, manteca—lard—was nearly impossible to find these days. "Thank you, Señor, for the beans at least," she said, turning her eyes to the kitchen ceiling, "although my ungrateful husband will complain anyway." Juana's pintos had come from her new backyard garden, a practice spreading quickly in the zones thanks to Jo.

While frying the mashed beans in a black iron skillet, Juana heard footsteps approaching the kitchen.

"Don't make anything for me tonight, Juana," Mano said wearily from the doorway. "I'm too tired to eat."

"It's been two days since you've had a bite, Mano. Eat something."

"Thank you, Juana. I'm not hungry."

"If you promise to eat something, I'll give you some news."

"News?" Mano asked anxiously. Jo was due back any day.

"Sit down and eat, niño," Juana said, bringing the skillet to the table. "Look, I just made some refried beans."

"Juana, please. I'll eat later. What's the news?"

Juana shook her head in frustration. "You're a good man, Mano. But sometimes you can be as hardheaded as my worthless husband." She then sighed and said, "Josefina is back. She was here looking for you."

Mano's face froze. "What did she say?"

"She said she'd wait for you at Ramon's library. I'll have more beans ready anytime you—"

Before Juana could finish, he was out the door.

Once on the street, Mano broke into a run. The library was over two kilometers away and he was exhausted, but his pent-up anxiety drove him ahead. Over the last eleven days, he had found that waiting helplessly to learn the fate of his family was harder than risking his life to save them.

As he arrived at the gutted restaurant where Ramon's collection of books was hidden, Mano stopped running. Like a man facing an execution, he tried to calm his mind, preparing himself to accept whatever fate awaited him.

He walked deliberately to the back of the building. The meat locker door was unlocked. Opening it, he saw Jo's back as she paced nervously.

When she turned to face him, her expression confirmed his worst fears.

Guillermo was sweeping the living room floor when Mano emerged from his bedroom carrying a heavy backpack, his head swathed in a turban.

"It looks like you're going outside the zone, eh?"

Mano nodded. "I am."

"That's good, Mano. You need to get back into the struggle again. Taking on the baldies will do you good. Look, I know learning about your daughter was hard. But life goes on, mi amigo," the old man said gently. "I know. I lost one of my own kids. It's been thirty-two years and it still hurts."

"A father doesn't expect to outlive his children, does he?"

"No. But only God knows why he takes them from us. It's our job to take care of those that are left... and ourselves."

Both men stood quietly for a time, recalling memories of children they would never see again. For the last twenty-four hours, Mano had done little more than grieve. Worse than the pain was the emptiness he felt at the loss of Elena.

Mano finally broke the silence. "Guillermo, I'm leaving now and I may not come back."

"No, Mano. You're made of iron," Guillermo said, smiling. "You always come back from a mission."

"It's not a mission. I'm going to the Relocation Community. Rosa and Pedro need me."

The old man scratched his head in disbelief. "Mira, Mano. I'm just a dumb old man who never got past the fifth grade. But even I'm smart enough to know this isn't a wise thing to do."

"You said it yourself, Guillermo. It's our job to take care of those who are left."

"Yes, if there's something you can do for them. But right now, your wife and son are still better off where they are. You'll be lucky if you make it to the camp alive. And even if you get there, what are you going to do for your family? Most likely, you'll bring more trouble on them than if you stayed away. If they're caught with you, they can be put to death, too."

"I know. But they're in danger in the camp, Guillermo. Trying to get them out is the best I can do."

"The best thing you can do for them is simple, amigo—keep

fighting. If we keep fighting, one day the gabachos will have to make a deal with us. That's how you'll get your family back. Don't throw your life away on a foolish gesture. Getting yourself killed is not going to keep your family safe." Guillermo grabbed Mano's hand. "Make a promise to an old man. Promise me you'll think about this one more day before you leave."

"All right, viejo. I'll think about it."

For the rest of the day, Mano wandered through the zone's battle-ravaged streets, mulling over the old man's words. He was aching with the need to act *now*. He wanted desperately to rescue his family. But in his heart, he knew Guillermo was right.

Near dusk, he reached a decision. It was a long shot, but it was the only hope he had left.

He would stay and fight—and he would make them pay.

THE QUARANTINE AND RELOCATION ACT:
Month 20, Day 14

Cresting a small rise in the road, Jesús Lopez caught his first glimpse of the brightly lit gate of Outpost Bravo. The beam of his headlights and the harsh floodlights of the outpost were the only breaks in the darkness of the surrounding landscape. Only last year, this had been a bustling suburb of Los Angeles. Now it was a desolate area full of dark and empty houses.

Approaching the garrison, Jesús eased the F-250 pickup close to the heavily fortified gate and rolled down the window. A corporal approached the vehicle, his M16 slung casually over his shoulder.

From the pocket of his weathered chocolate-chip fatigues, Jesús produced an identification card and printed orders, wordlessly handing them to the guard. The photograph on the ID card identified Jesús's ebony face as Private First Class Terrell Mayfield, a National Guard reservist. The orders directed Private Mayfield to report to Outpost Bravo for two weeks of active duty. To enhance the illusion, the truck's doors were equipped with magnetic signs that read "Mayfield & Sons Construction Company." The work-worn pickup looked authentic, with a tool compartment in the bed and a hydraulic winch on the front bumper.

While the corporal examined the documents, a second guard approached the truck with a dog that sniffed the vehicle for explosives. As the soldier conducted his search, Jesús tried not to glance at the Glock-32 tucked inside the door—a last resort if his cover failed.

The guard handed the papers back to Jesús with a sneer. An Army regular, the corporal disdained weekend warriors who came straggling in the night before their active-duty hitch was to begin.

"Do you know where to park personal vehicles, Private?" Jesús nodded his head.

"Proceed," the guard said, opening the mechanized gate.

Jesús drove inside slowly, passing the defensive emplacements that lined the entry to the outpost, and made his way toward the center of the garrison. On one side of the road stood a line of hastily built barracks. On the other side was a collection of buildings that had once been a school.

After driving past the structures, Jesús spotted the landmark he had been looking for: the transmission tower. As Jo had promised, it was easy to spot; the entire height of the twenty-meter tower was illuminated by blinking lights. Jesús still found it amazing that the U.S. Army would make one of its vulnerable points so obvious. But Jo had explained that after a widely publicized helicopter crash several years earlier, Congress had mandated that all military transmission towers be lighted for safety.

Jesús turned left toward the tower, winding through the camp's central utility areas. In less than half a kilometer, he reached his destination: the camp's military police command post. The garrison's commander had laid out the camp by the book. Fortunately for the insurgents, "the book" was available online, a resource Jo continually used to their advantage.

The MP command post was a windowless prefab structure housing the monitoring center for cameras that kept a constant vigil on the camp's perimeter. Adjacent to the building stood the tower used to receive the signals from the surveillance cameras.

In an overseas unit, the camp and its sentries would have been issued night-vision equipment. But the current commitment of forces on foreign missions—and the continuing fiscal crisis—left domestic units with less costly optical cameras. Although not at the cutting edge of military technology, the cameras, when supported by constant foot patrols, still provided formidable security for the camp.

Jesús parked the truck across the road from the relay tower and looked at his watch. It was 10:07.

He had two minutes to wait.

Sitting in the truck, uncertain of his fate, he reflected on the strange twists in his life that had brought him to this place and time. His father, a man he did not remember, had been his driving force.

As a child, Jesús had been reminded by his mother every day that his father, a colonel in the Panamanian Army, had given his life defending his country from foreign invaders in 1989. The invaders were from the United States.

Like many of Manuel Noriega's supporters, his mother fled the country following the invasion, taking refuge in Honduras with her three children. Raised in a squalid tenement in Trujillo, Jesús had grown up listening to his mother's continual lament—their poverty was the result of the Yanquis' arrogance. Jesús had learned to tune out his mother's litany at an early age. His father's glory was a relic of the past, of things long dead.

When the opportunity arose for Jesús to come to the United States, he'd jumped at the chance. Yet when Jo Herrera recruited him to fight against the U.S. government, he had not hesitated. Some part of his mother's hatred still lived on inside him—and it was now leading him to risk his life.

At precisely 10:09, Jesús emerged from the truck. Unhurriedly, he unlocked the winch on the front of the truck and started across the road, extending the winch's steel cable as he walked. Reaching the base of the receiving tower thirty meters away, he locked the cable hook as high as he could reach on the tower's tubular steel structure and started back toward the truck.

Near the road, the sound of an approaching vehicle made him startle in alarm. In a matter of seconds, the half-inch steel line lying across the pavement would be visible in the vehicle's headlights. For an instant, he thought of running. Then, like a night breeze, a calm came over him.

He began walking nonchalantly up the road toward the approaching vehicle. As the headlights of the Humvee washed over Jesús, he waved casually. The Humvee moved on without slowing. The distraction had worked. The soldiers in the vehicle had noticed nothing out of the ordinary.

Jesús needed to move swiftly now. The encounter with the Humvee had consumed precious seconds. He walked quickly to his pickup, locked the winch, and entered the truck. Easing the vehicle forward about ten meters, he put the truck in reverse and floored the gas pedal, bracing himself for a jolt.

The force of the resistance took him by surprise, whipping the back of his head hard against the pickup's rear window.

Jesús felt something wet moving down his neck—blood. Fighting to remain conscious, he looked through the windshield at the tower. It was angled but still standing.

Jesús drove the truck forward again, certain the MPs would emerge from the building at any second. Again he floored the truck in reverse. After a jolt of resistance, the tower collapsed in front of the truck, narrowly missing the hood. Jesús was relieved—but the danger was far from over.

The door of the MP command post opened and a soldier stepped outside. Jesús could see the surprise in the soldier's posture as he noticed the tower lying on the ground. The man instinctively reached for his sidepiece as his eyes followed the length of the tower leading toward the truck. Before the soldier could draw his weapon, Jesús leveled the Glock and fired three shots. The soldier clutched his chest and crumpled to the ground.

Jesús glanced at his watch. It was 10:14. He was four minutes behind schedule with the signal.

Moving to the rear of the truck, he opened the gas cap. Inside was a gasoline-soaked rag leading down into the fuel tank. He flipped back the top of his lighter, knowing that once the rag was lit, he would have less than five seconds to clear out. Before he could strike a spark, a pair of violent blows struck his left arm and hip, accompanied by the firecracker popping of a handgun.

Knocked to the ground, Jesús rolled painfully under the truck and drew his pistol. Peering around the tire, he saw a series of bright muzzle flashes from the doorway of the command post and felt a searing pain in his left shoulder.

Jesús knew there wasn't much time left now. He was badly wounded and would be overrun at any second. For a moment, he was surprised by his emotions. He was not afraid. Instead, he felt a deep sadness that the plan had not worked out better. There was only one more thing he could do to salvage his mission.

He pointed the Glock toward the doorway and fired the rest of his clip in quick succession. The ten-round volley sent the figures in the doorway scurrying inside. He hoped that would buy him the seconds he needed.

His left side paralyzed, Jesús crawled along the hard-packed soil and rose slowly to his knees near the gas tank. As he struck the lighter, he heard shots ringing out behind him. It didn't matter now. His job was nearly done.

Gracias, Señor, he said to his maker as a blue flicker raced up the rag, consuming it in flames.

Captain Michael Fuller picked up the phone and speed-dialed the CO's quarters.

"Colonel Prentiss," the gravelly voice on the line said.

"Colonel, someone's blown up a civilian truck near the MP command post and shots have been fired. Our perimeter camera array appears to be down."

"I heard the blast, Captain. It sounds like a terrorist attack. Alert the sentries to seal the camp. Who's on active status?"

"Charlie Platoon, sir."

"Have them converge on the site of the explosion and begin a sweep outward toward the camp perimeter. If we've got more Panchos inside the post, I want to clamp down on them before they get away."

"Begging the colonel's pardon, sir. What if this explosion is a diversion? If we commit our only combat-ready troops to an internal sweep, we're leaving the perimeter lightly defended to an attack from the outside—especially with the cameras down."

"I've been through terrorist attacks before, Fuller. You're giving these people credit for using military strategy. They just want to hit us and run."

"Yes, sir. I'll give the orders to Charlie Platoon."

Although Fuller was convinced it was a mistake, he could not bring himself to question the colonel's orders any further. After all, the man had served in both Gulf Wars. Still, Fuller mused, if Colonel Prentiss had been a first-rate officer, he would have been commanding a unit overseas, not a dogshit domestic garrison. In any case, one objection to a superior's orders was risky enough. Two in a row would be career suicide.

As he relayed his CO's orders, Fuller was certain the colonel was making a perennial military blunder—fighting today's war with yesterday's tactics.

———

Hiding in a dry riverbed outside the perimeter of Outpost Bravo, Mano glanced at his watch. It read 10:08. The signal from Jesús was due in two minutes.

He gestured for Angel and Tavo to remain prone and peered toward the corner of the camp's fence, fifty meters away. After scouting the camp for days, Mano knew the sentries would reach the corner in a few seconds and begin walking away from them, leaving the area unguarded for four minutes.

Mano would have never attempted this operation without the new Domestic Rules of Engagement the Army was being forced to employ. In an overseas garrison, the area surrounding the camp would have been lined with mines and sometimes even motion-triggered weapons. But Congress had forbidden these types of unattended defenses stateside to reduce the risk to civilians.

It was now 10:09 and Mano waited calmly. Angel and Tavo seemed relaxed as well. The vatos were proving to be cool under fire, most likely a result of their criminal past. *At least now they're helping their people instead of stealing from them,* he mused.

Mano's watch finally reached 10:10—the time for the signal from Jesús. As the seconds passed, Mano's expression began to betray his anxiety. The delay was not a good sign. The explosion of the truck would let him know Jesús had knocked out the cameras and would also create a distraction to buy them some time.

At first, Mano had been concerned about using Jesús to infiltrate the outpost. His thick Spanish accent would be easy to detect during any extended conversation. Ironically, Ramon and Jo had coached Jesús in the speech and slang of African-Americans. Hearing Jesús repeatedly pronounce "y'all" as "ju-oll" had provided a few lighthearted moments. But Mano had never doubted Jesús's courage and determination. If there was a way to get the job done, he knew Jesús would find it.

At 10:14, Mano saw a dim orange flash in the sky, followed by the dull boom of a distant explosion. The signal was four minutes late. The sentries would be back any second.

"We have to change our plans...entienden?" Mano said slowly to Angel and Tavo.

"Yes," Angel said. Tavo nodded in agreement.

"You two cut through there and continue with the original plan," Mano said, pointing toward the fence directly in front of them. "I'm going after the sentries."

Angel and Tavo again nodded their heads, grasping his change in plans.

Mano drew his pistol and moved in the direction of the sentries, staying outside the glare of the lights along the fence. He knew his only advantage against the guards would be the element of surprise. He was outgunned—and he had no cover.

After jogging less than a minute, Mano made out the shapes of the guards in the distance. To his surprise, they were not moving toward him but facing the center of the outpost instead.

Mano stood for a moment, dumbfounded by his luck. The diversion had worked better than he could have hoped. The soldiers seemed to be overreacting to the explosion within their camp, leaving the perimeter of the outpost undefended.

Returning to the corner of the fence, Mano was shocked to find the chain-link barrier intact and the vatos nowhere in sight. Had they turned tail? Then he looked at the fence more closely. The links had been snipped with almost surgical precision and returned to their original positions. Mano parted the fence, slipped inside, and placed the links in their original alignment as Angel and Tavo had done. After sprinting two hundred meters into the camp, he arrived at their target—the garrison's motor pool.

Angel and Tavo were already in position, crouching beside two of the motor pool's fuel tanks. Mano ran to the third fuel tank, pulled a wrench from his fatigues, and loosened the main drainage valve. Seconds later, six thousand gallons of high-octane gasoline began spilling on the ground.

Mano then rose, made eye contact with the vatos, and pumped his fist twice—the signal to ignite the fuel. He retreated from the gushing valve and produced a disposable lighter. Striking a spark, he locked the flame and tossed the lighter in a high arc toward the fast-growing puddle. Before the lighter had reached the ground, he began a mad dash away.

Mano knew the fuel on the ground would burn but not explode—otherwise, none of them would survive. Only after the flow of fuel through the valves was low enough to allow air to enter the tanks would the compressed fuel inside ignite and trigger an explosion. Those fifteen to twenty seconds would give them enough time to escape.

Mano, Angel, and Tavo had nearly reached the fence when the first tank exploded. The flash of the fireball was so bright Mano saw his shadow appear beneath the glare. The three men dropped to the ground as the heat of the blast wave singed their backs and the earth below them trembled. The other two explosions followed seconds later.

"Vamos! Vamos!" Mano said, helping Angel and Tavo off the ground as the blasts faded. Their location had just been advertised to every soldier in the outpost.

While pulling back the fence for the vatos, Mano saw a soldier stunned by the explosions stagger near them, his helmet and weapon missing, blood seeping from his nose and ears.

Angel had also spotted the soldier, and in a seamless motion he drew his pistol and took aim. Before Angel could fire, Mano slapped away his gun.

"He is enemy!" Angel screamed angrily. "Estos cabrones mataron a tu hija!"

Mano understood Angel's words: *These bastards killed your daughter.*

Mano looked calmly into Angel's livid face. "I'll avenge my daughter with honor, Angel," he said, pointing toward the helpless soldier. "There's no honor in this man's death."

Forty minutes later, the three reached a vacant bungalow where Jo had stocked provisions for them. The inconspicuous home would be their haven for the next few days.

As Mano settled into his sleeping bag, he looked south through the window. On the horizon was the glow of three fires blazing in the night sky. *These are the candles I've lit in your memory, mi hijita,* Mano thought. *I hope you can see them where you are.*

The fires were still burning at dawn.

THE QUARANTINE AND RELOCATION ACT:
Month 21, Day 2

Jo extended the antenna to its full length, trying to clear the static on the portable shortwave radio on her kitchen table. "I don't get it. We usually pick up the Canadian BBC feed without a problem." Seated with her at the table, Mano and Ramon leaned closer to the radio, trying to make out a broadcast amid the hissing and crackles.

Ramon scratched his head. "Any chance the baldies could be jamming that frequency, Mano?"

"It's possible, although it may not be intentional. In Afghanistan, the Army issued signal jammers for some of its vehicles—but it was to block the triggers on remote-controlled IEDs. The Army hasn't brought much of its RF equipment stateside, though."

Ramon's eyebrows rose. "Curious that we're picking up this static all of a sudden, no?"

"If the Army's started using RF jammers, it could work in our favor. We'll know they're around a lot sooner."

Jo tilted the antenna almost horizontally to the right. "There we go!" she said as a voice with a posh accent broke through the static.

"Can you turn it up?" Ramon asked, leaning forward. "I can barely hear it."

Jo twirled the dial. "That's as loud as it will go."

"I've got an idea that might boost the signal," Mano said. "Jo, have you got any tinfoil?"

Ramon laughed. "Oh, you're in big trouble, amigo. Jo thinks tinfoil is an ecological abomination."

"It's a trick we used to use as kids to watch the low-def channels," Mano explained.

"Well," Jo said sheepishly. "If it's for the cause...it so happens I've saved some scraps," she said, reaching into a drawer. Jo handed Mano the foil and he attached a series of strips to the antenna.

"Much better, Mano!" Ramon called out. "Even I can hear it now. These old ears of mine—"

"Hush," Jo said. "I think the news has almost started."

As the announcer finished the station ID and began the promos for the afternoon programs, Jo handed glasses of merlot to Ramon and Mano. This small indulgence had become part of a daily ritual begun nearly a week ago as they listened for the payoff to Ramon's behind-the-scenes political maneuvers. It was an experience they all clearly relished, although none of them would have admitted it.

After a story about the most recent divorce in the royal family, the news they'd been waiting to hear finally aired.

Almost three years after the Rio Grande Incident in San Antonio touched off a wave of riots across the American Southwest, the recognition of a rebel provisional government is being considered within the borders of the United States.

Today, only four months after the release of the rebels' Santiago Declaration, Venezuela has filed a motion at the United Nations that has stunned the USA and much of the world.

The measure calls for two delegates from the Hispanic Republic of North America to be granted observer status in the U.N. General Assembly. The Venezuelan motion claims the Hispanic Republic should be recognized as legitimate representatives of a stateless people similar to the non-voting status granted to U.N. representatives from the Palestinian Liberation Organization in 1974. Word among U.N. insiders is that the resolution is gaining considerable support.

In a statement released by the White House press office, President Carleton Brenner vowed that if the Venezuelan motion comes to a vote, the U.S. will permanently withdraw from the United Nations.

This is Nigel Blake, BBC News, New York.

Ramon tipped his glass toward Jo and Mano in a toast. "Salud, my friends," he said, his eyes growing misty. "I only wish this was champagne."

Jo touched each of their glasses with her own. "Nothing could taste any sweeter," she said, draining the rest of her wine.

THE QUARANTINE AND
RELOCATION ACT:
Month 21, Day 5

There are many who will abandon the struggle during
moments of difficulty. There will be many more who
will join the revolution when it appears it will succeed.
—José Antonio Marcha, 1987
Translated by J. M. Herrera

Nesto crossed the street as he neared the Whittier Boulevard checkpoint. He wanted to put some distance between
himself and the dicey situation around the North Gate.

A platoon of edgy troops was guarding four U.S. Army
six-by-six trucks idling along one side of the boulevard just
inside the entrance. The soldiers were swiveling their heads
nervously, clutching the trigger guards on their M16s. *Reservists*, Nesto thought with disdain. *A few weeks ago, these pendejos
were pushing paper. Now they're inside the big, bad QZ and scared
shitless. If one of these trucks backfires, they might open up on anything that moves.*

Behind the soldiers, volunteers from La Defensa del Pueblo
wearing sky blue armbands were hurriedly unloading burlap
bags of cornmeal from the open-bed Army trucks into a motley collection of pickups, vans, and sedans. *Those chumps at the
DDP are throwing away a sweet opportunity*, Nesto mused. The

U.S. government was providing the grain absolutely free and a smart operator could make some serious money distributing it. Nesto planned to get a piece of that action—very soon.

He continued east for several blocks, finally reaching a small house on Maple with four Verdugos hanging out on the porch.

A year ago, this encounter would have ended in violence. In fact, a year ago, he wouldn't have been in this barrio unless he had five of his own vatos with him, all heavily armed. But things had changed. It had started as a truce between the gangs and grown into something approaching mutual respect. Nesto never dreamed something like this could ever happen.

A smart player knows when to fold, Nesto reminded himself as he walked toward the house. He'd played the DDP card long enough and made a pile of cash. The money he'd collected from Ramon, plus the monthly fee from the CIA, had been very sweet. But Ramon and his bunch had brought the heat down on all of them when they went public with their Santiago Declaration. *The idiots.* Now the Agency was breathing down his neck. It was too dangerous to play this game anymore—especially since they'd passed the Terrorist Arraignment Act. There was no way he was going to risk a death sentence. The time had come to cash in his chips. Ramon's call for a meeting had been a real stroke of luck.

Although they appeared nonchalant, the vatos on the porch had been watching him closely. Los Verdugos, the palace guards for the DDP, were one of the most serious obstacles in what he was about to do.

"Y que, ese," Nesto said as he approached them.

"Y que," they responded, clearly expecting him.

Nesto walked onto the porch and one of the vatos gestured for him to lift his hands in the air. Nesto knew the drill. Being frisked for weapons and monitoring devices had become a familiar routine.

Each time Nesto had met with the leaders of La Defensa del Pueblo since he'd revealed his connection to the CIA, the procedure had been the same. They would send a message telling him where to show up. Once he arrived at the location, he would be met by DDP guards, patted down, and then escorted to Mano and Ramon, who were always somewhere else. A couple of the guards would remain at the original location to watch for anyone tailing Nesto. It was a security procedure Nesto knew would not be easy to defeat.

Led by two Verdugos, Nesto arrived ten minutes later at a second-floor apartment in a grungy two-story building. Ramon and Mano were already seated on two threadbare chairs in the one-room layout as he ambled into the room with his escorts.

Nesto glanced disdainfully around the seedy apartment and dropped onto a stained velvet couch. "Hey, you guys are movin' up in the world, ese," he said, smirking.

"I'm so glad you could join us," Ramon replied dryly.

"It's been a while, man. It's been a while. You haven't called me in nearly six months. You dudes seem to be pulling off a lot of jobs without my help these days. I seen the news of the attack on the Army camp last month. Was that you?"

Mano glared at Nesto. "Who wants to know?"

"Hey, ese, don't go accusing me of anything, OK?"

"I've never trusted you, Nesto," Mano said, his eyes locked on the mero. "I think you'll sell us out the day you think you've got a better deal."

Bluffing, Nesto rose to his feet. "That's bullshit, man. If you don't trust me, then I'm outta here."

"Nesto...Nesto...please forgive Mano," Ramon said. "He's only speaking his mind. But you must admit, amigo, your curiosity *is* a little suspicious."

Nesto dropped back onto the couch. "OK, man. Forget it. I was just going to stroke you dudes on pulling off some of these jobs without any real weapons."

"Weapons are what we're here to talk about. So let's get to it," Mano said.

"OK, ese. What do you need?"

"Two dozen AK-47s, twelve RPGs, and fifty pounds of Semtex."

Nesto's mouth gaped. "Are you shitting me?"

"We won't need your services this time, Nesto," Mano said. "Just the weapons."

As the shock subsided, images of money began churning in Nesto's head. This could be a really big score. If he played his cards right, he could get one final, monster payday before he dropped the dime on the DDP. "That's a lot of weapons, ese," he said, trying to mask his excitement. "How soon will you need them?"

"We need to have everything in our hands by the first week of May."

Nesto sucked in his breath. "Four weeks...That's not much time for all that material, man. I'm going to have to check this out. But I'm guessing it's going to be steep—at least a hundred thousand, all up front."

"Seventy-five thousand," Ramon said. "and you'll get half in advance as we've always arranged it."

"It's not going to happen, ese. You're not going to get that much material into the zone without some serious cash up front. I've got to grease a lot of palms, man."

Ramon shrugged his shoulders. "As you observed, Nesto, we haven't needed your services for nearly a year. So it's up to you. That's our offer."

Nesto rubbed his chin, trying to appear reluctant. "OK, man. I'll set it up. But I'm going to need the cash right away."

Ramon picked up a backpack next to his chair and tossed it into Nesto's lap. "Count it."

Nesto unzipped the bag and saw the bundles of small bills inside. "No need, man. You've never shorted me before. I doubt you're going to start now."

Leaving the dingy apartment with his escorts, Nesto was secretly exultant. He was about to save his skin with the CIA—and still score his biggest payday yet. All he had to do was play this right.

After returning to his barrio, he dialed the number for Bill Perkins at the CIA.

"Something big is going down in May, man," the mero of El Farol said into his baby blue vu-phone.

———

"Yes, Carol. I think we can trust our mole on this one," Evans said into his PC.

Looking at the glaring face of Carol Phelps on his computer monitor, Evans could tell his boss was unconvinced. "A report about a Pancho national offensive will have to go all the way to the White House, Hank. I don't have to tell you the consequences of getting this wrong."

Evans swallowed hard. "Yes, I know," he said cautiously. "But this can't be a trap. All our mole told us was about a big weapons buy, not a specific location. The rebels have nothing to gain by having us ready."

"The Panchos are not the only military threat we're facing. If we load up at home, we're going to be weaker somewhere else."

"I don't get it, Carol. You told me to put the squeeze on our mole and now you're balking because we came up with something big?"

Phelps stared at Evans coldly from the screen. "All right, Hank. I'm going to send this upstairs," she said icily. "But let me assure you...if this goes wrong, I will have your balls parboiled."

Two days later, preparations for a nationwide insurgent assault began. Military units throughout the Southwest were placed on DefCon 2, the highest state of alert short of war. The equipment of many homeland units was upgraded and reservists due for discharge were retained for another two-month stint. In addition, orders were issued for several elite units to be quietly shipped stateside, including the fearsome Delta Force, cleared for domestic operations for the first time since the 1987 riots at Atlanta's federal prison. As a final precaution, military reconnaissance satellites were temporarily diverted to domestic surveillance.

After months of being caught off guard, the U.S. intelligence community had finally produced a break. If a widespread attack was coming, the U.S. military would be ready.

THE QUARANTINE AND RELOCATION ACT:
Month 21, Day 29

All right. This is far enough. It's time for you two to go home," Ramon said to Jo and Mano as the three of them approached the hidden entrance to the tunnel. "You can't go all the way to Switzerland with me."

Groping in the moonlight, Mano found the entryway's concealed handle and lifted the camouflaged trap door. A handmade ladder led into the pitch-black below.

Jo leaned forward and kissed Ramon's forehead. "Adios, Ramon," she said, wiping her eyes. "Travel safe, hermano."

"Thanks, Josefina. I'll be fine," Ramon answered, patting her cheek. "Give 'em hell on Marcha's birthday."

Mano extended his palm toward Ramon. "Try not to freeze, old man," he said, trying to keep his emotions in check.

Instead of shaking his hand, Ramon spread his arms. "Don't be such a gabacho," he said, stepping forward and hugging his friend.

Mano felt his throat tighten as he gently clapped Ramon's bony back. "Vaya con Dios," he said softly.

Ramon stepped back and laughed. "Speaking Spanish? My God, Mano. You *are* taking this seriously. This is a farewell, hombre, not a funeral."

"Watch yourself near the border," Jo cautioned. "The patrols have increased lately."

Ramon winked as he adjusted the straps on his backpack. "The baldie hasn't been born that can catch *this* old gray fox," he said before climbing down the ladder.

Mano watched Ramon turn on his flashlight and disappear into the tunnel's darkness. If all went well, Ramon would reach Geneva in a few days. There, he would join Octavio Perez on a historic mission.

Three days earlier, the United Nations had passed Venezuela's resolution. Two representatives from the Hispanic Republic of North America would be granted non-voting seats in the U.N. General Assembly. Only the United States had voted against the move. Great Britain and Israel had abstained.

True to his word, President Brenner recalled the U.S. representatives to the United Nations the same day. In Washington, the White House began lobbying Congress for passage of the latest resolution by Congressman Melvin Bates calling for a full U.S. withdrawal from the United Nations and the expulsion of the U.N. from American soil. Anticipating the move, the U.N. announced it would be moving its international headquarters to Geneva.

Following the United States' withdrawal, U.N. secretary-general Balraj Mehra addressed the General Assembly from its complex on the banks of the East River in New York for the last time. In the speech, Mehra denounced the United States as a rogue nation behaving outside established international law—law, Mehra pointed out, the U.S. itself had helped create as a founding member of the United Nations.

At that moment, the globe's power structure began

dividing into two hostile blocs. In one camp was the U.S., the planet's last remaining superpower—and in the other, virtually the rest of the world.

Between the two lay the powder keg of the Marcha Offensive.

THE MARCHA
OFFENSIVE

THE MARCHA OFFENSIVE:
Day 1

Nesto followed the two burly Verdugos through the doorway of the abandoned Holiday Inn and found Jo in the litter-strewn lobby. "What the hell is going on, chica?" he said to her. "Your boys here got me out of bed at seven on a Sunday morning. This better be important, goddammit."

Before Jo could answer, the two young vatos closed to within inches of Nesto's face, glaring at him menacingly. Although Rafael and Enrique spoke little English, Nesto's tone of disrespect toward one of their leaders did not sit well with them.

"What's the matter, Nesto?" Jo said. "Are you worried you'll miss Sunday Mass?"

Nesto's indignation quickly cooled under the stares of the beefy guards. "OK, OK...What are we doing in this low-rent joint anyway?"

"Follow me," Jo said, leading Nesto and his escorts through a series of doors into the kitchen of the empty hotel.

The long steel counters, once used for food preparation, were now covered with a hodgepodge of electronic devices. On the left counter were four laptops, three fax machines, and a switchboard-style desk phone. Along the right counter, a bank of high-def plasma sets was tuned to the major networks and CNN. Behind the devices, a tangle of wires led to a gas-powered electrical generator, which operated near the empty pool in the facility's central courtyard.

"You trying to start some kinda pawn shop or something?" Nesto said, glancing at the mostly outdated equipment.

"We may need you for some information today, Nesto. We've got a nice comfy seat for you over there," she said, gesturing toward a collection of metal folding chairs in a corner of the kitchen.

Nesto scanned the room again. "I get it," he said. "Today is the big day."

Jo was not surprised by the mero's deduction. Nesto had become a leader by using his wits and cunning to best much bigger men.

As Nesto sauntered toward the chairs, Rafael and Enrique in tow, Jo was grateful once again to Mano for the foresight to bring Nesto here. The mero's exposure to the workings of the CIA might prove useful today. But more important, they had Nesto where they could keep an eye on him. On the loose, his knowledge might prove disastrous during the offensive.

Mano's principles had shaped the choice of targets for today's offensive: they would attack only unmanned facilities and military garrisons. Mano had insisted they minimize the risk to civilians. His ideals were not abstract political concepts. They were based on common decency and compassion. His unerring moral compass had made Jo face up to the ruthlessness of her own zeal.

She hoped the surprise she'd arranged for Mano today would help atone for her past failings. It had eaten up a great deal of her remaining wealth. But Mano's homecoming tonight would be one he would remember for the rest of his life. A pang of sorrow pierced Jo as she realized she could never be a part of that life.

You haven't got the time for sorrow—or guilt—right now, she told herself. There was work to be done. By force of will, she turned her attention to the array of machines along the counter in front of her. A flurry of readiness reports was coming in from their teams across the country.

———

Nesto was trying hard to mask his glee. In an incredible piece of luck for him, Jo had brought him to the control center of their operations on the day of their big offensive. Taking them out was going to be easier than he imagined. The first thing he needed to do was to send out the signal. To do that, he would need to distract the two vatos guarding him.

"Oye, ese, you guys got some cards we can play or something?" Nesto said to the young guard on his left.

When the vatos ignored his question, Nesto shrugged and rolled his eyes. Sighing heavily, he tilted his head back and let it roll lazily from side to side. As the minutes passed, he restlessly folded and unfolded his arms, crossed and uncrossed his legs. The two young vatos assigned to guard him assumed Nesto was bored and distracted—precisely the impression the mero sought.

Nesto wanted to accustom the guards to his fidgeting. It would make it easier for him to send the signal. As he continued his impatient squirming, the guards began to take less notice of his gestures, eventually turning away from him to convey their disdain. Certain that his random gestures would not draw undue attention, Nesto casually clicked his heels together three times.

The beacon signal had been sent. He had activated the transponders embedded in the heels of his Nike hightops. *Some pretty devious fuckers down there at the CIA. Just like in* The Wizard of Oz. Nesto chuckled to himself.

In the outskirts of Geneva, two aging radicals huddled around a high-end laptop, anxiously awaiting the reports from Jo on the progress of the offensive.

Ramon Garcia and Octavio Perez had rushed back to their modest chalet after an early dinner with two delegates from Argentina. The U.N. representatives of the Hispanic Republic of North America had spent another long day lobbying members of the General Assembly. Soon after their arrival in Switzerland, the two newly minted statesmen had discovered many nations eager to settle old scores with the United States—and the existence of the HRNA gave them an exceptional opportunity. Ramon and Octavio were exploiting this advantage to reach their immediate goal: full recognition by the U.N.

If they could negotiate a voting seat in the General Assembly and be recognized as a sovereign nation, many new doors would open to the Hispanic Republic. Legitimacy, economic support, even military aid might all be possible. They were poised to take a giant leap forward. But much of it hinged on the outcome of the Marcha Offensive.

From the backyard of a vacant mansion near the crest of a steep hill, Mano trained his binoculars on Outpost Bravo four hundred meters away in the flat valley below. It was Sunday morning and the camp looked peaceful. Except for the guards leaning casually against the sandbags at the main gate, there was no movement at the outpost. Mano glanced at his watch. It was 8:59. In one minute, the calm would come to a sudden end.

Beside Mano was Tavo Galvan, looking over the sights of his RPG at the outpost below, waiting eagerly for Mano's order to fire.

All four RPG teams under Mano's command had their rockets trained on the collection of camo-painted military vehicles parked near the perimeter of the camp. Mano had targeted the camp's Humvees and six-by-sixes for two reasons. First, the vehicles would be relatively easy to destroy. And second, taking them out would hamper the soldiers' ability to pursue them. By the time the active-duty platoon mounted up and rolled out after them, Mano hoped he and his men would be well on their way to their safehouse less than three kilometers away.

To prevent the camp's defenders from locating them by their rockets' smoke trails, Mano's teams would fire once and then move a hundred meters laterally along the slope for their final volley.

Mano looked left and waved. About two hundred meters away, Simon Potts waved back, indicating he was ready to begin videotaping.

Looking right, Mano made eye contact with the other RPG teams and lifted his hand in the air like a kicker about to start a football game. The other team leaders responded with the same gesture. They were ready.

Mano checked the time again. It was exactly 9:00. The big

man tapped the "send" key on his RF radio twice, transmitting a coded message to Jo's command center: "The attack is on."

He then slashed downward with his hand.

The deep, raspy hiss of four rockets pierced the morning stillness, their bluish-white trails curving like four claws reaching toward the outpost in the valley below.

Hank Evans raised his head abruptly when he heard the explosions and looked around the room trying to get his bearings. He'd been asleep at his desk, his head resting on his arms.

Saturday had turned into another all-night work session at the office. Since they'd received the warning of the coming insurgent attack, his team had been engaged in feverish, round-the-clock preparations.

Evans glanced at his watch. It was 9:01. *Is the attack finally here?* he asked himself as the fogginess in his head cleared. He stood unsteadily and was staggering toward the windows when Bill Perkins rushed into his office.

"I just heard from Captain Fuller! Pancho's attacking the outpost! I think this is it, Hank."

Evans's eyes widened. "They're hitting a military target—in broad daylight?" he said. "They've been a lot smarter in the past."

"We haven't got time to figure this out now. C'mon, let's get out of here!" Perkins shouted, running for the door.

Evans followed Perkins down the dank hallway toward the bunker they'd prepared in the maintenance room at the center of the former school. Nearing the bunker, Hank heard another round of explosions. These sounded different, a series of low *crumps* that came in waves a few seconds apart and seemed much farther away than the first blasts. Evans realized it was return fire from the outpost. Inside the bunker, he heard the thumping of helicopters passing overhead.

Hank felt a thrill of satisfaction. His office had alerted the military. As a result, they were ready, and Pancho was finally going to pay the price.

Mano and Tavo were running toward their next firing position when the big man heard three low thuds coming from the outpost, followed by a chorus of shrill whines. Mano instantly recognized the sounds he'd last heard in Afghanistan—incoming mortars.

He grabbed Tavo by the shirt, pulling him to the ground as the big man threw himself on his belly. "Get down!" he yelled to the six men behind him. "Abajo!" he screamed in Spanish, not sure if he was using the right word.

The two Verdugos closest to Mano instantly dropped to the ground. The four farther behind them were not as fortunate. They stopped running and stood in confusion. Their hesitation proved lethal.

The first mortar shell struck fifteen meters behind Mano and Tavo, hurling a mix of dirt and searing metal in a deadly fountain that sprayed into the air above their prone bodies, leaving them unhurt. The next shell arrived a second later and landed directly in front of the men of the third team, who were still on their feet. The two men were hurled backward by the blast, their bodies shredded by shrapnel. The third shell hit the last team directly, killing them instantly.

Mano knew they had only seconds before the next volley.

He jumped to his feet, pulling Tavo with him and gesturing to the others. "Run!" he yelled, pointing toward the crest of the hill some fifty meters away. "Vamos! Rapido!" As he followed behind the three survivors of his command, he kept his ears peeled for the sound of more incoming rounds. They'd run about twenty strides when Mano again heard the dreaded thuds and whines.

Mano hurled his huge body at the three smaller men running up the steep slope in front of him and managed to tackle them all in a single lunge. "Get down!" he yelled needlessly. Seconds later, the next volley of mortar shells began exploding on the slope behind them. The four men pressed themselves into the ground, feeling it tremble under their bellies. The shrapnel from one of the rounds tore through the tops of the trees above, raining small branches and leaves on them.

When the second volley ended, Mano was relieved to see no one was injured. The mortar gunners had zeroed in on the same position again. But there was a good chance he and his men would get out alive if they could get over the crest of the hill.

Then he heard a new sound rising from the valley below them, a distant, rhythmic thumping. He looked back and saw the angry-hornet profiles of two Comanche attack helicopters streaking toward them.

The big man now knew there was only one way any of them would survive. They needed to disperse. Huddled together, all four could be wiped out with a single missile from the Comanche.

"Listen to me carefully," Mano said calmly to the three

young men, who were shaken but still composed. "We need to spread out. Me entienden?" He tapped each of them on the chest and pointed in a different direction to reinforce his order.

"Sí...Yes, I understand," Tavo said. The others nodded in agreement.

Mano took the loaded RPG from Tavo's hands. "OK, now GO!" the big man said and gently shoved Tavo away. As the young men scattered, Mano looked back toward the helicopters. They were closing fast. He knew his unit's survival was a matter of luck now—and the odds did not look good.

———

At 9:21, the fax machine dedicated to Texas operations beeped into life, churning out a message. Jo started reading the sheet before it had completely emerged from the machine:

Garrison on high alert. Attack failed. Nine dead.

—TX-4

The message was from El Paso. Scrawled in an urgent hand, the fax was the latest sign in a disturbing pattern. Although most of the sabotage missions were being carried out successfully, all the insurgents' assaults against military installations were being decisively repulsed. The rebels were taking heavy casualties. Jo was now certain their attacks had been expected.

She thought again of Mano. He had not been in touch with her since his coded radio call confirmed he was launching the attack twenty minutes ago. If her suspicions were correct, there was a good chance he and his men had walked into a trap. The thought filled her with dread.

There was only one way the military could have been alerted—Nesto. She glanced toward the mero sitting in the corner between the two guards, looking very bored. What at this point could she do about his betrayal? The damage was done.

Before Jo could decide her next step, her walkie-talkie began to squawk. It was one of the Verdugos stationed several blocks south, reporting the approach of two helicopters. As he spoke, Jo heard the low throbbing of the chopper blades in the distance.

Now Jo faced a more immediate decision. Were the helicopters headed toward her location or merely flying over in response to the attacks Mano had launched against the outpost north of them? As a precaution, she sent Rafael outside to keep an eye on the approaching helicopters. If it looked like the choppers were about to land, he would return and alert them.

From the corner of her eye, Jo observed Nesto's reaction. The mero was still feigning indifference to the events around him. That seemed ominous.

As the door closed behind Rafael, Jo's RF radio screeched into life.

"Oso calling Rubia…"

Mano was calling.

Mano watched the three Verdugos scramble up the barren slope along different routes. There was little cover at the crest of the hill. Mano knew the Comanches would make short work of the young men if they were caught in the open. He needed to buy them some time. If he could disable one of the helos, it might give them a chance to make it over the treeless summit and into the dense woods on the other side.

Taking cover in an overgrown arbor, Mano saw the first Comanche appear above the tree line. It hovered for a moment, then charged up the slope, apparently spotting the men running near the crest. Mano could see the pulsing flashes of the chain guns mounted on the Comanche's stubby fins.

Mano knew he would have only one shot—and that shot would be at a fast-moving target. He brought the RPG to his shoulder, aimed at a spot about twenty meters in front of the Comanche, and squeezed the trigger.

Watching his rocket's smoky trail, Mano knew immediately he'd miscalculated. The Comanche was moving too fast. The rocket's trajectory was lagging too far behind the helicopter. His heart sank as he realized the rocket would miss. But as the missile continued its arcing flight, it grazed the back of the Comanche, shattering its tail rotor.

It was not a clean hit. But without the stability of its tail rotor, the Comanche went into a slow spin, and was forced to break off its attack. Mano felt momentary elation as the damaged Comanche was forced to land in a clearing about two hundred meters west. His men might make it to safety after all.

Then the other Comanche appeared.

The second helicopter picked up the pursuit its damaged partner had aborted, speeding up the hillside, its chain guns blazing.

Over the next several minutes, Mano watched helplessly

as the second Comanche hunted his men down and slaughtered them with methodical precision. The bitter taste of bile rose in his throat. He had failed to protect his men.

After destroying its targets at the crest of the hill, the second helo returned to the damaged Comanche, hovering above its wounded teammate, protecting it from further attack.

Mano was sure the outpost had tracked the position of his last RPG shot. But his proximity to the downed Comanche would spare him from another deadly volley of mortar fire. He now had a chance to escape.

In that moment of relative calm, Mano began assessing the disastrous events of the last twenty minutes. The rockets from their RPGs had evidently been detected by Firefinder radar. Mano was stunned that a domestic garrison would have this type of sophisticated hardware. And the Comanches were the most advanced attack helicopters in the U.S. arsenal, having been resurrected from congressional oblivion by the Brenner administration. Even more startling, both weapons systems had been on operational alert.

Clearly, his assault had been expected.

It could only mean one thing: Nesto had alerted the CIA to the planned offensive.

He thought instantly of Jo and felt a sharp pang of guilt. Bringing Nesto into the nerve center of this operation had been his idea. Although the rebel leaders now knew where to find Nesto, his presence could also endanger Jo—and he needed to warn her.

Mano turned on his RF radio, knowing the transmission might alert the outpost to his presence. As the only one left of his command, he would accept the risk.

"Oso calling Rubia. Oso calling Rubia. Over," he said into the radio.

After a few seconds of static, he heard Jo's voice. "Go ahead, Oso," she said.

"You have a snake in the kitchen. Over," he said, sure Jo would understand the message.

"Understood, Oso. We've also got some hawks overhead here. They're getting closer. I think—" Jo's words ended abruptly, replaced by a stream of static.

A chill traveled down Mano's spine. "Jo, get out of there. Get out of there, NOW!" he shouted, dispensing with any semblance of a code.

He listened for several seconds for her reply. The radio only belched static.

"Jo…Jo…can you hear me?" he asked, his voice hoarse with emotion.

The radio continued its meaningless squawking.

After almost a minute without a reply, Mano turned off the radio and tried to calm his mind. There was nothing more he could do to help Jo from here. Crouching inside the weedy arbor, he vowed to himself that Nesto would pay for his betrayal. But to do that—and to have any chance of helping Jo—he would have to get back to the QZ alive.

Moving east, he backtracked to his original position, offering a silent prayer as he sprinted past the eviscerated bodies of his men killed by the mortar shells. He planned to circle the hill through the thick, protective woods on the lower sections of the slope. That indirect route would put him back inside the walls of Quarantine Zone B by dark—if he could manage to evade the foot patrols the garrison would be deploying soon.

Nesto tried hard to control his excitement. Jo had just ordered one of his guards outside to watch for the helicopter. He was now being guarded by a single Verdugo. *This chica is making my next move a whole lot easier,* he told himself.

The wiry mero had been nonchalantly eyeing the kitchen for the last twenty minutes, looking for a weapon. At first, his visual search had been fruitless. The Verdugos must have combed the area beforehand. But they had overlooked one thing.

Along the ceiling, almost directly above Nesto, was a disconnected length of pipe that had once carried water into the kitchen's overhead sprinkler system. The pipe was dangling at an angle just above the head of the Verdugo beside him. If Nesto could distract the young guard for a few seconds, he could leap up, grab the end of the pipe, and bring it crashing down on the Verdugo's head. After disabling the guard, he'd have access to the gun he could see bulging in the pocket of the vato's baggy pants.

His plan of action set, Nesto now needed the right moment to act. He did not have long to wait. Seconds after the first guard left the kitchen, he heard Jo's radio squawk.

"...Oso calling Rubia. Over," the garbled voice on the radio said.

Jo walked away from Nesto toward the far corner of the kitchen. It was the break Nesto had been waiting for. If he attacked the guard now, Jo would not be close enough to help.

As he had been doing all along, Nesto stood and stretched. The guard was now used to his restless behavior and ignored it. With his hands in the air, Nesto unclasped his Rolex and let it drop to the floor.

The sound of the watch hitting the floor drew the guard's eyes downward. It was a fatal mistake.

"...Oso calling Rubia. Over," Mano's voice said from Jo's radio.

Jo carried the radio into the far corner of the kitchen, out of earshot of Nesto, before answering. "Go ahead—" she said, relieved to know Mano was still alive, but she was stopped in midsentence by a loud crash. She spun toward the sound and saw Enrique on his hands and knees with Nesto standing over him, a folding chair raised above his head. Nesto viciously slammed the chair against Enrique's skull, sending the young guard crashing to the floor.

For a heartbeat, Jo stood frozen in disbelief. Then she dropped the radio and charged toward Nesto.

As she closed on him, she saw the mero turn the lifeless guard over and retrieve the gun from his pocket. From nearly ten feet away, she dove.

She crashed into Nesto, managing to grab his gun hand as she landed. The two grappled for control of the weapon, Jo's advantage in agility an even match for Nesto's superior strength.

Locked in fierce combat, both Jo and Nesto were oblivious to the sound of a helicopter landing nearby, followed by a flurry of gunfire.

Jo succeeded in pinning the gang leader to the ground, only to have Nesto pull her down by the hair. She countered with a knee to the testicles that doubled him over, leaving the mero gasping for breath. While he writhed in pain, she slammed his hand against the floor, sending the gun spinning into the corner. Before he could react, she leapt to her feet and retrieved the gun.

Seconds later, she stood over the prone mero, the sights of the Glock-32 trained steadily on his forehead.

———

Staff Sergeant Michael Ellis burst into the kitchen through its double swinging doors, his M4 at his shoulder. The sight he encountered bewildered the Delta Force veteran.

Standing in the far corner of the room was a tall blonde, bleeding and badly bruised but pointing a handgun at a small Hispanic man cowering on the floor. The lifeless body of another man lay nearby, still bleeding from a head wound.

The sergeant's first thought was that the blonde was a Pancho hostage who had managed to overpower her captors. Still, Ellis had been trained to take no chances.

"Drop the gun, ma'am—now!" Ellis screamed through his black mask.

As the sergeant watched in amazement, the blonde turned toward him and began firing.

The dull stabs of the bullets striking his torso snapped Ellis out of his shock. The blows were painful in spite of his flak vest. He staggered backward. Then, in a reflex developed during years of training, the sergeant dropped to one knee and fired back at his assailant, his three-shot laser-guided burst striking the blonde in the head and upper chest. The force of the bullets hurled the woman's body backward, still holding the pistol in her hand.

Certain that the immediate threat was neutralized, Ellis

swung his sights to the man lying on the floor, his face wide-eyed with terror.

"Dorothy! Dorothy! Dorothy!" the little man on the floor shrieked, desperately waving his hands.

Sergeant Ellis nodded in recognition to the terrified man, keeping his weapon trained on him. "Dorothy" was the code word identifying their mole.

It was well after dark when Mano emerged from the Tunas Drive storm sewer inside Quarantine Zone B. His return had been delayed by the Army patrols and surveillance drones now bristling around the QZs—another surprise the Army had unveiled.

He moved warily along the deserted street, normally bustling during early evening. Something—most likely an Army raid—had driven people indoors.

He did not believe the Army would try to maintain a presence within the zone. The risk of a bloodbath was too great and the government was leery of casualties, both military and civilian. But after today's debacle, he was not certain of anything.

As he rounded the corner near the Holiday Inn, a trio of old men gathered round a barrel fire turned their heads toward him nervously.

"Have you seen any baldies around?" Mano asked, walking closer.

Looking at his black fatigues with approval, the oldest man pointed toward the hotel. "Two helicopters landed there this morning. There was a lot of shooting and then they flew away."

"Everybody's been afraid to go in there," added another.

"Gracias," Mano said, walking past them.

"Que vayas con Dios," the old man called after him.

A flimsy barrier of plastic crime scene tape left by the Army encased the Holiday Inn complex. Pushing aside the tape, Mano entered the hotel, making his way through the interior courtyard. In the dim moonlight filtering through the skylights, he saw that the electrical generator had been destroyed.

Just past the generator was the body of Rafael Rodriguez. The young Verdugo assigned to guard Nesto had been shot several times with a high-caliber weapon. Judging by the congealed blood around him, he'd been dead for several hours. The grisly sight raised Mano's sense of foreboding.

Mano produced a penlight from his fatigues and opened the door to the kitchen, his dread over Jo's fate growing with each step into the total darkness inside.

He waved the penlight around the room. The small light beam moved along the countertops, revealing the battered remnants of their communications equipment. Between the counters, Mano spotted the legs of a man lying on the floor. Moving closer, he saw it was Enrique Rueda, the other Verdugo assigned to guard Nesto. Enrique had been killed by a blow to the head.

Mano's anxiety mounted as he flicked his small spotlight around the rest of the room. Then his beacon found a flash of honey-gold hair. He stood frozen for a moment, summoning the courage to look. Finally, he let his penlight travel slowly over the body. Because of her hair and clothes, he was sure it was Jo. Her face was a grotesque mask, distorted beyond recognition by the wounds of two high-caliber bullets.

Mano turned out the light and stood motionless in the darkness. In that instant, his thoughts converged like a laser beam into a single thought: *find Nesto.*

Nesto's special Nikes were getting seriously soiled.

"Goddamn those CIA pendejos," the mero muttered angrily as he walked through the narrow channel of foul brown water trickling along the bottom of the storm sewer, the beam of his flashlight bouncing wildly inside the cylindrical passageway.

Nesto had been looking forward to the day when he got even with Mano and the DDP. Instead, it had turned out to be a shitty day.

The first setback had come shortly after the Delta Force troopers secured the rebel command center. Nesto had expected the soldiers to take him away to safety. He did not want to be around if Mano somehow managed to survive.

He was livid when the sergeant tersely explained there was no room in the chopper for him. But Nesto knew better. Apparently, his value to the CIA had ended. His anger soon turned to fear. He was now on his own in evading Mano.

After Nesto returned to his barrio, things got worse. He found his vatos had vanished. One of the hookers said they had disappeared after hearing about a heavy baldie crackdown expected after the big rebel push. Without the protection of his vatos, Nesto was left with little choice. He would have to flee.

Though terrified that Mano would appear at any moment,

he decided to risk a trip to his house. Approaching the large, tile-roofed structure, he noticed the front gate on the ten-foot fence surrounding the property had been left open.

Nesto entered cautiously and found his house guards gone. Fortunately, the secret cache beneath the floorboards of his bedroom closet was intact. Five minutes later, he left the house laden with all the cash he could carry in his baggy pants. He tucked a .380 Colt Pony into his waistband beneath a loose-fitting plaid shirt.

He spent the rest of the day sitting in the corner of a private cantina several blocks from his house, nursing a succession of Coors with his eyes constantly on the door.

After sunset, he lowered himself into the storm sewer main at North Boyle and made his way through the large concrete tunnel toward the L.A. River. His plan was to make it to Mexico and lie low until he learned Mano's fate.

He was now less than a hundred meters from the storm sewer's discharge point into the L.A. River.

Crouching inside a dense clump of arundo, Mano listened intently, methodically surveying the nocturnal landscape of the Los Angeles River. As was common during most of the year, the river was an inch-deep puddle meandering through the concrete channel. Because of the city's lack of maintenance over the last several years, an abundance of plants, in which Mano was now concealed, had sprung up through the cracks in the concrete. Mano was grateful for the cover.

Coming to the river had been a long shot. Mano knew he had only a few hours to find Nesto. By morning, the wily mero would be long gone. Mano was counting on one thing:

unless Nesto was in government custody, the gang leader would probably head south along the river after dark.

Lying in wait along the river was not without risk. Twice in the last hour, a trio of Army Humvees had crossed the bridge just to the north of him.

Mano had chosen his intercept point in the riverbed carefully, roughly one klick outside the border of Quarantine Zone B. No matter which of the many tunnels Nesto might use to escape, his trail would lead him here if he was heading south.

The moon was rising higher, casting a cold gray light over most of the river, leaving a narrow band of darkness along the left bank. Mano knew Nesto would travel in the shadows. This was where he waited.

Blocking out the pale glare of the moon with his hand, Mano scanned the left bank with his peripheral vision, which was more sensitive to light.

There, he almost said aloud as a blur of movement appeared near a willow about fifty meters away. He spotted the movement again. This time, he could make out the outline of a figure darting in his direction between the clusters of vegetation. All he had to do was wait.

For the last two hours, Mano's mind had been in stalking mode. Any feelings of grief and loss had been pushed aside. Now, as his quarry drew near, a surge of emotion coursed through him that felt very alien. Killing Nesto quickly would not be enough.

He wanted to see Nesto suffer first.

Mano drew his Glock as he heard the soft scrape of footsteps on the pebble-littered concrete. Through the willow branches, he saw Nesto stride into view. In a single motion,

Mano rose to his feet and swung his left forearm, catching Nesto below the chin in a clothesline tackle, sending the mero down on his back.

"I've been waiting for you, Nesto," Mano said, his voice cold and dry. "You got a lot of good people killed today...and now you're going to pay for it." He leveled his pistol.

"Wait...please...wait," Nesto pleaded, his pupils dancing wildly, desperately searching for the words to save his life. "You said it was good people that were killed today. Well, I know something about Jo—something she did that wasn't so good."

Mano kept Nesto in the sights of his Glock, but without knowing why, did not pull the trigger. "You think smearing Jo's memory is going to save your worthless life?"

"There's a lot about Jo you don't know, Mano," Nesto said, starting to regain his composure.

Mano's hand holding the gun relaxed slightly. "What are you trying to say, Nesto?"

"You remember the first L.A. cops who were killed in the riots around three years ago?"

"I do. So what?"

"After they were killed, the riots got a lot worse...and the vigilantes started raiding the barrios. You remember all that, right?"

"If you've got a point, Nesto, you better get to it quickly."

"That was the start of the real trouble, man. A lot of people have died since then because those cops were killed," said the gang leader, propping himself up on one elbow.

Mano said nothing. But he knew Nesto was right. Julio and Elena, his niece, and countless other innocents would be alive today if this whole mess had never started.

"Why are you telling me this, Nesto?"

"Because Jo was the one who ordered those cops killed."

"You're lying."

"No, Mano. I *know* Jo ordered those cops to be killed because she paid me to do it. Ramon arranged the whole deal."

Mano was stunned. Could it be true? He recalled his first weapons deal with Nesto years earlier. It had seemed clear then that Ramon had dealt with Nesto before. Mano stood speechless, his mind racing for an explanation.

"She played you for a chump all along, man," Nesto added with a touch of sympathy.

The words struck Mano like a blow.

Had he misjudged Jo? Was she capable of murder? Did she deliberately incite the violence that led to the deaths of his children? Engulfed in a churning eddy of doubts, his gaze turning distant, Mano slowly lowered the pistol to his side.

It was the opening Nesto had been hoping for. He reached for the Colt Pony under his shirt.

Nesto's sudden movement snapped Mano out of his trance. The mero's hand was arcing toward him holding a stubby silver pistol. Instinctively, Mano kicked at Nesto's hand.

As Nesto's gun discharged, the .380 caliber bullet intended for Mano's torso tore through the flesh of his right forearm, knocking the Glock out of his hand.

Ignoring the searing pain in his arm, Mano launched himself at Nesto before he could fire again. With his uninjured arm, he grabbed Nesto's gun hand and squeezed as the mero screeched in agony. When he released the pressure, the gun fell from Nesto's bleeding hand.

Mano then trapped Nesto's head in his good arm and gave

a violent twist. A sickening, low-pitched crack of shattering bone and cartilage marked the death of Ernesto Alvarez.

Mano staggered to his feet, staring at the gang leader's body. His death brought no satisfaction. Worse, his lofty image of Jo had been turned on its head. He no longer knew what to believe. Was Jo a fraud—and their cause as well?

The death of Nesto released the flood of emotions Mano had been trying to hold in check. A wave of despair washed over him as the blunt reality of their defeat sank in. Jo was dead. Their most trusted men had been slaughtered. The nerve center of their operations was lost.

A succession of painful memories surfaced in Mano's mind. The death of the Jimenez twins...the loss of his niece...the killing of his son...his separation from his family...the loss of his daughter...Jo's brutal death...It had all been for nothing.

They had chased the pipe dream of a loser.

THE MARCHA OFFENSIVE:
Day 2

The supreme challenge of any revolutionary is not the struggle against a larger, better-equipped adversary. It is the struggle against hopelessness.

—José Antonio Marcha, 1989
Translated by J. M. Herrera

Through the windows of his house, Mano could see a glint of pale light. There was a chance the soldiers had somehow uncovered the location of his home during the raid on the command center. A squad of troopers might be waiting for him inside.

Beyond caring, he opened the door.

In the living room were Guillermo and Juana. Although it was well after midnight, the old couple were still at work by the dim light of a gas lantern, Juana mending a shirt and Guillermo folding laundry.

Juana smiled with relief when Mano entered. "Mano! Gracias a Dios, you're alive. There were many explosions and gunfire all day."

"And helicopters, too," Guillermo added. "People are saying a lot of our fighters were killed."

"It did not go well today," Mano said flatly. He could not bring himself to say more. After intercepting Nesto, he'd returned to the command center and buried Jo and the young Verdugos. With only one good arm, it had been slow and painful work.

He was drained of all strength...and all feelings.

Mano walked toward the bathroom to clean the wound on his arm. As he crossed the living room, Juana noticed his injury. "Mano, did you hurt your arm?"

"It's nothing, Juana. I can take care of it."

Juana folded her arms and frowned. "Manolo Suarez, don't you disrespect me. Come here and let me see your arm."

Mano complied, and within minutes Juana and Guillermo were eagerly attending to his wound. As Juana finished tightening a fresh bandage around his bulky forearm, she could no longer contain her excitement.

"Mano, we have a surprise that should cheer you up," Juana said, grinning widely.

Guillermo scowled at his wife. "Don't give it away, old woman."

"Be silent, old fool. I know what I'm doing," Juana said to her husband. She then turned to Mano. "Josefina stopped by this morning and left a surprise in your room," she said, gesturing toward his bedroom door.

Despite the bleakness in his soul, Mano had no desire to offend Juana and Guillermo. They were trying to cheer him.

He rose and walked wearily down the hall toward his room. The anticipation of a gift from Jo only deepened his despair, another painful reminder of her death. Still, out of respect for the old couple, he opened the door and looked inside.

There were two sleeping figures in the room. One was on his bed, the other curled in a pallet on the floor. Even in the faint light, Mano recognized his wife and son.

A sliver of light penetrated Rosa's eyelids. After four nights of hard travel and little sleep, she unconsciously fought the urge to open her eyes and returned to her dream.

She was in a grassy field bathed in afternoon sunlight, looking up at Mano and Jo, who stood on a slope high above her. Mano waved in greeting and began descending the hill. After he reached her, he looked back up the slope toward Jo, now a silhouette in the glare of the setting sun.

Rosa squinted as Jo's shape began to vanish in the blinding glow. Rosa raised her hand to shield her eyes from the piercing brightness, and the setting suddenly changed.

She was in a dark room, looking toward the light that entered from the doorway. The outline of a muscular figure stood at the door.

"Mano?" she called out softly, unsure if she was awake or dreaming.

Mano entered the room wordlessly, tears welling in his eyes, and lifted Pedro and his blankets from the floor. As Mano carried the boy into the living room, Juana and Guillermo beamed smiles of approval and quietly retired to their room. Mano tucked the sleeping child into the sofa and returned to the bedroom.

At last alone with Rosa, Mano kissed her. The kiss began tenderly, then quickly rose in passion. In that moment, Rosa forgot the pain and the grief she had endured in the camp. In Mano's arms again after more than a year, she felt only the longing of a woman too long separated from her man.

Rosa was surprised when Mano suddenly broke off their

kiss. He sat up in the bed and stared at the floor. "Querida…
so much has happened…"

Rosa lifted his face with her hand. "Whatever happened
before doesn't matter anymore, mi amor. All that matters
now is that we're together."

"You don't understand, Rosa. We launched an attack
today. Many of us across the country took part—and it failed.
A lot of people were killed, including Jo."

Rosa suddenly felt the hollow ache of grief. "May God have
mercy on her soul," she said, making the sign of the cross. "I
hated Josefina before she came to the camp. But I came to
know she never meant us any harm. She was a good woman,
Mano. She was just very mixed up inside. In fact, she's the
reason Pedro and I were able to leave the camp. She bribed a
lot of people to get us here."

"Juana and Guillermo told me. But there's more about
Jo you don't know, Rosa." Mano hesitated, uncertain if he
should continue. "Jo may have been a murderer," he finally
said.

"I don't believe it," Rosa said gently. "Where did you hear
that, Mano?"

"From a gang leader. He said Jo paid him to kill some
policemen three years ago. He said Jo did it to provoke more
trouble, and it worked." Mano lowered his gaze. "Julio and
Elena might still be alive today if those policemen hadn't
been murdered."

Rosa placed her palms softly on her husband's cheeks and
looked into his eyes. "Mano, God knows Josefina was not a
saint. But she was not a murderer. She did not do this thing."

"How can you be sure?"

"Because Josefina told me herself. She admitted she paid

that gang leader to start the trouble. But she said she had no idea he would kill those policemen in cold blood. Their deaths were one of her greatest regrets."

"Why did Jo tell you this?"

"Mi amor, women share things men will never understand."

———

Mano awoke to the sound of birds in morning song, the gray light of dawn glowing in the window.

Half awake, he lapsed into a strange memory, recalling a book from Ramon's library about the making of a Samurai sword. The steel of the blade was heated, folded, and beaten down over and over—until it was finally quenched in cool water to harden its strength.

The image of the steaming sword was accompanied by the delicious realization that Rosa was nestled next to him. After their long separation, her nearness was strangely familiar, a half déjà vu.

Mano recalled with tenderness their passionate lovemaking of a few hours earlier. His energy had surprised him. The previous day had been the longest of his life.

He had seen good people die. He believed their rebellion had been crushed. He'd even doubted the honor of Jo and their cause. But on this placid morning, yesterday's events seemed part of another era, a distant past remembered without pain. His vision was turned forward. He was burning with a sense of certainty.

Mano was determined to carry on the fight.

EPILOGUE

The fortunes of war do not govern the success of a
revolution. It is not what happens on the battlefield that
changes history. A military victory is worthless if it fails
to win the battle of public opinion.

—José Antonio Marcha, 1988
Translated by J. M. Herrera

Few Americans alive on May 20 would ever forget what
they were doing on that fateful Sunday.

Like December 7, November 22, and September 11, the
date of the Marcha Offensive was a day that would be permanently etched into the American psyche.

Reports of the attacks surfaced shortly after noon Eastern
Time. Within the hour, the news was spreading across the
nation with the momentum of a nuclear reaction.

For some, the first stunning report came during church
services. For others, the initial reports rocked the calm of a
quiet Sunday at home. Many heard the news from a friend or
relative. The flurry of vu-phone calls ignited by the attacks
overloaded circuits across much of the nation.

The early reports came from local TV and radio stations.
As the scope of the violence became apparent, the national
networks picked up the story, rushing their anchors into
the studios. In their most sonorous, serious-news voices, the

anchors described the widespread scale and coordination of the attacks, creating an atmosphere drenched in alarm and uncertainty.

The networks soon trotted out their talking heads on Hispanic culture. Among the first bits of information gleaned from these pundits was the significance of the date: May 20 was the birthday of José Antonio Marcha, the patron saint of the insurgents. Cutaways to reporters standing before yet another smoldering facility frequently interrupted these background interviews.

Less than ninety minutes after the first reports, the network anchors were updating hastily generated computer maps that charted the extent of the attacks across the nation. On the CBS map, yellow starbursts recorded the locations of sabotage. Stylized soldiers marked the sites of armed assaults. The number of icons on the map grew by the minute.

The media reported the detonation of explosive devices at a frightening array of locations—electrical transformers, telephone relay stations, vu-phone towers, naval docks, and airport runways. Government offices were another prime target. Bombs of varying sizes exploded at post offices, state highway depots, truck weighing stations, and one county courthouse. There was no official death toll from the attacks yet, but many in the audience feared the worst.

Preliminary reports also indicated that heavily armed combatants had attempted to storm more than thirty government installations. Among those targeted were U.S. Army garrisons outside the Quarantine Zones in Los Angeles, El Paso, and San Antonio. A number of local law enforcement posts across the nation were also struck.

Fresh footage of the devastation was aired the moment it

arrived as each network vied to scoop the others. One of the most dramatic clips came from California. Shot from a distance, it showed the bluish-white trails of four rockets arcing toward a U.S. Army outpost. The missiles burst in the air above a collection of military vehicles, shrouding them in smoke. As the haze cleared, soldiers appeared, chaotically scrambling to douse their blazing trucks and Humvees. The camera then quickly shifted to a wooded hillside where a large suburban home was seen exploding under a barrage of artillery fire. Moments later, an attack helicopter zoomed up the slope, raking the hillside with its weapons. The chopper was hit by ground fire and sent circling to the ground as another helicopter joined the fray.

No living American had ever witnessed a military action on U.S. soil. As the chilling scenes of battle and the news of widespread sabotage flooded the nation, fear and alarm began to grow. *Where will it end? Is my neighborhood next?*

By early afternoon on the East Coast, the panic was escalating. Many barricaded themselves in their homes. In some neighborhoods, armed civilians formed ad hoc militias. Anxious shoppers stormed grocery stores, stocking up on staples. The lines around most gas stations extended for blocks. People separated from their loved ones tried desperately to reach home. Hordes of travelers jammed the airports. Many others were afraid to fly. Rental cars were in hot demand. Interstates across the nation were clogged with desperate, frightened drivers. The fear was contagious.

At 4:30 p.m. Eastern Time, President Brenner made a television appearance. He assured a shaken nation that all was well. The attacks, while widespread, were "not catastrophic," he said. The president also announced that all the armed attacks had been repelled with few government or civilian casualties. Most of the attackers, though, had been killed or captured, he said. Assuring that the unprecedented wave of violence was over, he urged all Americans to stay home and remain calm. They were not in danger.

The president's message turned the tide of panic. The terror and fear that had spread across the nation began to subside. In reality, few civilians had ever been in jeopardy. Within military and intelligence circles, the Marcha Offensive was seen as a severe blow to the rebels. But among the mainstream public, overwhelmed by the media onslaught, the raw shock of the attacks had taken a toll. Those terrifying hours had shattered a confidence so deep, few Americans had ever considered a possibility that now seemed very real...

The United States was in a civil war—and there was a chance the rebels might win.

READING GROUP GUIDE

Characters

Who was your favorite character? Why?

Who was your least favorite character? Why?

What emotions drove Mano's conversion from loyal citizen to insurgent?

Do you think Mano's actions were immoral? Why or why not?

Under the same circumstances as Mano, what would you have done differently?

How did Mano's view of their rebellion differ from the views of Jo and Ramon?

What experiences ultimately radicalized Rosa?

Do you think Rosa's reaction to her predicament differed from that of a mainstream American woman? If so, how?

Stereotypes and diversity

Did the story make you question your assumptions about the people and culture of Latin America? For example, were you surprised by the diversity of the Latino characters in the story?

What role has the media played in fostering Hispanic stereotypes?

What are the positive and negative aspects of using an ethnic label like "Hispanic" or "Latino"?

Immigration and demographics

Did the story change your perspective on U.S. immigration policy? If so, how?

Do you think a separatist movement like that proposed by fictional character José Antonio Marcha could ever take root in the U.S.? Why or why not?

What can we do to prevent the social turmoil presented in the story?

The media

Where is the balance point between the news media's responsibility to highlight social problems and the exploitation of those problems to attract viewers and readers?

Short of censorship, how can we protect ourselves from the economic impetus to "sell the news"?

Historical parallels

The events in *America Libre* are similar to some real-life events in U.S. history, such as the race riots of the 1960s and the internment of Japanese-Americans during World War II. Do you think that today's society has changed to prevent events such as these from happening again? If so, how has it changed? If not, what are examples of how society has stayed the same?

Could the U.S. recognition of the State of Israel in 1948 ever be used as precedent for a Hispanic homeland within current U.S. borders? Why or why not?

Do you believe any of today's public figures are using the immigration issue for political gain? If so, how?

GUÍA DE LECTORES

Caracteres

¿Quién era su carácter preferido? ¿Por qué?

¿Quién era su carácter menos preferido? ¿Por qué?

¿Qué emociones condujeron la conversión de Mano de ciudadano leal al insurrecto?

¿Piensa usted que las acciones de Mano eran inmoral? ¿Por qué o por qué no?

Bajo las mismas circunstancias que Mano, ¿qué habría hecho usted diferentemente?

¿Cómo es diferente la opinión de Mano de la rebelión de la de Jo y de Ramon?

¿Al fin, cuál experiencia le convirtió a Rosa en una radical?

¿Piensa usted la reacción de Rosa a su lío diferenció de el de una mujer americana de corriente? ¿Si es así, cómo?

Estereotipos y diversidad

¿Cambia usted sus asunciones sobre la gente y la cultura de América latina a causa de la historia? Por ejemplo, ¿fue sorprendido por la diversidad de los caracteres latinos en la historia?

¿Qué papel han desempeñado los medios en fomentar estereotipos hispánicos?

¿Cuáles son los aspectos positivos y negativos de usar una etiqueta étnica como "hispánico" o "latino"?

Inmigración y demográficos

¿Cambió usted su perspectiva de la politica de inmigración en los E.E.U.U.? ¿Si es así, cómo?

¿Piensa usted que un movimiento separatista como eso propuesto por el carácter ficticio Jose Antonio Marcha podría echar raíces en los E.E.U.U.? ¿Por qué o por qué no?

¿Qué podemos hacer para prevenir la agitación social presentada en la historia?

Los medios

¿Dónde es el punto del balance entre la responsabilidad de los medios de destacar problems sociales y la explotación de esos problemas para atraer espectadores y a lectores?

Corto de censura, ¿cómo podemos protegernos contra el ímpetu económico "para vender las noticias"?

Paralelos históricos

Los acontecimientos adentro *América Libre* sea similar a algunos acontecimientos de la historia de los E.E.U.U., como los alborotos de la raza de los años 60 y el internamiento de Japonés-Americanos durante la Segunda Guerra Mundial. ¿Piensa usted que la sociedad de hoy ha cambiado para evitar que sucedan los acontecimientos tales como éstos otra vez? ¿Si es así, cómo ha cambiado? ¿Si no, cuáles son ejemplos de cómo la sociedad ha permanecido igual?

¿Podría ser posible usar el reconocimiento del estado de Israel por los E.E.U.U. en 1948 como precedente para una patria hispánica dentro de las fronteras de los E.E.U.U.? ¿Por qué o por qué no?

¿Cree usted que hay algunas figuras públicas de hoy que están utilizando la cuestión de la inmigración para su propio aumento político? ¿Si es así, cómo?

ABOUT THE AUTHOR

A longtime resident of the U.S. Midwest, Cuban-born Raul Ramos y Sanchez is a founding partner of BRC Marketing, established in 1992 with offices in Ohio and California. Besides developing a documentary for public television, *Two Americas: The Legacy of Our Hemisphere,* he is host of MyImmi grationStory.com, an online forum for the U.S. immigrant community.

For more information please visit www.RaulRamos.com.

The fight isn't over.
Look for the upcoming sequel to *America Libre*,

EL NUEVO
ALAMO

After the disastrous Marcha Offensive, Manolo Suarez stands alone, the sole leader of the insurgency in war-torn Southern California. Despite heavy rebel losses during their nationwide attacks on military installations, public demands for reprisals lead to a siege of the Quarantine Zones. Denied food, water, and medicine for nearly two years, the insurgency appears ready to crumble. But the hardships spawn a rebel splinter group: El Frente—an ultra-radical faction bent on terror attacks against U.S. civilians. Reunited with his family, Mano finds himself at odds with his wife, Rosa, who wants an end to the fighting, and his son Pedro, who joins El Frente. When Mano learns El Frente plans to destroy a Midwestern city with a smuggled nuclear weapon, he must make a dreadful decision: will he betray his son or let millions of innocent people die?

Now turn the page for a sneak peek at
El Nuevo Alamo

THE MARCHA OFFENSIVE:
Day 2

Some things had not changed. The dawning sun in East Los Angeles was still a feeble glow in the gray haze, but the city's infamous smog was no longer a residue of its endless traffic. These days, the smoke of cooking fires clouded the sky. The vehicles that had once clogged Los Angeles were now charred shells littering a war-scarred city divided into two walled-in Quarantine Zones.

A rooster crowed outside a white stucco cottage on the north side of Quarantine Zone B. Inside the small house, Manolo Suarez got out of bed and began to dress.

Lying naked on the bed, his wife, Rosa, stirred, her eyelids heavy. "What time is it?"

"Time for me to go, querida," Mano answered, fastening his weathered jeans.

Rosa sat up abruptly, her eyes flashing. "What? How can you leave now, Mano? This is our first day together after a year and a half apart and—" She stopped, the anger in her voice suddenly gone. Rising from the bed, she slipped on a tattered robe. "I'm sorry, mi amor. I understand. Will you have time to eat?"

"No, it's nearly daylight," Mano said, opening the bedroom door. "I should have left an hour ago."

"When will you be back?"

Mano looked into her dark brown eyes. "When I can."

"Is this how it's going to be, Mano? Not knowing if I'll ever see you again each time you leave?"

"This is a war now, querida. I wish it could be different."

Rosa pulled the robe tighter around her. Thirteen months without her husband in the Relocation Community had changed her. She'd come to understand Mano's dedication to the rebel cause—and even to support it. She sighed and embraced him. "At least we're together again. May God keep you, mi amor."

Mano gave her a reassuring squeeze, then walked into the living room where he peered cautiously through the windows before leaving the house. Once outside, he moved along the deserted street with a resolve borne of necessity. He had nothing left to lose. If captured by the government, Mano would be charged with treason and sentenced to death under the Terrorist Arraignment Act. Even his wife and son faced a similar fate under the draconian law passed five months earlier. Mano shook his head, trying to clear his mind of the ever-looming threat. He had a more immediate crisis.

The start of yesterday's Marcha Offensive had been derailed by a mole who'd alerted the government to the rebel's nationwide attacks. A terrible question now plagued Mano: how much damage had the mole caused?

Guided by the mole, the Army had discovered the rebel command center in Los Angeles directing their nationwide offensive. Mano had returned from his raid to find their communications equipment seized or destroyed and his comrades killed—including Josefina Herrera.

The enormity of Jo's death was too much to contemplate.

Mano could not afford to dwell on grief. Most of the insurgency's leaders were now out of touch or dead, leaving him as the sole survivor of the inner command in the area.

A quarter hour later, Mano approached a duplex on Fraser Avenue. The man who lived inside was his last resort for help—Angel Sanchez, the mero of Los Verdugos, a street gang that had become the palace guard of the rebel leadership in Los Angeles.

Mano needed to see Angel right away—if the gang leader was still alive.

The armored column raced through downtown Los Angeles stirring eddies of dust in the empty streets. As the vehicles crossed the viaduct over the vacant Union Pacific rail yards, the voice of the column's commander came on the radio.

"Tango Five to all units," Captain Michael Fuller said. "Convoy halt."

Moving in unison, the five vehicles rolled to a stop and Fuller emerged from the Humvee leading the column. Studying the road ahead through his binoculars, a tight smile formed on Fuller's face. The rusting steel doors of the North Gate into the Quarantine Zone B were open, creating a glowing portal in the long, early morning shadows cast by the ten-foot concrete wall topped with razor wire. *So far, so good*, Fuller thought with relief.

The North Gate was one of only two passages into the twenty-two square miles of Quarantine Zone B. Although it was a likely place for an ambush, Fuller was betting the rebels would not be lying in wait at the gate this morning.

He climbed back into the Humvee and picked up the

radio handset. "Tango Five to all units. Deploy in combat formation and proceed into the Quarantine Zone."

The four tanklike Bradley Fighting Vehicles behind Fuller's Humvee began moving into position at the head of the column. As the Bradleys lumbered past the Humvee, Fuller's driver nervously stroked the blue figurine taped to the dashboard. "All right, Hefty," he whispered to the grinning Smurf. "Pancho's waiting for us inside. Get us through that gate, dude."

"Don't worry, Springs," Fuller said to his driver. "Getting inside won't be a problem." *Save up Hefty's luck for later,* Fuller kept to himself. *We're going to need it.*

Angel Sanchez entered the living room of his duplex apartment, cranking the dynamo on a shortwave radio.

"Good," Mano said. "You found it."

The self-charging radio was one of two acquired by Josefina Herrera for the rebel cause in Los Angeles. The other device, a more elaborate model with better range, had been lost during the Army's raid on their command center yesterday.

After charging the battery for several minutes, Angel handed the radio to Mano, who tuned it to the familiar setting for the BBC and placed it on one of the steel milk crates that served as chairs and coffee table in the sparsely furnished living room. Most wooden furniture in the Quarantine Zones had been burned for fuel, along with almost anything else combustible.

Following a report on the London Stock Exchange, the dulcet-toned BBC announcer reached the news Mano and Angel had been waiting to hear.

... and now our top news story: the widespread Hispanic insurgent attacks across the United States being called the Marcha Offensive... Mary Ann Kirby reports.

The scratchy quality of the female voice now on the air indicated her report had been recorded over a telephone line.

When the reporter had finished, Angel turned off the radio and faced Mano. The gang leader had understood much of the news despite his limited grasp of English. "Muchos muertos, eh?"

"Yes, a lot of dead," Mano answered, grim-faced. If the news report was accurate, they'd lost nearly half their fighters, many not much more than boys and girls. Not surprisingly, very few had surrendered. They all knew the consequences of the Terrorist Arraignment Act.

Mano closed his eyes and rubbed his temples, swamped by a wave of guilt. He was the architect of the Marcha Offensive; he had insisted their fighters attack military installations and not civilian targets. The price for avoiding the tactics of terrorists had been very high. *At least very few civilians died*, he reminded himself.

Mano knew the element of surprise was a guerrilla's primary weapon. The informer had robbed them of that advantage—and the Army would be quick to exploit their heavy losses.

Mano rose to his feet. "The baldies will be coming, entiendes?" he said, striding toward the door. "We need to be ready."

"Si, Mano," Angel replied, falling into step behind him. "I talk con mis vatos. They tell me when baldies come."

Captain Fuller leaned forward in the Humvee's seat, scanning the rooftops visible over the Quarantine Zone wall for snipers. He was relieved—but not surprised—to find their entrance into the zone unopposed.

Most Army patrols entering the nation's Quarantine Zones over the last year had suffered heavy losses. Michael Fuller, however, was determined to avoid that fate for the five vehicles and forty-three soldiers under his command. That's why he'd chosen this time and place to enter. Still, the thirty-one-year-old captain had qualms about his decision. He was breaking an unwritten truce with the Panchos by launching an armored patrol into the zone during the Army's weekly delivery of food.

Once inside the solid steel doors, Fuller's convoy skirted past a line of open-bed Army trucks loaded with sacks of cornmeal parked along the boulevard. Civilians in blue armbands were hastily transferring the sacks from the six-by-six trucks into an odd assortment of civilian vehicles while a platoon of National Guardsmen stood warily nearby. The civilians stopped their work, staring hard at Fuller's trespassing column.

From the rear bench of the Humvee, Lieutenant Gerald Case gazed expectantly out the window. "You think we're going to see some action, Captain?"

"Not if I can help it."

"C'mon, Cap. What's wrong with stirring up a little firefight? I missed out on the action at the outpost yesterday. A combat commendation would be a fast way out of this shithole."

Case's words stung Michael Fuller—mostly because they were true. A domestic assignment in today's Army was for bottom feeders. Overseas duty was the fast lane to promotion. "Stow it, Case. I'm not going to risk getting anybody hurt to help your career...or mine."

"We ain't likely to get anybody hurt with a platoon of Brads around, Cap," Case said, nodding toward the four treaded vehicles trundling ahead of them. Each Bradley was armed with a turret-mounted 25mm chain gun and carried seven heavily armed troopers.

"What about civilians, Case? Don't you think...Watch the kid, Springs!" Fuller yelled to his driver as a naked toddler wandered into the path of their vehicle. The screeching of the brakes brought the boy's mother running into the street.

"Sorry, Captain," Springs said, his face pale. "I didn't see the kid. I guess I was looking out for the Panchos."

Lieutenant Case sneered. "Wouldn't have made much difference if you'd taken him out. They breed like rats," he said as the boy's mother swooped up the child and retreated into the doorway of a dingy apartment building. "Why we fight these people on one street and feed them on another one is beyond me, Cap."

"If we starved the QZs, every person inside would be fighting against us, Case. Beans are a lot cheaper than bullets. And besides, it's the right thing to do."

"They teach you that kind of bleeding-heart crap at West Point, Captain?"

"Yeah, right after the mandatory class on the virtues of appeasement."

Case stared at Fuller blankly. "Appeasement?"

"Never mind, Lieutenant. We don't have the time right now."

"Well, explain this for me, will you, Captain...How the hell did an Academy ring knocker like you wind up with this dead-end posting anyway?"

Fuller turned slowly toward Case. "Lieutenant, your mouth is going to get you in deep shit one of these days...possibly very soon."

As their convoy drove deeper into the zone, Fuller silently cursed the politicians who'd hatched the Quarantine and Relocation Act—and then left the military to clean up their mess.

Two years after the bill was enacted, most Americans now saw the attempt at the largest ethnic internment in the nation's history as an epic failure. The government had halted construction of new Relocation Communities for Hispanics in North Dakota after the deaths of over two thousand internees during the first winter. Meanwhile, the once-temporary Quarantine Zones—built around Hispanic urban enclaves to end the bloody street battles between vigilantes and Hispanics—had become rebel strongholds from which the Panchos launched strikes and then melted back into the civilian population.

The last twenty-four hours, however, had changed the game.

Yesterday's nationwide offensive had been a disaster for the Panchos. Thanks to a rebel informer, the Army had anticipated the insurgent attacks on U.S. military installations and decisively repulsed the assaults. But their mole had delivered an even bigger win. They had uncovered the rebel command center directing the nationwide attacks—an abandoned Holiday Inn near the center of Los Angeles Quarantine Zone B.

A twelve-trooper Delta Force team arriving in two choppers had wiped out the enemy personnel at the command center and hauled away all the rebel communications equipment the helos could hold before hurriedly pulling out. Deep in Pancho-held territory, the small Delta team risked being overrun if they'd tried to hold the position. Now the brass wanted a more thorough intelligence sweep of the Pancho command center.

The Pentagon had created Fuller's ad hoc task force to ferry an intel team to the rebel command center. His orders were to let the G2 wonks snoop around and then escort them out. The mission was considered so important the generals had even assigned an air surveillance drone to Fuller's task force—a first for a stateside unit.

From the touch screen on the Humvee's dashboard, Fuller studied the drone's-eye view of the road ahead. What he saw made the captain shiver under his flak vest despite the eighty-degree heat: a barricade of rubble and abandoned cars blocked all four lanes of Whittier Boulevard.

After nearly a year of duty in Southern California, Fuller had come to know the insurgents' tactics well. No matter which detour he chose, he was certain the Panchos would have an ambush waiting.

13.99   6/1/11